a big boy did it and ran away

christopher brookmyre

timewarner
paperbacks

A *Time Warner* Paperback

First published in Great Britain in 2001 by Abacus
This edition published by Time Warner Paperbacks in 2002

Copyright © 2001 Christopher Brookmyre

'Crime Scene Part One' written by Greg Dulli.
© 1996 Kali Nichta Music/Warner-Tamerlane Music BMI.
From the album *Black Love* by The Afghan Whigs.
Lyrics reproduced by kind permission.

A CIP catalogue record for this book
is available from the British Library.

Typeset by Palimpsest Book Production Limited,
Polmont, Stirlingshire
Printed and bound in Great Britain by
Clays Ltd, St Ives plc

Time Warner Paperbacks
An imprint of
Time Warner Books UK
Brettenham House
Lancaster Place
London WC2E 7EN

www.TimeWarnerBooks.co.uk

For Jack

THANKS: Marisa, Id Software, Greg Dulli, POTZW.
They must all share the blame.

Christopher Brookmyre was born in Glasgow in 1968, and has worked as a journalist in London, Los Angeles and Edinburgh, contributing to *Screen International*, the *Scotsman*, the *Evening News* and *The Absolute Game*. In 1976 he became a St Mirren supporter. He remains unsure whether this was constructive.

His first novel, *Quite Ugly One Morning*, was published in 1996 to popular and critical acclaim, and won the inaugural First Blood Award for best first crime novel of the year. This success was followed up with the bestsellers, *Country of the Blind*, *Not the End of the World*, *One Fine Day in the Middle of the Night* and *Boiling a Frog* which won the 2000 Sherlock Award for Best Comic Detective.

'A stonking good read, redolent with arch Scottish cynicism and laced with observational humour . . . Sharply satirical and poignantly funny, this is a gripping and highly entertaining read'   TIME OUT

'An intelligent, laddish thriller with lots of attitude'
                                                                                   DAILY MAIL

'A compulsive page-turner which will steal a day or two of your life but reward you with some of the wittiest one-liners and most hilarious set pieces you will find on any bookshelf'
                                                                               THE BIG ISSUE

'Aggressive stand-up, filled with riffs on oil money, rock music and hotel room service'   GUARDIAN

'Brookmyre is a brilliant satirist . . . An absolute must read'
PUNCH

'There are an impressive range of voices, various narratives, scene-setting and cutting. It is fast paced and heavily plotted, producing moments of genuine suprise . . . hilarious, exhilarating entertainment'   THE HERALD

Also by Christopher Brookmyre

QUITE UGLY ONE MORNING
COUNTRY OF THE BLIND
NOT THE END OF THE WORLD
ONE FINE DAY IN THE MIDDLE OF THE NIGHT
BOILING A FROG

This one's true as well

To be oneself is to kill oneself.
– *Henrik Ibsen*

PROLOGUE

Tonight, tonight I say goodbye
To everyone who loves me
Stick it to my enemies tonight
Then I disappear
Bathe my path in shining light
Set the dials to thrill me
Every secret has its price
This one's set to kill

Too loose, too tight, too dark, too bright
A lie, the truth, which one should I use?
If the lie succeeds
Then you'll know what I mean
When I tell you I have secrets
To attend

Do you think I'm beautiful?
Or do you think I'm evil?

—Greg Dulli, *Crime Scene Part One*
from *Black Love*, The Afghan Whigs

things to do in stavanger when you're dead

SSCs. Death was too good for them.

Seriously.

These fuckers deserved to live forever. The sleepwalking suburban slave classes in their Wimpey mock-Tudor penal colonies. A jail that needed no walls because the inmates had been brainwashed into believing they wanted to be there. Incarceration by aspiration, all the time mindlessly propagating and self-replicating, passing on their submissive DNA to the next generation of glazed-eyed prisoners.

And every day they'd get up and pray that emancipation never came: 'Dear Lord, protect us from uniqueness. Grant unto us eternal conformity, and deliver us from distinction. Amen.'

There was one up his arse right then, flashing the headlights on his MX3, the bloke's eyes widening and nostrils flaring in time with the admonitory illuminations. An absolute fanny. Risking his life in an attempt to overtake before the crawler lane ends, so he'll be one car – *one car* – up the queue when he reaches the traffic lights. And what did that tell you about the life he was risking?

Exactly.

Suburban Sad Cunts. This was the real reason for road rage. It wasn't a symptom of growing traffic congestion (though it shared the single car-usage factor), it was that this was the closest they got to defiance, the last ghostly remnant of the will to assert some identity. It was the only time they got to express any sense of self: when they were behind that wheel, on their own, jostling for position with the rest of the faceless. Overtake the guy in the bigger, newer, shinier car, and it made you forget all the other, truer ways in which he was leaving you to eat his dust. Someone gets in your way, holds you back, and you transfer all your frustrations to him because it reminds you of just how many obstacles there are between where you are now and where you want to be. The car in front is your lack of self-confidence, bequest of your over-protective mother. The car in front is your fear of confrontation, inherited from your cowed and broken father. The car in front is the school you didn't go to, the golf club you didn't join, the Lodge you don't belong to. The car in front is your wife and kids and the risks you can't take because you've got responsibilities.

But the most tragic part is that you need the car in front, you need the obstacle, because it prevents you from confronting the fact that *you don't know* where you want to be. You'd be lost beyond the penal colony. It's scary out there.

You wouldn't fit in.

That was why billions were spent every year advertising near-identical vehicles as a totem of personal taste and discernment. Toyota, Nissan, Honda, Ford, Vauxhall, Rover, each with their hatchback, their coupé, their saloon, each model barely distinguishable from its competitor by anything more than the badge. The ads featured lantern-jawed beefcakes rescuing children, battling sharks, shagging like heroes, anything to keep your attention off the actual car. 'The new Vauxhall. Its headlights are shaped slightly different from the Nissan. Because *you*'re slightly different.' Maybe not, eh?

But then that was where the four-by-fours and sports models came in. Guys driving off-roaders to the fucking video shop; the only time the thing was actually off the road was when it was in the driveway outside their Gyproc and plywood 'dream home', or when it was in the workshop after you took a bend at more than forty and rediscovered your respect for aerodynamics over sheer bulk. Sometimes there was a Dependants Carrier for the wife, or maybe just a four-door saloon, salary dictating. So you saved and strived and kissed ass to pay for that MRII or CRX or GTi, to hold on to some pitiful fantasy of your enduring virility. You might have the wife, the mortgage, the weans, and the in-laws round for dinner every Sunday, but part of you would *never* be tamed. Another slice of Viennetta, anyone?

This was the reason that no matter how steep the petrol price hikes, however many park-and-ride schemes were subsidised, urban traffic congestion was never going to diminish. In that journey to and from work, that half an hour you were at the controls of your thunderous roadbeast (going the same speed as the 2CV in front), you were able to live a pitiful little dream of yourself.

We would never car-pool. The SSC would rather sit in tailbacks every day, waiting for that brief moment when he can put the foot down and pretend he's going somewhere important, somewhere he wants to go, and fast. That power surge borrowed from the engine, the feel of the steering wheel in his hands, and Bryan Adams on the stereo. In that moment, he's cool as fuck: he's a secret agent, a maverick detective, an assassin, a terrorist. As opposed to an insurance adjuster.

What never occurred to him was that, if they existed, the secret agent, the maverick detective, the assassin and the terrorist would actually be driving some nondescript SuburbanSadCuntmobile, because they needed to blend in. Sure, maybe they drove something flashier on their days off, but you could bet it wasn't a fucking Mazda. And you could bet they weren't fantasising about being a family-man wage-serf while they burned rubber.

The SSC's fantasies are uniform and predictable because he has no imagination. He needs advertising to do his imagining for him. That's why, bereft of independent opinion or any informed sense of judgement, he thinks Denise Richards is sexy, that Sony make good hi-fi equipment and that drinking Becks makes him cooler than the bloke standing next to him with a pint of heavy. That's why he thinks he looks like a different guy driving the family six-seater than at the controls of his overpriced (and para-doxically worth every penny) ego-chariot. He thinks assassins and terrorists tool around in sports cars, and if you asked him what kind of motor Death would drive, (after you'd told him a hearse was too literal) he'd probably describe the vehicle of his ultimate fantasies, styled, of course, in black. A Lamborghini Countach or Ferrari Testarossa, or maybe some minor variation on the Batmobile; a sleek, powerful, dark and incomparably macho machine.

And he'd be wrong. Miles out.

Death would drive an Espace.

He'd drive an SSC family slave-wagon just to underline that the life He was taking wasn't worth living anyway; with plenty of seats in the back for the next generation when their turn came.

He was on the dual carriageway now, five minutes away from the airport at any other time of the week, but ten today, it being Monday morning. What better day for a new beginning than the start of the working week, the day that would for everyone else usher in yet another 104-hour vigil as they prayed for the deliverance of Friday night.

However, every new beginning was also an end, every rebirth first required a death. It would be respectful, even decorous (not to mention fun) to contemplate this life he was about to leave behind, this life that had so few hours left to run. With that thought, he reached to the stereo and popped out the cassette, then stabbed at the pre-set channels until he found the local commercial station. Might as well have the appropriately dismal soundtrack. A grim smile crept across his face as he recognised the song currently playing, the new chart-topping single by EGF. It was the standard homogenous Euro-dance number, another near-identical slice off this endless turd that was being shat out of the Low Countries via the Mediterranean teen-copulation colonies.

EGF. It stood for Eindhoven Groove Factory. Seriously. There had been a time, not so long ago, when if you had any ambitions for a career in the music biz, being from continental Europe was something you had to keep quiet, unless you were Einstürzende Neubaten and quite clearly too mental to care. It was commercial and credibility suicide. You just couldn't *be* from Europe and expect to sell records in the UK or US, the two biggest music markets.

The Scandinavians were inexplicably tolerated, benefitting perhaps from a cultural exemption that owed a little to geography and a lot to a natural preponderance of strapping blondes. From Abba to The Cardigans, via Roxette and Ace of Bass, it had never hurt the album sales to have a frontwoman who was blonde with legs all the way up to her head. At least you had to give the Scans credit for having sussed that this was the only recipe viable for export. All points south, however, they continued to labour under the misapprehension that their sub-Eurovision drivel would be interpreted in Blighty as something other than an act of international aggression. Hence, very little made it through quarantine at Dover. The occasional specimen was imported for zoological curiosity value, or more accurately to fuel our innate sense of musical superiority, such as *Rock Me Amadeus* or *The Final Countdown*.

There were those who believed the third Antichrist of Nostradamus's prophecies was, in fact, the European Union, and certainly something Satanic had been loosed around the ratification of the Maastricht Treaty in the early Nineties. How else could you explain the fact that the British public subsequently started buying records from the same forsaken region as had been found irrefutibly guilty of *Live is Life* and the ongoing catalogue of atrocities that was The Scorpions? What other explanation could be given for the traditional hard-working, hard-drinking four-piece being usurped as the pre-eminent group blueprint by two or three Evian-drinking spotty tossers playing synths in their mum's garage somewhere in the Benelux?

The latest (culminatory, as far as he was concerned) infestation was EGF, and their inescapably ubiquitous (it's really big in the clubs!) 'song', *Ibiza Devil Groove*.

There was never much to differentiate the work of any particular bunch of these mindless fuckers from that of their peers, but EGF had nonetheless managed the unlikely feat of truly distinguishing themselves in his eyes and ears. They had done this through their choice of which obligatory past standard to sample from (in lieu of spending two minutes coming up with a hook, or even a lyric). Not for them an old Andy Summers riff or Topper Headon beat;

Eindhoven's finest had built the summer's biggest smash around the chorus of Cliff Richard's *Devil Woman*.

Rock and fucking roll.

He turned up the volume for maximum effect. It felt like the last day of school before the summer holidays in those odd classes where the teacher didn't let things slide: you could perversely luxuriate in the tedium of a double Maths lesson, immersing yourself in what you *wouldn't* have to put up with tomorrow.

He couldn't kid himself, mind you, that where he was going there'd be any escape from *Ibiza Devil Groove*. Christ, even if he topped himself he probably wouldn't escape it; the old Sparks track *It's Number One All Over Heaven* sprang to mind, and there was no doubt EGF was number one all over Hell. However, what he *would* be escaping was . . .

'. . . Silver City FM, bringing you a wee kick in the Balearics there, ha ha ha, with the magnificent EGF. It's just coming up to eight forty-nine on May the twenty-sixth, here in Europe's Oil Capital, where the temperature is eleven-point-five degrees . . .'

Europe's Oil Capital. Honestly. The first time he heard the expression, he'd assumed it was a bit of self-deprecatory humour. That was before he learned that there was no such thing as self-deprecatory humour in Aberdeen, particularly when it came to the town's utterly unfounded conceit of itself. It was a provincial fishing port that had struck it astronomically lucky with the discovery of North Sea oil, and the result was comparable to a country bumpkin who had won the lottery, minus the dopey grin and colossal sense of incredulous gratitude. The prevalent local delusion wasn't that the town had merely been in the right place at the right time, but that it had somehow done something to deserve this massive good fortune, and not

11

before time, either. Nor did the billions ploughed into the area's economy stop them whining about every penny of Scottish public money that got spent anywhere south of the Stracathro motorway service station.

He didn't imagine the locals had first asked anyone else in the European oil industry whether they concurred before conferring this status upon their home town, but working in marketing he at least understood the necessity of such misleading promotion in face of the less glamorous truth. 'Scotland's Fourth City' wasn't exactly a winning slogan, especially considering that there was a dizzyingly steep drop-off after the first two, and it *still* put them behind the ungodly shit-hole that was Dundee.

The also self-conferred nickname 'Silver City' was another over-reaching feat of turd-polishing euphemism. It was grey. Everything was grey. There was just no getting away from it. The buildings were all – *all* – made of granite and the sky was covered in a thick layer of permacloud. It. Was. Grey. If Aberdeen was silver, then shite wasn't brown, it was coppertone. It was grey, as in dull, as in dreary, as in chromatically challenged. It was grey, grey, grey. And the only thing greyer than the city itself was the fucking natives. A couple of quotes to illustrate.

'An Aberdonian would pick a shilling from a dunghill with his teeth.' Paul Theroux.

'There's nae folk sae fine as them that bide by Don and Dee.' Lewis Grassic Gibbon.

Apposite as the former might be, it was actually the latter that offered a deeper insight, though not quite in the way the author intended. To understand, you first had to take a wild stab at what part of the globe you thought Grassic Gibbon might hail from. Then having miraculously plucked that one out of the ether, you might begin to develop a picture of a people who either didn't get around much, or wilfully failed to absorb anything if and when they did. How else could they remain ignorant of the existence of even the most basic foreign customs, such as smiling?

Living in Aberdeen had taught him the difference between the parochial and the truly insular. The parochial was defined by a naïve, even innocent ignorance of the world beyond its borders. The truly insular knew fine there was a world outside, they just *didnae fuckin' like it*, and had *nae fuckin' need for it*!

Living in Aberdeen had also taught him that as you only got one shot at life, it was way too precious to waste living in Aberdeen. The inescapable nature of this truth had only fully dawned on him when he realised that his life here had become just that: inescapable. It was the kind of place you only went to in the first instance because you assumed you wouldn't be there for long; you'd bide your time, serve your sentence and get back to civilisation at the first opportunity. But what you hadn't foreseen was that that opportunity might never come, and in the meantime circumstances could wrap themselves around you like the coils of a snake.

So if you only got one shot, what were you meant to do when you found yourself doomed to spend it here? Surrender and join the SSCs? Aye, right. Find some form of compensatory vice, like fucking your way around the neighbourhood's housequines on your flexi-time midweek days off? He'd tried. It grew tired very quickly, mainly due to the brain-deadening quality of their post-coital conversation. Five minutes after they came, some Pavlovian trigger mechanism invariably caused them to start wittering on about their progeny. That was if they weren't

13

already kicking you out of bed because they had to go and collect the little bastards from nursery or wherever. You could kid yourself on that it was making you feel good, but to be honest you might as well take up golf. It was just your choice of recreation in the prison's exercise yard.

What did that leave? How about buying a fucking lottery ticket, and joining the acolytes of Britain's saddest new religion? It was also Britain's biggest, and no wonder, because unlike all the others, it was the only one that offered you a second shot in this life rather than the next. And yes, you *could* get a second shot, theoretically. Only one rule of life was truly hard and fast: the same one that demanded you make the most of it, and mocked you for your efforts from the wheel of its Espace.

But those precious second shots came to a paltry few, fewer even than the fourteen-million-to-one lottery winners, most of whom were far too dull to do anything remotely interesting with their new resources. Once they'd returned from the mandatory Caribbean cruise and bought the Ferrari, the motor launch and the new pad in a part of town where the neighbours will treat them like shite off their shoes, what next? Consumerist nirvana? Come on, there was only so much gear you could buy at Argos. Twenty mill could buy you a whole new life, but only if you knew where to shop. Otherwise you were just buying a bigger cell. Truly reaping the potential reward was a little more complicated than picking up a giant greenback from a B-list celeb and a tart in a bikini.

To get a second shot, he now knew – even if you were shackled here in the mock-Tudor gulag – you didn't need to win the lottery. What it took was the will to walk away. Quit whining, quit bitching, just quit.

Walk away. As simple, and as difficult, as that.

Leave everything behind.

Making the realisation was the hard part; taking the decision. Then from the other side of the resolution, it all looked laughably easy.

Leave your partner. No problem. Already done, in fact. The people they'd each once been had blown town years ago. Scratch that; the person he'd once been had been lost in transit during the move to the Sliver City. How did the song go? If you love somebody, set them free. He didn't love Alison, but he owed her that much at least. It wasn't just himself he'd be granting a second shot.

Leave your job. Are you kidding? What incentive was there – or had there ever been – to stick with that? Oh yeah, of course: security. As in maximum.

These chains only held you as long as you clung to them.

The machine spat out a parking ticket and raised its barrier as he pulled the cardboard chit through the open window. He dropped it on to the passenger seat and drove slowly forward, joining the automotive satellites in their outward-spiralling shallow orbit, making wider and wider circuits as they were forced on each pass to seek a space that bit further out from the terminal building. They'd spend five minutes, maybe more, doing that to save themselves an extra twenty seconds' walk. Right enough, most of them probably had a whole briefcase to carry. Or perhaps they thought they were more vulnerable to being picked off by predators if they appeared to be straggling outside the pack.

The parking ticket was the first thing that caught his eye as he killed the engine. 'Do not leave in car,' it said. It was one of many instructions that no longer applied to him. He popped it in his pocket all the same. There was no room

15

for decadent gestures. This life had to be lived as normal and by all of its petty little rules right up until his connecting flight took off from Stavanger. The only concession right now was that he was wearing a polo-neck instead of a shirt and tie, necessary to cover up the change of clothes he had on beneath. He didn't want anyone to notice him leave, so when he walked away, he would already be a different person.

He still had the mandatory jacket and trousers too, but had picked something that would plausibly go with the polo-neck, affecting that 'business traveller dressing as casually as he dares but still wanting everyone to know he's a business traveller' look. It had to be one of the great equalising points against the female inequality grievance list that *they* had an endless variety of business garb to choose from, but guys were stuck with – let's be honest – minor variations on the monochrome theme of 'grey suit'. That there could be so much snobbery over the labels, styles and cuts was fucking laughable, but it was perhaps understandable (if pathetic) that any evidence of distinctiveness should be so seized upon. After all, there were probably angler-fish that were considered particularly unattractive by their peers, even though the entire species looked like Anne Widdecombe after a heavy night.

The worst of it was that he seemed to be in a minority in this sense of sartorial frustration. To the SSCs it was like a security blanket. They felt naked and exposed in anything else, and by God, they thought they looked *good*. The ties around their necks might be partially restricting their respiratory function, but it was also a comforting sensation, the pressure of a paternal hand reassuring them that their status was ratified and visible: they were suit-wearers, they had a suit-wearing career in a suit-wearing profession, and nobody, *nobody* was going to mistake them for faceless nonentities, oh no.

All around the car park, they were marching towards the terminal building as though spiritually drawn, suited to a man, briefcase fitted as standard. If you were travelling on business, on *company* business, the suit would be compulsory, but for these bastards the compulsion was coming from within. It overrode all other considerations, such as practicality. It wasn't comfortable attire for air travel, where the seat size, leg room and safety belt seemed designed to do roughly the opposite of a Corby Trouser Press, to say nothing of the constant precipitous fear that your in-flight meal, drink and tea or coffee (sir?) would end up in your lap. But still there endured this misguided notion that you had to look your best to fly, something that presumably had its roots in the earlier days when only the rich could do it. He remembered family package holidays as a kid, early Seventies, going to Palma or Malaga out of Abbotsinch. His dad told him you could always spot the wee Glasgow guys on their first-ever flight, because they looked like they were due in court. They'd wised up by the time they flew home, when they remained equally identifiable by their oversize comedy sombreros and near full-thickness burns covering all exposed flesh.

Time, experience and new generations had seen the discount leisure-travel look evolve, but it wasn't any more flattering. He'd always meant to investigate whether Airtours wouldn't actually let you board the plane unless your entire family were wearing matching shellsuits and had a combined kilogram weight in four figures.

He'd increasingly heard it said that cheap air travel was clogging up the skies, with dire accompanying predictions of an escalating incidence of disaster. The skies were indeed congested, and more so all the time, but as far as he was concerned, the blame shouldn't be laid at the Reebok-clad feet of the wobbling classes; at least there was some purpose to their trips, even if it was merely the opportunity to devour saturated fats in a warmer climate. The true cause of all these near-misses and twenty-minute holding cycles was all around him right then: pointless, unnecessary business trips.

This was the communications age, the era of video-conferencing, virtual exhibition software, emails, web catalogues, and yet every day, from every airport, suited SSCs were hording on to planes to fly to meetings where nothing would be achieved or agreed that couldn't have been resolved to equal satisfaction through a phone call or even an exchange of letters. They'd say it was about the personal touch, or the value of face-to-face relations, and while these things were to some extent true, the real purpose was to delude the SSC drones into thinking they were valued and important employees. It was certainly cheaper than raising their salaries, and the tax-deductible block bookings probably came with the sweetener of a few first-class long-hauls for the boss and whichever secretary he was banging.

It broke up the monotony if every few weeks you bunged them off somewhere overnight; made them feel they were on some kind of classified mission with which the firm had entrusted them. It made them more than suited professionals, it made them suited professionals who were so important, they had to fly places. No mere tooling around the sales territory in a Ford Mondeo for them. The vast majority of the time, however, the only practical consequence was to clog up the airports.

The check-in area was mobbed and chaotic, as per for Monday morning, with the added joy of a party of Euroteens milling around with that particular gormlessness which only hormone-addled post-pubescent continentals could truly evince. The air was thick with the smells of Clearasil and damp backpacks. He listened apprehensively to their chatter, trying to get a handle on the language, praying it wasn't Norwegian. They sounded Italian, possibly Spanish. It was hard to make out which check-in desk they were queuing for, so sprawling was their mass, but it was soon evident that they were BA's problem today, and therefore not his.

He handed over his tickets at the ScanAir desk, where he was greeted with a smile from the girl behind the counter. The namebadge said Inger, which explained the unAberdonian flash of gnashers. Probably worked her ticket in the cabin crew then opted for a ground staff post as soon as she'd snared a well-heeled oil exec.

They went through the usual formalities of seat allocation and mutual flirtatiousness, before she got to the mandatory security questions: did you pack this bag yourself, has it been out of your sight, did somebody else ask you to carry anything, is that a surface-to-air missile in your pocket or are you just pleased to see me? The purpose of these exchanges escaped him. You'd definitely have to stay behind after class at terrorism school if that little polite query had you spilling your guts. Maybe it was about reassuring the passenger that all protocols were being followed to ensure their safety; if so, it was likely to have roughly the opposite effect, if that was the measure of their counter-terrorist savvy. What did they do if someone actually got through with a gun? Ask him nicely to put it down, crucially remembering to say please?

A more advanced version of the same pointless tokenism awaited at the passenger security check, where you queued up to have your hand luggage partially irradiated and your sides lightly patted if you'd forgotten to drop your house-keys in the dish. He'd had more intimate handling being measured for his suit. They were so tentative as to make an appropriate mockery of the whole process: they didn't want to get too fresh in case you took the huff and pointed out what they well knew: that nobody had ever been – nor was ever likely to be – stopped with a gun down their jooks at this Legoland apology for an airport. And if that astronomical improbability ever did come to pass, did they think the gunman, having been asked to stand aside while they patted him down, would wait till they'd found it, give them a bashful grin and say 'Well, you gotta try, aintcha?' Unless, of course, that illuminated ad for the Scottish Tourist Board was concealing a false partition behind which a battery of heavily armed cops waited at all times, their trigger-fingers getting ever itchier through unuse.

'Do you mind if we have a wee look in your briefcase, sir?'

'No, help yourself.'

All these flights down the years and he still couldn't guess what the selection criteria were for them opening your hand luggage. Sometimes they stopped him, some-times they didn't, with no consistency as to his appear-ance, destination, whether he was alone or in company, anything. Was it something unusual spotted by the glazed and constipated-looking bastard peering with chronic ennui at the X-ray monitor? Was it utterly random, to meet a percentage quota? Would they at that particular moment rather open your neat, shiny briefcase than the forbiddingly grubby overnight bag of the eye-stingingly sweaty gut-bucket ahead of you, who'd required a shove to squeeze him through the metal-detection arch? Or did they just fancy a nosey sometimes? He'd have no respect for them if they didn't.

The bearded security officer gestured to him to open the case himself, an ostensible intimation of courtesy disguising the fact that he didn't want to look like a twat by fumbling cluelessly around the latest needlessly complex latch-trigger system. He simultaneously pushed the buttons on either side, like it was a pinball machine and the ball was rolling lazily between the flippers. Turning the case smartly through one hundred and eighty degrees, he released the lid, its impressively gentle ascent smoothed by the telescoping aluminium supports that had added at least twenty per cent to the price.

There wasn't much to see. A couple of folders, a magazine, a newspaper, mobile phone, hand-fan, Walkman, king-size Mars bar and two cartons of juice. Hard to imagine any of that lot had appeared particularly suspicious going through the conveyor. Nonetheless, the guy had stopped him now, so he had to make it look worthwhile. Beardie started with the mobile, raising and lowering it on his palm to emphasise its weight as he handed it over.

'Would you mind turning it on?'

'Yeah, no problem.'

He pressed the button, eliciting a cursory glance at the LCD window before Beardie took it back.

'That's fine. Bit of a monster, isn't it?'

'Tell me about it. Why d'you think I'm carryin' it in the case? My new one's knackered, so they've got me luggin' this thing around. Surprised they let me take it on as hand luggage. Has to happen when I'm goin' away as well.'

'Sod's law.'

Beardie moved on to the Walkman next, getting nodded

assent to press Play himself. The tape turned to his satisfaction, though he evidently gave no thought to whether the passenger might have painstakingly cued up his favourite take-off track. He then held up one earphone. A quick tinny burst sufficed, the palpated hiss sounding, unfailingly, like Speed Garage, which presumably was the only musical genre to sound exactly the same whether your cans were on or not.

Beardie resumed his examination, undeterred by the lack of anything much to examine. He gave the fan a whirl; picked up the folders, magazine and newspaper, flicking through each in turn; then either out of admirable thoroughness or mild pique, checked out the Mars bar and finally the juice cartons as well. These last being his final chance to exert some authority, he gave each an inquisitive stare, before following it up with an investigative shake, which was the ultimate proof of the utter uselessness of the entire 'security' charade. If he was worried that the Ribena cartons actually contained nitroglycerine, would the advised procedural protocol be to give them a good shoogle?

'Right, thank you, sir. Enjoy your trip.'

It was only once he was on board the aircraft, and had heard the enduringly futile announcements on what action you could take in the event of the fuel-laden plane plummeting vertically from the skies, that it occurred to him to worry about the implications of these two-dimensional defences. Because let's face it, if this plane was sabotaged and crashed before he made it to Stavanger today, he would be one very unhappy dead person. To say nothing of the colossal fucking irony.

Oh well. Just as long as it didn't mean you spent the afterlife in Aberdeen Hell.

* * *

22

The plane had touched down at 11:20 local time. Conditions clear and sunny, outside temperature eighteen degrees.

Stavanger. An appropriately inauspicious conduit in his grand scheme. There were no new beginnings to be found here, only transit lounges, flight information and a store selling cuddly gnomes and smoked salmon. Most of the times he had been here, it had been merely to get on another plane and travel somewhere else; somewhere else he didn't particularly want to be either. Other people's jobs took them to Barcelona, Milan, Athens, Paris. His took him to every austere, hypermasculine, over-industrialised fastness in Scandinavia, including – but more often via – Stavanger. For once, a flight would take him from here to where *he* wanted to be, but as ever, it wasn't until he had got on and off one more plane that his journey would be ended, and another one truly begun.

He sat in the departure area, choosing a bench by the window upon his return from the toilets. The plane was sitting on the tarmac, yards away, the livery's colours distorted by the bright sunshine, but the name legible on the fuselage: Freebird. He smiled. Couldn't have named it better himself.

The clock read 11:55. Fifteen minutes to boarding. This was the hardest part: it wasn't long to wait now, but waiting was all there was left to do. Waiting and thinking. There was no avoiding the former, but he sincerely wished he could prevent the latter. Seeing the jet through the window, it was difficult not to contemplate the enormity of what lay so imminently ahead, but he had to tune it out. Throughout these minutes, he knew, it would seem easy to back down, call it all off. Easy to feel the comfort of your chains.

It was the longest quarter of an hour of his life, limping its way through each minute that brought him tantalisingly

23

closer to the point at which the torment of choice would cease. Once he handed over his boarding pass and walked down that gangplank, there would be no going back. Not without some very uncomfortable explaining afterwards, anyway.

Somehow, the laws of temporal physics prevailed, and the clock conceded.

At 12:12 the departure was announced.

At 12:15, he boarded the aircraft.

At 12:37, it took off.

At 12:39 and eighteen seconds, when the plane had reached exactly three thousand feet, a bomb exploded towards the rear of the passenger cabin. The charge wasn't particularly big, but neither did it have to be, placed as it was within feet of the fuel tanks. The tail section was severed completely, causing the remainder of the aircraft to arc and then spin as it plummeted towards the fjord beneath.

That was the truly transforming moment, when life, whatever it had meant before, suddenly became unconditionally precious.

The job, the daily commute, the enslaving mortgage, the faceless suburb, the crumbling relationship, the arguments, the bills, the crushed ambitions, the castrating compromises: in an instant they went from being an inescapable hell to a lost paradise.

And the rate at which they underwent that change was ten metres per second squared.

At 12:40 and nine seconds, the front section hit the water, breaking the fuselage into two more parts and killing everyone on board.

sending a message to the man

This was a new kind of nervous. It wasn't like the nervousness he felt before a match; that was more of an impatience, an unsteady feeling that set him off-balance until he got his first touch, sent his first pass, made his first tackle. After that, all was familiar, whatever challenge the opposition presented. And, thank God, it wasn't like the nervousness he'd felt on Thursday, waiting for her to go on her break, trying to get the timing right so that it seemed natural and she didn't know he'd been hanging around, worrying that her rota had changed and he'd already missed her; all of which being *before* he had to actually speak to her. He'd feared his voice would disappear, and then when it didn't, that she could read his thoughts even as he chatted and joked. When he finally asked, he'd felt his words soften and tremble in his throat, his lips seeming to numb as though he had some kind of palsy, hardly presenting the strong-jawed image that would enhance his chances.

Her name was Maria. He'd known her for years in as much as they were in some of the same classes at school, but he hadn't known her to talk to until recently. The guys just didn't talk to the girls at school, not unless they wanted to lay themselves open to all manner of teasing and ridicule. Even among themselves, nobody talked about who they fancied, unless they meant models and movie stars. It was as though it was a sign of weakness, or something the others could use against you. Worse still, they could tell her, and then you might as well commit suicide.

Maria had a job at one of the big department stores over the summer holidays, and he had genuinely bumped into her on her break on Monday. It had taken him by surprise that they had been able to talk so comfortably, but what surprised him more was the way he felt after she was gone. He couldn't think about anything or anyone else. From being just a girl he knew of, she became the only girl in the world he wanted to know.

He went back the next day, thinking he'd just try and catch a glimpse of her, but not let her see him (what would she think?), but it turned out to be her day off. On Wednesday he had to help his father lay chips in the garden, and the truck didn't turn up on time, so the job wasn't done until late in the afternoon. He thought about going into town and waiting to catch her coming out when her shift was over, but when he came downstairs after having a shower, Jo-Jo was in the kitchen, waiting for him to come and join a kick-around in the park. He would go tomorrow, he told himself, and he wouldn't just sneak a glimpse, he would speak to her. He would ask her out.

She didn't say yes. Instead she began nodding and smiling before he had even finished his tremulous, stumbling sentence, making it plain that she *had* read his thoughts, had known what was coming, and already knew her answer. It felt amazing.

They arranged to meet outside the cinema. She had surprised him by saying she wanted to see the American movie *Close Action 2*, which Tony hadn't considered ideal date material, and he came close to blowing their relationship before it started when he suggested she must fancy the star, Mike MacAvoy. Maria didn't regard herself as a

26

'girly' girl. She listened to The Offspring and Nine Inch Nails as her classmates drooled over the latest bubble-gum teen-idols, and while they gossiped about soaps, she could tell you everything about *The X-Files* and *The Sopranos*.

She was late. Not very late, not late enough for him to start seriously worrying about being stood up – yet – just late. The sense of anticipation had been present in varying degrees of intensity for at least thirty-six hours, but what he was feeling now was something different, something unique. This was a good nervous, an exciting nervous. He was trying to remember how she smelled, to picture what she'd wear, how she walked, the way she smiled, and marvelling that so many wonderful and fascinating things could be contained in one small frame. It tingled in his stomach and it quivered in his chest. It was as though he had to remember to breathe.

And then he saw her, suddenly emerging from behind two old women dressed in widows' black. She wore a corn-flower-coloured sundress that made her look like she ought to be barefoot and the pavement knee-high grass. Last month he'd scored from a direct free-kick in injury time in the last game of the schools season to clinch the point his team needed to win promotion.

This felt *far* better.

It was a miserable night, rain bouncing off the tarmac, swamping every windscreen and rendering the cars in front a mere blur of red tail-lights. Miserable, that was, for everyone else. For Nicholas, there was a paradoxical pleasure to be had in the sheer hideousness of the weather. Even having to drive through it had an inversely comforting effect, for the simple reason that at the end of the trip, he knew he'd be able to close the front door on it all and sit down to dinner with his wife.

He'd enjoyed stormy winter nights ever since he was a child, when he used to spend ages at the front window of his mother's flat, looking down at the rain-washed street or watching the water streak the glass. It enhanced the feeling of snugness and security, made the place seem all the more cosy and his mother's presence all the more warm. When he had first moved in with Janine, he had been pleased to discover that the feeling survived into adulthood. They'd always enjoyed the sense that sometimes they could shut the world out and exist only for each other, and it seemed accentuated when the wind was shaking the trees and the rain lashing the glass.

It was their second wedding anniversary, but the first one they'd be spending together, Nicholas having been abroad on business last year. It was also the last one they'd be spending alone for the foreseeable future, with Janine expecting next month. Nights like this made work worthwhile, like the wind and the rain made a small but double-glazed apartment a palace.

The traffic wasn't particularly bad despite the rain, just slowing a little in the usual bends and up-slopes. Maybe it was lighter because people had knocked off early when they saw the deluge through their office windows. Nicholas looked at the LED clock on the dashboard. He'd be home in forty minutes at this rate. Janine would greet him with a kiss and a glass of Merlot, while he would reciprocate with the new dress he'd bought her. She wouldn't be wearing it for a while, but he remembered his sister saying how just such a gift had meant a lot to her when she was advanced in her pregnancy. It helped remind her that she hadn't always been in that condition, although it often felt that way, and gave her something to aim at for getting back into shape afterwards.

With that, his mind turned to what might be on the menu. A cassoulet perhaps, he thought, breaking into a broad smile. That's what she'd made a night last week, but when he arrived home she discovered she'd forgotten to turn on the oven, and they'd had no choice but to have a bath and make love while they waited for it to cook. They were like teenagers these days, doing it all the time. Perhaps it was hormonal on Janine's part, or perhaps it was some natural inclination to draw closer together in advance of becoming a family. Who knew? Who cared?

He hit the disc-shuffle button to cue forward to the next CD, *OK Computer*. Not an ostensibly romantic choice, but it had come out when he and Janine first moved in together, and hearing it always made him think of that time. The traffic began to pick up speed once he was over the hill, past the cement factory. He could revise his ETA to nearer half an hour.

Tanya was beginning to wish she had been born in a future century when teleportation had supplanted all other means of transport, though she'd settle for one in which personal hygiene had become enforceable by law and trains didn't resemble some Communist-era social experiment on wheels. The carriage was, as ever, packed beyond capacity, and in accordance with the first law of public transport, the ratio of genetic sub-species and mental inadequates to normal human beings was ten times that of the normal per-capita average. She had managed to secure a seat at the window, which meant trading off the freezing draught against only having some soap-allergic plebeian squeezed up against her on *one* side. In this case it was a cabbage-smelling old crone whose leather complexion and rasping voice suggested she smoked more than a laboratory beagle.

She was, mercifully, abstaining on this trip, presumably in deference to the toddler wedged into her lap, who was not so much eating a boiled sweet as breaking it down into its molecular constituents, the better to spread it as far around his sticky little person as was physically possible. His glistening hands swayed precariously close to her good coat every few seconds, and when Tanya tried to compact herself closer into the wall, the old bag simply took up the slack and brought her syrup-coated runt back into smearing range.

Directly across from her, there was an ostentatiously snogging couple who had come up with an ingenious way of compensating for the over-crowding by attempting to occupy the same space simultaneously. If Tanya closed her eyes it would be easy to mistake the slobbering noises for the bubbling of a volcanically heated mud-pool, though the infant was still producing more drool on his own than the pair of them could collectively muster. They were like a shape-shifting entity, every so often metamorphosing to thrust forth a different limb or appendage, the effect all the more grotesque due to at least one of the male's arms being inside his partner's blouse the whole time. There were three moving indentations on one side of the girl's chest, squirming knuckles where a solitary nipple should have been. The old bag tutted every so often but it would have taken a bucket of ice-water to break them apart.

Next to them was the statutory mutterer, a bespectacled middle-aged man who looked as though he had been collecting nervous tics as a hobby since early childhood. He sat there, eyes darting furtively but randomly around the carriage, while his fingers fidgeted and his mouth poured forth an incontinent torrent of unconnected words and sounds.

A curse on her parents for not giving her the air fare. They said they'd already given her a sum for the coming term, and it was up to her to manage it, but for goodness sake, they knew she hated the train. Did they want her to have to take a bite out of it before the Christmas break was even over? It was because of her exam results for last term. They hadn't said anything – they never did, just huffed around and waited for her to read their minds – but she knew that's what this was about. It wasn't as though it was her fault. The urchin she'd paid to do her essays had proven to be a dud, and she'd ended up with Cs all round. Typical of her luck: everyone did it but she had to be the one who backed a loser.

She wiped the window clear of condensation with a paper handkerchief, not daring to touch the grimy pane with her bare hands. It was the last one in the packet, and it had crossed her mind to offer it to the brat to clean some of the adhesive gloop from his paws, but she needed the distraction of a view. Hardly worth it, of course. Nothing but snow. She saw some soldiers by the side of the track, which suggested they would be passing the army base soon, thank God. That meant there were only about forty-five minutes more to endure.

There had been some soldiers at the Christmas party at Peter's place, an old school friend of his and three of his comrades. And God, could they drink. Her head throbbed at the mere memory. It had gone well beyond the usual outrageousness, and of course it had to be Helena who outdid herself. She had gone down on two of the soldiers in the middle of the room, with everyone cheering and looking on. Talk about trying too hard. She badly needed to learn the difference between decadence and stupidity. The idea was to not care what anyone thought of you, as

31

opposed to merely having a complete lack of self-respect. Socially, it should have been the end for her, but the guys would undoubtedly still let her hang around for obvious reasons.

Through the window she saw the army base's outer-perimeter fence, whizzing past in a blur of posts and wires. She let her focus blur by staring at the snow, while around her the kissers squelched, the mutterer burbled and the sprog finally ended the tension by wiping a palm on her thigh. Tanya looked down to examine the damage but was promptly thrown back against her seat as though the train had been cracked like a whip. The carriage had suddenly jolted to one side, accompanied by a shuddering creak of steel and a grinding rumble from beneath. The couple and the mutterer were thrown forward into the gap between the seats, while those in the aisles fell to the floor or on top of the seated passengers on either side.

Around her the air filled with gasps and screaming, above which the grinding still boomed, the derailed train driving forward with terrifying momentum. The carriage shook and bounced as its passengers struggled to support themselves. Her forearm was gripped by the now disentangled female on the floor, while the woman at her side tried to curl herself around the now bawling infant. All faces were filled with fear, eyes widened, breath held. Each new jolt or shunt spilled body against body while voices cried in pain or strain. The girl in front fell forward as she tried to right herself, her elbow landing in Tanya's thigh like a spike. Her boyfriend sprawled sideways, nose streaming with blood after the mutterer's head struck him, the mutterer himself slumped against the old woman's knees like a marionette.

The shuddering intensified, the carriage shaking left and

right, faster and faster as it bludgeoned forward, building and building until there was a cracking, smashing, snapping sound from up ahead. Tanya instinctively braced herself, pulling her legs up and huddling into a ball against the seat-back and the panel separating the windows.

The initial derailment had been merely the overture; now the symphony of destruction truly began. The carriage was flipped from end to end along the horizontal, then turned on its side and rolled a full three hundred and sixty degrees, all the while still skidding forward through the gravel and snow, until brought to a standstill by its collision with the side of a barracks building, which it partially demolished.

The effect inside was like a liquidiser.

Tanya only knew that the carriage had halted because the thunderous rumbling stopped. Inside, there was still motion as bodies tumbled and rolled, those still conscious struggling to extricate themselves from the tangle and crush; those less fortunate lolling helplessly at gravity's dictates.

She knew she was alive because she could hear screaming and she could feel pain. Her left ankle had been snapped like a chicken-bone, but she couldn't see the damage because she was trapped from the waist down under the combined weight of the girl and the old woman, both of whom appeared to be dead. The girl was lying face-up, her head at an impossible angle, neck broken, eyes open. The old woman was face-down, motionless, blood puddling beneath her.

The screaming was everywhere, but its omnipresence seemed curiously to mute it; either that or she was losing consciousness. Amidst it, however, she could hear a slightly different cry: higher, insistent, younger. It was the child. Tanya turned her head and looked either side. She could see him, under a seat which had miraculously not collapsed. His face was red with crying, a look of frightened confusion in his eyes. From somewhere she summoned the strength to reach out and grab one of the seat's supports, trying to pull herself out from under the two bodies. Agony seared through her leg at the first hint of movement, but it was enough to cause the old woman to slide off to one side. After that, Tanya was able to roll the dead girl off too, then dragged herself close enough to reach out a hand to the child. He didn't respond at first, still too enveloped in his little world of distress to notice her. Then, when he did, he tried to shrink away.

'Come on,' she attempted to say, her voice a broken whisper, inaudible amid the cacophony.

Her hand touched his foot, then he tentatively took hold of her fingers, before finally crawling forward from his refuge.

She heard a shout from outside, through the shattered window. There was a soldier looking down at her, offering his hand through the empty frame. Her voice still failing, she pointed down until he noticed the child. The soldier pulled himself part of the way inside and took hold of Tanya around the torso, hauling her through the gap as she continued to voice her hoarse concerns for the tiny creature still down on the floor.

'I know, I know,' he said quietly, setting her gently down on the ground before clambering back into the train. Tanya looked around. There were soldiers attempting assistance all along the side of the carriage, one end of which was sticking into the barracks. In the opposite direction she could see the other carriages, all of them having crashed through into the compound. Soldiers were running from every building towards the scattered wrecks.

Her own rescuer re-emerged, the toddler under one arm, suddenly quiet. The soldier handed him to her as she sat in the snow, then commenced another sortie inside the mangled compartment. The child began sobbing again, throwing his little arms around her neck and burying his face in her coat. She closed her eyes and pressed her cheek against his hair, the pain in her leg seeming momentarily that bit more distant.

Then she heard the bang.

Tanya looked up and saw the front-most carriage and the locomotive disappear in a ball of fire. The ground shook beneath her as the explosion grew and expanded, faster and faster, ever outwards, unstoppable, inescapable. In a fraction of a second she saw it consume soldiers, carriages, buildings, billowing forwards like a tidal wave of flame.

She clutched the child and closed her eyes.

A brilliant flash lit up the rain-blackened night. Nicholas presumed it to be lightning, as his wipers battled to make an impression against the downpour and the spray. It was followed in a fraction of a second by a clap of thunder that shook the sky, the ground and the car, though this last was through his startlement at its suddenness, its volume and its awesome power. Nicholas refocused on the tail-lights in front, all of them turning red to brake as the wipers bought him another millisecond's clear view. The flyover ahead was collapsing, the vertical columns crumbling and buckling as the top section crashed down on top of the traffic in huge broken segments.

He stepped hard on the brakes but the Audi slid on the drenched road surface, aquaplaning at ninety kilometres per hour towards the car in front, itself still hurtling forward, brake lights no more than a panicked wish. As he skidded he heard a series of bangs, like his fellow condemned being executed by gunshot while he awaited his own bullet. He covered his head with his arms as the Audi slammed into the car in front, the airbag bursting out to envelope him before he was jolted again by an impact from the rear.

He was hyperventilating, but at least he knew he was alive. Behind him he could hear more crashes; in front of him he could see only the airbag. His arms were pinned, but he could move them a little, and his legs were mercifully intact also. He attempted to slow his breathing, compose himself. He was okay. Shaken, probably looking at back pains for months, but he was alive. *Überleben durch Technik*.

There was another bang from ahead, louder than any of the crashes, followed by another, then another, the relentless sequence accelerating as it continued. At the top of the windscreen he could see red and yellow light dancing in the raindrops.

Fire.

Nicholas clawed at the airbag, struggling to escape its now deadly embrace. He reached below for the seat-adjustment lever and slid backwards, giving himself the precious inches he needed to manoeuvre.

The car in front exploded as he pressed the seatbelt release.

He closed his eyes.

'Janine.'

The first thing Tony saw when he opened his eyes was his hand, balled into a fist in front of his face. It was still holding the banknote he'd proffered at the concessions stand for Maria's ice-cream, the only thing she'd agreed to let him pay for. Beyond that was a haze of smoke and dust, so much dust. It billowed around him, obscuring all but his immediate surroundings, occasionally allowing a glimpse of what lay a few more feet away: a cornflower sundress, the figure face down, twitching, convulsing.

Breathing didn't work. He sucked in air, hissed it forth, too fast, irregular. Everything felt cold.

Between him and the cornflower sundress he could make out a pair of legs amid the rubble. One foot was missing, the other hanging by a ragged remnant of flesh. The shoe looked like his. He owned a pair just like it, but he hadn't put them on today. He hadn't put those shoes on today. He'd worn the other ones, the older ones.

Please.

Tony reached down with his right arm.

He tried to call for his mother, but his throat filled with liquid. Blood washed back over his face, covering his eyes, and he saw no more.

MONDAY, SEPTEMBER FIRST

we've got hostiles

The briefing room was like *3D House of Chins*, row upon row of lantern jaws atop stiff shoulders. The last time she'd seen so many males trying to look simultaneously stern and cool was at a school disco. There were seats on the near side, but she decided to walk across the floor in front of the dais, milking reactions. Every head turned, every eye followed her, though she was under no illusions why. It wasn't just that she was the only woman in the room; it was probably as much that there was a woman in the room at all. The weaker sex weren't unheard of in Special Branch, but not many forces were going to delegate one to a pee-the-highest gig such as was taking place that morning. This wasn't a reflection on the forward-thinking liberalism of the Strathclyde force, more a means of communicating how little they anticipated this latest alert would affect them. They were right, too. According to the international terrorist's atlas, Great Britain was a kidney-shaped island ringed by something called 'the M25'.

She met a few eyes as she walked, challenged their scrutiny, offering a coy smile to let them know she could read their thoughts.

'What's she doing here? Positive discrimination, probably. Look at the size of her, too. Wouldn't want that backing you up in a ruck, would you? Must be a graduate fast-tracker. More qualifications than collars. All brains and no bottle.'

Maybe that wasn't what they were thinking, but she'd certainly heard all of it in her time.

There were nods from a few familiar faces, but just a single smile, John Millburn the only one risking disciplinary action by discarding part of the morning's official uniform. He gestured to her that there was a free seat nearby on his row, then unceremoniously nudged the balding officer next to him to move one along, allowing them to sit together.

'Angel X. How you doin', pet?'

'Not bad, pal,' she said, unable to stifle a yawn. 'Sorry. Half-six shuttle. Glad to see everybody got the serious expressions memo. They look like the government's just announced a tax on Freemasonry.'

'Oh, tread carefully there, pet. Someone's gotta help the widow's son. In't that right, Brian?'

The balding cop glowered and shook his head. Why did he have to pick a seat next to the class clown? And will it be marked down if he's caught sniggering?

'So what's this about? Do you know? Apart from . . .'

Millburn shrugged. 'I know as much as you. And that the people who know more than us are very worried.'

She looked round the gathering, a hubbub rising as fifty-odd people had the same conversation.

'Still, won't end up on our patches, will it?' she observed. 'We were probably invited as a courtesy as much as anything else.'

'Speak for yourself, pet. I'm down here in the Smoke now. As of a month ago.'

'Really? Congratulations. I think. Hasn't Newcastle descended into anarchy without you?'

'Aye, except we don't call it anarchy on Tyneside, we call it Saturday night.'

A door opened to the left of the dais, and through it emerged the gangling figure of Commander Tom Lexington, head of the anti-terrorist task force. The clamour ceased as swiftly as though he'd pressed a Mute button. It was an instinctive action of respect in part for the man and perhaps more for what his presence represented. He remained by the door, holding it open. There were three seats next to the lectern.

First to appear was a bespectacled, peely-wally, child-molester-looking type. MI5, she thought. If you cut him in half, it would be written all through his body like pepper-mint rock. He was wearing a pair of black trousers that she instantly thought of as being food-stained and held up by a piece of string. Intelligence analyst, out on a day pass from a basement in Millbank. He'd have been blinking in the daylight all the way here.

Behind him there followed, in grey military fatigues, a specimen of concentrated manhood potent enough to wither every thrust-out jaw in the room. She could tell by his relaxed body language, the way he carried himself and his neutral, almost tired expression. Nothing to prove to any man. Nothing to fear from any man. He was powerfully built but looked light on his feet. Next to Lexington he seemed quite short, but then most people did. There was a razor-nick on his otherwise smooth-shaven chin, a delightfully incon-gruous blemish on his otherwise formidable appearance.

The two new arrivals took their seats as Lexington stepped up to the lectern and placed some papers on it.

'Good morning,' he said, though circumstances sug-gested heavily that it was anything but. He had the voice of a Radio Four newsreader. It sounded soft but authori-tative at any volume, with a measured tone that both calmed and compelled. 'First of all, let me thank you all for coming down here this morning, and let me apologise for the lack of information as to why your trip was neces-sary. I am only too well aware that there is nothing we coppers like less than someone else knowing all the secrets. That is something I am about to rectify.'

He cleared his throat as he fingered the papers in front of him, briefly turning a page over and back again.

'I don't know how much attention any of you have been paying to foreign affairs recently, so please bear with me while I put this in the same context for everybody. On the tenth of March this year, General Aristide Mopoza emerged from two years in hiding to lead a successful military coup in the former British colony of Sonzola. The General himself was ousted as the country's dictator following his failed attempt to annex the neighbouring state of Buluwe. British forces, you will remember, played a significant role in this conflict, as well as in the General's subsequent toppling and the establishment of a democratically elected presidency. It's safe to say this did not sit well with sections of the Sonzolan military, many of whom have remained secretly loyal to Mopoza. They deeply resented Britain's involvement in the Buluwe conflict, which they believe they would have won otherwise. To colour the picture further, over the past decade, Sonzola has had about as many changes of power as Italy and has been in a state of almost constant civil war, throughout which Buluwe often harboured and assisted the pro-democracy rebels.'

Puzzled looks were starting to be exchanged. Lexington paused, enough to acknowledge both that he was aware of them and that he would like them to desist. They did.

'General Mopoza's forces struck on the day the country was celebrating the second anniversary of his overthrow. Like all students of history, he has a fondness for significant dates. This particular student, incidentally, read his history at Cambridge and once described himself as an Anglophile, but under the circumstances, I think we should remember

44

Oscar Wilde's remarks about what each man does to the thing he loves. In the 1960s, he fought in his country's struggle for independence and sees himself as forever tied to its destiny – a destiny in which there is no role for the country of his alma mater, other than vengeance.

'In a nation such as Sonzola, however, the only certain destiny is that sooner or later someone will stab you in the back. Yesterday morning, at zero-fifteen hours, Captain Adrian Shephard of Her Majesty's Special Air Service led an operation to evacuate General Philip Thaba, a member of Mopoza's inner circle who had communicated his wish to defect. Captain Shephard will take over the briefing from here.'

SAS. Of course.

Shephard got up, looking slightly less effortlessly assured in front of the assembly. Maybe it was easier facing down an enemy than an audience.

'Good morning,' he began, sounding less than certain about this. 'The . . . eh, reasons for General Thaba's defection were never made clear. He maybe didn't feel he was getting a big enough slice of the pie in return for his loyalty in the coup; alternatively, his own position of strength may have made him a likely candidate for a bullet in the head if Mopoza was getting nervous. We don't know. What we did know was that he claimed to be in possession of information regarding a terrorist threat to the British state, and that he was prepared to exchange this for safe passage and certain other, ehm, guarantees.

'This was therefore an entirely clandestine handover. My unit was deployed to escort General Thaba from a location twenty miles outside Freeport, across the nearby border into Buluwe. He was accompanied to the handover site by a small guard of his own loyal troops. My unit crossed the

45

border at zero fifteen hours, as Commander Lexington said. At approximately one hundred hours, we were in sight of the rendezvous when General Thaba's party came under rocket fire from helicopter gunships. The armoured car carrying the General suffered an indirect hit and was rendered inoperable by splash damage. Our radar did not pick up any prior aerial activity, and it was our conclusion that the helicopters took off from cover within a mile of the rendezvous. Ground forces were also in immediate attendance, and a firefight ensued. Despite suffering heavy casualties, General Thaba's troops did manage to transfer him to an operational vehicle and deliver him into our hands.

'By this time, unfortunately, the General had suffered serious – ultimately fatal – injuries, and remained conscious for only a few more minutes. I asked him to tell me whatever he could, but he was seldom coherent, and when he did speak it was to demand morphine and that we drive faster. I instructed our medic not to administer morphine until the General divulged whatever he knew. Our medic disobeyed. Upon receiving the injection, General Thaba began to lose consciousness, but before he did so, I asked him again to tell me what he knew.'

Shephard was blushing. Maybe it was the heat in the room, or not being used to being on the spot, but she suspected it was at the paucity of what he was about to offer.

'General Thaba was . . . less than lucid. He said only: "The Black Spirit. An eye for an eye." He repeated this twice when I asked him to elaborate. These were his final words.'

There were tuts and sighs all around the room. It was, as far as they were concerned, a big shaggy-dog story with a duff punchline. A few, however, responded with intakes of breath. They were the ones who read further than the sports pages and had heard of the Black Spirit.

'Are you sure he didn't say "Rosebud"?' cracked a voice from the back of the room, to approving laughter.

'Or "there is another Skywalker",' added a second wag, fortified by someone else having tested the water.

Shephard smiled bashfully. A man's man, he no doubt knew well when to take his lumps. Lexington looked less indulgent, and silenced the room by getting back to his feet.

'My personal favourite is "Don't let the awkward squad fire over me",' Lexington said, his tone somehow commanding without sounding stern. 'And I don't intend to this morning.'

'Come on, sir, it's a bit bloody cryptic, isn't it?' appealed Rosebud.

'Oh you think that's cryptic, do you, Willetts? Well let me assure you, that's the clear part. Captain?'

Shephard looked around his audience again, even more discomfited than before, plainly unused to needing anyone to bail him out.

'I'm afraid the Commander is right. The nature of the ambush indicated that General Mopoza knew well in advance of Thaba's intention to jump ship. This begs the questions of how much else he knew, and when he knew it. The permutations are frustratingly abundant. Did Mopoza also know Thaba was trading on information about a planned terrorist attack? Did he even feed Thaba this story in the first place because he suspected a betrayal? Did Thaba bolt because he had been cut out of the loop, hence the scarcity of his information? Like everything else in Sonzola, it's one big morass of double-crosses.

'In a military analysis, I find it almost incredible that Thaba was evacuated from the ambush, so there remains the possibility that Mopoza let him get away, knowing or

47

not knowing he was fatally injured. In short, we don't know whether Thaba's information was genuine, whether Mopoza knows what we know, or even whether Thaba made the whole thing up to buy his ticket.'

'So, with all respect, sir,' Rosebud asked, 'what has any of this got to do with us?'

Shephard looked to Lexington, who dismissed him politely with a nod and said a quiet 'thank you' as the soldier sat down.

'To answer that question, Superintendent, let me introduce Mr Eric Wells of Her Majesty's Security Service.'

Child Molester sprang up eagerly. He looked like he ought to be even more nervous than Shephard about facing the room, but probably lacked the self-awareness. Maybe just as well, given the nature of the crowd. After the support act's frustrating performance, the headliner was really going to have to deliver.

'I can't shed any more light on the questions Captain Shephard posed,' he said quietly, prompting immediate requests from all round the room that he speak up. She'd seen the type plenty of times before, an overflowing fount of information, but used to being tapped by a maximum of about three people at once.

Wells coughed a little, then resumed, his voice more projected but still not carrying particularly well. She estimated he had about thirty seconds to grab them by the throats before he'd be lost in a flood of impatient mumbling. Thirty seconds would be plenty, though, if she'd guessed right about his area of expertise.

'It is possible that General Thaba's information is as worthless as it is vague, in which case I am now wasting everyone's time. I sincerely hope that I am wasting everyone's time.'

The last remark cut dead a dozen sarcastic mumbles. Wells had more stagecraft than she'd thought, though he did have heady material to work with.

'General Thaba may have been delirious, he may have been dying, and he may even have been lying, but he mentioned the Black Spirit. *That* is what it has to do with you, officer, and that is why you've all had to come here this morning. The possibility we are facing is that one of the world's most dangerous and ruthless terrorists could be planning his first strike on British soil.'

A smattering of scornful tuts and sighs grew into a wider undercurrent of discontented mumbling. Lexington stayed put, significantly less protective of the wispy Wells than the SAS man. That significance, however, remained lost on most of the assembly.

'It's hardly grounds for a national alert, is it?' said one, a dumpy wee bloke she recognised from a placement she'd done in London last year. Hart, his name was, and like many in the big city he was used to a more tangible terrorist threat, with specific times, locations and codewords, not this airy-fairy bollocks.

'Not yet,' Wells said flatly, an unmissable admonition in his tone. 'But if it gets to that stage, then you're going to be very glad you paid attention to the speccy bloke from MI5. Because make no mistake, this is not just another homicidal fanatic with a shedload of Semtex, howling at the moon. The Black Spirit is a whole new species. He is a contract terrorist: you give him money and he kills people, that's the deal. He doesn't have a cause, he doesn't have an agenda, he doesn't have a leader, he doesn't have a sponsor and he doesn't have anything that could possibly ever be mistaken for a conscience. He does it because he gets paid, and believe me, his services are in demand, because he is very, very good at it.'

Wells was fairly warming up now, banging out the goods with an undisguised relish. He'd been surprisingly unruffled by the early heckling, and her guess was that this was because, like most obsessives, he was obliviously confident that his audience would share his enthusiasm once he reached the meaty part.

'He first flashed on to our radar screens just under three years ago, when he blew up the American embassy in Madrid. You may remember that responsibility for the bombing was claimed by Islamic militants. In truth, they merely paid the piper. The Black Spirit played the tune. The audacity of the attack was, analysts believe, intended as an overture, and the theme of high civilian casualties has remained central to the symphony. As well as gutting the embassy of the self-pronounced "most powerful nation on Earth", the explosion also demolished a cinema in the adjoining building, killing forty-eight people. They were watching the film *Close Action 2*, which for those of you lucky enough never to have seen it, is about an elite US anti-terrorist unit. The timing of the blast was not thought to be coincidental.'

Wells could now have reverted to his previous quieter tones if he'd wanted. In fact, he could have whispered. Little chance of that, though: he was having way too much fun.

'Since then, his CV has included the sinking of the Black Sea cruise-liner *Twilight Queen*, the deputy Prime Minister of Georgia among the eighty-one dead; last year's poison-gas attack in Dresden, which claimed fifty-five victims, and January's St Petersburg railway disaster, in which he effectively turned a passenger train into a moving bomb then derailed it through a Russian army base. The death toll for that one broke the three-figure mark. And these are only the ones I'm allowed to tell you about. He's been responsible for others, but his involvement in them remains classified.'

A hand went up amid the hush. It was Willetts, he of the Rosebud remark. He wasn't looking quite so jovial.

'How do you know these were carried out by the same guy?'

'Oh, he makes sure we know. He leaves us a sign, a, ehm, calling card, you could say. Like most terrorists, he's very protective of his work. He's not giving anything away, though, he's not stupid. It's his way of identifying the ones he *wants* us to know were his. We're certain he's carried out others anonymously, and if we could match him up to those we might get a better glimpse of his identity. The problem is, there's sixty terrorist incidents around the world per month, on average.'

'And what's the sign?'

'I'm afraid that's classified too.'

Groans echoed round the room. Lexington was right: cops hated secrets. They weren't missing much this time, though; she had seen the Black Spirit's little territorial piss-stain, and there was nothing mysterious about it. The reason it was classified was so that they could be sure when they were looking at his work, which helped to join a few dots; even if, as Wells admitted, they were only the dots he wanted them to join. If the signature became common knowledge, then every bampot with a bomb could spread it around to claim second-hand kudos and cloud the picture.

'Why is he called the Black Spirit?' Hart asked, unknowingly skirting the answer to Willetts's question. 'Can you tell us that much?'

'It's just a name,' Wells lied.

51

The reason wasn't important, but Wells didn't want to get their backs up further by telling them that *that* was classified too. It was verboten because it referred to the also classified signature: a crude, line-drawn, almost shapeless black blob given a face by two white ovals and an oblong grid of grinning teeth. It had generated a number of similar nicknames – the Dark Phantom, the Grinning Ghost, the Black Ghoul – but 'the Black Spirit' had been the English rendering that stuck around Interpol. Wells had stumbled when referring to it as a 'calling card', afraid he was giving something away. This was because that was exactly what the cheeky bastard left behind, printing the image on dozens of white business cards, which ended up blowing around the bodies and debris afterwards.

'Well, no, in fact it's more than a name,' Wells revised. 'At least, it has become more, and that's been his design all along. This individual has gone from obscurity to being one of the most wanted terrorists since Carlos the Jackal in the space of three years. And the explanation for this meteoric rise is not that he's the best, the baddest or the most prolific, though he's in with a shout at all those titles. It's because he has, effectively, marketed himself. I said he was a new species, and I didn't mean just because he kills for cash. This isn't merely contract terrorism: this is designer-brand contract terrorism. The reason he leaves his mark on his most high-profile works is so that his notoriety grows. So for your million bucks or whatever he charges, you don't just get your terrorist atrocity, you get your terrorist atrocity with the Black Spirit label attached. And as his notoriety grows, so does the marketability of that label. The bad guys know they can trust him to deliver, and the good guys shit themselves when they hear the name.'

Or cream themselves, as seemed a growing possibility in Wells's case.

'Normally, that kind of exposure works two ways. The downside of waving it in everybody's face is that you're increasing the risk of being fingered. Not this guy. He's been operational for three years and we know next to nothing about him. We don't know what he looks like. We don't know what nationality he is. We don't know his age. We don't know his associates. We don't know his inter-mediaries. We don't know his aliases. We don't know *anything* that's going to give us the slightest chance of iden-tifying him if he gets on a plane and walks through immi-gration at Heathrow.'

The grumbling began to resume, but it had a very different edge to it now. It had changed from the impa-tience borne of not believing they were needed, to the discomfort of not believing there was much they could do anyway.

Millburn's hand went up, and all eyes fell on him, perhaps hoping his question would expose the threat Wells had built as merely a house of cards.

'How do you know this Black Spirit is one man? If you've no descriptions, couldn't it be a group, a gang?'

It was Wells's turn to look impatient. Though he had an answer for it, he obviously hated this question. He didn't like it when the children threatened to stop believing in Santa Claus.

'That possibility was considered for a while, yes. There is absolutely no doubt that he has collaborators, but people in this line of business tend not to operate on a democratic basis. No matter how tightly knit the group, someone has to be calling the shots, and the Black Spirit's exploits have been nothing if not egotistical. We also have . . . *some* intelligence: second-, third-hand accounts of, well, variable veracity would be the euphemistic way of putting it. People saying they heard this or met that person who heard someone tell someone else . . . You know the deal. Terrorists and their associates are no different from other criminals in that they will either tell you nothing or tell you lies, but now and again there's the occasional inadvertent titbit dropped among the garbage. Anyway, for what they're worth, the accounts are consistent on enough points to confirm that they are talking about an individual. Unfortunately it's an individual nobody ever claims to have met or even seen.

'Normally with terrorist groups, there's so much factionalism and internal politicking that members eventually start turning dissident and selling out their former comrades. Again, this hasn't applied to the Black Spirit. For one thing, there are no ideological tensions because there's no ideology to argue about. But our anecdotal evidence suggests that there are two stronger reasons for the loyalty he has enjoyed. One is that his collaborators are handsomely remunerated. The other is that he has a long memory and nobody in their right mind wants to get on the wrong side of this bastard.'

No, course not. All the fanatics, psychopaths and assassins round the globe, they all skip a beat at the mention of his name. He eats guns and shits bullets. He bathes in blood and dines on body parts. Oh God, keep talkin' baby, keep talkin', ooh yeah baby. He's the baddest of the bad. He's a killing machine. Ooh you say it so good, you say it so nasty, ooh, ooh, ooh, ooooooh . . .

Fuck off.

Lexington had probably told Wells to ham it up in order to light a fire under everybody, but there had been no need for such priming. If the Black Spirit had walked in the door right then, the MI5 creep would have dropped to his knees and swallowed every inch.

He's a whole new species. He's audacious. He's resourceful. He's ingenious. He's cool. He's bad. He's scary. He's got a two-foot cock.

Aye, very good.

He's a wanker, that's what he is.

All terrorists are wankers. Whatever flags they wrapped themselves in, whatever religions, histories or myths they attached to their crusades, they were, to a man, just wankers. They told themselves and anyone bored enough to listen that they were in it for the glory of their cause or the welfare of their 'people' (few of whom were ever consulted about this), but the truth was that they were in it because they liked killing people. Every last fucking one of them.

Listening to Wells eulogise about this tosspot was making her itch. Her spine was stiffening, her fingers stretching taut by her side, clenching and unclenching. 'Designer-brand terrorism.' Listen to yourself, you prick. Oh yeah, it's mass murder, but it's mass murder with *style*. The victims should be bloody well honoured to die at the hands of someone with such panache. It was laughable to hear him talk about how inventive, how proficient, how *good* the Black Spirit was at terrorism. You didn't have to be 'good' to be a terrorist, you just had to be, well, no better way of putting it: a wanker. You just had to be prepared to do despicable things; there was no genius required in their execution. You could walk up behind Captain Shephard eating in a restaurant and smash him unconscious with a whisky bottle – that didn't mean he wouldn't plaster you across the four walls in a square go. The whole point about terrorism was that any arsehole could do it, anywhere, anyhow. That was where the 'terror' part came from – society not being able to protect itself from a threat that could come from any source and strike at any target. It was all about attacking the unsuspecting and the undefended.

The cops and the politicians could be relied upon to go on TV and denounce every terrorist incident as 'cowardly'. The perpetrators would be smirking at this flimsy little insult, or justifying it to themselves as a legitimate tactic against a much larger foe. But it *was* cowardly. Planting bombs in unguarded places took no balls at all.

How hard was it for the Black Spirit and his wankers-in-arms to blow up that train in St Petersburg? You wouldn't get far in an airport with a suitcase full of C4, but at a railway station, you could simply climb on board, stick your luggage in the rack, then walk away again, which was what they did. No checks, no X-rays, no sniffer dogs, and no-one in the carriage left alive to give a statement.

Madrid had taken slightly more sophistication, but for Wells to describe it as 'audacious' was a generosity borne of infatuation. The word he was looking for was 'sneaky'. For effect, Child Molester had said the explosion 'also' demolished the adjoining cinema, which was true but more than a trifle disingenuous. It was the cinema itself that was bombed, its adjacency proving the point of least resistance in attacking a heavily guarded target. The intelligence agencies racked their brains to decipher the political ramifications of it being the Spanish US embassy that was singled out, before they were forced to conclude that there were none. It had an accessible public building backing on to it and other US embassies didn't, that was all. The nationality was irrelevant.

Not that the cinema was entirely a soft touch. There were very few capital cities in the world where you could catch a flick without first having someone root through your handbag, and given ETA's on-going bloodlust, Madrid wasn't one of them. However, no matter how security-conscious the staff were trained to be, if there was one thing guaranteed to inspire credulity in modern-day Europe, it was bureaucracy. People are sceptical of what seems too good to be true, but if something sounds like a pain in the arse, they've no problem believing it must be for real. The Black Spirit's outfit posed as officials from the city's Health and Safety department, complete with IDs and paperwork, there to perform a spot-check on the cinema's alarms, fire extinguishers, smoke detectors and sprinkler systems. They removed all of the extinguishers, saying they didn't meet the latest specifications, then fitted their own replacements. According to the house manager's death-bed statement, they even got him to sign a receipt, telling him an invoice would follow shortly. It sure did.

Audacious?

When she was nine, someone wrapped a dogturd in newspaper, placed it on her doorstep, set it alight, rang the doorbell then fucked off. Her father answered the door and immediately began stamping on the flaming parcel, covering his slippers in shit. That was roughly how audacious the Black Spirit's activities were. Neither perpetrator had the guts to look their victims in the eye.

It wasn't the only thing they had in common, either. They were both bullies, both cowards. They picked on the little guy and then they ran away.

Teachers the world over faithfully preached the message that bullies were cowards. In her classroom, the bullies had smirked, the way she pictured the terrorists smirk. Load

57

of shite, they were telling themselves. They weren't cowards; cowards shat it, and *they* shat it from no-one. They were some of the hardest guys – and girls – in the school, no question they could look after themselves in a barney. But funny, they didn't go picking fights with the other hard cases. If they wanted to look tough, surely that's what they should have done?

Don't be stupid.

Human experience taught that when people wanted to look tough, they picked on easy targets. A short-arsed megalomaniac picked Jews. A Lilley-livered political mediocrity picked single mothers. A deludedly ambitious cardinal picked gays. A bloated Ugandan dictator picked Asians. And endless halfwit nonentities in Leeside had picked the wee darkie lassie with the funny name.

Consequently, she had serious anger-management issues around the whole bullying thing. And the whole racism thing, and the whole sexism thing, though they were really just parts of the same whole. Her parents and her brother had all handled the abuse a lot better. Mum and Dad, having been expelled by Amin with a two-year-old son and a baby well on the way, perhaps had a wider perspective on it. A council house in Renfrewshire was a bit of a comedown from the lifestyle they'd once built for themselves, but under the circumstances it was sanctuary, and if some of the locals called them names or left turd-bombs on their doorstep, then it was still a lesser form of racial abuse than what they'd already survived.

Her brother, James, had always been thick-skinned and easy-going to the point of irritating. He got his share of verbal and physical abuse, arguably more than her, being older and therefore first into each of the educational snakepits. It just never seemed to get to him; at least not in any way that he let anyone see. Perhaps that was how he coped, in combination with being too bloody affable to make many enemies. It helped that he was good at football, which accorded a certain respect as well as the protection of his fellow school-team members. When he reached secondary age, he also had the subsidiary benefits of going to Parkhead every other Saturday, which seemed to place him in a context that made him easier to accept, even to the bampots. Maybe especially to the bampots.

She had never enjoyed any comparable advantages, being far too short to get picked for netball, the only game the girls were ever offered at St Mary's primary school. At Sacred Heart secondary, she did make the hockey team, but sporting prowess was not the same source of kudos among the female peer group. Clique politics and popularity power-struggles were far more important. Athletic ability only counted for something if it was one of the in-crowd that had it; hence the hundred metres was a big deal in first and second year when Maggie Hanley won it. When the wee darkie girl with the funny name won it in third year, it was because Maggie wasn't interested in 'that wee lassie stuff' any more (though the wee darkie girl with the funny name remembered Maggie looking pretty fucking interested as she overtook her with ten metres to go).

By that age, she'd been too long the outsider to want anything to do with the fake sorority of all that fickle faction-alism. Bereft of anything substantial that they had in common, the cliques were usually united solely by who they didn't like. Across the various parties, this tended to be a reciprocal list, but most of them had room on it for her too. This was because she 'didn't make it easy for herself', which she took to mean she didn't drop to her knees in gratitude whenever one of these bitches condescended to actually be polite to her for a change. The other inference was that she had to expect a certain amount of racial abuse and she shouldn't be so sensitive; or to state it more simply, she should know her place. And to put this attitude into full perspective, it had to be appreciated that the source of the quote was the assistant headmistress.

The occasion was significant too. After years of Pilate-class hand-washing on the part of the teaching staff any time she reported being punched, kicked, spat on or merely insulted, it was suddenly a serious matter the first time the abuser came off second best. She had 'over-reacted', she was 'hyper-sensitive', even 'volatile'. Yeah, maybe she was. Maybe it was that junior-sibling syndrome, being ultra-assertive, over-competitive, always wanting to leave her mark or have the last word. Or maybe it was that since the age of five she had been taking shit in the classrooms and playgrounds of schools where other than herself and James, the closest thing they had to an ethnic minority was the Byrne twins from Dublin.

'Chocolate Button' had been her unwanted nickname since Primary Two, applied because she was small and brown, get it? Chocolate was, in fact, the prefix for any number of hilarious remarks, all of which only got funnier the more she heard them. If she was a Proddy, she would be a Chocolate Orange. No, please, stop, these pants have got to do me all day. Granted, it wasn't the most offensive term she would hear ('She'd diarrhoea an' she thought she was meltin' - ha ha ha ha'), but the term itself didn't matter. What mattered was that she heard it every day, and every time it was used, the intention was to remind her that she was different and she didn't belong.

That was why she 'over-reacted' and 'brought shame on the school' during a third-year hockey match against St

Stephen's. 'All' her opponent had done was sing the chorus of that Deacon Blue song, *Chocolate Girl*, every time she came within earshot. The girl hadn't meant any offence, she said later (though it had sounded more like 'mmm hmm hmm mmf hmm mmf'). She had heard it on the radio at lunchtime and just couldn't get the song out of her head all afternoon.

Sure. Same as the Sacred Heart winger didn't mean to hit her. The hockey stick accidentally flew out of her hand and into the poor girl's face. Twice.

But did it solve anything? No. Did it change the other girl's racist attitude? Probably not. Did it make her instantly popular and respected in the eyes of her classmates? Don't be daft.

And did it make her feel better?

Oh, *fuck* yeah.

It was an epiphany.

Like she was reborn. It would be facile to say that she found her vocation in that violent catharsis, but its roots could certainly be traced back to there. In that moment, all the mouths that had ever called her chocolate this or darkie that became as one: one that was spitting teeth, dripping blood and thoroughly wishing it had stayed shut.

Her parents hadn't been entirely enamoured of the idea when she professed her intention to join the police. Their experience of uniformed authority had understandably not made it something to which they wished their children to aspire (though to be fair, in their adopted home, they had been reassured enormously by the gormless plods telling them 'we're looking into it' after each instance of harassment, vandalism or flaming jobbies). She therefore acquiesced when they suggested she go to university first, an undertaking they were undoubtedly sure would shake this undesirable notion from her head. It didn't. She flirted with new ambitions on a daily basis – that's what university is for, isn't it? – but flirting was as far as it went: she and the polis were betrothed.

Campus extra-curricular activities often led graduates down previously unforeseen paths, but in her case, she hadn't been able to plausibly envisage any financial or long-term prospects in Tai-kwon-do, Shorinji Kempo, Karate or pistol-shooting. There was, however, one line of work in which she reckoned they might prove useful.

The degree came in handy too, not least the languages, which had tipped the balance in her favour when she pitched for the Interpol liaison post. Her mother was Belgian by birth, so she and James picked up a solid grounding in French as both a product and necessity of eavesdropping on their parents. To that she had added Spanish and Dutch at university, this last proving the most prized by her senior officers due to so many investigative roads leading to Amsterdam, where she found herself cultivating links with Interpol. This led in time to a three-month placement in Brussels and ultimately her liaison role for the Strathclyde force. It wasn't a post ever likely to occupy her full-time, more a responsibility that fell to her as and when, but it made her contacts, got her face known far and wide, and consequently opened a lot of doors.

It was in Brussels that she got her inside gen on the Black Spirit. She was there when he hit Strasbourg, one of the 'classified' atrocities Wells had alluded to. He engineered the collapse of a disused flyover on the autoroute at the height of rush hour, killing seven people instantly and twenty-eight more in the ensuing pile-up.

An 'official' inquiry blamed structural fatigue, accelerated by the vibrations of haulage traffic. It was never made public that the disaster wasn't an accident, let alone who had been behind it. There was no paymaster on that occasion, no Looney-Tunes collective trumpeting their responsibility, hence the option to keep the truth quiet. This one he had done for his own satisfaction, a little 'fuck you' to the European Parliament, which had recently agreed new international protocols to speed up the extradition of wanted terrorists. The protocols would, according to their architect, 'drive a high-speed road between the courts of every nation'. Extradition wasn't even something the Black Spirit was likely to be bothered about, not unless he was planning to get himself arrested any time soon. It was sheer sabre-rattling, a reminder to the authorities that his dick was still bigger than theirs.

The fall-out turned into an all-hands drill across every Interpol bureau, which was why she got access to files and individuals she would otherwise never have been allowed near. Interpol was like the Internet: it wasn't so much a body in itself as a means of connecting other disparate entities. It was therefore constructed around a number of nodes, which ranged from fully-staffed offices to individual liaisons such as herself.

Brussels being the nearest thing Interpol had to an HQ, she met a number of terrorism intelligence experts there, people who had followed the Black Spirit's 'career' from the start. They knew a shitload more than Wells, and their attitude to their subject was a great deal less reverential, mainly because they had seen the bodies. The men and women who had been on-site to collect the Black Spirit's calling cards kept their disgust beneath – but close to – the surface, where they needed it, to drive the fight no matter how bleak it looked.

Enrique Sallas had been involved in the hunt since

Madrid, and he knew better than most how bleak it could get. He had been on the force thirty years and told her he had never encountered a phenomenon that scared him more.

'This is a guy who truly doesn't give a fuck, and I don't even mean about the victims. That goes without saying. But this guy doesn't give a fuck about the causes he's assisting either. He doesn't even give a fuck about the money, that's my opinion. He does it because . . . *he can*. He does it because it makes him feel good. We can't negotiate with him, we can't compromise with him. A change in politics can't sideline him. One conflict is resolved, he's offering his services where the next one emerges. Others call him the Black Spirit because of the picture on the card. I think of him as the Black Spirit because I fear he will always be with us, in one form or another. He is bloodlust, he is murder, and he will shape-shift and remanifest wherever hatred is to be found.'

Impassioned as he was wont to become, even Enrique didn't miss the irony that the Black Spirit was trading on a mystique they had played a large part in giving him. It wasn't just Wells who couldn't help but be fascinated by this shadowy figure, even if only because he posed so many questions. She was guilty of it too, though she might put that down to foreign terrorism naturally seeming more exotic than the version she was familiar with. In the UK, terrorism meant Ulster sectarianism, a repetitive cycle of violence in which the horror was the only thing greater than the boredom. From a professional perspective, if she was interested in moronic neds obsessed with Anglo-Irish history, she could always volunteer for Old Firm match-duty.

Having said that, there were few better illustrations of terrorism's perverse allure than the vicarious thrill-seekers and their braindead paraphernalia at Ibrox and Parkhead.

She remembered overhearing some of James's halfwit mates talking about a banner they had seen at the match one day. It had incorporated the tricolour and the Palestinian flag, and read: 'IRA – PLO. Two peoples, one struggle.' They thought it was 'really cool'. None of them ventured to explain the cool part about nail-bombs and dead children, but there was no question this romantic-sounding ideal had some kind of aura for young and simplistic minds. Fighting for freedom, battling against oppression, blowing up the Death Star. The question was, would 'the struggle', any struggle, still have the same aura if guns and bombs weren't involved? Well, nobody had ever turned up at Parkhead or Ibrox with a 'Gay Rights' or 'Free Tibet' banner. It was about boys and toys. No guns, no glory.

However, the not so young and simplistic were fasci-nated too, so maybe it was something deeper, perhaps even something primal. In the uncertain, ever-changing adult world, was there something paradoxically comforting about believing there was a manifest embodiment of evil on the loose out there? Were we like the boys in *Lord of the Flies*, dreaming up 'the beast' because it was less fright-ening to believe in a malevolent being than to confront the chaos of the truly unknown? Perhaps the Black Spirit was a repository for our fears and insecurities about crime, violence and ultimately death: we could combine them all as one totem and fear that; rather than have countless numbers of them scuttling around our heads like hatching insects.

Whatever he represented, in reality the Black Spirit couldn't be all the things she, Wells, Sallas or Interpol believed him to be. What was certain, however, was that he did exist, he *was* out there, and according to Lexington, he was heading this way. Wells having mopped up his spilt jizz and sat down, the bossman was back at the lectern.

'I know what you're all thinking, so let me state as clearly as I can that you can't afford to think it. General Thaba's delirious remarks may have been cryptic, but remember that he traded his way out on the specific mention of a terrorist threat to the British state. Those were his precise words. "A terrorist threat to the British state." All he gave us in the end was "the Black Spirit", the meaning of which should now be frighteningly clear, and "an eye for an eye", which, the Good Lord's proprietary claims notwithstanding, is the war cry of those intent upon vengeance. General Mopoza, it is fair to say, falls into that category.

'As I mentioned earlier, Mopoza has a proven fondness for historically significant dates. Had the late General Thaba been in a clearer frame of mind, he might have mentioned that Sonzola annually celebrates its independence from the British state on September the sixth. That's this Saturday, ladies and gentlemen.'

'Well it still sounds like bollocks to me.'

The band had left the stage with no clamour for an encore, only the sound of chairlegs squeaking on the floor as the gathering began to disperse. Wells had circulated briefing packs, the facts and figures padded out with speculatory analysis and a seriously reaching psychological profile which she'd seen before.

Like the Eskimos' enhanced vocabulary for describing snow, she thought there should be a panoply of terms to distinguish the subtle but significant varieties in tone and nuance of the low grumbling that followed every police briefing. With experience, she had learned to recognise most of them. This one was an unusual blend of 'it won't even concern us' mixed with subtly discordant elements of 'we're being fucked about here' and 'there's something they're not telling us'.

'I'm not saying I wouldn't be worried if this Black Spirit bastard showed up on my patch, but what have we really got to go on? This Thaba bloke wanted an exit and he had to give them something, so what better than flinging in a name that's guaranteed to frighten the horses?'

'Why are they taking it so seriously? I think either that Wells bloke has been blowing smoke up Lexington's arse, or they're not giving us the full picture.'

'It's a wild-goose chase.'

'Total wind-up.'

'Ants in their pants all because someone mentioned the Bogeyman.'

'Understandable caution, really. Keep your eyes and ears open just in case.'

'Nothing we can do if we don't bloody know anything.'

Millburn held the door open for her as they exited to the lobby.

'You're keepin' it close to your chest, X. Either that or you were bored into catatonia.'

'Bit of both.'

'I'm bettin' you know more about this heid-the-baw than that MI5 bloke.'

'That's classified.'

Millburn smiled.

'Don't suppose it'll be botherin' you up there in the People's Republic. Terrorists are like tourists. First stop London, every bloody time.'

'You were the one who ran away to the big city.'

'Aye, but not for career reasons, you understand. You canna get United tickets for love nor money in Newcastle, and London's got five Premiership teams. That's five away games, pet.'

Millburn was under the mistaken (but never corrected – she hated anyone thinking she was one of the boys) impression that she wasn't interested in football, which was why he saw it as a challenge to crowbar it into their every conversation. Tutting and rolling her eyes, she gave him a playful push to send him on his way.

He was one of the good guys, and a very smart cop, but he was wrong about whose doorstep the Black Spirit was more likely to end up on. That was why every force in the country had been represented this morning. London was the last place he'd think of hitting. Armed police all over the shop, public areas evacuated if anyone left so much as a McDonald's bag lying around. Forget it. Vulnerability was what he sought first and foremost. Look at Strasbourg. He didn't go near the parliament itself, nor did he need to to make his point. His style was to attack places that no-one had thought to attack before, meaning that neither had anyone thought much about defending them. Even in St Petersburg, where he hit the more traditional terrorist target of an army base, he had done it using a civilian passenger train.

The truly scary thing was that they didn't even know what to be scared of. He could attack anywhere, using any means. There would be no coded warnings, no 'legitimate targets'. No-one knew who he was or what he looked like, and he had never stuck his own head above the parapet. Nonetheless, there was one thing she was determined about, one thing she had sworn to herself back in Brussels and felt even more strongly about now.

If the Black Spirit set foot on her turf, Angelique de Xavia was taking him downtown.

WEDNESDAY, SEPTEMBER THIRD

real life™

What do you want to be when you grow up?

That had always been a hard one for Ray to answer, even back in the days when each of the aspirational possibilities had its own Fisher-Price play-figure: fireman, policeman, doctor, soldier, train-driver, bus-driver, binman, sailor, pilot, spaceman. In retrospect, there had been a distinct leaning towards the public sector in those moulded plastic role-models, but this had undoubtedly been less to do with socialistic vocational ideology on the part of the manufacturer and more to do with the greater marketing opportunities afforded by professions associated with a specific vehicle (sold separately). Still, this kind of thing was bound to have a subliminal effect; strictly speaking, even the astronaut was on the public payroll, and these toys were sold in the days well before bus deregulation, back when Brian Souter was probably barring gay Weebles from riding his Dinky Toys double-decker.

Ray guessed that many of those Fisher-Price product lines had by now succumbed to the toy industry's most feared affliction – irreversible anachronism – but maybe that was preferable to a modern new range that included IT specialists, call-centre drones and burger-flippers. The accessory range wouldn't be a knock-out either.

'Dear Santa, I have been a good boy all year, apart from that time I put the hamster in the washing-machine but Mum says that's okay because I was only trying to get the chewing gum off his fur though she wasn't happy about that because I'm not supposed to eat chewing gum because you can choke to death on it and it makes you look like a ned. Can I please have a Fisher-Price management consultant please and if it's not too much please can I please have the flipchart and team-building equipment kit please.'

The first thing Ray could remember wanting to be was a welder. He was in Primary Three at the time and didn't have the first idea what a welder did, but that was hardly relevant under the circumstances. It was the long lunchtime (teachers' payday, last Thursday of the month) and they were playing Colditz. Ray wanted to be on the goodies' side for a change, but the goodies' leader, Tommy Dunn – seven-year-old detached cool personified – had stipulated that you only got on to his team if you wanted to be a welder when you grew up. Tommy's dad was, if Ray remembered correctly, a consultant maxillofacial surgeon, or possibly a welder.

'Make it' was the command by which their playtime world was shaped, a good dozen years before Captain Picard added the stylish but redundant 'so'.

'Make it that I've dug a tunnel through intae the sewers an' it comes oot behin' the kitchen bins,' Tommy had decreed, before cautioning his fellow captives: 'An' make it that I've got tae go ahead masel' an' yous have tae cover up fur me until I come back an' say it's safe.'

The subsequent absence of the welding evangelist had precipitated a discussion between POWs and Jerries as to what they each *really* wanted to be, something that Ray was instantly aware of never having thought about. It was quite a concept; dizzying and daunting, exciting and intimidating. You could be anything: you simply had to choose what. The possibilities were suddenly endless, but the time for contemplation was more finite. At seven years old, he felt rushed into a decision, hoping as soon as he had committed that it wasn't binding. Twenty-six years later, little had changed.

'I want to be an astronaut,' he ventured. He'd liked SF stuff, from *The Clangers* upwards. If adult careers were being offered like crayons from the teacher's box, might as well go for the brightest. All of a sudden, his future extended beyond the next Christmas or birthday, and was coloured as never before, with spaceships, teleports, airlocks and moonbases.

'Astronauts risk their lives, so they do,' warned Brian Lawrence, recently prospective policeman, lately lost to the welding profession. 'You could get kill't. Mind there was a fire in one of the rockets in America, and sure there was that one when the air ran oot, and they nearly died as well. They never died, but nearly, so it just shows you.'

'Eh, well I don't want to be an astronaut any more,' Ray amended. It was an age when the instant climbdown carried no ego penalties; at least a decade off that first shameful resort to the phrase 'not as such'.

He wasn't pressed for an alternative, as Tommy Dunn had returned with the news that his tunnel was clear, and the Jerries had acquiesced in his escape scenario ('Make it that I've brung back a gun an' we're takin' wan o' the Jerries wi' us as a hostage so's the other yins cannae touch us until we're through the tunnel, right?').

Tommy's tunnel, as it transpired, no longer emerged by the kitchen bins, but instead led (still via the sewers) into a system of caves, also known as 'the sheds'. The sheds, Victorian-built playground shelters dividing the infants' area from the Primary Threes, Fours and Fives, lent themselves memorably to children's willing imaginations, the underfoot conditions and perennially damp walls perhaps tendering subliminal suggestions.

'Make it that there's a river runnin' through the caves, an' we're wadin' through it until it gets too deep an' then we have to duck under an' haud oor breaths an' swim through the dark an' come up in a big pool except still in a cave, right?'

Ray remembered it as though real, that extended lunchtime seeming to stretch far beyond an hour and a quarter, their adventure in the caves unhindered by the girls bouncing sponge-balls against the walls nor by the other boys using the support poles for goalposts. Mainly he remembered the smell of wet stone, incongruously warm, inexplicably comforting; perhaps it was only those things after that, because of that.

'Make it that I've caught up wi' yous an' snuck up under the water,' said Mick Hetherston, having arrived at the sheds and been brought up to date with the state of play.

'You'd never have caught up – we've been in these caves for a whole night noo. You can stay in the sheds, but you're over there, you're miles back. You've still tae go through an' up oot the pool, hasn't he, Raymie?'

'Aye.'

'But make it I'm really a British secret agent pretendin' tae be a Jerry, an' I was helpin' yous escape aw the time, an' that's how yous were able tae take Bobby hostage back at the castle.'

'Aye, that's gallus,' was the impressed consensus.

'An' make it I was a British secret agent tae,' appealed Bobby, doing the arithmetic and reaching a disturbing conclusion.

'Naw, then there'd be nae Jerries left. Make it that you escape fae us an' we have tae hunt you doon.'

'But I don't want tae be a Jerry anymair.'

'It's ma game, so you have tae.'

'Och, that's shite.'

No, Bobby, that's life. Some suckers were just stuck with their role. Question was, were they better off than those who couldn't find one? In the space of half an hour, Ray had moved on to a third vocation, though he had at least remained true to his wartime allegiance.

'I think I want to be a pilot.'

This one wasn't a pressure decision. Given a little time to get used to the whole idea, he realised that this was a notion that had been knocking around his head for a while. He liked flying. He'd been on an aeroplane six times: to Spain and back, then to Bulgaria and back twice. Coming back wasn't as much fun. There was still the thrill of take-off, but after that you were just going home, and your holiday was well and truly over. Taking off on the way out was the greatest feeling in the world. If he was a pilot, he'd get to fly every day, get to feel that amazing take-off sensation all the time.

He loved the airport too, loved being there. The check-in, the conveyor belts, the departure lounge, and of course, the planes. Everything was modern at the airport: shiny, all plastics, metals and glass; not like school, where everything was old, dull and wooden. When they drove past it on the motorway, he used to fantasise that his parents were about to turn their vehicle towards the car park and surprise him, say the boot was full of secretly packed luggage and they were heading off for a fortnight. When he had kids of his own, he'd told himself, he'd surprise them that way for real.

75

They also went to the airport to collect relatives, which was exciting because he got to see the planes, but it always left him with a sense of disappointment. The place looked just as fascinating, as space-age, but the sense of magic wasn't there when you knew you weren't going any further than the arrivals hall. It was like seeing the new toys at someone else's birthday party. The better they looked, the greater the feeling of missing out.

Airports had never ceased to tantalise him as he got older. They were places for beginnings. There was always a sense of potential about them; of adventures waiting to be had beyond their gleaming corridors, high-tech portals to a better place than the one you were used to. In childhood, they were where holidays began, the wrapping paper on a present bigger and better than anything you could get for Christmas, but nonetheless a present only your parents could bestow, and like Christmas, but once a year. In adulthood, admittedly something of a courtesy title in his case, they offered the constant, autonomous possibility of escape, whenever you wanted, and whatever you wanted that to mean: from a spontaneous cheap winter week in Hammamet to, well . . .

To what, Raymond Ash? Say it.

To a ticket the fuck out of your life.

That, after all, was why he was at the airport right then, wasn't it? To be tantalised, to contemplate the possibilities in a place where possibilities proliferated, as opposed to home or work, where they shrank, withered and died. Or was he really going to swallow that shite he was telling himself about going there to buy his PC magazine because the airport was on the way home and the parking was about the same price as New Street? He'd bought the magazine half an hour ago, and the parking was in twenty-minute increments, so why wasn't he on his way?

Ray was sitting on a bench in the upstairs concourse, watching the screens, the destinations, the *possibilities*. Watching the passengers, wishing he was one of them, knowing that such a transformation was one credit-card transaction away. Make it that I'm getting on that flight to New York. Make it that I'm getting on that flight to Toronto. Make it that I'm not a rookie English teacher anchored to his unpromising new career by a wife and three-month-old baby. Make it that I don't have to go home to them tonight, to see her in desperate tears and to hear him screaming because the pain won't stop. Make it that I don't have to humiliate myself in the face of another shower of psychopaths tomorrow.

What do you want to be when you grow up?

Ray still didn't know. He was thirty-three and he still didn't know. Father? Teacher? They'd both sounded good for a while, but then so had astronaut and pilot. Astronauts risk their lives. Pilots, it turned out, also needed a little more vocational commitment than he had anticipated: viz, being prepared to fly to foreign destinations without going on holiday for a fortnight once they got there. He hadn't foreseen all the drawbacks to his latest pursuit either, but had proceeded through faith in the dual, contradictory self-assurances that: a) he would be able to surmount any obstacles through the drive to provide for his family; and b) if he didn't like it, he could always do something else.

Also known as denial. Denial, however, was peace of mind on tick, and sooner or later, the bill always arrives, plus interest.

So now here he was, a father and a teacher. He didn't like either and he couldn't do something else, not any more. That was why he was at the airport, wasn't it?

Possibilities.

/Start new game.

This will abort the game in progress. Are you sure?
Yes/No.

No, not sure, but thinking about it very carefully. The game in progress wasn't looking good. Health was low, energy was lower, morale was flashing red and the battle just kept getting harder. He had been badly misled about the skill level.

After sex, there could be no facet of human existence that people lied about more than parenthood. It was a mammoth, worldwide, multicultural, ecumenical, cross-generational conspiracy of porkies that would shame the Warren Commission, but without which, presumably, the species might well have died out. People didn't just fib about it to your face, either; the shelves of every bookshop and library were teeming with volume upon volume of whoppers, theoretical and purportedly anecdotal information, guidance and advice that bore no resemblance to reality as he and Kate were experiencing it – on average twenty hours a day.

For three months, their lives had passed in an excruciatingly slow, trance-like haze, never fully asleep, never fully awake, as they struggled to cope with a tiny creature who didn't seem particularly pleased to have been called into existence. It had been a planned pregnancy, but within a couple of weeks they had learned that while they might have wanted a child, they definitely hadn't wanted a baby; and definitely not one like this poor wee scone.

Misery, thy name is colic.

It began in the afternoons, around three, sometimes earlier, and ended around three in the morning, sometimes later. Within about ten minutes of each breastfeed concluding, Martin would draw his wee legs up to his stomach, arch his back, open his mouth and howl, tears on his temples, pain and confusion on his face. Ray had very quickly appreciated what the word 'inconsolable' truly meant. There was nothing he could do to alleviate his son's suffering, save wearing a path in the carpet as he walked up and down holding him, stroking him, singing to him, patting him, all of it utterly, utterly futile.

The evenings, in particular, were a blast. They each took it in turns to fail to console the junior Munch model while the other grabbed a quick bite to eat through in the coveted oasis of peace that the kitchen had become. It was surely a sign of sensory deprivation that he often found himself wishing a Tesco microwaveable cannelloni could last forever, because as soon as it was finished, it was back to face the enemy.

They usually had the TV on, both to provide distraction and to give some sense of time, but unless Martin was clamped to the nipple, they were reliant on their new favourite number – 888 – for Teletext subtitles. This had its limitations for the genre they were in most need of (the phrase 'comic timing' clearly meant little to whoever programmed the computer to present the feedline and punchline one atop the other on the same screen), but did have an unintentionally reciprocal effect on live news and current affairs shows. The poor sod frantically pummelling on the phonetic translator could seldom keep up, particularly during interviews, so you were often treated to the closing arguments of one item when the talking head or cutaway footage was already up for the next. The sight of Carol Vorderman being inadvertently captioned as 'a cancerous blight on our society that we seem powerless to stop' had been an invaluable chink of light in an otherwise very bleak few hours, matched on another occasion by Baroness Young appearing to tell David Frost that she deeply regretted posing topless for *FHM*.

Adding to the siege effect was the fact that unlike most new fathers, Ray hadn't had the escape of a job to go to by day, the start date for his post being ten weeks after the birth. It was an interval that had once seemed cosily serendipitous, leaving him free for a natural nesting period during which the three of them could rest, recover, bond and contemplate their Mothercare-catalogue blissful future.

Ray used to wonder how torturers could carry out their atrocities, as their victims' screams of pain would be unbearable to anyone with the merest vestige of humanity. He now reckoned that the first qualification would be parenthood, as there could be nothing that inured you to the sound of screaming better than hearing it for hours on end, every day of every week.

There were far darker thoughts than that, though, thoughts that you weren't supposed to admit to, that you couldn't unburden to anyone, and that there was definitely no page in the parenting manuals offering advice on. This was, of course, because he was the first new father ever to think them, just like Kate was the first new mother to intersperse worries that her newborn might die in its sleep with wondering whether she'd feel bereaved or relieved.

This was the gigantic lie, masking truths that nobody talked about, nobody acknowledged. You were supposed to be all smiles and chunky jumpers now, posing in photos, smiling down at your beatific bundle, whose very presence just filled your heart with warmth and your head with pride. Parenthood was hard work, sure, but bountifully rewarding, and it cast a sparkling spell of love, joy and fulfilment about every minute of your soft-focus existence.

Didn't it?

When he looked down at Martin, the main thing Ray felt was tired, and instead of gazing towards the bright, beckoning adventure of their lives ahead, what most frequently filled his mind was the question of how he could get back the life he had. He had many times contemplated the same desperate scenario as Kate, knowing as she did that it was merely a symptom of distress. That was why as soon as the baby did fall silent for any length of time during the night, his first response was to get up and check that this wasn't because the bugger had spontaneously snuffed it. In fact, he remembered breaking down in helpless floods of tears on the living-room floor one afternoon while Kate was asleep upstairs, the emotional collapse precipitated by the idea of another possible way out: what if they gave him up for adoption? They were clearly not cut out for raising him, you only had to look at the state of the pair of them to see that. Surely someone else could do a better job, could ease his pain, stop the crying. Wouldn't that be better for all of them? Then he had looked at Martin, at that moment awake and uncharacteristically calm. He saw him two, maybe three years older, standing in a room with other children, other adults, looking a little nervous, a little confused, not knowing the man who was kneeling down to say hello to him. That was when Ray lost it. He ended up walking around the living room, holding Martin to his shoulder as ever, but with Ash *père* taking on the crying role for a change.

Despite this, the question refused to go away, whether or not he had a satisfactory answer for it. He wanted his old life back, and who wouldn't. This wasn't life; this was barely subsistence. And yeah, he knew – they both knew – of all the ways it could be worse, the things they ought to be grateful for. Martin was, colic aside, a fit and healthy baby, with none of the defects every expectant parent can't help worrying about; not even ginger hair. Wonderful, magic, spiffing. Can I go to bed now please? Can I have some time to myself? And could somebody remind me who I used to be?

It'll get easier, people kept telling him. He wanted to believe that, and rationally knew he ought to, but it was a hard thing to have faith in when the evidence to hand didn't appear to support it. They'd struggled through weeks, months of this, and the only thing that had alleviated was the pain when Kate breastfed, a development she attributed to having lost all feeling in that area. Ray worried that he'd suffer the same effect emotionally, so worn-down and hollowed-out did he feel. These days, he barely felt like an individual, never mind the specific individual he'd been a few months ago. Instead, he was an enslaved appendage, existing only to serve the unknowingly tyrannical infant. He could plausibly envisage parenthood turning the pair of them into these miserable, embittered cyphers, bearing no resemblance to the two people who had opted to become parents in the first place. It'll get better. Yeah, and what if it does but I don't?

That was the true fear, wasn't it? Not that he'd never get his old life back, but that he'd never get his old self back. His 'old life' was far too nebulous a concept to know exactly what part or period to feel nostalgic about. For much of Kate's pregnancy, he'd been a glorified student, for God's sake, in his bloody thirties. Not exactly heady days, he'd have to say, but they had been days of genuine optimism, and a certain belated sense of maturity. Baby on the way, responsibility close at hand, time to 'put away childish things' to quote St Paul, from Ray's shortlist of least favourite expressions, irritatingly appropriate given that he had been making a living from computer games before opting to train as a teacher. He hadn't looked back then, but admittedly if there was one thing Ray was truly cut out for in life, it was packing in whatever he was doing and starting over elsewhere.

Save current game before quitting? Y̲es/N̲o.

N̲o.

Since graduating from university, a wince-inducingly long time ago now, his CV had become a testament to his versatility and constant thirst for fresh challenges, to quote the job-interview spin. Another way of looking at it was that he had the attention span of a hyperactive budgie and the applied perseverance of a butterfly. The truth was probably a combination of the two, and he left it to individual interpretation what one made of a previous employment list that included, in no memorable order: bartender, waiter, video-shop clerk, local radio researcher, occasional local radio contributor (unpaid, usually in reparation for screwing up the researcher part and leaving a hole in the schedule where a missing guest should have been), local council desk-jockey, call-centre drone, computer assembly-line operative, computer relocation technician (and no, that wasn't a euphemism for thief), archery instructor, minicab driver, typesetter, PC gaming entrepreneur, cartoonist and rock star.

This last didn't actually appear on his CV, though it was true, kind of in the same way as playing for East Stirlingshire meant you could describe yourself as a professional footballer. Simply 'drummer' would be more accurate, which was probably why he had opted to excise it altogether from the official version. You were obliged to admit to your criminal record, but fortunately there were some stigmas the law couldn't force you to reveal.

In a working life spent flitting hither and yon, the hardest change should have been the most recent one: selling up The Dark Zone and training to be a teacher; giving up a project he had invested time, money, energies and hopes in, for a career offering more stability but demanding vocational commitment (ooh, scary). At the time, though, it had felt right; more right, more defining than any decision he had ever made. The business was only that – a business, another project he could (and inevitably would) walk away from. What had always really mattered was him and Kate. They had begun to talk seriously about having a baby, and though she had never spelled it out, he knew that it wasn't something she'd embark upon while he was still living out his extended adolescence. Even when the business was making money, he'd never have kidded himself that it was viable in the long term. Maybe he'd have got a few more years out of it (and maybe the bank would have closed it in another month), but what he and Kate were planning put the timescale into perspective. Making the decision even more straightforward was the fact that The Dark Zone was listing into the red when the council's offer came in to buy him out, so he recognised fate's beckoning finger and did the grown-up thing.

Mistake.

One week in the job and he could still see fate's hand, but it was showing him a different finger.

/set skill level nightmare.

/set opponent_num 30

AWAITING GAMESTATE

LOADING REAL LIFE™ ENGINE.

LOADING MOD: 'ENGLISH TEACHER'

LOADING SOUNDS

LOADING MAP: BURNBRAE ACADEMY [burnb.bsp]
LOADING GAME MEDIA
LOADING PENCIL
LOADING RUBBER
LOADING RULER
LOADING JOTTER
LOADING BLACKBOARD
LOADING OTHELLO
LOADING LORD OF THE FLIES
LOADING ROBERT BURNS - SELECTED POEMS
LOADING WEAPONS: PUNISHMENT EXERCISE
LOADING WEAPONS: HOMEWORK ESSAY
LOADING HAZARDS: WINDOW-POLE
LOADING HAZARDS: FIRE ALARM
LOADING HAZARDS: MALEVOLENT FART ACCU-
SATION
LOADING OPPONENTS
AWAITING SNAPSHOT . . .
RAYMOND ASH ENTERED THE GAME
What do you want to be when you grow up?
Not this.
/Start new game.
This will abort the game in progress. Are you sure?
Yes/No.

Not such an easy decision away from the PC. In the virtual world, you could live a million lives, take on a host of personas, and there was no such thing as regret because you could reload a saved game, go back to before the point where you went wrong, or quit and start over again. Even online, in deathmatch, there was no ultimate price for your mistakes: when you died, you just respawned elsewhere on the map and plunged back into the fray.

That's what he'd been doing all these years, wasn't it? Quitting and starting over again when it wasn't going to plan. Respawning in a new job, thinking it didn't really matter if things didn't work out. That was why he was here at the airport, here where he could buy a ticket to anywhere and just disappear. Ray was looking at the Quit screen because he needed to know that it existed. He wasn't really thinking the unthinkable, just standing on the edge to see whether it made him feel like jumping in or running back.

Ray looked at the clock on the departures board, wondered where Kate and Martin would be right then. Out for a walk with the pram maybe, passers-by stopping to offer their tuppenceworth, having heard the bawling from a hundred yards away.

'Fine set of lungs on him, eh?' Every fucking time. Every fucking one of them.

Or more likely she'd be pacing the carpet, music up loud for the dual purposes of soothing the baby's soul and drowning his howls. He ought to get home, he knew. Home, where he'd be handed Martin as soon as he got in the door, Kate retreating to the bedroom, bathroom or kitchen for an hour's respite.

Christ, five more minutes. Just five more minutes, please, to be tantalised, to sit within touching distance of what might be, what could be. He glanced down at the magazine, his phoney excuse for being here, made all the more phoney by the knowledge that he wouldn't get a chance to read it, never mind play the games it was talking about.

Then he looked up again, and saw a ghost.

It was just a face in the crowd, one of dozens barrelling through the Domestic Arrivals hall, fresh off the Heathrow shuttle. The incident lasted barely two seconds, perhaps four striding paces amid that teeming bustle, but it was enough to leave Ray paralysed, sitting on the bench as though frozen in time, with the crowds whizzing around him like a frames-per-second time-demo test.

Look long enough at any busy corridor – any airport, any railway station – and for a second you'll glimpse a face you think you know, the mind having an incurable habit of filling in the blanks with its own available resources. Ray couldn't look at a pair of back-lit flowery curtains without seeing eyes, jawlines, profiles; clouds against a blue sky became a stratospheric sketchpad. However, this was slightly more than a glimpse, and the guy looked back. Stared back even, though he could have been doing so because Ray was staring at *him*, and he was maybe wondering if he was supposed to know the nosey bastard.

Then just as suddenly he was gone, as though swept under by the human current, leaving Ray white and gaping. He'd been looking at the guy before he realised he knew the face, staring at the face before he could put a name to it; and then the face vanished, just as he worked out that seeing it was impossible.

The hair was different; so different as to put the entire head distractingly out of context. A flowing, back-combed blond mane forever framed the visage in Ray's memory, which possibly explained the delay as he made sense of it beneath a militarily close bullet-crop. In fact, he might never have made the connection at all but for the woman alongside slowing to dial her mobile, giving Ray the briefest uninterrupted view of the figure's unmistakable gait. He walked as though he was wearing a cape, or as his mate Div used to put it, 'like he thinks there's two cunts blawin' trumpets either side of the doorway'.

Simon Darcourt.

Sixteen years ago, he'd walked into Ray's life with that same regal stride, a sweeping procession that seemed simultaneously too effortless to be entirely affected, too self-conscious to be entirely natural. His very physicality was pure theatre, a presence that commanded any room he entered and turned it immediately into his stage. Even the way the bloke smoked a cigarette was like a ballet. Ray never saw him do it upright, standing at a bus stop or walking along the street. It was always a seated performance, indoors: a graceful play of head, legs, arms, throwing back that mass of hair as the first jet of smoke was exhaled at forty-five degrees, right ankle cast over left thigh, left leg rigidly straight down to the heel, fag-bearing right arm languidly draped over the armrest of his chair. Ray used to watch it and wonder, like the tree falling in the deserted forest, whether Simon bothered to light up if there was no-one there to see it. If so, what a waste, like Neil Young playing to an empty hall.

He was magnificent, once upon a time, in those far-off student days. Like a comet blazing through wherever he passed, a coterie always in his trail, helplessly drawn by his aura and buffeted in his oblivious wake. They'd all been in his thrall once, all basked in his light, even if some would later be too proud or too wounded to admit it. Ray had stayed longer and flown closer to the heat than most, and got correspondingly burnt the worst too. All the others' wax wings melted and they soon fell away. Well, all bar one, and she had her scorchmarks too.

Nobody would ever, could ever forget Simon Darcourt. Ray had known him for less than four years, but in the time since, he had remained as fresh and vivid in Ray's mind as after that first Geography tutorial, or that last bitter exchange. Even glimpsed in a crowded airport, his should have been one of the most instantly recognisable faces in Ray's memory, but two things had temporarily clouded his judgement, one of them being the buzz-cut. The other was that Simon Darcourt had been dead for three years.

Ray had even gone up to Aberdeen for the memorial service, admittedly partly out of curiosity to see whether Div had been accurate in predicting that the only friends present would be the ones Simon had made in the last month, having systematically alienated everyone else. In the event, there was a pretty big turnout, but it was hard to tell how many really knew the deceased. There was a large representation from the firm Simon worked for, as well as a sizeable delegation of civic dignitaries, including several local MPs, MSPs and even the then First Minister. It was a courtesy, maybe an apology, that the state offered to those it had failed to protect, as well as an honourable (if futile) gesture of dignified defiance towards their murderers.

Ray had waited until the bereaved parties, the official parties, the official parties' security guards and even the old wino in the hooded duffel coat (a statutory fixture of Scottish cemeteries) had gone away, then went to the head-stone to read the name and the dates, still hardly able to believe they referred to the right guy.

Poor bastard. It was never supposed to be like this. Simon had the awesome charisma of one who was born for greatness; if accompanied by the detestible arrogance of one who knew it. Whatever they had all come to think of him, he had made their world a more interesting place, and even once he had gone from Ray's life, he still antici-pated Simon one day pitching up again somewhere of celestial prominence. Ray didn't buy the *NME* these days, but any time he saw the front page on a newsstand, he half-expected to see those intense grey eyes staring back from it. And sure, some people's lights shine bright in a confined space – school, uni – then dissipate against the wider sky, but Ray had never known anyone more naturally cut out for celebrity. It didn't seem right that he should just be erased, rendered a footnote to some foreign conflict, a notch on the rifle-butt of a terrorist scrote and his infantile sense of grievance.

'Sorry, mate,' Ray had said, standing over the stone. 'We should have met up for a pint, eh? Sorted it all out. I'll miss you, man. I think I always did.'

It wasn't sentiment; Ray had occasionally thought about getting in touch, going for that pint, but it had been easy to procrastinate. They had their whole lives, hadn't they? Their paths were bound to cross again sooner or later.

In Real Life™, without a 'reload saved game' function, you most regret the things you *don't* do, never more so than when the last chance has gone. Simon's death had been a valuable lesson in *carpe diem*, enough in fact for Ray to propose to Kate shortly afterwards, following years of living together. And maybe that's what this was too, via his stressed and fatigued mind playing tricks with him. It couldn't have been Simon he saw, just a similar face, his brain distorting it to fit. The bloke certainly didn't acknowledge him, there was no flicker of recognition before he looked away again. Even that distinctive walk must have been a projection; after all, how many nanoseconds did he actually see of the guy's full length?

This was his subconscious's way of telling him to stop feeling sorry for himself, go home and get on with it. It was reminding him, as he contemplated airborne escape, that journeys from airports don't always take you to better places.

So he was having a hard time as a new father and a new teacher. Boohoo. He was shit at online deathmatch as well when he first started that, remember? Respawn and plunge back into the fray.

It will get easier. It will all get easier.

Ray winced, as ever, as he put his key in the lock, steeling himself for whatever awaited within. He had his lies prepared too, to explain being home late. Bad traffic on the M8. Should have known, his own daft fault for trying a shortcut.

Kate emerged from the living room, Martin in her arms. She was smiling and so was he.

'Look at this,' she said.

'What?'

'He's calm,' she explained, laughing a little. 'No colic tonight. Do you recognise him?'

'Just about.'

'How are you? You look like you've seen a ghost.'

Best not. He'd have to say where, for a start.

'D'you want a wee hug?' she asked, meaning with the baby.

'Yes,' Ray said, and meant it. He took hold of Martin, held his warm, tiny face to his cheek. The wee man barfed on his shoulder.

He laughed, and so did Kate.

'So how was it today?' she asked.

'Ach, no' bad.'

There were few things he didn't confide in his wife, but under the circumstances, the fact that he detested his new career was something he hadn't considered it prudent to share. He was aware she could read his reticence well enough to know that it wasn't the dawn of an invigorating new voyage of self-fulfilment, but equally she knew that if he didn't want to talk about it right then, it was best not to pry.

'You?'

'All right. He's been a wee bit better today. Oh, and Lisa from the ante-natal group popped round with her wee Rachel, so we got a wee blether. I didn't get any dinner sorted out again though. Sorry.'

When they'd both been at home, they'd been fighting each other to cook, as it meant time alone in the kitchen with a glass of wine and some music on while the other wrestled the infant. On your own with him, though, you were lucky if you got the chance to open a tin of beans.

'I'll rustle something up while he's on the breast.'

'Can you be bothered?' Kate asked. 'How about a take-away? I've a hankering for curry.'

That sounded perfect. They hadn't had one for months, it seeming a waste of money if they couldn't sit down and enjoy it together. But even if they were eating it in shifts, a Ruby would do them the power of good. It would also give Ray the excuse for a walk, which he could really do with that night.

It was nearly nine by the time he got out, having allowed Kate time for a long soak and given Martin his nightly dook as well, in the absurdly optimistic but nonetheless enduring hope that it would send him off to sleep. It was raining a little, some light drizzle. Nothing compared to the miserable July they'd endured, a month of merciless downpours that had curtailed trips out with the pram and threatened to drive them cabin-crazy. August had been better, comparatively, but it had been a stinker of a summer in every possible way.

The rain wouldn't have bothered him that evening

anyway. He needed time with his thoughts, something best spent outdoors even before the advent of his offspring. What he had seen – or rather, what his mind had presented him with – had left him shaken, and not merely by its initial fright. It had been a psychological slap in the face with a large trout, distracting him from his depressed tunnel vision and knocking him off-balance enough to look again at what was in front of him.

Don't quit. Respawn and plunge back into the fray. Notch up some frags, man, the game's just starting.

The baby game was just starting too. Sceptically reluctant as he'd been to believe it, people had assured him that the colic would simply stop, as suddenly as it had begun. Three months, according to some, thirteen weeks said others. Martin hadn't been that bad the night before, and seemed unrecognisably placid tonight too. It was going to get easier, better. As predicted by the health visitor, he had even started to smile. Maybe one day Ray would too.

He walked along their street, Kintore Road, a little enclave of Sixties-built modest semis amid the sandstone grandeur of Newlands' nineteenth-century merchant-class avenues. At the end was a path leading to the footbridge across the Cart, a river that normally looked little grander than a large burn at this time of year, but which was swollen almost to winter depths by the recent monsoons. Across the bridge were the tenement-lined streets of Langside, divided by water from its more affluent neighbour. You could usually smell curry as soon as you crossed the bridge, though that would be from a tenement kitchen. The takeaway was quarter of a mile further on.

He heard a car door open behind him in the cul-de-sac as he reached the path. He glanced back. It was one of those people carrier efforts, with a guy in a sweatshirt and jogging pants standing outside the passenger door, apparently giving directions to whoever had dropped him off. The people-carrier pulled away and did a one-eighty, heading back up towards Cathcart Road. Ray slowed his pace, planning to let the jogger pass before the bridge, but the bloke in the sweatshirt was walking too. Maybe dropped off after a kickabout somewhere.

Ray stopped on the bridge, again hoping the guy would at least overtake. He didn't want to have to hurry his trip, and he hated walking too close to people.

The river looked worthy of the name for a change, the water even high enough to cover the shopping trolleys and bike frames. Ray glanced to his side, where the guy in the sweatshirt was tying his shoelaces. It was the kind of thing that he knew ought not to make him nervous. If the bastard was planning to mug him, what was all the fannying about for? Foreplay? Or was he waiting until he'd bought his curry so he could rob that?

Daft.

Daft, but still, but still. It had been a freaky enough day already. He decided to pick up the pace and hope the guy went the other way once they were over the bridge.

The not-jogger resumed walking as soon as Ray did, which prompted a serious internal dialogue as to the dignity versus security issues of breaking into a run. He compromised on walking faster, and vowed not to look back. The trainer-cushioned footfalls remained behind him, but he couldn't tell whether they were gaining ground. His vow lasting a good four seconds, he glanced back, ready to sprint if the response demanded it. However, the guy wasn't looking at him, he was looking past him. Ray faced the front again and saw what he was looking at.

The people carrier was heading towards the bridge at

speed, having made the loop to the other side of the river via Langside Drive. Ray turned to look at the not-jogger, who was pulling up his sweatshirt to reveal an automatic pistol taped to his stomach. He tore the tapes away and began screwing a silver-grey silencer to the muzzle. Up ahead, the people carrier slewed across the end of Cartside Street and its driver jumped from the door, also holding a silenced pistol.

Ray blinked, closing his eyes tight for a moment. Chronically knackered and unprecedentedly stressed, he'd already been seeing things that weren't there today. Dead people at the airport and now double-trigger assassins on the Southside. Granted, the latter weren't unheard of these days, but they generally didn't bother with silencers any more than they bothered with English teachers. When he looked again, the driver had reached the far end of the bridge, and he most definitely *was* carrying a weapon. He stood with his feet apart and raised the gun in both hands. Five yards behind Ray, the not-jogger was doing the same thing.

This wasn't possible. It wasn't even plausible. Then Ray remembered a story about a student in Dennistoun answering his front door and getting kneecapped by two neds who were supposed to be hitting the bloke upstairs, a hash dealer who shared the unfortunate student's surname.

He threw his hands in the air like a bank clerk in a cowboy picture.

'I'm the wrong guy,' he shouted. 'Fuck's sake, don't shoot, I'm the wrong guy.'

'Raymond Ash?' the not-jogger asked, clearly and slowly, in the clipped, precise English of a fluent but non-native speaker. Ray turned to face him.

'Jesus Christ.'

'No, I think Raymond Ash.'

Ray tried to swallow, but it felt as though his throat was blocked. He should have had a dozen questions, but could only think of Martin and Kate. The not-jogger slid the lever on his automatic, chambering a bullet. Ray heard the action repeated at his back.

Martin.

Kate.

The names, the faces gave instinct a kick in the arse. He dived for the railings, expecting the lethal blows to cut him down as the first muted shots sounded in his ears. Somehow those impacts never arrived, but the next one was guaranteed. He hit the water before he could think of all the junk he was likely to impale himself upon, and instantly became the first Glaswegian grateful for the summer rain.

Sheer instinct had taken him from the line of fire, but the same reflexes put him right back there when he automatically surfaced, seeking his breath and his bearings. Above him, both gunmen were leaning over the railings, scanning the opaque and rain-dappled river. They opened fire as soon as they saw him.

Ray ducked under again, hearing bullets zip past him through the water. His feet found the bottom. It was only about a metre and a half deep, but he was invisible as long as he stayed below. The zipping sounds ceased, the assassins biding their time, saving their ammo. Ray could feel the current pulling at his clothes. He was pretty sure he'd pissed himself, but it was hardly a concern now. The river bent sharply amid thick cover of trees just twenty or thirty yards downstream, next to the playing fields. Unfortunately it also got wider and shallower around the same stretch, but it was the only chance he had. He tucked his hands around his ankles, curling himself into a ball, and then lifted his feet from the riverbed, letting the flow carry him along in small, bouncing movements.

His last bounce ran him aground just as his breath gave out, the water still deep enough to cover him but not enough to keep him afloat. He gasped in the air and looked up. The bridge was out of sight, but through gaps in the bushes he could still see parked cars up on Cartside Street. The gunmen were bound to be up there somewhere.

He scrambled to the bank and threw himself flat among the trees, where he lay still and listened, but his water-logged ears heard only his own heavy breaths and the sound of blood pumping round his head.

dead man wanking

Simon had barely walked the length of the room and hung up his jacket before he heard a knock at the door. Damn sharp service: the British hotel industry had benefited immeasurably from being largely bought over by the Yanks and the French and generally having as little local management input as possible. Some might whine about cultural imposition, but he hardly thought it a great loss to the national sense of identity that it was now in attendants and waiting staff's job descriptions to actually do what they were fucking paid for and not look like they were being anally raped while they were about it.

The bellboy carried his case inside and set it down on the rack, then gave him the textbook room-features break-down, a service particularly useful to those travellers who hadn't yet worked out what the light switch was for, or were perhaps planning on using the telephone to dry their hair. Ostensibly it was a courtesy, and a chance for the guest to make any enquiries he or she might have; but the true purpose was to hang around long enough for you to get hold of your wallet. Simon slipped him a couple of quid, opting as always for a decent but not over-generous tip. Too mean or too ostentatious and they were more likely to remember your face.

The TV was on, as per, displaying the hotel's welcome message and menu over a soundtrack of Vivaldi, the Muzak of the corporate age. He looked at the name addressing him on the screen, different almost every time he checked in somewhere. This trip, he was Gordon Freeman. He'd chosen the Christian name to sound inconspicuously Scottish; while the surname was an indulgence, a celebration even. He'd been back before, of course, but never on business, and that was what made it so special. That Friday feeling, folks, and it was only Wednesday. Break out the Crunchies.

Talking briefly to the receptionist downstairs, it had been strange to hear himself speaking in his old accent, something he had found himself doing before he realised it. He seldom spoke English anymore, and when he unavoidably had to, he rendered it as Euro-neutral as he could. None of the people he worked with had ever known his nationality (or former nationality), and he insisted that they didn't enquire or speculate about each other's either. They spoke French – the international language of their profession – unless circumstances required otherwise, as was the case now. But for this op, codenamed Mission Deliver Kindness, all communications, at all levels and across all media, were to be in English. He ordered them even to think in English, particularly those assigned 'speaking parts', who had each been on a satellite-fed diet of specific British soaps for the past two months: some on *Corrie*, some on *Brookie* and the rest on *Stenders*, poor cunts. The benefit of this was to roughen up the edges of their word-perfect pronunciations and ground them in regional colloquialisms so that they didn't sound like a bunch of homogenous Euro-twats. It seemed to have worked too, and apparently without any of the feared side effects. As far as he had noticed, Deacon's occasional Estuary English inflections hadn't come at the price of a complete failure of dress sense or a tendency to fend off sorrow with the aid of a singsong round the old

Joanna, while Taylor had been pig-ugly *before* his introduction to the time-warped and genetically deficient world
of Weatherfield. May, being an explosives expert, was
bound to feel at home with the unfeasibly combustible
environs of Brookside Close, though Simon had no way of
knowing whether he'd been prone to bouts of depression
prior to his concentrated immersion in Scouse misery.

The accent he would be using, he told them, was learned
from a show called *Taggart*. He feared all these years of
speaking French might make him sound as Glaswegian as
deep-fried foie gras, so he had to come up with an equally
unauthentic source just in case someone was nosey enough
to check it out.

Simon switched off the TV, probably the last time he'd
see the name 'Freeman' in intended reference to himself.
For the duration and execution of MDK, he would be
'Mercury'. No-one in the team ever learned their comrades'
real names, an indispensable precaution in a world where
loyalty only lasted as long as it took to pull off the job and
trouser the greenback. They weren't allowed to name themselves, either, as who knew what traceable elements might
lie in their choice of handle. Simon gave them their names,
and always used those of major-league rock stars: easy to
remember and international enough not to betray a
parochial and thus identifiable frame of reference. He was
sure Shub would approve, master that he was of the art of
self-obscuring.

Hotel rooms like this were a pleasure that never faded
with familiarity. A lot of them were indistinguishable, and
minus the logos, you could easily forget which chain name
you had just checked into, but there was actually something comforting about that. Yeah, they all had the same
features, but they were features he liked, so the effect wasn't

so much a home from home as a reason to be happy you were on the road. Two double beds, well-stocked mini-bar, room-service menu, desk in the corner, towelling gowns in the wardrobe, marble in the bathrooms. When his schedule allowed, he savoured the ritual relaxation of unpacking and undressing, before pouring himself a drink and having a long, slow soak, after which the stresses and cares of mass murder just washed down the plughole with the suds.

Tonight, however, the ritual had to wait. There was pressing business to attend to, an unforeseen complication that had to be incorporated into their plans. He placed his laptop on the desk and plugged the phonejack into its socket, then booted up and double-clicked an icon marked Assembly.bat. The program ran a number of executables, dialling to page the three command-rank members of his team, then connecting to a password-protected relay chat server that only the four of them knew the address of anyway. In what might accurately be called the Surveillance Age, there was no such thing as guaranteed privacy, but this came close. The server and all clients were firewalled out the arse, so there was no way of intercepting data going in or out, except as scrambled gobbledegook. The only flaw was that one of the participants could log the chat session and later toss it to the cops, but only if he really wanted to know what a power drill felt like inside his abdomen.

Deacon responded immediately, by way of an automatically generated text message, which meant he was still in the air and therefore unavailable. Taylor showed up in the chat session first, having pulled into a layby to do so, probably screeching the tyres now he had an excuse to crank up his new cellular modem. They all had them, but, for security reasons, Simon had rigidly restricted their use to these firewalled blethers and looking up pornowhack.com.

May joined the session shortly after that, dialling in from their temporary HQ.

The alteration to the schedule was in motion within half an hour. Deacon would be brought up to date when he reported in, but he wasn't needed. May had it in hand, dispatching Joe Strummer and Mick Jones to go rock the little drummer boy's Kasbah whenever he next exited his address, which was helpfully listed in the phonebook.

Simon closed the chat session, grabbed two Bourbon miniatures from the mini-bar, then turned on the taps in the bathroom. Now that its potential consequences were being capped, he could afford to reflect on what had happened at the airport, and was in fact having some difficulty thinking about much else.

What were the odds? Really, what were the fucking odds? Ha! Shorter than anyone might think.

There'd been a woman with a drooling toddler beside him on the flight; the comparative anonymity of economy class coming at the usual price to comfort, dignity and olfactory wellbeing. She'd been telling the pudgy little spawn about God, as precipitated by their being above the clouds and the gnome asking predictably stupid questions. 'God is everywhere,' Mummy had explained, enough sugar in her voice to rot every last milk tooth in the cretin's chubby head. This being the case, God had to be a Glaswegian, because they were fucking everywhere too. It didn't matter how remote a part of the planet you cared to explore, when you got there, you were bound to run into somebody you'd last seen on Byre's Road or the Central Station taxi rank.

Actually visiting the place practically guaranteed an impromptu reunion with *somebody*, even if you were only passing through the airport. In fact, especially if you were passing through the airport. When he was younger, he thought it was just because everybody went on their holidays at the same time. Later in life he'd found that the time of year or even the time of day didn't matter: if you flew in or out of Abbotsinch, you usually saw someone you knew. It was the funnel effect, skewing the probability, channelling all the city's air travellers through one small space. Kind of thing you had to bear in mind in this game. Playing the percentages was negligence, no matter how well you thought you knew them: what comfort would it be as you bit the barrel of your own gun to know that you had been statistically unlucky?

Last time he'd flown into Glasgow, he'd seen Lucy Klesk, a student-era conquest of his in the 'ten pints down and no-one else in sight' weight-class. She was sitting in one of the departure-lounge cafés, captivated by *Hello!* magazine and a king-size Mars bar. The years and the calories had not been kind, and it took him a moment to recognise her under that full-thickness extra layer of pale flesh. She'd been too engrossed in fending off the imminent threat of malnutrition to notice his scrutiny, but even if she had looked up, eye contact was a luxury he knew he could afford, as long as it was kept brief.

It took some getting used to, took some believing. Like putting on Gollum's ring that supposedly made you invisible, you wouldn't go straight down the female changing-room at the local pool without making sure that it was working, and Simon's problem was that there was no-one he could ask for independent confirmation. The first time he returned, he must have looked like such a tit, walking around with sunglasses on indoors, wearing hats and hoods: all to obscure a face that was already hidden behind the world's greatest disguise.

When the true proof of this came, it was back on foreign soil, where he took no such absurd precautions. He was walking through Schipol, connecting to his flight home to Nice, when he passed Rob Hossman on the opposite travelator. Rob had sat two desks away from him at Sintek Energy for four years; he'd even been to an abysmal dinner party at the guy's house, one of those desperate suburban purgatory-with-salad affairs, where all the men pretended they were listening to each other's conversations while they fantasised about fucking each other's wives. They had traded greetings in corridors a thousand times, observing that etiquette whereby you clocked who was coming but pretended not to notice them until you had reached the crucial ten-foot passing zone. At Schipol they glanced across the concourse simultaneously, and Rob was half a second from performing that twitchy nod of his when the magic ring did its stuff.

The look on Hossman's face was one that Simon would see repeated many times down the years, up to and including Larry the little drummer boy that very evening. It began with a narrowing of the eyes, the spark-of-recognition stage. Next the forehead made like an accordion as they ransacked their memory banks and tried to work out why his mug was familiar. Then, at what would normally be the Eureka moment, they hit the buffers with a thud. After that there was blank incomprehension – the Photo-Me-booth first-flash look – followed usually by a slight shake of the head or some more accordion action, by which time he was gone.

If their brains were computers, they'd need a manual re-boot. One simple line of data unfailingly crashed the programme. How did Sherlock Holmes put it? Once you've ruled out the impossible, whatever you're left with, no matter how implausible, must be the truth. Their problem was that the impossible *was* the truth, so once they'd ruled that out, all they were left with was confusion.

Holmes was still right, though. They just weren't possessed of all the relevant information. What they believed to be impossible, wasn't. What they believed to be the truth wasn't either. It wasn't public knowledge, but was nonetheless a fact, that Simon Darcourt's body had never been recovered. According to the inquest, it was officially 'impossible' that he could have survived the explosion, given where he'd been sitting, never mind the ensuing crash into the fjord's icy waters. Officially impossible because the officials weren't possessed of all the relevant information either.

Hard to blame them, really. The Stavanger disaster must have been a bitch to investigate, what with the debris being scattered and submerged in a stretch of deep water that was only accessible by boat or seaplane. It took the diving teams and salvage crews almost a month to conclude their efforts, and though they eventually raised all sections of the plane, they worked in the soul-destroying knowledge that the currents and shifting sands were every day claiming a further share of the evidence. His wasn't the only body never to be recovered, the passenger manifest providing the only means of calculating the death toll. The bomber's tracks weren't merely covered, they were all but washed away. Whoever had blown up ScanAir flight 941, the investigators concluded, really knew what they were doing.

Well, yeah, sort of. But as even the most gin-addled, volunteer-fondling stage magician could tell you, the secret of a good disappearing trick is to keep the audience distracted: give them a loud bang and a bright flash so that they don't notice your discreet exit, making sure you also whip the props away before they start trying to suss how it was done.

Of course, he hadn't blown up a passenger airliner merely for the purpose of faking his own death; that would constitute a profligate waste of human life. There'd be no pay-out, for a start, and in any case, he wouldn't have been able to lay hands on the hardware. It hadn't even been his idea. Okay, the not-dying part had been his idea – what he regarded as a sensible modification of the suicide bomber's traditional remit – but the attack itself was at someone else's instigation.

Finland had extradited the fugitive Urkobaijani guerrilla leader, 'Artro', to Moscow, where he was wanted for organising a bombing campaign in support of the region's (yawn) struggle for independence. Artro's speciality had been marketplaces: security low, surveillance non-existent, very busy, very public. Having now seen a couple of Russian markets, the only downside Simon could envisage was that it would be difficult to tell the difference between the state of the place before and after the bomb went off. It certainly couldn't smell any worse.

Artro's geopolitical knowledge didn't extend very far beyond Russia being the Great Satan and the US being the Great Satan as well, and it was widely rumoured that he'd gone on the lam to Finland in the disastrously mistaken belief that Scandinavia was an entirely autonomous continent, politically separate from Europe. That said, misapprehension wouldn't necessarily have led to apprehension if he'd followed the first rule of lying low, which is to lie low; or in his case, to not get puggled on three bottles of Finlandia then start glassing Russian sailors in the centre of Helsinki.

Artro's militia vowed revenge on the Finns, their feelings towards the Russians already having been made fairly clear. Their problem was that Artro had been very much the balls and the brains of the outfit – the latter admittedly wasn't saying much – and the credibility meter was starting a rapid countdown on their vow. In fact, with their leader behind bars, the potency of their entire organisation was under serious scrutiny; in the world of terrorism, perception is everything, so if nobody is scared of you, you might as well not exist. They needed to do something high profile and they needed to do it soon.

Naturally, they went to Shub. Sooner or later, everyone does.

And if you've been very, very good (or, depending on your moral standpoint, very, very bad), Shub sometimes comes to you.

Shaloub 'Shub' N'gurath. Probably the most dangerous man in the world, if only the world knew he existed. That wasn't his real name, of course, only what he'd told Simon for communication purposes, and it was rumoured he never gave the same name to two people. 'I don't like being talked about,' he said, and by Christ he meant it.

How to describe him? The Bill Gates of international terrorism? The anti-Kofi Annan?

The Bill Gates comparison was probably better, in that no matter what you were up to, your cause, your enemy or your methods, you could be sure he was seeing a slice of the action, financially speaking. Another valid comparison would be with the Great Oz, as it was difficult to equate this bald, bespectacled and pot-bellied little man with the power he wielded and the reputation that preceded him. The aura of mystery and secrecy surrounding him functioned as part of his security and defence.

Though rumours proliferated, they tended to be rendered even more shadowy and confused by the difficulty in two conversants establishing for certain who they were talking about, not to mention their mutual reluctance to confirm that he *was* who they meant, lest it ever get back to him.

Despite this, Simon had still heard plenty of stories. Some sounded like campfire tales, others Bogeyman myths likely to have been started or at least encouraged by the man himself, but one he had little difficulty believing was that Shub was represented on the boards of several of the world's leading arms manufacturers. Certainly if he hadn't existed, they'd have done very well to invent him (even though all of them – and their shareholders – deep down sincerely wished their products weren't necessary and that the world could be a happier, more peaceful place). His far-reaching efforts kept the fires of armed conflict well stoked around the globe, and those conflicts had made him an extremely wealthy man. In explaining his business to Simon, Shub had concentrated on the area of terrorism because that was to be his field of activity, but it was obviously only one slice of a very large and very bloody pie.

'Terrorism is merely an agent, an irritant,' Shub said. 'It causes the rash, the irritation, and governments are forced to scratch. Then, as every child is told, scratching makes it worse. More soldiers, more guns, more training, more unrest, more repression, more revolt, more terrorism, more irritation, and for me, for my friends, for you, for us all: ka-ching, ka-ching, ka-ching.' He had smiled, rubbing his thumb against his fingers in the internationally recognised gesture.

'Blood money' was the politicians' poe-faced and over-used phrase, more accurate than they probably knew. Terrorism pumped cash around the globe like a heart:

weapon sales, weapon smuggling, training camps, professional hits, kidnapping, drug-running, fundraising, protection rackets, money-laundering, security systems, surveillance technology, defence contracts . . . ba-bump, ba-bump, bang-bang, bang-bang, ka-ching, ka-ching. And if terrorism was the heart, Shub was its pacemaker. World Peace would be a very bad day at his office, which was why strenuous efforts were being put in at all times to make sure such a cataclysm never came about.

Terrorism didn't just move money, either: it generated the stuff. In the most impoverished areas of the world there might not be any cash for food, but if you threw in some ethnic tension or an independence struggle, the war chests just filled up as if by magic. Most people would only associate Urkobaijan with Channel Four news footage of tearful refugees wading through mud, pulling all their earthly possessions on wooden carts, but that didn't mean Artro's mob couldn't spare a three hundred K advertising budget for letting the world know they still meant business.

The IRA had their deluded sugar daddies drinking Guinness in Bostonian Plastic-Paddy theme pubs, but they weren't unique. Every festering little conflict on the planet had its overseas fanclub, ex-pats or second-generation romantics trying to buy a sense of their own fading ethnicity as the world threatened to homogenise around them. Plus they could usually rely on further generosity from foreign parties who shared their antipathy towards the target nation and/or the target nation's allies, which was one of the many areas in which Shub specialised.

Gadaffi had infamously made Libya an international centre for terrorism. He brought people together from many nations and conflicts, gave them funding, helped them share resources, contacts, networks; offered them training camps, accommodation, swimming pools, room service and conference facilities (well, just about). However, this hospitality was only extended to those who fitted the left-of-centre ideological bill. It was like terrorism as a nationalised industry. Shub N'gurath, on the other hand, represented the free market end of things, and would never let something as crass as politics get in the way of making a deal.

The ScanAir bombing was a great example of Shub's ability to match people's needs and resources. In Brazno, Urkobaijan, Artro's shower had the money and the motive but not the means and definitely not the time. In Bridge of Don, Scotland, Simon had the nous but not the hardware. In Ghent, Belgium, a man named Michel Bruant had the hardware but no way of getting it out of the country. And in Le Havre, France, there was a freight firm running an unofficial sideline worth eight times its declared turnover. Shub put them all together, and took a minimum forty per cent at every step.

Serendipity doo-da.

Shub also had a talent for recognising not only the right man for a job, but in some cases the right job for the man. Bruant's package was designed as a suicide bomb, and Artro's brigade all liked the idea of Urkobaijani independence so much that they had every intention of still being there if and when it finally happened. Nonetheless, Shub would have had little difficulty finding them a volunteer if the price was right; he'd done it before.

There was nothing expressed the depth of your belief, courage, resolve and all-costs fanaticism quite like a suicide attack, but according to Shub, these rare qualities tended to be found only in 'those who were closest to their god'. By this he didn't mean the fundamentally religious, but the terminally ill, with little time left to do much but worry about their family's future welfare. 'Assisted euthanasia' he called it, the assistance being primarily financial in nature – though strapping twenty pounds of C4 to your chest and detonating it in a public place obviously helped you on your way. Quick and painless, too.

Shub had brokered plenty such deals, and might have organised another but for two factors. Factor one was the Urkobaijanis' stipulation that the target should be a civil aircraft, putting them into terrorism's elite bracket: the mile-high club. In the past, all he'd needed was someone capable of staggering from their oncology ward to the local police station or government building, but negotiating European airport security would take a sharper mind and a fitter body.

A suitable candidate would still have been found but for factor two, which was that Shub had been alerted to the existence of someone who might have the brains to do it without staying ringside for the show; someone who was showing great potential and might be ready to take off the stabilisers; someone who might be swayed to view it not so much as a task as a once-in-a-lifetime opportunity.

Simon got more than a hundred and fifty thousand dollars for blowing up flight 941, which was enormously generous considering Shub probably guessed he'd have done it for nothing, given the ancillary benefits. There was an element of investment in it though, or maybe even 'nurture' was the word. In Shub's eyes, the people he did business with were split into two camps: customers and contractors. Those who were motivated by factors other than the financial were the customers, politicised fools just waiting to be parted from their money. Those cashing in were the ones he respected, the ones he could relate to.

Simon was, at that stage, doing it principally because he enjoyed it, which was why Shub no doubt felt it mutually beneficial to teach him that the money could be enjoyable too.

Before flight 941, before Shub N'gurath, it was just a hobby, no matter how good he was getting at it; something he did for kicks in his spare time. Despite the enormity of what he had already achieved, and despite even the cash he had accrued, turning full-time pro was a far from simple progression. It wasn't as though he could turn to Alison one night and say, 'Honey, I'm going to follow my dreams before life passes me by. Are you with me?'

He could tell himself the respectable job and suburban existence were merely a useful cover, but his growing sense of frustration argued convincingly otherwise. They might provide a facade, but it was a facade he could only come out from behind for limited spells: glimpses of a world of freedom that he had to keep walking away from. He was earning a sight more from this 'hobby' than from his recognised job, but he couldn't touch the money. If he suddenly rolled into the driveway in a Beamie Boxter, Alison was bound to ask a few difficult questions, and the Inland Revenue were going to be curious too. He wasn't doing it for the money and he didn't particularly *want* a Beamie Boxter, but it encapsulated his problem. What he wanted was a life that seemed so tantalisingly within reach, a life he now knew he was born for, but first he had to get out of the life he was in.

Walking away was not the obstacle. He had to make sure he wasn't followed, and that was the tricky part. If he simply disappeared, went out one morning and didn't come home from work, there wouldn't be an official investigation, but people would forever be picking over the facts, sniffing for a trail. Alison was unlikely to spend the rest of her life or even the rest of her week asking 'why?', and she certainly wouldn't need to hire a detective to find the biggest answers, but when something isn't closed, curiosity remains. Add the element of mystery and you compound it tenfold. All these years later, people were still claiming to have seen someone who just might have been Richey Manic: spinning the cycle, feeding the enigma. The number of people who might think they'd recognised Simon's face in a foreign crowd was considerably smaller, but the principle worked the same. Someone somewhere would always be looking for him, and that was *without* knowing he'd killed anybody.

Shub N'gurath turned out to be his fairy godmother, the major-label A&R man who spotted him jamming in a pub band and said, 'Kid, you've got what it takes. How would you like to be a star?'

The timescale was tight – little more than a fortnight – with the Urkobaijanis in a hurry to get back on the newswires before the end of the month. That had suited Simon fine. It took minutes to devise his plan after Shub told him what was required, and with Bruant supplying the bespoke hardware, he only had to procure a couple of items himself and then fly the route to refresh his memory. The last thing he'd have wanted was a few spare weeks to dwell on all the ways it might go wrong, not to mention extending the task of acting normal at home and, in particular, at work. Keeping the fucking grin off his face around Sintek Energy just for those two weeks had been the biggest challenge of the entire undertaking.

He booked his flights, as ever, through Slipgate.com, invoicing the first journey to himself and the second to Sintek. Doing it through Slipgate on the web allowed him

113

to select his seats and, equally important, verify the type of aircraft. He'd flown the Stavanger-to-Helsinki leg at least half a dozen times on Sintek business, and it was usually an Avionique 300, but there was one time it had been an Aerospace 146 (which might actually have been with a different airline) and he needed to be sure. Slipgate confirmed 300s for flight 941 on both trips: the reconnoitre and, six days later, the real deal.

He organised the first run for the preceding Tuesday, which he booked off work in lieu of a recent trip to Oslo that had eaten into a weekend. The date of the target flight had already been selected as Monday the twenty-sixth, the fate of those on board not decided by himself or even by the Urkobaijanis, but by Harald Johansen in Sintek's Helsinki office. Simon needed an official reason for his journey, and Monday was the only day of that week Harald was free for a get-together. There was a satisfying irony about it: having clocked up so many thousands of miles in pointless business travel, he was going to bow out en route to one final, utterly unnecessary meeting.

The recon trip was more than a memory-refreshing exercise. He needed a Stavanger airside ID and there was only one place to get it. Well, on-site there were a number of places, but having killed time there so often, he knew which one would be the easiest. There was a troll in the souvenir shop who always hung her jacket over the back of her chair, presumably so that none of the transit passengers would be denied the sight and smell of her permanently sodden armpits. She made frequent lumbering sorties around the store, leaving her laminate unguarded behind the cash register, itself in safely plausible loitering distance from the greetings card rack. When Simon got there, however, she was nowhere to be seen, and in her place was a diminutive, rodent-faced adolescent, eyeing up the customers with a suspicion that suggested it would absolutely make her day if she spotted one trying to purloin a Toblerone. Needless to say, her jacket was firmly on and she was sporting her ID badge like it said 'I AM THE LAW'.

This necessitated an otherwise highly inadvisable course of action: a trip to the coffee stall further along the concourse. He waited until the queue had cleared (ha ha), and ordered a large cappuccino, something nobody was ever likely to do twice, then made a fumbling show of trying to find the correct Norwegian coinage. All of this helped give the bored-looking Euro-dork behind the counter the impression that Simon was a wide-eyed and bumbling ingénu, something he then compounded by tumbling the Styrofoam cup from the counter and spilling the cappuccino across the floor. The gangling teen had a resigned look on his face as he reached for a cloth; it wasn't the first time it had happened, but presumably the customers normally tasted it first. Simon was profuse in his apologies, and fussed around him as he crouched down to mop up the mess, the dork too concentrated on keeping his sleeves out of the puddle to notice his laminate being gently unclipped as it dangled from his chest. Simon pocketed the ID, then made a show of being out of local currency when asked if he wanted a refill. The dork was understandably in no mood to offer a freebie, but Simon couldn't complain. He'd been generous enough already.

After that, he took a walk round to flight 941's departure gate and watched the in-flight caterers load up their shrink-wrapped gastroenteritis. They wore sky-blue overalls, as he remembered: separate slacks and shirts, company logo on the breast pocket. He picked up a similar set later in the week at a workware store in George Street and scanned the logo from a napkin he'd lifted on the flight, transferring it using a kid's iron-on T-shirt kit from the computer section at Toys R Us.

High-tech terrorism *ou quoi*?

The package from Ghent arrived on the Friday, as scheduled, but Shub made him sweat on the final element: his new passport, onward ticket and blank Amex cheques not showing up until late Sunday afternoon. Before they did, he'd been climbing the walls, concerned that the whole operation was going to be aborted due to this one failure. It was to prove a valuable experience, as from then onwards, on every job he set up, there was always one element that didn't quite fall into place until very close to showtime. The lesson was not to get frazzled and start channelling all your anxieties into this one thing, as the danger was that the distraction could cause you to miss a more significant unravelment elsewhere. In this case, it was only after the courier turned up at his doorstep that he remembered to check all the battery levels, and discovered the ones Bruant had put in the Walkman were on their last legs, presumably from over-rigorous testing.

Bruant's device was intended to be taken into the passenger cabin as hand luggage, and was consequently built around objects one might plausibly be carrying on board a flight. The components were housed in a modified briefcase with concealed compartments below the lid and above the base. These compartments would not show up under airport X-ray scanners for the simple reason that they would at that point be empty. What they were intended to contain was meanwhile accommodated in plain view for the inspection of security staff: two fruit juice cartons lying loose in the main body of the case. The cartons, in fact, each contained one constituent of a binary liquid explosive, perfectly harmless until mixed (unless of course you bunged a straw in and drank the stuff).

The briefcase's telescopic support arms detached at the base, and a few twists of their bottom-most sections brought forth tapered plastic injectors, to which you attached the cartons once you were airside. A modified Walkman supplied the pumping mechanism, connecting to an insulated port at the centre-rear of the case, its busy little cogs also turning a tape for the benefit of security inspectors. The pump drew the liquid into the concealed compartments above and below, where it mixed, ready for detonation. Mixing and detonation were controlled via a necessarily bulky mobile phone, the anachronistically large Ericsson housing the detonator and a digital altimeter, as well as an LCD display that projected the expected graphics when you pressed its buttons. The altimeter could be set to trigger mixing and detonation at specified altitudes. Simon selected three thousand feet, being the height the in-cabin display had read on his recon trip when they were directly above Boknafjorden.

To all of this he had added an object of his own: a battery-operated personal fan, as sold in the travel-gadgets section of every airport. This one had a few modifications, one of which being that it was now remotely operable via his electronic car key. Completing the briefcase's contents were some work folders from Sintek in a zip-locked PVC binder, to which he added a newspaper, a magazine and a king-size Mars bar at the airport newsagent.

He only had to clear security once, at Aberdeen, which he regarded as a soft point of entry. It was just too insignificant to have all but the most bog-standard cursory surveillance, with the most dangerous articles passing through the detectors being contraband half-bottles smuggled by the North Sea roughnecks. Once airside, he didn't have to pass any further checks, as at Stavanger there was no need to leave the departure area between flights.

The first thing he did when he got there was to visit the now once again troll-monitored gift shop, where he made the highly appropriate purchase of a bottle of champagne, plus a pair of jeans and a plain white T-shirt. Next, he went to the gents' toilet, locked himself in a cubicle and carefully assembled Bruant's device, before undertaking the preparatory work on his own gizmo. This consisted of unravelling the champagne's wire restraint and partially loosening the cork, before replacing the wire and connecting it to a conduit at the head of the travel fan. He gave the bottle a good shake and put it, with its entangled attachment, in the duty-free carrier bag. Lastly, he squeezed the jeans and T-shirt into the PVC binder, sealed it, then placed it delicately into the cistern.

He had booked an aisle seat in the backmost row, mere feet from both the toilets and the fuel tanks. The 300 was boarded by steps at the front and rear, and despite his seat allocation, he entered fore. He got the fare-inclusive smile from the stewardess on the door as she counted the passengers aboard, then joined the queue behind the familiar log-jam of travellers storing their hand luggage, getting up to let each other in or playing pass-the-parcel with the statutory in-flight screaming infant. Amid this anxious settling-in activity, no-one paid much attention as he placed his duty-free bag in an overhead locker and then moved further on up the plane.

Another stewardess was on meet-greet-and-count duty at the aft steps. He gave her a 'silly me' smile and shrug as he approached from the wrong direction, waiting until she was obscured by another boarding passenger before taking his seat, so that she didn't take specific notice of where he was sitting. He placed his jacket – containing wallet, passport and return tickets – in the overhead locker, and sat down.

The flight was quiet, as expected, which was why he'd selected the midday run rather than early morning or late afternoon. It would be preferable if he had no-one sitting next to him or indeed opposite, something further ensured by choosing the back row, which was the last to be allocated by the boarding computers. Another passenger nearby wouldn't be a disaster – as no matter how many times he'd seen people get up and move seats prior to take-off, he was yet to see someone query it with the cabin staff – but it was prudent to minimise possible complications. He held on to the briefcase in the meantime: ideally he would place it below the seat, but if he had company, he'd stow it overhead, out of sight, out of mind.

After a few minutes, the aisle was clear but for a ski-bum type having one more go at stuffing his Michelin-man inflatable anorak into the locker above his seat. The trolley dollies were exchanging confirmatory looks. It was almost time. He slid the briefcase under the seat next to him and pretended to read his magazine. A blue figure brushed past him, heading down the plane: the aft stewardess going to meet her fore counterpart, the dolly-in-chief, to add up the numbers. That left one more behind him, sliding metal drawers and banging hatches as she performed her pre-flight catering preparations.

At the front, the dolly-in-chief was handed a copy of the final manifest by a smiling ScanAir official, with whom she appeared to be exchanging cheerful banter. Her ratification of the tally would mean the doors would be closing imminently, but only after one last confirmatory headcount,

119

which the aft stewardess was now embarking upon. She moved swiftly through the cabin from the front, the scarcity of passengers meaning her arithmetic would be done well before she reached the back.

Simon put his magazine into the seat pocket and took careful hold of his car key. He kept his head down to avoid eye contact, watching her legs approach, waiting for the turn that would mark the end of the count. It came. He lifted his head, focusing on the front again. The fore stewardess, having got the nod, was going for her door; the aft one likewise. Action stations.

He pressed the Unlock button on his electronic key. Six rows from the front, his travel fan spun into action, unwinding the wire from the shaken champagne bottle and unfettering the straining cork. There was a thud from the overhead locker, followed by a sudden cascade of liquid on to the head of the passenger below. The aft stewardess turned around again to investigate, the now irate passenger already getting to his feet in response to his baptism of Taittinger. The passenger opened the hatch to investigate, microseconds before the aft stewardess could stretch an arm to prevent him doing precisely that, and received a further drenching for his troubles. This, understandably, did little for his mood. You didn't have to speak Norwegian to understand that he was very forthrightly asking the passengers around him whose bottle it was, like anybody was going to own up. By this point the dolly-in-chief had closed her door and was moving in to assist, while the aft stewardess signalled to her colleague at the back to bring something to mop up the mess.

That was his cue. Simon waited until dolly three had urgently brushed past, then stepped into the toilet, where speed was the reward for the otherwise unthinkable indignity of wearing slip-on shoes. He quickly removed his polo-neck and trousers, revealing the blue overalls underneath, then stuffed his old clothes into the wastepaper chute and stepped back into the cabin.

The prepared line was going through his head – '*Tristjeg måtte bruke toalettet*' – for if he encountered one of the crew, but the diversion worked better than he'd hoped. He'd hit the jackpot in randomly placing the champagne above a distant relative of Thor, whose trip was not about to get any better. Closing the toilet door quietly behind him, Simon skipped lightly down the rear stairs then walked briskly but not hurriedly across the tarmac to the terminal building.

Once inside, he made his way back to the gents, where he retrieved the ziplocked folder and got changed into his new clothes, removing his replacement passport, ticket and traveller's cheques from the discarded garments. He sealed the overalls and ID laminate inside the folder, then carried it out to the departure lounge, from where he watched flight 941 push back, taxi and take off. By the time it exploded, he was already checking in for his flight to CDG.

To say it was amateurish would be too kind, even allowing that his subsequent standards were a lot higher. It was crude, sloppy, seat-of-the-pants stuff, a miracle of sheer jamminess that it came off. Some said you made your own luck, that fortune favours the brave, but he wasn't seduced by these retrospective sentiments of the negligent-but-spawny. All these years later, he still had gut-tightening flashbacks in which he vividly envisaged all the ways it could have gone wrong, all the individual factors that he'd had no contingency for if even one of them hadn't run exactly to plan.

In this game, you couldn't rely on being lucky, and after

any operation, it was vital to acknowledge and analyse the ways in which he had been. This worked both ways, in identifying not only the shortcomings of Simon's own plans, but also any unforeseen defence weaknesses he had inadvertently exploited. In the case of flight 941, he might have enjoyed a large rub of the green, but he also learned a salutary lesson about the biggest, most gaping and indefatigably enduring flaw in anti-terrorist security worldwide: people simply don't expect to be attacked.

Those trolley dollies must have sat through dozens of briefings, training courses and rehearsed scenarios, all intended to raise awareness and condition their response to a potential terrorist threat. They might even have been put 'on alert' (whatever that meant) in light of the bombastic teddy-throwing that had followed Artro's arrest. In practice, none of it meant a damn thing, because practice was four flights a day, five hundred a year, throughout which the most realistic threat was posed by the pilot's hangover, and the principal thing they had to be 'alert' to was half-cut businessmen in first class trying to grope their tits as they leaned over to serve another G&T. The procedures they were following on flight 941 were intended to ensure that nobody missed the plane and that they weren't carrying anyone who hadn't sprung for a ticket. They were too busy getting on with their jobs to worry about terrorism. Christ, who wasn't? The average person didn't get up in the morning and start pondering whether today was the day someone would try to blow up their commuter train. He'd even heard people admit that their response to IRA bomb scares – and explosions – at London railway stations was to think 'Oh, well in that case, I'd better take the District Line'.

It wasn't just that people didn't think about it – it was

that they didn't *want* to think about it, and who could blame them? The odds didn't make it worthwhile. People only had so much worry-time built into their daily thought processes, even for their more irrational imaginings. Going home at night, you maybe worried about the train crashing, or getting jumped on that stretch of pavement where the streetlight is knackered; not that the sportsbag in the luggage rack opposite is packed with Sarin gas, or that the next parked car you walk past might explode. If you did, you'd never be able to leave the house.

Yes, he had been lucky, and yes, he'd taken risks he'd never repeat, but he'd got away with it because to the terrorist, despite global-wide counter-intelligence and ever more sophisticated surveillance technology, this was still that oft-mourned world where people never locked their front door. Sure, someone had made him a very clever bomb that effectively got itself through airport security, but it didn't change the fact that a suburban marketing executive had been able to blow up a civilian passenger flight with the aid of some overalls, a stolen badge, a battery-operated fan and a bottle of bubbly.

Once he actually knew what the fuck he was doing, the possibilities were endless, especially given that officially, he no longer existed. His old life, his old name, in fact Simon Darcourt's entire identity perished in the crash, and in that moment he became traceless, invisible, a ghost upon the Earth. He had no name, no files, no records, no past, and only one other person knew he'd once been someone else. People who'd known him could look into his face and dismiss what their eyes were telling them. Even Larry the little drummer boy had looked but failed to comprehend.

Still, that didn't mean the incident could be ignored. Simon didn't believe in destiny – he left that to the deluded,

123

self-important bastards who paid his invoices – but he did know to respect omens. Not in any supernatural, David-Warner-plate-glass-interface kind of way, but as the mind's little shorthand Post-it notes: incidents or images that reminded you to stay sharp and pay attention. Having come so far these past three years, he was back in Scotland for the execution of the biggest project he'd ever devised, and within minutes of landing he'd seen someone who could potentially unravel everything. The only thing preventing that chain of events from initialising was that the little drummer boy simply couldn't believe he was looking at a dead man. From there, it wasn't too far a leap to simply not believing the man he was looking at was dead. Not too far, and definitely not far enough for peace of mind.

With Mopoza unsure how much Thaba might have blabbed, there was an outstanding role to be filled in this production: that of a doomed, tragic fool; and merely by being there, by looking into Simon's eyes, the little drummer boy had successfully auditioned for the part. The irony, in hindsight, was that it had been Simon Darcourt who was looking at a dead man. Raymond Ash just didn't know it yet. And in payback for everything that had passed between them, Simon was going to enjoy giving him the message.

THURSDAY, SEPTEMBER FOURTH

a cautionary tale against sensible decisions

The driver was patrolling back and forth on the walkway above, training his weapon on all possible approaches in turn. Ray couldn't see the not-jogger, who might well be down in the water too by now. As long as he stayed under the bridge, he was likely to remain out of the driver's line of sight, but he'd have to make a move soon, as the other gunman could be at his back any second. The familiar sight of the rusted ladder was dead ahead, dangling down from the centre of the bridge into the murky water beneath. He breathed in, lunged the last few feet and began climbing, his stomach tightening with the awareness of his vulnerability. On a ladder, you were the easiest of targets: moving slowly, in a rigidly straight line, your intended destination obvious to any predatory observer.

He reached the top intact, his position still hidden from the driver by the column in the centre. One side of the bridge was a dead-end, leading straight to the enemy. The other offered his only chance of escape, though at the cost of moving briefly into view. The driver would have time for just one shot, but if he was accurate, it would be enough. Ray started running, fixing his sights on his footing, not daring to look back. The path turned hard right at the far end of the bridge, and would take him out of the firing line temporarily if he ever got there. He was going flat out but it didn't seem fast enough, like he was moving through soup, or had bungee cords attached to his waist. He looked ahead.

The not-jogger came round the corner, levelling his weapon. Behind him, the driver jumped down from the walkway.

Ray jumped over the side as they fired, disappearing into the flooded circular pit. His submersion muted the sound, but he could still hear the noise of one of them grabbing the Quad Damage power-up, multiplying the impact of his weapon by four. He then heard them both splashing into the water behind him, by which time he was already swimming through the tunnel. Q2DM5: The Pits. Ray knew every inch, every pixel. He had enough of a start to reach the lift and leave them trapped down in the armour room while he got away, unless they got lucky with the trajectory of a grenade bounce, or a prediction shot from the rocket-launcher.

There was a high-pitched, pulsing, screaming sound in his ears, getting closer, louder, then he felt something hit his back. Light flashed everywhere and the room spun wildly around him. A quad-impact, and yet somehow he had survived. The sound grew louder still, now less pulsing and more constant. Again he felt the thump in his back.

'Ray.'

'Huh?'

He sat up suddenly, opening his eyes to see a flurry of blue fleece in the cot at the end of the bed, where Martin was pouring out his signature howl. Kate was sitting up alongside, her bedside light on, the clock beside it informing him that it was four forty-one.

'I think he's filled a nappy. Can you do the honours while I get ready to feed him?'

'Eh? What? Oh, yeah. Sorry.'

Ray climbed unsteadily out of bed, not quite awake, stalling in that transitory state in which the dream world and the one he'd woken up in had still to be fully separated and distinguished. Martin was playing a vocal part in sorting them out, but Ray remained confused about which immediate memories belonged to his dream and which to the evening preceding it. He remembered the airport. That was for real, wasn't it? Then there'd been . . . no. That must have been dreamt. He was dead. Ray still dreamed about him every so often, evidence that despite the years and even death, Simon was still creeping around his subconscious. Sometimes they were reconciling, catching up on what happened to each other; sometimes they were way back when, having the same arguments. Even in his dreams, Ray still came off second best.

Ray lifted Martin out of the crib and placed him on his shoulder, the familiar whiffs of puke and liquid keech surrounding him like an unwelcome aura. After the airport there'd been . . . no. That was dreamt too. They'd all ended up on a *Q2* map, for Christ's sake. He thought he could picture them with pistols rather than railguns, but that was equally absurd, particularly the fact that they'd both missed.

Holding Martin in one arm, he switched on the bathroom light then knelt down and rubbed the changing mat to take the chill off it. He placed the infant carefully on the PVC and reached for the baby-wipes, which was when he caught sight of the washing basket, a still-dripping trouserleg dangling over the side.

'Aaawww, fuck.'

After that, the true events of the evening played back like a demo.

It was difficult to select a highlight, but the polis probably shaded it from the assassins and the imaginary dead flatmate. They had an almost effortless way of making everything seem worse, arguably eclipsed by their equally reliable ability to make it all seem your fault as well.

129

Within moments of the interview commencing, he was wishing he'd just kept the whole thing to himself. He'd already lied to Kate about what happened, saying he'd been thrown over the bridge during an attempted mugging. Why didn't he just tell her he'd fallen in trying to save a drowning puppy? There'd have been no cover story for him visiting the cop shop, and at least that way, only one person would have looked at him like he was a sad, attention-seeking fantasist. She had said Ray should call the cops and ask them to come to him, but he didn't want her present when he gave his statement. He wasn't in the habit of hiding things from his wife, but reckoned she had enough on her plate these days without worrying that her husband was being hunted by hitmen or even just going out of his mind.

In Ray's experience, the quintessence of what was so infuriating about dealing with the polis was the incomparable frustration of being patronised by a stupid person. Naturally, mentioning what happened at the airport didn't help. He hadn't meant to; might even have made a point of not doing so if he'd retained any control over what he was saying. Once he started talking though, it just sort of fell out, along with everything else, as though the cop's half-interested promptings had opened some kind of narrative fuselage.

'You said you'd just come home from work. Were you aware of anyone following you then?'

'No, but I didn't come home directly. I went via the airport and to be honest I was a bit freaked after that so I wasn't paying . . . I mean I wouldn't have noticed if someone *was* following me.'

'What were you doing at the airport? Seeing someone off? Picking someone up?'

'I went there to buy a magazine. I did see someone, I mean I thought I saw someone I knew but it wasn't, I mean it couldn't have been so I suppose I didn't see him.'

'I'm sorry, you say you went to the airport to buy a magazine?'

'Well, it's kind of on the way home and the parking's about the same as in town and there's not such big queues to get on to the M8 at that time of day.'

'And to confirm, you did or didn't see someone you knew there?'

'I didn't. I thought I did but it couldn't have been. It doesn't matter.'

'You say you were "a bit freaked" after visiting the airport. Why was that?'

'Just as I was telling you. It was the person I thought I saw – I couldn't have seen him because he's dead. Died in a plane crash.'

'And you think you saw him.'

'No, I *thought* I saw him, as in momentarily.'

'Right. What was his name?'

'It doesn't matter.'

'It's best if we have a comprehensive record, Mr Ash.'

'A comprehensive record including the name of someone I definitely didn't see tonight? What about the people I did see? The ones with the handguns.'

'We're looking into it, Mr Ash, but we'll need a full statement from you, especially as you seem to be the only witness at this point.'

'At this point? It only happened less than two hours ago.'

'PC Mackay was close to the area at the time, and he's down there now, making enquiries at the flats overlooking the Cart bridge. You're right, it's early days, but so far

131

we've had no reports of anybody seeing anything suspicious, or of hearing shots being fired.'

'They were using silencers, I told you.'

'Right. So you did. And there was no-one else in the vicinity of the bridge or the path throughout this incident.'

'No. It tends to be quiet round there that time of night.'

'Of course.'

And so on, until:

'A new baby in the house, you say?'

'Yeah. Three months.'

'Got two myself. Grown up a bit now, though. Nine and six. You sleeping much?'

'Not really.'

'Stressful time, isn't it? Especially the first one. You're never sure you're going to cope. A new job too. How long have you been there?'

'Couple of weeks.'

'That can't be very easy on you either. Lot of pressure, lot of stress, not much kip. Difficult combination.'

Go fuck yourself. What would you know about it.

'It's the kind of thing that can make you feel . . . People can want to cry out for help, but they don't quite know how.'

'Are you saying you think I'm making this up?'

'I'm not saying anything, Mr Ash, just trying to make you weigh up the possibilities. People under stress can do irrational things. I can't say you didn't see these men; I'm sure you saw something, but maybe it wasn't what you thought you saw, like the other thing you *thought* you saw, at the airport.'

'Listen, I'm not in the habit of jumpin' into fuckin' rivers on my way out for a takeaway. I was shot at tonight by two men who confirmed my name before they opened fire,

132

and you're tryin' to be my fuckin' shrink? Are you gaunny take this seriously or should I just go home?'

'Calm down, Mr Ash, please. We will be conducting a thorough investigation, but I have to caution you that wasting police time is a serious offence. In the meantime, I'd recommend you get back to your wife and baby and get yourself a good night's sleep.'

In an exchange generously endowed with understated sarcasm, that parting shot really took the honours. By the time Ray got back into his car, the usual nightly fatigue was taking hold, augmented this evening by his exertions and the after-effects of so much adrenaline flooding his system. Combined with his humiliations at the hands of Sergeant Bawheid, the cumulative effect was to dissipate his sense of self to the extent that he was beginning to doubt the veracity of his own account. The men had been there, unquestionably, but like Simon at the airport, had he projected something, mentally filled in the blanks in a way that made sense to his stressed and paranoid brain? Something similar used to happen when he was playing way too much *Duke Nukem*, back in the days when people thought the Build engine created a realistic 3D perspective. Any time he saw a ventilation grate or a fire extinguisher, he'd automatically think 'switch to pistol' with the intention of blowing a hole through to the next room. Then he'd remember he was standing in the Marks & Spencer's food hall, and the nearest thing to a weapon in his current inventory was a tub of low-fat houmous. Still, despite years of playing his way through every 3D-shooter, every sequel and every mission pack, there remained no precedent for imagining that ordinary people standing in front of him were actually holding guns. Nor was there any explanation for the fact that they'd known his name.

Complicating it further was the fact that if they knew his name, they would almost certainly know where he lived too, and if so, why hadn't they just come up to the door? Why did they ambush him on the bridge? And having failed, why weren't they waiting there for him when he made his soggy way home? These were questions that had kept him awake despite his exhaustion, and that presented themselves again upon his confirmed return from a depressingly fleeting visit to the Land of Nod.

Possibly worse than the continued absence of plausible answers and the hanging shadow of mortal threat was the heart-sinking realisation that despite all of it, he still had to go to fucking work. There was no choice, no option for respite. Corn to be earned, offspring to be provided for, pursuing murderers or the onset of insanity notwithstanding. What was he going to do, get a sick note? 'Please excuse Raymond from school today because he has ~~diorea~~ ~~diarre dihor~~ is being hunted down by hired assassins.'

Maybe Sergeant Bawheid was right. Maybe it *was* a cry for help, a smuggled note from inside this prison of responsibility, this forced march through the long-term career gulag at the order of a diminutive despot. Making it worse was the knowledge that he was trapped by his own decisions, confined through his own free will, and the road to his personal hell had been paved with only the best intentions. He'd given up The Dark Zone voluntarily, and it would have been difficult, even for Ray, to miss the developmental significance of preparing for fatherhood by moving on from a venture that attempted to provide a living through playing games. Choosing instead the role of teacher – mentor to the real children – merely underlined his subconscious intentions.

The Dark Zone hadn't ever really been a career move

anyway. It had been a pub conversation that got out of control, a drunken idea that unexpectedly failed to look daft in the cruelly honest light of dawn. Bloody Id Software, that's who was to blame. Saint Paul would never have made any glib mutterings about putting away childish things if the bastard had played *Doom*. That was what changed everything, or at least the beginning of what changed everything; what changed computer games from a diversion to a lifestyle, a sub-culture and even, he'd thought, a career.

It was on 24 February 1996 that a ravenously awaited piece of code named qtest was released on to the net by Id. Div, with no wife or girlfriend needing use of the phone, got a complete download at around two in the morning of Sunday, 25 February. Ray was round at his house by two-thirty, with his machine and a serial cable.

After the usual start-up bugs and tweaking, Ray and Div played for nine solid hours, pausing only for toilet breaks and to make fresh coffee. It was an early test release with a small number of maps and a large number of glitches, but it was enough to demonstrate that computer games were about to be revolutionised. Not only did it look 3D, rendered in textures so detailed you could almost smell the slime on the walls, but it was negotiable in 3D, whether you were climbing stairs, riding lifts, swimming through pools or tumbling from castle walkways.

All of this was unprecedented, but what truly changed the face of gaming and had a fair crack at taking over Ray's life was *Quake* deathmatch. Up until then, the appeal of computer games was in an interactive experience that was nonetheless narrative-based and in many ways comparable to cinema or television. Multiplayer *Quake*, with its solidly tangible physics and a 3D engine so realistic it could induce motion sickness, provided an experience comparable to sport.

Even Ray wouldn't have argued that it was the new rock'n'roll, but he would make a case for comparisons with Punk, with its DIY ethos and a sense that it belonged to the participants. Every day saw the release of new maps, new models, and whole new modes of play, from 'Capture the Flag' to 'Catch the Chicken'. Players formed themselves into 'clans', and from there leagues sprang up amid thousands upon thousands of websites, the photocopied fanzines of their day. Friendships and enmities were forged, as well as relationships and even marriages. (Divorces too, no doubt, but most likely in households where only one spouse was a Quaker.) All life was to be found on the servers and chatrooms, but you could usually tell from clan-tags what a person's attitude was likely to be. Someone who played for Anorak Death Squad [ADS], Hash Bandits UK [HB–UK] or Cows with Fluff [CwF], for instance, was unlikely to be throwing tantrums if he or she got gibbed; whereas a more egotistical approach was suggested by names such as Elite Alliance [EA], or the labouring-too-hard-in-search-of-a-desired-acronym Extremely Violent Intelligent Lollipops [EVIL].

Everyone fantasises about somehow making their hobby their job, though the route was more obvious (if no less easy) for those whose hobbies were playing golf or football. The pastime of blowing people to pieces with absurdly powerful weapons in virtual environments did not yet have its Tiger Woods. What it did have was an ever-growing number of participants, a great many of whom had their enthusiasm for their games tempered by the frustrations of trying to play them over the erratic and unstable Internet. The only way to host a truly fair competition was to network a bunch of PCs so that everyone was the same negligible distance from the server. It was something he and a few pals had occasionally done over a winter weekend, and it was one such Sunday night, once all the machines were packed away again, that the pub post-mortem spawned something more than the usual arguments over whose flat should next play host to this retarded-development self-help group.

At the time, he had been working for Div's firm, Network Transplant. They dismantled, transported and reinstalled PC networks during office relocations, ensuring that all of the machines made it from A to B, and that they still did what they used to when somebody hit the On switch. Div's relations with systems managers all across Scotland meant Ray had been able to tap into a valuable supply of second-hand hardware, the rate of depreciation in the computer business being steep enough to make a Ford Focus seem like a gilt investment.

He found a low-rent basement premises just off Victoria Road, there being few businesses for whom a lack of natural light was regarded as a locational advantage, and minimised decor costs by painting the place black from floor to ceiling. Thematic highlighting came in the form of promotional posters the games' distributors were happy to throw in when you were buying a dozen copies at a time, and after that it was merely a matter of hanging his hand-painted sign outside, sticking some Sonic Mayhem on the sound system and he was ready for action.

He'd toyed with calling the place The Level Playing Field, but Kate's marketing judgment prevailed as she opined that it sounded like a sports shop and lacked a certain futuristic resonance, or as she put it, 'it's not nearly geeky enough'. He opted instead for The Dark Zone, which scored high on the target geek-identification scale (you could never go far wrong with the word 'zone' when you were pitching to the SF/fantasy demographic). The fact that the place was like an experimental environment for inducing seasonal affective disorder may also have been a subconscious factor.

He recruited a couple of part-time assistants and launched in September with a free-play evening, leafleting the SF bookshops and hobby stores, student hang-outs, metal/indie-inclined pubs and games retailers. The winter months were pretty good, word-of-mouth having spread around throughout the autumn. December even saw office parties descend on the place as a novel supplement to the traditional programme of turkey lunch and photocopying each other's arses. Watching a respectably dressed professional woman in her forties clench a fist in her colleague's face as she yelled 'Eat that, loser' almost made Ray feel that his work on this Earth was done.

The lighter evenings, however, heralded a dramatic downturn. Even what passed for summer in Glasgow was enough to tempt much of his target market outdoors to have a go at games based on the Real Life™ engine, usually teamplay mods such as Football and Cricket, or that ever-popular two-player pursuit marketed variously as Dating, Winching and Lumbering. By the end of August, he was well into the red and, even more depressing, having to turn business away because customers were wanting to play new games that he didn't have the cash to buy, let alone the new graphics cards needed to run them.

To his and his bank manager's relief, the fluctuation proved seasonal, and business did start picking up again as the nights drew in, but much of the cash was swallowed by hardware upgrades as he struggled to keep pace with the latest fads. This was when he was forced to confront the flaw in his alcohol-tinted vision of hobby-as-business. There were dozens of new titles being released every month, and even though only a deserving few would snare the interest of the notoriously discerning multiplayer market, it was still a wider range than Ray could spread his enthusiasm across, never mind his money. If he was being honest, he had set up The Dark Zone as a digital coliseum for hardcore 'first-person shooters' – *Quake*, *Unreal*, *Half-Life*, *Duke* – and had accommodated the rest very much as a commercial necessity. As more and more customers came to the desk asking for an hour on games he'd never played, he began to fear he'd soon be in charge of a business he no longer entirely understood, like a metalhead record-store owner being asked for the latest 'bangin' Euro-trance'.

Nevertheless, it was still those FPS games that continued to bring in the bulk of the money, and it was his reliable understanding of that particular sub-culture that really made him fear for The Dark Zone's future viability. Quite simply, the Internet was becoming a more stable environment for gaming. At The Dark Zone, people could turn up and play against whoever else happened to be there, which could be ten others or could be just Ray. Over the Net, they could scan for servers and play against thousands of opponents – known and unknown – from all over northern Europe, and they could do it without leaving the house on a wet January night. Ray knew this better than anyone: despite having his own dedicated network a few feet from his desk, he often passed the quieter business hours fragging mercilessly on Barrysworld servers, based hundreds of miles away.

The game was changing, and his passion for keeping up with it was already on the wane when the baby question began to dominate the domestic agenda. He found himself recoiling from the lengthening days and the lean months they were sure to bring, so it wasn't that difficult a decision when the local council made their approach. They wanted to set up a community Internet centre, providing online access to people – particularly schoolchildren – who otherwise wouldn't get near a PC. The Dark Zone was earmarked because not only did it have all the hardware and a functioning network, but it was already a popular haunt for the local kids they intended to reach. They bought him out down to the last mouse-mat, even retaining all the games software in the knowledge that it would be easier to get the weans surfing educational websites if they were promised a deathmatch gib-fest at the end.

Selling up wasn't without regrets, but he was smart enough to know when he'd been jammy. He got out with a lump sum instead of a major debt, and regarded the cash as a fortuitous chance for a fresh start at something long-term, something grown-up. Something specific, in fact.

In an adult life that had been coloured by a vocational promiscuity bordering on the sluttish, the one notion that just kept coming back was teaching. During his university years, it had been a running joke among fellow arts students, regarding the credibility gap between their encouraged ambitions and their realistic future employment prospects. Whenever they got the beer-filled crystal ball out and waxed aspirational about where their degrees and desires might one day take them, it became traditional to end the discussion by saying 'but we'll probably all end up teachers'. For some, it had seemed like a superstition, a genuflection before providence in supplication that they be spared this unthinkable fate; and with that, no doubt, came the corresponding fear that it would be a self-fulfilling prophecy.

Ray had been less horrified by the prospect. In earlier

student years, this was because the world of employment appeared too comfortably far off for him to worry about, and by the time the real world was months rather than years away, he was still able to exempt himself because he had his music-biz delusions to obscure the view. However, it didn't stop him wondering, and when he wasn't dreaming of a world where drummers were recognised as the true geniuses of rock, he could think of worse outcomes than being an English teacher. The pay would be dismal, sure, and he'd probably have to keep dipping into the vessel of unnecessary pain that was *Othello*, but something about it did appeal, other than just the long holidays.

Most likely it was the latent, unexorcised fantasy of a powerless schoolkid: oppressed, depressed or just plain bored, telling himself he'd do it differently, he'd do it better, given his own shot at the blackboard. School, at the time, had seemed an endless duration, and he doubted he was the only one there to dwell daily on the many ways in which it could be improved. In some people, this matured into formulating a vision – which they needed little invitation to share – of how they'd run the country were they Prime Minister (and what a happy-go-lucky state we'd be living in if any of those little dreams came true – 'Live from Wembley Stadium tomorrow: this month's mass execution of people who indicate wrongly at roundabouts!'). Ray, though, had merely zipped it into his 'What if . . .?' archive, from where it extracted itself again every few years.

Maybe the idea would have taken hold earlier, but the circumstances had never been right. Even before his graduation ceremony he was already in a patchwork of piecemeal employment, giving archery and crossbow lessons at the Castleglen Hotel & Country Club when he wasn't waiting tables or pulling pints. Casual and part-time jobs overlapped and superseded one another throughout his early twenties, when he was working merely to fill his hours and his pockets, living for nights and weekends. In those days, he had nothing but time.

When he hit twenty-five, he started finding it harder to ignore that bloody question – What do you want to be when you grow up? – and equally hard to believe that each job he took was anything other than a salaried procrastination. Remembering those student dream-extinguishing salutes, teaching loomed before him as the grown-up path to take, what with the *Guardian* still not advertising vacancies for Rock Gods or Professional Computer-Gamers. The obstacle back then – or maybe it was the excuse – was that he didn't think he could finance a post-grad year, not now that he and Kate were used to having some disposable income and a decent flat to live in. Maybe in a couple of years, he'd thought; after all, he was still young.

After The Dark Zone, he was out of time and out of excuses. He was also, to be honest, fed up with this consumer-age existentialism, fed up having to think of the answer at parties when someone asked him what he did for a living. Everybody was 'a' something. What did that make him?

The lump sum was a chance for a fresh start, a scarcely deserved second shot at adulthood. Maybe, he even thought, it was the ticket to somewhere he'd always been meant to go. Who knew? He'd find out when he got there, and he travelled hopefully in the meantime. Well, 'travelled desperately' might be a more accurate description of the journey's latter stages, as he counted down the days to having a worthy excuse for being out of the house, far away from the family he would be supporting.

Travelled hopefully, travelled desperately.

Then he arrived.

the best days of your life

'What you meant to be havin' next?'

'Double English. Mr Ash.'

'Mr Ash? Awww, *he* is a fuckin' fanny, man. That's who I'm meant to have right noo. We ripped the pish right oot him last time.'

They were dogging first double-period, going in late. Well, strictly speaking, only Wee Murph was dogging it, having slept in. Lexy had been to the dentist's for a check-up, so he had a note as cover, but he wasn't saying. He'd run into Wee Murph on the Hazelwood Road and they made their way up together from there, checking their pace against their watches to make sure they didn't arrive before the first lesson was finished. No point in letting some swine poke about your gums with a jaggy stick if you still showed up in time to get homework, and in English it was guaranteed. New teachers always gave it out, partly so's they didn't look like soft touches, but mainly because they never got you to do anything during class.

Mr Ash's had been a case in point: pure murder. He couldn't get Lexy's class to shut up, so he ended up losing the place and shouted at them at the top of his voice. It had gone tensely quiet for a second, until Johnny McGowan burst out laughing, and that set everybody off again. Mr Ash asked Johnny for his name, to which Johnny responded 'Andrew Lafferty', so after that everybody gave names of kids in other classes. The stupid bastard started checking the register, no clue what was going on.

'By the time he'd given up tryin' tae sort it oot,' Lexy told Murph, 'it was nearly time for the bell, so he just gave us the books an' tell't us we'd tae read up tae chapter three for the next class. Optimistic, is he no'?'

'Aye,' Murph agreed. 'Specially wi' Cammy in the class. Never mind read it, he'll have sell't it by noo. He'll be doon the toon seein' if he can get part-ex on hauf a Silk Cut.'

Wee Murph was a laugh. He hadn't been at the same primary as Lexy, but he'd been one of those names you heard about as soon as they all started at the big school. He always had lots of patter. Not just whatever was the new cool phrase everybody was trying to force into conversations to show off they knew it, but real patter, words and expressions that just poured out. The things he said made Lexy laugh even when he wasn't trying to make a joke. Wee Murph was in 2s3, Lexy in 2s6, which meant that although they weren't in the same class, they got the same teachers for most subjects.

'I heard one o' the fourth-year classes gie'd him a right session as well.'

'Aye,' Wee Murph said, his eyes lighting up. Lexy knew what had happened, but he wanted to hear Murph telling it. 'He opened wan o' the windaes, so Jai McGinty's big brer goes: "Get that shut" – an' Ash done it!'

'Jai McGinty's big brer's mental.'

'Total bampot. That's the fourth-year spam class as well. They shouldnae have handed that tae a new teacher. Like puttin' a coo in charge o' the lions' cage.'

'What did your mob dae tae him?'

'He was talkin' aboot images or somethin', how the wummin in the poem was meant tae be like a sheep. He asked us tae say whit animal the person next tae us made us think of. Marky Innes is first, an' he's sittin' beside Margaret Gebbie, so he says a dug.'

'A hound.'

'Aye. We aw pure pished oursel's. Ash goes "you've got tae say *how* she's like a dug". Marky says 'cause she looks like wan. So then Gebbie says Marky's like a pig, 'cause he smells like wan.'

'Who were you beside?'

'Charlie. But Linda Dixon's on the other side o' me.'

'She's a doll.'

'I know. So I said she made us think ay a beaver.'

'Aw man.'

'I know. Ash says how? I says 'cause she's always dead busy, a hard worker an' that. He was aboot tae turn tae Charlie, an' I goes "Plus, she builds dams oota trees." Charlie pure decked himsel'. He'd snotters comin' oot an' everythin'. You know Charlie. He'd laugh at a door shuttin'.'

'Aye.'

'Aw, but wait tae I tell you what else. He asked us tae write a hingmy, a composition, aboot goin' tae the swimmin', which was a mistake considerin' hauf o' that class don't know what a bath looks like, never mind a swimmin' pool. Somebody passed the message roon, an' when we aw handed in wur papers, every guy in the class had just drawn big knobs, no' even written a word.'

'Aw, man, that's brilliant. Whit did Ash dae?'

'It was gallus. You could tell he was pure squeezin' his baws, tryin' no tae laugh. He came on dead serious instead, makin' oot he never takes shite. Learner driver, man. No' got a clue.'

'Did he go an' get Doyle?'

'Naw. Cannae blame him. Imagine goin' tae Doyle's

office, or the staff room, an' tellin' everybody your class aw drew big wullies instead o' writin' their essays.'

'It would be a pure beamer.'

'He said we'd aw tae dae the essay for homework.'

'Have you done it?'

'Have I fuck. My big brer was oot last night.'

'Aw, excellent.'

Wee Murph's big brother, Big Murph, was doing some computer course at Paisley Uni, and Wee Murph got to play with his PC when he was out. Lexy had been round there once. The games on it were ancient, stuff you could get the Sega and PlayStation versions of for about two quid in the exchange shops. Some of them were still a good laugh, though, like that *Grand Theft Auto*, which had first come out when Lexy was about eight and still playing with Action Man. He remembered his big cousin Peter talking about it, but his mammy didn't let him have it because she'd read in the paper that it would make kids want to steal cars and go joyriding. This was not a concern that Wee Murph considered very realistic.

'As if. The weans roonaboot here that are intae stealin' motors don't need computer games tae spark the idea. It's like sayin' *Tomb Raider* would make you want to grow tits.'

They went the long way, round the new estate, planning to come in through the teachers' car park instead of the path through the playing fields. The first years had PE at that time, and they just *knew* Miss Walsh would pull them up if she saw them sauntering past, even though it was nothing to do with her.

'She's a cow,' Lexy ventured.

'You'd think it was oor fault she's ugly,' Murph added.

There was a big grey lorry parked round the corner from the school gates, looked like a removal truck.

'Check that,' Murph said. 'Belly Kelly's packed lunch is gettin' delivered.'

'Naw, that's just his play-piece.'

Wee Murph laughed, which pleased Lexy. There was no greater brass neck than a joke that died on its arse.

The rear of the lorry had its fold-down ramp extended, resting on the tarmac, and the roller-shutters were open a few inches at the bottom. Murph stopped and had a trial push at them. They were stiff, but they moved up a bit with perseverence.

'Murph, whit ye daein'?'

'Shoosh. Just havin' a wee nosey.'

'The man'll come.'

'There was naebody in the cab. Keep the edgy for us.'

'Aw, fuck. Hurry up, well.'

Murph crouched on the ramp and pulled the shutters until he could get his shoulder under them. Lexy stood at the side, looking both ways along the road, thinking of what to do if he saw someone. He'd pretend he'd stopped to tie his lace, give Wee Murph a shout and then just walk on. Bloody spam-case, jumping about in a lorry right outside the school.

'You better no' knock anythin', right?' he warned.

'Fuck's sake man, steady the buffs. I'm no' a thief.'

Murph disappeared inside the truck, leaving Lexy to scope left and right like he was at fucking Wimbledon, occasionally rehearsing his drop-to-lace-tying emergency drill. There was nothing coming. The road only led into the school or back into the estate; it wasn't exactly Argyle Street.

'Gaunny hurry up?' Lexy said in a half-whisper, though he knew it was pointless. There was still a good fifteen minutes until the morning interval, and Murph now had a major distraction.

147

'Aw, *man*,' he heard Murph gasp, sounding genuinely astonished, which didn't bode well for getting him out of there any time soon.

'Whit?'

'Aw, fuck me. 'Mon up here a minute, Lexy.'

'I'm keepin' the edgy. Whit is it?'

'There's naebody there. 'Mon, fuck's sake. You've got tae see this.'

Lexy had one more glance in each direction, then quickly scuttled his way under the shutters. The inside was empty except for a row of packing crates at the very front, and beside them in the corner a huge pile of those grey dustsheets that the removal men put over your furniture to stop it getting chipped. There were also dustsheets hung on the walls, partly covering the wooden lattice frames the removers tied tall objects to. Wee Murph was standing in front of one of these, his hand on the cloth.

'What's in the boxes?' Lexy asked.

'Nothin'. Empty.'

'So whit did ye – aw, fuckin' hell. No way.'

Murph had pulled back the dustsheet to reveal two machine guns strapped to the lattice. He giggled nervously, but both of them knew this was no longer a laugh. They were also aware that they'd be looking at more than a punishment exercise or even a good kick up the arse if they were caught.

'Dae ye 'hink they're real?' Lexy felt compelled to ask.

'Naw, they're fuckin' water-scooters. Feel them.'

'I'm no' fuckin' touchin' them.'

'They're metal. Solid.'

'Aw, fuck, man. We better get oot o' here, Murph.'

'My thoughts exactly, Lexy.'

Wee Murph had one last lingering look at the glinting weapons, then let the sheet slip down again.

148

'C'mon. Hurry.'

'Don't run. Stay quiet,' Murph advised.

They began walking to the rear of the container, then Murph stopped and put a hand on Lexy's arm.

'Whit?'

'Shoosh. D'you hear a car?'

'Fuck. Aye.'

They both dropped to their honkers and looked out through the gap. There was a silver Rover moving towards the truck, slowing as it did so.

'Aw, fuck, man. No way.'

They heard the engine idling, the car having stopped behind the ramp.

'Whit we gaunny dae?'

'Hide.'

'Fuck. Where?'

'Here. Quick.'

Murph dived for the heap of dustsheets, Lexy at his elbow. They burrowed a space behind the pile, their backs to the wall, pulling sheets over the gaps just as they heard the shutters rolling up, the noise amplified by the empty space. After that, they heard the car drive inside the truck, all the way to the front, tyres rolling only feet away. The engine was killed. A door opened and shut, followed by the clunk of the locks being closed by a remote, then foot-steps as the driver walked out.

Lexy was about to have a peek from behind the blan-kets when he heard the car's door handle rattle a couple of times, followed by a series of muted thuds.

'Don't move,' Murph warned, in as quiet a whisper as Lexy had heard, even in evil Mrs Stewart's maths class.

The thuds stopped, and there was silence. Lexy felt Murph's hand on his forearm, a signal that it was too early even to have a fly swatch. He was right, too. They heard another car approaching, then the dulled clang as it also went up the ramp and into the container. This time the door was opened and closed, but not locked. The first car's handle rattled again, preceding another thud as the second driver walked to the back of the truck. A moment's more silence ensued, then there was a huge bang, causing the pair of them to cling on to each other; must have been the ramp getting pulled up. The roller-shutters came down with a crash, followed by a dense metallic click as the door was locked.

Lexy made to move, but still Wee Murph gripped his arm.

'There' some'dy in wan o' thae motors.'

From beneath, they felt the low shudder of the engine starting up, and a few seconds later, the truck began to move.

'Aw, man, I hope they arenae stolen,' Murph whispered gloomily.

'The guns?'

'Naw, the motors.'

'How.'

''Cause we could end up in a boat tae fuckin' Moscow, an' I've forgot my dinner money.'

interesting times

There was a bottle of Loch Dhu on Angelique's desk when she came back from the sandwich shop with her breakfast. It was a gimmick whisky dreamed up by a marketing man rather than a stillman, its hopefully saleable distinction being that it was black. Really black. Not just darkly peaty like Laphroaig, but black enough to suggest it shouldn't be taken internally. Some whiskies were matured in sherry casks, some bourbon; this one was evidently aged in a treacle barrel. She just hoped it didn't taste like it. It could have been worse, though. They could have gone with some muck like Tia Maria or Kahlua, which would have been the cheaper option.

Cops were never done whining about how little they got paid, given the hours, the danger and the canteen lasagne, but no expense was spared when it came to wind-ups and daft jokes. Still, it was proof of changed days that it wasn't intended to refer to her skin. Her sex and her stature were still tediously fair game, but you had to be grateful for any advances in a profession where cultural progress moved like a greased glacier.

The road to Special Branch had not been an easy one. In her uniform and CID days, her height had always been as much of a problem issue as her colour and her sex, due to the singular prejudices of the Action-Man tendency, who frequently bemoaned the relaxation of restrictions that had allowed smouts like her on to the force. It was usually not said to her face, but deliberately loud enough for her to overhear. Eventually she challenged one of them about it in the canteen, a bloke called McMaster, who instantly went into that patronising-but-oh-so-reasonable mode his ilk could effortlessly affect.

'No offence, hen, nothin' against you personally, but we deal wi' some bad, bad people oot there. What's a wee lassie like yourself gauny dae if there's a big bear like me comin' at you?'

'I'd follow procedure and radio for back-up, and ask for a big bear like you to come and assist.'

'And what if I'm no' available?'

'Do you want me to tell you, or to demonstrate?'

Gleeful anticipation had rippled around the room, entertainment in store. At the centre of the ripples there was only growing tension. Then her boss, DS Clark, had dispelled it all by calling her to heel and leading her out of the nearest door; to the kitchen, as it happened.

'What the hell are you playing at?'

'I'm fed up listening to shite like that.'

'You're like a West Highland terrier noising up an alsatian. The guy weighs two hundred pounds. Did you think all that kung-fu stuff was going to work?'

'Well, I guess we'll never know, will we?'

There was the rub. Both parties left the canteen telling themselves the other had a lucky escape, but only one had doubt in his eyes. Granted, in front of so many colleagues, McMaster had a lot more to lose and precious little to gain, but there was no question he was the more relieved to see the situation defused.

When the dust settled, it became apparent that this display of feisty defiance had earned her the big man's respect and made the lads look at her in a completely different light from then on. Or did it tread on their inse-curities and generate even more resentment? She couldn't quite remember. It was definitely one of them, though.

Given her size and her qualifications, they just couldn't wait for her to get promoted to where she belonged: as far away from the street as possible. The day after she made detective, she was called into the DCI's office for a congrat-ulatory chat, and offered the 'perfect' post: co-ordinating the division's ethnic minorities liaison efforts. He'd been told she spoke three other languages. What were they? Gujurati? Urdu? Hindi? That would be invaluable in working with 'her community'.

'What community?' she asked. 'Catholics?'

The DCI made a valiant response to being knocked down this unseen hole, by whipping out his shovel and getting on with some digging.

'You're . . .? I mean . . .? I thought . . . But . . . You say you're a *Catholic*?'

'No. I was brought up one though. I went to a Catholic school. My mum's Belgian. They take it very seriously.'

'I'm sorry. I'd no idea.'

She resisted the temptation to observe that, in the Glesca Polis, folk thinking she was a Jungle Bunny rather than a Jungle Jim was probably the only reason she'd got this far.

'And you don't speak . . .?'

'Nope.'

'But you must have close ties to . . .?'

'Nope.'

There was a long silence.

'I've heard there's an opening coming up in the drugs squad, sir.'

'Ehm, yeeees.'

If the DCI was discomfited, some among the lower

153

orders were fuming. It was positive discrimination, and she wasn't playing the game in return. She only got promoted because she was from an ethnic minority at a time when the force needed a few higher-profile brown faces. She could at least show some gratitude by going off to work among her own. Wasn't that what the likes of her joined up for in the first place?

Well, no, actually. But neither had she thought the job *wouldn't* be full of arseholes who'd resent her very presence on a daily basis. It didn't present much of a deterrent, however, being something she was used to dealing with since the age of five.

There was a note attached to the neck of the whisky bottle. It said, 'I'll come quietly, guvnor. It's a fair cop.'

She turned round to check who was looking. There were lots of heads suddenly buried in files and paperwork, guilty schoolboys each and every one.

'Weans,' she said. Maclaren and Wallace sniggered. 'And I suppose you think I'll be sharing this?'

A couple more heads perked up – McIntosh and Rowan – now that the gag was out in the open and she hadn't taken the huff. They feigned hangdog expressions at her threat.

'All right, tell you what. I'll open it on Sunday night if you experts are right and nothing happens on Saturday. Fair enough?'

'Aye.'

'Sure.'

'Sounds good.'

Angelique placed it on the windowsill, leaving the alternative unspoken, but knowing the bottle was getting opened whatever happened over the weekend. If the Black Spirit did strike on Sonzolan independence day, they'd all be needing a drink afterwards.

The likelihood of that wasn't something she felt qualified to comment on either way. Angelique knew plenty about the terrorist, but information about whether the UK featured in his imminent plans remained extremely thin on the ground. She hadn't assumed the role of prophet of doom; in fact the whisky was as much their way of winding her up about being the one who had landed such a pointless task. In that sense, there was a tacit hint of gratitude about it, or at least acknowledgement. There but for Gracie's dog, as Millburn would say.

The days were counting down and in the absence of any clues, leads or developments, it was getting harder to feel worried, even though part of her knew that theoretically the opposite should be true. It was a lot easier to steel yourself to the task of finding a needle in a haystack if you at least had a halfway convincing reason to believe the needle was even there. You'd also have the advantage of knowing what you were looking for.

The regular sources were dry, the Black Spirit not having exposed himself via the politics or supply lines that normally entangled terrorism and organised crime, and from where information leaked via cash, grudges and betrayal. With him being a freelance operative, there was no splinter-faction to sell him out, no power-struggles to take his eye off the ball. The exercise had consequently been reduced to the embarrassing desperation of actually putting out a national request for officers to report to Special Branch 'anything weird that isn't obviously drugs-related'. The definition of 'weird' was left to the individual's discretion, but it was presumed they understood that this was within the context of a possible terrorist threat. Beyond that there was the further filtration process of regional knowledge, best summed up by one duty sergeant's requested confirmation as to whether she meant 'weird generally or weird even for Fegie Park on a Saturday night'.

Nonetheless, this still meant a lot of worthless absurdity was being referred, 'just in case'. Yesterday's top waste of time was the theft of two drums of chemical fertiliser from a farmer's yard in Barrhead; DIY pipe-bombs weren't really the Black Spirit's style, and anyway, in that part of the world, the neds just stole stuff on impulse and checked out what it was later.

It looked like they were starting early today. The clock hadn't reached eight before she was taking a call about an alleged shooting attempt in Langside last night, the sergeant apologetic but nonetheless bound by customary thoroughness to mention it. She could picture him blushing at the other end of the phone as he wearily added that the complainant had also mentioned seeing a dead person at Glasgow Airport earlier in the evening.

The only piece of intel to stimulate much of a response all week was the initially worrying news that Mopoza's eldest son had been AWOL from his college digs at Oxford since Friday. The timing of his disappearance seemed at last to provide some form of corroboration of what General Thaba had claimed, but it evaporated when the lad turned up for his Classics tutorial on Wednesday morning, wearing a smile that corroborated only his boast to have got seriously laid over the weekend.

It didn't tally with the Black Spirit's known practices anyway. The efficiency, discretion and loyalty of his accomplices suggested he was extremely discerning in their recruitment, and he was understood to be highly protective of the edge he believed the dispassionate professional enjoyed over the emotionally involved. He didn't carry passengers and he definitely didn't tolerate liabilities.

After that, they were back to the fumbling conjecture of Monday's briefing, leaving them with two possibilities. The first was that this would join the long list of tedious and ultimately unsubstantiated alerts that were nonetheless a necessary part of the policeman's lot; and the second was that all of their security efforts were about to be circumvented by a new kind of enemy who they were embarrassingly powerless to fight. Odds and experience favoured the former. Nonetheless, up and down the country, every force's Special Branch had some poor mug who'd have to put his (or very occasionally her) ongoing investigations on the back burner for a few days until the word came to stand down.

The only way to chase the feeling of being in limbo was to stay busy, not such an easy prospect when the few local leads to be pursued were the likes of the Great Borrheid Fertiliser Robbery or the case of the Southside Fantasist. At a national level, no-one was coming up with anything other than their own regional variations of the same barely remarkable absurdities, incidents and reports that could come in any day, any week, any year. The whole exercise seemed resigned to its own futility, as though it carried an asterisk admitting *may not apply*. The only truly tangible factor worth investigating was the Black Spirit himself, so Angelique had occupied much of her time appraising the latest intelligence.

The briefings out of Lexington's office were broken down by their relevance to two questions: 'Who is he?' and 'What might he hit?' The hope was that any advances in answering the first would better inform their speculation on the second, which thus far only had his track record to go on, a depressingly varied repertoire.

Mopoza, as with any of the Black Spirit's clients, wouldn't have been permitted to get entirely specific about his desired target, as the contract terrorist's efficacy stemmed from his capacity to invent, adapt and improvise. It wasn't true, however, so say he could strike anywhere. He had a deft touch for feeling out vulnerable points of attack, but there always had to be a degree of prestige about his targets, or at the very least an element of semiology. He bombed a cinema to take out a US embassy, he bombed a train to devastate a Russian military base, and when he demolished a motorway flyover, it was to send a coded message to the heart of the European Parliament. For the purposes of his own marketability, he had to be more than a cartoon anarchist lobbing a big black fizzing bomb into the public square, as any eejit could do that. And even in exploiting what appeared in retrospect to be gaping flaws in security, there was a dark kudos in having been the one who thought of it first.

A list of possible targets had been compiled, annotated with various parties' opinions as to greater or lesser probability. It was based on the Security Service's standard catalogue of locations identified either for their potential vulnerability or strategic/ideological significance. Given Mopoza's martial motives, emphasis had been placed on military sites, and records of British operations during the Buluwe conflict had been combed for specific incidents that the General may have considered as particularly demanding of vengeance. Instances of collateral damage were highlighted, making very cold reading under any circumstances, but all the more chilling in this context of possible retribution. The myth of precision airstrikes, long since dispelled by the Kosovo conflict, had been thoroughly buried in the rubble of a city as populous, ramshackle and cramped as Freeport. The missiles didn't have to miss to inflict unintended casualties. Schools, hospitals, churches, buses, bars, markets and factories had all seen multiple fatalities, every category therefore legitimised for belated retaliation.

The dossier contained a map of central London with the major rail routes picked out in bright red to emphasise where they ran beside or in some cases directly beneath significant buildings. Angelique had scorned the idea of the Black Spirit wanting to operate in such a security-conscious city, but the map demonstrated that he didn't necessarily have to. He could put a bomb on a train three hundred miles away, rig it with a GPS tracker and then remote-detonate the thing at any point, accurate to within metres.

There was a note from Eric Wells doubting the likelihood of the Black Spirit repeating a stunt, on the grounds that 'he wouldn't want it to look like he'd run out of ideas'. Lexington's own comments acknowledged the point, but cautioned that it didn't constitute a good enough excuse for getting suckered twice by the same punch. For that reason, British embassies overseas had also been put on alert, with particular notice taken of those adjacent to publicly accessible buildings.

The size of the 'What might he hit?' file was inversely proportionate to what it could usefully tell them, a bulging testament to there being far more possibilities than they could ever hope to guard against. Meanwhile, the slimness of the 'Who is he?' folder said everything about what they knew. When the most substantial single document in a case file is the psych profile, you know you're grasping. There'd been a few instances in which these shrink-raps had proven useful (or at least retrospectively accurate once hard work and harder evidence had tracked the subject down), but in

Angelique's experience they usually amounted to screeds of vague or highly speculative theorising, padded out with liberal doses of the staggeringly obvious.

'This is a man who has little or no empathy with his fellow human beings [oh, no shit, Sherlock]; even his accomplices will be regarded as mere bit-part players in the greater drama that is his life. For this reason it is difficult to envisage him in a role other than that of loner or leader. In his mind, others exist to serve him, please him or praise him, and anyone who does not fulfil one of these functions is irrelevant or despised.

'There have been no code-worded warnings, no attempts to limit the civilian death-toll even when his principal target is military. The bodycount glorifies him. He doesn't see the casualties of his actions as victims, enemies or even trophies: just numbers. He sees only what the accomplishment of his mission brings to him in terms of personal achievement and notoriety. His sin is not anger, but pride.'

All quite plausibly true, but not much help in telling them what they were looking for. The only part that shed any light in that respect was, paradoxically, the passage dealing with why they knew so little about him.

'The meticulous caution he has exercised in his endeavours – and in protecting his identity – suggests a fear of being caught beyond that which normally attends a criminal's prudence. He fears being caught because he has never been the naughty boy before and does not know how he would handle it. I would doubt that his true name appears on any police records, and

160

consider it even less likely that he has ever been imprisoned.

'He will have been at one time – and ostensibly may still be – a respectable individual from a normal background. By this I mean that, unlike most terrorists, he was not raised amid a criminal, paramilitary or conflict-scarred culture, where a resignation to fate, martyrdom or sacrifice is engendered by the prevalence of brutality, incarceration and violent death. Violence does not touch him; he doles out death from a distance without fear of reprisal. It is violence by device and by remote-control, not requiring him to overcome a single individual in personal combat. In this respect, he is a tourist, which is why we can find no footprints on the paths his like have usually trodden.

'Something, therefore, had to precipitate his descent into this underworld. A personal tragedy, perhaps, involving the loss of a loved and respected authority figure; a parent or mentor who fulfilled a super-ego role. He would not have been able to carry out his subsequent acts if he thought this person might ever learn of them, and this figure was probably also what tied him to the life of respectability and responsibility he lived before.'

Yeah, but where's the bit where it says he's a wanker?
The obligatory purple prose and psycho-babble aside, the profile got one thing balls-on. This guy rose without trace. He made his grand debut amid the bloody fanfare of the Madrid bombing, but there was no way he had simply sprung fully formed from the loins of Zeus. It had often been postulated at Interpol that they were looking at a man who had no orthodox crooked pedigree, but they

knew he still had to have cut his teeth, learnt his trade and earned some respect in certain quarters in order for him to get the Madrid gig in the first place.

Enrique Sallas had, in fact, made this a particular line of investigation, convinced that valuable clues were to be found if they could identify the works of his bloody apprenticeship. The complete file of 'possibles' made Lexington's bulging brief look like the Geri Halliwell Guide to Self-Awareness, but with time on her hands and little worthwhile to fill it, Angelique had got a copy couriered from Brussels.

It contained extensive bumf on literally dozens of 'unsolved' terrorist attacks and high-profile murders believed to have been professional assassinations, almost certainly his route into the bigger game. The 'unsolved' status ignored the matter of attributed (or more usually claimed) responsibility, as there was seldom much doubt over who had been behind the atrocities. Rather, the file dealt with incidents for which police had no solid suspects, concentrating on those claimed by newer and lesser-known factions who did not enjoy the resources or infrastructure of their more established counterparts, Hamas, ETA and Hezbollah not being known to rely on hired help.

The dossier came with an up-to-the-minute cover document detailing Enrique's own analysis, but even from photocopies it was obvious what were the most thumbed pages, revealing Enrique's instincts and fixations just as vividly. However, there was no point to Angelique's own exercise if she was anything less than methodical, so she had been slogging her way through the whole thing over the past two days in between phone calls, coffees and snacks, such as the croissant she was demolishing now, detailed carnage proving no impediment to appetite.

Enrique had focused on larger-scale incidents rather than the individual hits, though a couple of those had also caught his attention. Despite her attempts not to prejudice the experiment, she was inclined to second his judgement. Many of the attacks just seemed too crude, too *obvious*, in target, method and execution, to have been their man, even on a steep learning curve. Vanilla terrorism: car bombs, mortar attacks, ambushes; taking out police stations, army patrols, judiciary, political offices. These were the cartoon anarchist again, with his big black fizzing bomb.

The more likely candidates were those that had some imagination involved, sickening as it was to so credit them. The attack on a Lisbon garden party hosted by the Peruvian ambassador, for instance, in which two people died and fourteen were injured when a remote-controlled, explosives-laden model plane was flown in on a miniature kamikaze mission. Or the campaign that successfully decimated the tourist economy on France's independence-seeking Pacific island colony, Anjou: one hotel swimming pool was pumped full of hydrochloric acid, killing the first two guests who simultaneously dived in for their early-morning swim; another pool had a Portuguese man-of-war released into it during a busy aquarobics session.

The only inclusion she was minded to dissent was flight 941 to Helsinki, which exploded minutes out of Stavanger courtesy of an Urkobaijani guerrilla movement with an utterly unpronounceable name. Granted, it was a major departure, both geographically and operationally, for a rebel militia more used to mining dirt tracks and blowing up public markets, but the Black Spirit wasn't the world's only freelance operator, and taking out a passenger jet was big-league stuff for a supposed beginner. It was also arguably too passé for such a precociously self-conscious innovator. Nonetheless, the screeds of annotation were testament to Enrique having a particular interest in this one, and she wanted to know why.

'It lacked his, you know, style,' Angelique contended, once he had finally picked up his phone.

'Style as in methods or style as in panache?' Enrique asked.

'Both.'

'And I would say that it *had* both. He prefers a vulnerable point of entry: this was a regional airport in Norway. How many terrorists ever go to Norway? Do you think there are armed police patrols up and down the departures hall in Stavanger?'

'I've never been, but I'll give you that one.'

'And as for panache, is there not a certain flourish about bringing a plane down in a deep fjord from where very little evidence was ever to return? No remnant of the device was recovered, nor were the authorities able to reconstruct the plane sufficiently to know even whether it was planted in the hold, or the cabin, or was externally attached. No-one survived, no-one on the ground saw anything unusual. This was as close to the perfect crime as I would care to imagine, and something I can*not* imagine is that it was the work of the knuckle-dragging farm hands who claimed it.'

'That's a given. But that doesn't mean it had to be him either. And if, as you say, it was so bloody clever, why didn't he put his signature on it?'

'Perhaps the printer's shop was closed when he went to pick up his little cards.'

'Don't take the piss, Enrique. It's a fair question.'

'I know, but it's one I cannot answer.'

'Okay, so here's another one: don't you think a civil airliner was a bit ambitious for our boy at that stage of his career?'

'Ambition is not something he has ever lacked. But by that I take it you really mean it may have been too great a task for someone . . . inexperienced in his profession.'

'Pretty much.'

'That one I can answer. Firstly, we do not know how much or how little experience he had, even by that stage. But as regards the difficulty of the task, I see that as barely relevant. It is you who imagines it as difficult, while nothing has distinguished the Black Spirit's deeds more than his ability to make them easy for himself. Without knowing precisely how that plane was destroyed, we cannot tell how simple a task it may have been for the destroyer.'

Angelique shuddered as she put the phone down, the ramifications of Enrique's argument starting to course through her like nerve poison. He was right. She had imagined blowing up a plane to be enormously difficult, willingly seduced by the reassurance of X-ray machines and metal detectors. Airports had more security than any other transport terminus, arguably more than any public place, but she was beginning to wonder whether that really meant anything, whether it mattered. London was one of the most security-conscious cities she had seen, but she now knew that the Black Spirit could strike there without setting foot in the place.

There were locations that she had perceived to be well-guarded and others that she considered vulnerable, based as much upon conditioning as knowledge or experience. The Black Spirit was aware of those perceptions, aware of how many people held them, and aware of why. But most crucially, he was aware of how to exploit them.

She looked at the bottle on the window-ledge, thinking how she would welcome even the annoying gags bound to accompany its opening come Sunday night if it confirmed the week to have been a complete write-off. 'May you live in interesting times,' was an ancient Chinese curse. The people pictured in the file, lying in the rubble, the people on flight 941, the people in that Strasbourg pile-up, they all knew what it meant. Right now, boring sounded pretty good. Paranoid fantasists, stolen fertiliser and Barrhead farmyards sounded pretty good.

McIntosh walked over to her desk, carrying a slip of paper, which he placed down in front of her.

'This guy called while you were on the other line there. A Sergeant Glenn from over on the Southside. I said you'd give him a ring back.'

'Cheers.'

Glenn. The apologetic duty sergeant who'd reported the alleged shooting. Probably phoning to say the bloke had bubbled and they were charging him with wasting police time. She wondered whether they could get Thaba for that, posthumously.

She dialled the number.

'Aye, hello DI de Xavia, thanks for gettin' back to me. It's ehm . . . we've had a few reports come in since I spoke to you, folk getting up and finding things, you know?'

'What things?' she asked, stifling a yawn.

'Eh, well, couple of cars on Sinclair Drive had windows shattered. One had the windscreen and rear-left side window broken, the other front-right and rear windscreen. Owners never heard anything, just spotted the damage when they went out to go to their work this morning. We're assuming it was last night. And, eh . . .'

He sighed, much as he'd done earlier, wishing he didn't have to say whatever he was about to.

'A wee wummin in Cartvale Road, corner close, a Mrs McDougall. Eh, apparently her budgie exploded last night.'

Angelique burst into laughter, unable to help it. It was the tension from Enrique's file. Oh, who was she kidding. It was hilarious under any circumstances.

'Her budgie exploded? Has anyone claimed responsibility?'

Glenn laughed too, but there was a weariness about it, and an impatience that she wasn't sure she liked. Impatience meant there was more.

'Naw, she didnae phone us at the time. Didnae phone the vet either, I don't imagine, from what I've heard. Poor wummin got a hell of a fright. She's a widow, lives on her own. Got her daughter to come round and stay. It was the daughter that noticed it this morning.'

'Noticed what?'

'A hole in the window, level with the cage. And another one in the wall behind it.'

Angelique had a feeling this wasn't going to be funny any more.

'Thing is, I've plotted the locations on the map, and you can draw a straight line from Mrs McDougall's through those two cars. Know where else it goes through if you extend it?'

'I think I can guess.'

'The bridge to Kintore Road, where Raymond Ash said he was shot at. The times match too.'

'I'd better have a word.'

'You'll understand if I'd rather not be the one who brings him in.'

'Sergeant Sarcastic was on duty last night, then? Don't worry, I'll have him picked up.'

'He'll be at Burnbrae Academy.'

'Thanks,' she said.

Thanks an unflushed bog-full.

apprehension

'Sir, this Bottom bloke, he's a bit of an arse, is he no'?'
  Oh God.
  PLAYING: TWENTY_EIGHT_THIRTEEN_YEAR_
  OLDS_IN_HYSTERICS.mp3
  READING: A_MIDSUMMER_NIGHT'S_DREAM.txt
  LOADING GAME MEDIA: DESPAIR
  LOADING GAME MEDIA: HUMILIATION
  LOADING GAME MEDIA: FATIGUE
  LOADING POWER-UPS: CAFFEINE
  LOADING POWER-UPS: LATENT SIMMERING
  MISANTHROPY
  LOADING OPPONENTS: PETER 'PED' BROWN
  AWAITING SNAPSHOT . . .
  Ray thought he had dodged a bullet when he spotted
an empty desk where Jason Murphy should have been
seated. The class wasn't short of headbangers, but that
particular one had proven the most adept at playing to the
gallery, and was high on the list of suspects for originating
last week's 'big wullie' conspiracy, whereby half the class
submitted crudely drawn dicks instead of essays. Thinking
back to his undergraduate career, there had been a few
times when Ray might as well have done the same, given
the marks he got from certain of the more curmudgeonly
professors.
  The hardest part had been stopping himself from
laughing, exacerbated by the almost critical need for some-

thing to put a smile back on his face. It seemed a waste to have to suppress it, especially with the weans all having gone to so much trouble in pretending to look busy while they worked on their individual contributions. The sketches themselves couldn't have taken more than a few seconds, each being the classic line-drawn cartoon knob with the mandatory spunk-blobs firing out of the top. It was unlikely to be the last time he'd set a composition assignment and get a pile of wank in return.

With the Laughing Gnome AWOL, he thought he might have a better chance of exerting some kind of control, via the recommended expedient of allocating them each a named role and letting them do horrible things to Shakespeare. That way, they tended to concentrate on when their own next line was coming up rather than how they might next disrupt the lesson, though he was kidding himself if he thought it aided their absorption of the text by somehow animating the drama. What was it Olivier used to say? You've never truly experienced the Bard until you've heard Renfrewshire teenage sub-literates monotonally stumbling over their stanzas in between scratching their sprouting pubes and flicking rolled-up snotters at each other.

It was going well for a while too, until Ray discovered that there was something worse than a classful of thirteen-year-old ignorami-with-attitude; and that was one thirteen-year-old with attitude and half a brain. Usually the 'brainy wans' tended towards the reserved, either through actually having some central-nervous-system activity to process incoming information, or through the ostracism that stemmed from placing some value upon your own education. According to Ray's colleagues, there were a few others whose fear of the latter made them play dumb when they were far from it, but nobody had warned him about the unstable cocktail of contradictions that was Ped Brown, recently returned from the school football team's trip to Gothenburg. He was one of those man-boys that seem to tower above their classmates during that randomly unfair staggered-start phase of pubescent growth, and as such could apparently flaunt his intelligence without fear of anybody giving him lip. As captain of the Under-14s, he was also about as likely a candidate for ostracism as an umbrella salesman on the day it rained shite. Unfortunately, this developing body and mind were nonetheless thirteen years old, same as the others, and Ped found it just as rewarding as his classmates to rip the pish out of his teacher. The difference his having half a brain made was that he was extremely good at it.

'Sorry, sir, I meant to say "ass".'

'Of course you did, Peter. Which means you've read on a bit further than the scene we're at just now.'

'Saw the film. Her oot *Ally McBeal* was in it, supposed to be in the buff but you never saw nothin'.'

'I know,' Ray agreed regretfully, before remembering where he was. 'Ehm, Calista Flockhart *was* in it, yes.'

'He is an arse though, is that no' the point?'

More laughter from the chorus. The comedic magic of the word 'arse' would never die as long as there were authority figures there to frown upon it.

'I thought we'd agreed on ass,' Ray said, trying the disingenuous-clarification tactic to avoid acknowledging a moral ruling on the word either way.

'Naw, I mean he's a balloon, an eejit. He gets on everybody's tits.'

Christ. Further hilarity. The king of comedy, Arse, is dead. Long live Tits.

'Calista Flockhart hasnae got any tits,' observed one of the girls, who going by her own build was basing her scorn entirely upon optimism for the near future. Maybe she'd a big sister and knew what she was looking forward to.

'You're absolutely right.'

'Who? Me or Carol?'

'Both, but Peter's observation was more pertinent. Bottom is an eejit. He's over-full of enthusiasm but has absolutely no awareness of his own limitations.'

'Like Robbie Williams,' offered someone in the second row. Ray couldn't remember all their names, but Gary sounded about right.

'Shut it you, Robbie Williams is brulliant,' came an impassioned retort from the distaff side, sounding like she was prepared to back up her opinion with weapons if necessary.

Ray had to close this one down before it degenerated, which would have to be at the price of not congratulating Gary for an inadvertently superb casting suggestion. Robbie Williams could have been born to play Nick the Weaver; just as long as he didn't bloody sing.

'Bottom acts like an ass, and that's why he is later turned into one, as we'll find out if we read on. Kylie, I think it was your line.'

'Who am I again?'

Jesus.

'Hermia.'

'Sir, was he not turned intae an ass because of Nob and Tit?'

Right. Now it was as bad as it could get, and not just because he was going to have to perform CPR on those members of the class currently approaching asphyxia. The precocious bastard had obviously caught a documentary

171

called *Within a Dream, Within a Play*, which went out on Channel Four about a month back. Ray had been marching up and down the living room with Martin at the time, but from the subtitles he had gathered that the programme was exploring the psychological and mythical aspects of the play in the context of various noted productions. Nob and Tit had been nicknames for Oberon and Titania, dating from an allegedly more innocent theatrical age, though it was difficult to accept that anything to do with those characters was ever less than charged with sexual significance. That, in fact, was the aspect Ped was now unavoidably going to bring up. The odds of him having watched the documentary all the way through were long, but if he had, it was evens he'd remember one particular fact.

''Cause, you know the expression "hung like a donkey"? Is it no' that Oberon wanted him changed intae an ass so that Titania would, you know . . .'

God in Govan, was *Buffy* not on that night or something? **LOADING POWER-UP: SUDDEN NIHILISTIC RECKLESSNESS**

'What, Peter?' Ray asked brightly. 'Shag him? Are you insinuating, perhaps, that Shakespeare was aware of the ass having supposedly the stiffest phallus of the animal kingdom and that it was a kinky prank on the part of Oberon to have his mischievous minion Puck bewitch Titania into taking this creature as her lover?'

There was complete silence throughout the room, but for the sound of pages turning as some of the weans tried to find the bit he was talking about. Ped thought about it, calculating how best to handle the situation now that his adversary was effectively cheating.

'Eh, aye.'

'Well you are one hundred per cent correct. This entire

play is, yes, about sex. Look at the setting: it's the night before a wedding celebration, for God's sake, so humping is high on the agenda, but it's not just any night, it's Midsummer's night, *the* numero uno pagan fertility rites shagfest on the calendar. As well as Theseus and Hippolyta, you've got the four horny and confused young lovers who get drawn *deep* into the dark forest, which is itself frequently a metaphor for what, Peter?'

'Eh . . .'

'Come on, it's a bit late for getting coy on me, and I know you know the answer, 'cause I saw the programme too.'

Ped swallowed.

'A fanny?'

'Very good. And once inside they become the playthings of Puck, also known as Robin Goodfellow, also known in myth as the Green Man of the forest, the Green Man being a pagan symbol of fertility, fertility being, in other words, Peter?'

'Shagging.'

'That word again. And the lord and lady of this arboreal realm are, as you informed us, Nob and Tit, who are having a bit of a tiff because Titania has been concentrating her devotions on an adopted child, with what frustrating consequence for Oberon?'

Ped was beaten to it by Gary.

'He's no' gettin' his hole, sir.'

'Exactly, Gary.'

'It's Charlie, sir.'

'Charlie. Whatever. He's not getting any. And you better believe Titania, being the queen of the fairies, is one hell of a shag to be doing without.'

Ray looked around the class, where the expressions of

confusion and amused disbelief told him they had been collectively outflanked and he was, for once, in control. Whether he'd still have a job by the time they'd told their parents and were next due on his timetable remained to be seen.

He walked to the blackboard, seizing the moment.

'So let's recap before we recommence our reading. A few keywords to write down. First one: shagging.'

The board was still covered in text from a previous lesson, a colleague inflicting one of Ted Hughes's animal cruelty collection on his unfortunate charges. Ray reached for the duster, but it was missing from its rest. Instead he grabbed one of the section dividers and hauled down the next panel with a squeak of the rollers. There was a four-foot cartoon knob staring back, the spunk blobs spurting towards him at head height.

The laughter was like a wall of water, crashing against him and making it impossible to turn around.

What to do next, he told himself, was the kind of test that distinguished the experienced pro from the floundering newbie. The former would, perhaps, simply roll the board on to another panel and pretend nothing untoward had happened; maybe crack a joke about what the last class had been learning, dispel any sense of confrontation. The more authoritarian might freak out and go into full intimidatory investigative mode, threatening every clichéd repercussion and turning the uproarious atmosphere into one of fear and regret. Ray, of course, didn't have a fucking clue, but was sure that it augured poorly for his future in this career that he found the incident funnier than anyone else in the room. He knew also that if he let himself start laughing, he'd end up on his knees, tears streaming down his cheeks, with the catastrophic side effect of sanctioning the knob motif in the eyes of the weans. It would be common knowledge by the end of playtime, and thereafter follow him around forever: jotters, essays, blackboards, folders, you name it. He might as well change his name to Mr Knob.

However, even a newbie can get jammy; pick up a railgun and nail someone point-blank out of sheer instinct or sheer luck. He can also, of course, pick up a rocket-launcher and fire it fatally into the nearest wall. Ray wasn't aware of any thought process directing his actions, but found himself writing on the board, as though unfazed, only his handwriting betraying a slight tremble as he fought to suppress his own laughter. He wrote 'shagging' above the tip of the knob, and for a flourish, enclosed it in a bead shape so that it appeared to be part of the ejaculation. The guffaws continued, but the edge of onslaught had been blunted; they were well on their way to laughing *with*.

'What else did we say?' he asked, hoping no-one was observant enough to spot the tears welling up. 'Come on?'

'Nob and Tit,' someone responded.

'Nob and Tit.' He wrote that too, encircling it in another bead, arcing along the same trajectory. 'Any more?'

'Oberon not gettin' his hole, sir.'

'"Not getting any", very good.'

'Fanny, sir.'

'That's right, the dark forest.'

'Big donkey's wullie, sir.'

'Of course, how could we forget the importance of the phallus, as has been so beautifully illustrated here by someone with a deep understanding of the play. Now, have you all written this down?'

'Yes, sir.'

'And have you all drawn a knob?'

Head-shakes and unsteady giggling all round.

'Come on, then. Get on with it.'

Ray folded his arms impatiently and waited. Eventually they realised he wasn't kidding, and set pen to paper.

'All done now? Hold them up where I can see them.'

Twenty-eight jotters were held aloft, all having faithfully and diligently completed the exercise.

'Good. Now, I think we're ready to resume reading. Kylie, I believe it was your line.'

Kylie, unfortunate spawn of the late Eighties, fumbled for the book, then recommenced the group assault on the undefended verse. Ray walked to the door, causing the next reader to stop.

'Keep it up. I'm just nipping outside for a second, but I'll still be listening. Go on.'

Ray closed the door quietly, the sound of a lisping Lysander muffled behind him, then unleashed a lung-crumpling sigh. He waited for his own laughter to begin, but it didn't come. It might yet ambush him later on, but for now it seemed he had succeeded in stemming the flow. Pity, really. Maybe he'd get the benefit later when he told Kate, or maybe it had just seemed all the funnier because he knew he couldn't laugh at the time. He remembered a truly fearsome Maths teacher with an intimidating resemblance to Oliver Reed, in whose class the most infantile whispered remark could seem eye-streamingly hilarious through the terror of incurring his volcanic wrath and his unrivalled belt-technique.

After a few minutes, Ray reckoned he was ready to go back into the class, where, miraculously, the play was still being read aloud. Best to be sure, though. He tried visualising the giant chalk knob, remembering the impact of that moment when it suddenly appeared. A smile crept over his face, letting him know the giggles were still too close to the surface. Another few moments, then.

There were footsteps approaching along the corridor, quick and deliberate. Adult, male, plural, he guessed. Bugger. He didn't fancy explaining his unscheduled break to another member of staff, so he decided he'd just have to take a deep breath and plunge back in.

The breath, as it turned out, was too deep. They were round the corner and in sight as he gripped the handle.

'Mr Ash?'

It was indeed two men, but not members of staff. He didn't know all the teachers by face or name yet, but he knew how they dressed, and this pair were far too smartly suited and booted. Polis would have been his guess, even if they weren't holding up warrant cards, which were in themselves less confirmatory than the standard-issue moustaches.

'I'm Sergeant Boyle, this is DC Thorpe, Special Branch.' The accent was English, maybe Lancashire. Ray felt his insides tighten. This was it: they were going to charge him with wasting police time, and they'd sent the heavy squad in to make it as intimidating as possible. 'We need to speak to you about the incident last night.'

'I'm in the middle of a class at the moment. I'll be free in about ten minutes.'

'We need you to come with us right now, Mr Ash. It's a very serious matter.'

'I didn't make it up.'

'We know. That's why we're here.'

Ray didn't know how to react. Vindication would have felt good last night, especially with that smug cop sitting across the table, but now their confirmation just brought the reality of the danger back down like an anvil.

Boyle put a leading hand on his shoulder.

'What about my class?'

'We've spoken to your boss, it's been cleared.'

'Is someone coming down?'

'Yeah. Come on.'

'So did you find something? A witness?'

'We'd best wait till the station to talk, Mr Ash.'

They walked very briskly out of the school, that no-nonsense cop-stride that exuded self-importance with every pace. Thorpe diverted at the front exit 'to bring the Head up to speed', while Boyle led Ray out to a grey Rover and ushered him into the back seat before taking the wheel himself. Thorpe emerged from the building a couple of minutes later and climbed into the rear next to Ray, upon which Boyle turned around and stuck a silencer-fitted automatic into Ray's chest.

'Fuck me.'

'Give him your car keys or I will,' he ordered.

Thorpe – presumably now not his real name – was already patting Ray down, removing his keys and mobile phone from his inside jacket pocket.

'What is it you want from *me*, for fuck's sake?'

'These'll do for just now, mate,' probably-not-Thorpe replied, a hint of Scouse revealed in his accent. 'Which motor is it? And don't fuck us about unless you really want to know what a bullet in the nuts feels like.'

'Black Polo,' Ray said, trying to sound swiftly cooperative.

'Which one?'

'The fucked one.'

Thorpe exited, then there was a clunk as Boyle engaged the central locking. He withdrew the pistol and put the car into gear.

178

'The bullet in the nuts offer stands until further notice, okay?'

'While stocks last,' Ray mumbled.

The car turned left out of the car park and promptly pulled up behind a massive lorry, parked about a hundred yards from the school gates, a ramp leading to its rear.

'No tantrums, please, Mr Ash,' Boyle said, taking the keys out of the ignition. 'Best to conserve your energy.'

'What fucking energy?' Ray said, watching Boyle head up the ramp.

He hauled open the roller-shuttered door then returned to drive the car up into the container. Once inside the truck, Boyle got out of the Rover again, locked the vehicle and walked away.

Ray tried the doorhandle but it merely bent back and forth with no effect. He tried walloping the side window with his elbow a few times, but it was clear which one would break first, and anyway, if he climbed out, where the hell was he going to go? He looked out of the rear windscreen, expecting to see Boyle close the shutter. Instead he saw his own car rolling up behind the Rover, Thorpe at the wheel.

'Pricks.'

What did they want with his car? And what the bloody hell did they want with *him*? They weren't cops, yet they knew about last night, so they had to be connected, but last night they were trying to kill him and today they were abducting him; disappearing him, even.

The roller-shutter was pulled down at the rear, leaving him also in literal darkness. He knew he should have been more fearful for his life, but the sense of threat was clouded by his having no idea where or who the threat was coming from. Inexplicable as it was, however, he could forget all that mince about subconscious projection and stress-related hallucinations. The events of last night may have passed in a panic-fuelled blur of action, emotion and instinct, easily confused and jumbled in the memory, but right now he was conscious, composed and alert, and he was quite definitely locked in a car, quite definitely locked in a lorry, having quite definitely been abducted at gunpoint.

It occurred to him to keep track of the turns and attempt to picture the route from memory, but the Rover's suspension did too good a job of cushioning the lorry's movements. He checked his watch so that he'd at least have some idea of how far he was travelling. After that, there was nothing to do but sit in the dark and ponder his situation, though even baffled contemplation needed information to fuel it, and he was fresh out.

Ray searched the most tender recesses of his conscience for traces of what he might have done to bring this upon himself, but was coming up well short. He didn't have any enemies; certainly none that he was aware of, and it was difficult to imagine generating this level of animosity without noticing. The only people he had even argued with in recent times had been online opponents, and even among the less stable of them, their idea of retribution extended to spamming poorly spelled insults in IRC chatrooms or bombing your mailbox with bazillions of auto-generated messages. So what did that leave? Some *Angel Heart* alter ego leading an unconscious life of crime? Hard to see where he would have fitted that in around the nappy changes and floor-pacing. Had he witnessed something he wasn't supposed to? Exhaustion and self-absorption could take their toll, but he still reckoned he would notice if an incident of mortal consequence happened in his line of vision.

Shit, of course! That had to be it: he'd forgotten to check his mail this morning for mistakenly addressed microfilms. There were probably nuclear launch codes lying on the doormat at that very moment, just waiting for Martin to spew all over them. Fuck, it was as likely as everything else that was going on at the moment.

He hadn't crossed any drug-dealers, hadn't racked up debts to some bloke with more scar tissue than Cher, hadn't joined any subversive underground movements and hadn't slept with anybody's wife (seldom even his own these days, *Mastitis Fetish* magazine and *Sex for the Sleep-Deprived* not being on the household subscription list). He hadn't even raised his voice in anger to another human being since . . .

Fuck. No. Don't go there, m8.

So yes, owning-up time: he had slept with . . . well, she wasn't the guy's wife, just his girlfriend, but this was more than ten years ago. The statutory limitation would have been well exceeded even if the injured party hadn't died in the meantime. And anyway, given the circumstances under which it happened, it wasn't something that had exactly plagued Ray with guilt. If it had, it might have provided another explanation for what he'd imagined he saw at the airport, but it still wouldn't explain *this* carry-on. Manifestations of conscience could reputedly be powerful things, but he didn't remember Banquo's ghost toting an automatic or kidnapping Macbeth in the back of a truck.

Nonetheless, the chronology demanded a connection. Since seeing/not seeing/imagining/astrally projecting Simon Darcourt at the airport last night, Ray's world had ceased to obey its normal rules: somebody had hacked the Real Life™ engine and left the server utterly borked. Was it entirely coincidental that the last time his life had gone anything like this crazy was the last time he and Simon's paths had crossed?

Surely. But if anyone could possibly fuck you over from beyond the grave, it would be that vindictive bastard. Simon kept score of every slight, every dispute, every 'disappointment', to use his spine-curling term; never mind full-scale betrayal.

He hadn't always been like that though. Well, maybe he had, but at least there had been a time when Ray was not so acutely aware of it.

Simon was the hero of the alsatian incident; you had to chalk that one up to him (though there had still been a casualty). Hillhead, nineteen-eighty-cannae-remember. First year. Ray had grasped the opportunity of broadening his horizons through higher education the way most good Scots lads did, by staying home at his mammy's and commuting to the nearest uni on a daily basis. You could pick out the West-of-Scotland home-dwellers at ten paces, even without hearing their accents: they didn't look malnourished, their eyes were bright from occasionally going to bed at a sensible hour and their clothes were always clean and ironed. The downside was that spontaneous, uncontrolled socialising – the quick pint following the last lecture that turned into a flat-party via two more pubs, a takeaway and the union disco, for some the entire purpose of university – was often curtailed by the logistical concerns of getting home to towns not particularly well-served by public transport during daylight hours, never mind three in the morning. The standard solution, when available, was to crash on somebody's floor, an option particularly welcome on what used to be known as school nights.

On this particular occasion, Ray had enjoyed the hospitality of the late Mr Darcourt and his housemate Ross, after a quick pint following the last lecture etcetera etcetera. He'd spoken to Simon a few times before that, and sat next to him in a couple of classes, silently entertaining each other by scribbling oh-so-hilarious remarks and doodles about the lecturer on their notepads. However, this had been the first time they'd really got talking, and they'd enjoyed one of those youthful, beer-fuelled meetings-of-the-minds that gave the impression university was bung-full of fellow visionaries. Sitting in the Queen Margaret Union bar, named at the time after the statutory dead black South African, their conversation covered every aspect of life: music, books *and* films. (Ray made a judicious rule of never bringing up the subject of computer games in Arts faculty company. Might as well turn up in an Anthrax T-shirt with a copy of *The Foundation Trilogy* under your arm.)

They seemed to agree on a lot of things, though as tended to be the case with such conversations, each participant probably switched off during the bits when his counterpart was enthusing over something he didn't like or hadn't heard of, impatient for his own turn. Memory subsequently retained only edited highlights. Ray, for instance, didn't remember Simon eulogising about This Mortal Coil, but he must have held forth on the subject that night because he would later play *It'll End In Tears* repeatedly until Ray wanted to track Liz Frazer down and force her at knifepoint to sing in a proper fucking language, he didn't care which one.

Arguably more important than what you liked was agreeing on what you hated, and nothing forged a bond quite as strong as a shared detestation of a prevalent orthodoxy. In this case, their unifying sacrilege was that they both despised The Smiths, a heresy that distinguished them as being *terribly* individualistic and raised them above what Simon described as 'all the bequiffed, designer-miserablist twats poncin' around the QM hopin' someone notices the volume of Oscar Wilde stickin' out their jacket pocket'. In the mid-1980s, The Smiths were the student equivalent of stadium rock. Saying you hated them was, in that context, about as daringly iconoclastic as saying you hated the Spice Girls, but it still felt good to unload about it. Listening to Simon unload was even better.

Scorn was Simon's true idiom. Nobody did withering derision quite like him, and it was a treat to hear him train the heavy armoury on what they both regarded as legitimate targets. On form, he was like Jerry Sadowitz without the warm sentimental streak, and the bigger the audience, the better the performance. Ray had a quiverful of barbs of his own, eliciting delighted approval from Simon when unsheathed, but he was limited in his dislikes. The scope of Simon's contempt was boundless.

'There's nothin' more depressin' than wakin' up next to a lassie and spottin' *Meat Is Murder* lyin' next to the turntable. My own fault for not askin' I suppose, but they should really have the decency to tell you. I mean, they'd tell you if they'd any other disease. No, actually, there *is* somethin' worse: pickin' up *Meat Is Murder* and findin' an Everything But The Girl album underneath. You're fuckin' doomed at that point. Before you get out of that flat, you're gaunny hear all about her parents' fuckin' divorce and two hours of how nobody understands her, and all for the sake of one shag. Not fuckin' worth it.'

Simon had had sex. The contemporary significance of this could not be overstated. Not only had he had sex and talked about it matter-of-factly (assuming, which Ray loved, that

Ray had had some too), but he'd even had *bad* sex. As far as Ray was concerned, while this was not unthinkable, it hinted at a degree of experience and maturity which at that stage he couldn't even aspire to. The idea of actually getting to do it seemed purely conceptual to a fairly shy seventeen-year-old who was only in the QM bar because (like every other seventeen-year-old in the place) he'd lied about his date of birth when he registered for his membership diary. This didn't mean he couldn't identify with what Simon was saying, mind you. He'd only been a student for a term and a half, but it had been time enough to teach him that possession of an EBTG album, badge, T-shirt or Tracy Thorne bowl-cut was nature's way of telling you not to strike up a conversation with that particular girl unless you feared you were feeling just too damn positive for your own good.

Still, Simon moved in a world where student girls lived in flats and had casual sex, even the scowling depressive ones, and that world was a lot further from Ray's than Houston was from Hillhead. For that reason, it thrilled him to be in Simon's company, speaking, drinking, laughing, on terms. He knew it didn't mean he was now one step from having sex *that he could complain about* with female Smiths fans, but it meant that he no longer had to worry about feeling like a sixth-year schoolboy out of uniform. It constituted a validation of proper student status.

Unfortunately, he feared it would be immediately revoked again when some more of Simon's friends turned up and it was suggested that they 'hit the disco and really make a night of it'. Ray could imagine his Clash T-shirt metamorphosing into a school tie and blazer as he pondered how best to phrase the admission that he had to get home to Mummy and Daddy's house for hot cocoa and a biccie before night-night.

He settled for 'I don't think I can make it but I'll hang around for one more pint,' neglecting to further elaborate. Simon, however, was insistent.

'Come on, man, you've got to. We're just gettin' started here.' That was in between making enthusiastic introductions, depicting Ray to his intimidatingly grown-up-looking pals (greatcoats, stubble and roll-ups) as a soulmate of exquisite taste, intellect and wit. Ray was therefore now even more fearful of being 'found out' as a wee, Ayrshire-dwelling virgin who'd merely cracked a couple of well-timed gags about Morrissey and been bluffing when he made out he'd heard of Père Ubu and Frazier Chorus.

'I've nowhere to crash,' he said, which deftly avoided the issue of where he'd normally be crashing: viz, a semi in the sticks.

'It's cool, you can crash at ours, can't he, Ross?'

'Aye, nae bother.'

And so Raymond's Big Adventure in the Land of Vicarious Cool continued.

'Ours' turned out to be a terraced townhouse converted into six student bedsits. 'If you get here the right time of day, you can hear the same Smiths album bein' simultaneously played on four different shitey tape decks,' Simon claimed. 'At least I think it's the same album. Every track sounds the fuckin' same to me.'

The three of them ate endless rounds of toast relayed in turns from the communal kitchen, washed down with black and watery tea (no milk, natch; one last tea bag heroically giving its all for six cups). Music was played, of course, a handful of shared favourites punctuating an eclectic plethora of obscure selections Simon insisted Ray would love. As it turned out, his strike rate was pretty high. It was an education for Ray, not only in terms of being introduced to a number of new bands, but in realising that while he thought he knew about music, to Simon it was a scholastic discipline. He provided a running commentary on every track, like the Shakespeare annotations that often took up more space on each page than the text itelf. Innovation was everything: if it had been done before, it was worthless, pointless. In other company, Ray might have been able to make a case for the ain't-broke-don't-fix-it ethic of the finely crafted song, or the sheer visceral impact of a well-timed power chord, but on this occasion it would have been like suddenly announcing he was a Jehovah's Witness and trying to flog Simon *The Watchtower*.

Père Ubu, as it turned out, were not bad, but Frazier Chorus were absolute steg.

Ross retired to his room when the tea and toast ran out, which was long before Simon's enthusiasm for furthering Ray's musical horizons. Eventually Simon did decide to go to bed, a spontaneous decision taken while Ray was down in one of the bathrooms having a pee. When Ray returned to the room, Simon was fast asleep in the only bed, and utterly unrousable. The only reaction Ray found it possible to elicit, via nudging, was a low, threatening growl. Asking whether he had any spare bedding seemed over-optimistic.

Ray was consulting his watch and trying to remember how early the buses started when he heard a toilet flush, and was able to intercept Ross on his way back from syphoning off the beer. Fortunately, it turned out he had a spare sleeping bag. 'I keep it in case Simon has guests,' he said archly.

He woke up around nine, after about five hours' fitful kip. The bedsit's curtains didn't reach the bottom of the window, so the wintery sunshine had beamed directly on to his face where he lay on the floor. If that hadn't done it, his bladder would have probably roused him soon anyway, after five pints and then all that tea. When he looked at Simon's bed, he was surprised to find it empty. Simon hadn't struck Ray as the type to clap his hands and jump up when the alarm went off, but he vaguely remembered him saying something about meeting a guy to buy an amp.

Simon barrelled into the room, buttoning his shirt, his face still damp from washing.

'I'm gaunny be late for this guy if I don't head now. You needin' to go too?'

'I've missed my first lecture. Next one's not until eleven.'

'Lucky bastard. Just let yourself out, yeah?'

'Sure. Where's the bog again?' Better be sure before his host departed; last night was still very hazy, and he didn't want to walk into somebody's bedroom by mistake.

'There's two. One on the first-floor landing, and another off the downstairs hall.'

'Cheers. Burstin'.'

Ray sat up and extricated himself from the sleeping bag.

Woof.

'Did you hear that?'

'What?'

'Sounded like a dog.'

Woof.

'I heard *that*. Fuck, that was inside.'

'Does one of your flatmates have a dog?'

'Do they fuck. Are you kiddin'? It would need a housin' benefit book before the landlord would let it in.'

Woof.

'That's definitely inside,' they both said.

Simon headed for the door, Ray hurriedly pulling on his jeans to follow. Just the movement of walking made it feel like someone was squeezing his bladder. When he emerged on to the landing, Ross was already out of his room and looking over the banister. Below them, they could see two females on the lower landing, also staring down towards the bottom hall. One was in a dressing gown, clutching a towel, the other dressed in jeans and a Bunnymen T-shirt.

Woof.

'There's a dog in the flat,' announced Bunnygirl, looking up, an English lassie Ray recognised from his literature-in-translation class.

'And there's me thinkin' it was an antelope,' Simon replied. 'How did it get in?'

'Somebody must've left the door open,' suggested Ross.

'Fuckin' Yasser Arafat probably. He never shuts it. Still thinks he's livin' in a fuckin' tent in the desert.'

'Don't be so racist,' the English girl countered. 'You're always on at Ali.'

'I'm not bein' racist. Unless it's a custom in Morocco to leave fuckin' doors lyin' open.'

'He's from Tunisia.'

'Whatever. He's the only one not here. His first lecture's at nine, every day. Serves him right for daein' medicine.'

'It could've been the postman.'

'Does it matter?' Ross enquired. 'What kind of dog is it? Has anybody seen?'

Woof woof woof woof growl.

'Oh fuck.'

Attracted by the raised voices, the dog had emerged into view to investigate the source, then began bounding up the stairs when it saw all the staring faces. Both girls immediately retreated into the nearest room and closed the door with a slam. The alsatian (it had to be an alsatian, in accordance with the rule that decreed every uncontrolled, ownerless dog running wild in a public place must be one

189

of those sabre-toothed and over-aggressive bastards) stopped outside it, standing up on two legs and scratching the paintwork.

Simon laughed, which caused it to turn around and bark angrily at him. All three of them dived into Ross's room, it being directly behind where they'd been standing.

'What the fuck is it doin' here?' Ross asked.

'That prick Yasser. I'm gaunny tie the door shut wi' his fuckin' headscarf.'

'I've got a tutorial at ten,' Ross moaned.

'I'm burstin' for a pish.'

'An' I'm meant tae be meetin' a guy on Byres Road in fifteen minutes. Doesnae look like any of us are goin' anywhere until we get rid of Cerberus doon there.'

Ross opened the door a little, peering through the crack.

'It's stopped barkin' anyway. I cannae see it, though. Think it might have gone back doonstairs. Christ, how we gaunny get rid of it? I hate thae fuckin' things. Wan o' them bit me when I was wee, never forgave the cunts.'

'That's whit your mammy tells you anyway. "You were gorgeous until that big dug bit you, Ross son."'

'Fuck off. This is serious.'

Simon laughed. 'I know. No' much point in me buyin' this guy's amp if I cannae play my guitar 'cause my arm's been bitten aff.'

'I've got tae hand in an essay at this tutorial. I'm already on an extension.'

'Well here's your big chance. Chuck it doon there tae the hound of the Baskervilles an' you can genuinely tell your tutor a dug ate it.'

'One more word an' I'm chuckin' you oot my room. You think you could make it next door withoot gettin' savaged?'

'It's only about four feet.'

'A long four feet with the jaws of death closin' in on you.'

'How far's the bog?'

'You'd never make it, Ray. You'd have pished yoursel' before you got there anyway.'

'I don't doubt it. Anybody got a ginger bottle?'

'Don't even think about it.'

'Seriously,' Ross implored, 'whit are we gaunny dae?'

'I know,' Simon said. 'We can phone Gerry roon the corner. Tell him to come to the house, then when he opens the door, the dug can get back oot. Either that or we can all get past while it's eatin' Gerry.'

'Have you got a phone?' Ray asked, wondering whether this was another of Simon's gags or a genuine solution.

'Aye,' Ross replied. 'Payphone. But it's on the ground floor.'

'Bugger.'

'Well, I think if I went to the landing and peed, I might wash it out the door.'

'I reckon we should just all make a run for it,' Simon ventured.

'You reckon you could outrun an alsatian?' asked Ross.

'I wouldnae need to. I'd just need to outrun you.'

'Charming.'

Simon looked at his watch.

'Christ. The guy's probably got umpteen folk lined up to buy that thing. Let me out.'

'You goin' for it?'

'Just gaunny have a wee look.'

Simon exited the room, Ross waiting a less than valiant few seconds before returning to their banister vantage point. Ray wasn't feeling very brave either, but the fear of exploding like a urine-filled balloon was urging him forward. By the time Ray got there, Simon had made it to the first landing, where the girls were peeping out of their doorway. The alsatian was nowhere to be seen.

'I think it's away.'

'Is the front door open?'

'Cannae see.'

Woof.

'Jesus,' said Ross.

Simon stayed where he was, tentatively looking over the banister.

Whine.

'Can you see it?' asked one of the girls.

'Aye. It's kinna cowerin' at the bog door, right at the back. I think it's more scared than us.'

'That'll be right,' Ross doubted.

'I'm goin' for it. I need that amp.'

Yes, go, go, thought Ray.

'Christ, is it worth dyin' for?'

'Ross, it's a dug, no' a fuckin' lion.'

'I cannae watch this.'

Ross stepped back from the banister as Simon began walking slowly down the last flight of stairs, Ray's bladder stretching thinner and tauter with every step. Behind Simon, the girls kept their door open in case he needed a handy exit. Ray moved delicately around the banister to get a clearer view of the bottom hall, in time to see Simon reach the door and calmly pull it open. There was a brown flash accompanied by a flurry of canine footfalls as the animal immediately bolted out of the house.

'Tell Ross I died well,' he called up the stairs.

'Up your arse.'

'You headin' out the now, Ross?'

'Aye.'

'C'mon then. We'll be safer from the wildlife if we walk in pairs.'

Ross rolled his eyes at Ray and popped back into his room for his essay, then trotted down the stairs.

'Thanks, Simon,' said the girl in the dressing gown.

'*De rien*,' he replied, holding the door open for Ross with an exaggerated bow.

'See you in the bar later, Ray, awright?'

Oh fuck, don't mention beer.

'Aye, sure.'

The front door closed, and with it the need to retain any semblance of cool was gone. Ray bounded down the stairs in his bare feet, but was only halfway to the next landing when the girl in the dressing gown nimbly stepped into the bathroom, now able to perform her ablutions without fear of being gored.

'Aw fuck.'

There was another bog in the bottom hall, Ray remembered, and tore down the remaining flight as though the dog was indeed at his back. At the bottom, he grabbed the end of the banister and pivoted around it, eyes fixed on the mercifully open and unoccupied second bathroom door.

As opposed to the carpet.

He didn't go quite the way of Jesus in Connolly's crucifixion; merely slid a little, almost but not quite toppling. The first thing he was aware of was the sensation of something underfoot that was not textile. It was soft, clay-like and disturbingly above room temperature. And it was between his toes.

'Aaaaww fuuuuck. Awww naaaaaw.'

Ray wobbled on his clean foot, face contorting beyond his control, skin having a determined go at leaving his

193

body. Outside of pain, there can be fewer less desirable sensations than lukewarm alsatian jobbie squirming through the gaps around your little piggies. If he'd had a chainsaw handy, he'd have been tempted to lop the foot off just to make it stop.

He hopped through the door, holding his befouled leg at the knee so that it didn't brush against anything, in particular other parts of his person. Once inside, he discovered that it was a bathroom merely in the euphemistic application of the term, containing as it did only a toilet and a minuscule wash-hand basin. There followed a difficult moment of pondering which to use first, before he decided that he could tolerate the vile clinging sensation just a little longer than he could tolerate the pain in his bladder.

He steadied himself with one hand on the wall as he pissed, the extended duration made even less welcome by the whiffs of alsatian keech that kept wafting up and threatening to make him gag. After that he had to execute a gymnastic manoeuvre inexplicably missing from the Olympic compulsory programme: that of plonking one foot in a tall but tiny basin while keeping the other one flat on the floor *and* having two hands free – not touching any walls for support – so that he could operate the taps and do . . . well, what he had to do.

The single mixer tap was a brilliant, invaluably useful and ingeniously simple innovation. It allowed you to regulate the water temperature merely by balancing the flow, so that you didn't have to scald yourself or wash your face in freezing-cold water. This pygmy's christening font, of course, didn't have one. Nor did it have any soap. On the plus side, the cold water did dull the smell a little, and after a few minutes his toes were so numb that he could barely feel the sensation of canine faecal matter grudgingly peeling away from his skin.

Maybe he should have read the signs. Perhaps if he'd been brought up religious he'd have sought a semiology in every event, as though trying to hack the code for the preset programme of his life. But even if he didn't believe in signs, he knew retrospectively that it was definitely an overture. The first night he'd spent with Simon Darcourt, he'd ended up literally in the shit.

There'd been other signs too, genuine evidence, as opposed to symbolic moments. The one that most stuck in his mind wasn't in any way dramatic, but it was the first time he could remember alarm bells ringing. He'd chosen to ignore them, and if he had his time again he knew he'd ignore them still. It took a particular brand of sociopath to operate a 'one strike and you're out' social policy of identifying fatal character flaws.

Simon, Ray and two or three others – he couldn't recall who – were sitting in the Grosvenor Café on Ashton Lane, a popular spot for a coffee and cheap, generous grub in between (and as often instead of) lectures. They were talking about *The Young Ones*, which had by that time gone through both the trendy-to-like-it and subsequent uncool-to-still-like-it cycles and was therefore ripe for rehabilitation. It was one of those gut-wrenchingly funny coffee-time discussions, seemingly all the more savourable for the clock counting down to a class that conscience dictated he must attend. Everyone was contributing classic moments, provoking cumulative laughter round the table. Sharing their recollections somehow rekindled how hilarious the scenes were first time around, before their impact was dulled by irresistible repeat viewings.

'Mind the bit when Vyvyan's heid got knocked off on

the train, an' he ended up kickin' it along the railway line.'

'"You took your time, you bastard."'

'An' that time he was diggin' for oil, nuttin' the floor.'

'An' the pickaxe went through his heid, aye.'

'"Don't worry, Neil, it was bound to happen . . . sooner or later." Wallop!'

All that stuff. You had to be there. Then Simon said:

'Remember the party one. The *best* one.'

This immediately struck Ray as an odd thing to say, and he was sure it wasn't just Simon's figure of speech. He didn't offer it, he pronounced it. There was something in the way he said it that invited – no, assumed – agreement, and as he spoke he looked around the table, meeting every eye in a sweep that was expecting rather than seeking approval. He didn't say 'my favourite one was' or even 'the funniest one was' with its implicit, unspoken 'imho' qualification. 'The *best* one.' It was as though it didn't actually occur to him that anyone else could have a different opinion. This wasn't the case, of course. Simon knew fine that there were people who had different opinions from his own. He even had collective terms for them.

A less impressionistic warning came on another late night in the QM, when the pair of them were really hitting it off, setting the world (or at least The Smiths) to rights. In a rare departure from the comfortable common ground of standard subject matter, Ray mentioned how a girl in one of his classes had thus far failed to return some lecture notes he had lent her. Ray just wanted to let off steam, maybe hear Simon go into one of his entertainingly colourful rants about the girl in question, preferably including details of some sexual involvement he might have had with her.

Instead he said merely: 'I find people really disappointing, don't you?' Ray got the impression he would join their number if he answered in anything but the affirmative. Again, to paraphrase the playground rhyme, 'it's not so much the things he says, it's the nasty way he says 'em.' He had heard plenty of weary and embittered or merely posturing misanthropy even by that age, but never spoken with such a cold certainty, such irredeemable condemnation. Ray was talking about some daft lassie much remarked to have a mind like a colander, and Simon sounded ready to wipe out the entire species.

'Em, sometimes, aye.' Ray left it at that, figuring a Capraesque advocacy of the human capacity for warmth and goodness was unlikely to melt Simon's heart.

People did 'disappoint' Simon, individually as well as generally, though their (sometimes unknowing) transgressions were often subject to a somewhat singular interpretation on his part. 'He/she disappointed me' was, in Ray's frequent experience, the phrase that heralded their being airbrushed out of the official records and ignored with a Stalinist dedication.

This social totalitarianism was in ironic symbiosis with an unmatched faculty for liking and being excited by people. In short, when you were in, you were very, very in, and when you were out, it was final. When he met someone new, he had the ability to make him or her feel like the most interesting person on the planet, perhaps because to Simon, at that precise moment, they were (behind him, of course). Any time you ran into him, he gave the genuine impression that the day had just improved immeasurably, simply because you had shown up. The effect was doubly charming because the feeling was reciprocated, in spades. Simon was someone towards whom interesting people and exciting events just couldn't help but gravitate, and yet he could still make you feel like you were the one brightening up *his* universe.

Until you disappointed him.

Ray could feel the truck slowing down again. It had stopped several times, presumably at junctions, but hadn't done so for at least an hour. He couldn't hear anything from outside, which would have suggested they were somewhere remote and secluded if it hadn't been that he couldn't hear anything from outside at the point he reckoned they were bombing along the motorway through the city. He was dying for a pee, the combination of caffeine, travel and fear having a powerfully diuretic effect, further exacerbated by not knowing when or if he would ever see a lavvy again. Whizzing on their front upholstery had seemed a temptingly vengeful recourse, but in opposition, as well as the smell, there was the thought that they could mete out vengeance too, and they had the option to piss lead. He'd decided to hang on for another ten minutes, after which the driver's seat was getting it out of sheer necessity.

The truck came to a standstill and the engine cut out. Ray enjoyed a millisecond's feeling of relief that the journey was over, before his thoughts turned to what might be about to happen next. Better to travel hopefully, indeed. Better to travel shit-scared and bursting for a single-fish, in fact, than to arrive in the custody of pistol-packing bampots.

The rear shutter rolled open. Boyle and Thorpe, or whoever the fuck they were, strolled purposefully into the container, Boyle carrying something black in his right hand. He opened the door and gestured to Ray to get out.

'Face the front.'

'Yes sir,' Ray said. It was meant to sound defiant, but

his voice cracked up. Daft, really. There was no point in pretending he wasn't terrified.

The black something turned out to be a bag or a hood. It was passed over his head and tightened around the neck. Boyle placed his hands on Ray's shoulders and turned him around.

'Walk.'

Ray moved slowly, his feet picking cautiously at the ground before each step. A hand grabbed his shirt around the chest and pulled at him to go faster. He was led down the ramp and over what felt like grass, then inside a building, the floor underneath smooth like lino or tiles. It felt cooler inside the building than out, and there was a fusty smell about it that suggested Mister Sheen and his pal Ajax hadn't dropped by for a while. The smell was that of abandonment and decay, to which Ray could add hopelessness, isolation and fear.

A door was opened for him and he was nudged through it on to bare floorboards, dust and traces of rubble rolling between the wood and his shoes. He was thrust down on to a chair and had his hands pulled behind him, where they were tied tightly together. His feet were then secured to the metal chairlegs, before the hood was finally removed. He saw layers of peeling wallpaper, bare plaster and a fireplace, the ceiling a diseased-looking plague of blistered paint and crumbling cornicing. There was one window, broken and partially boarded up, allowing a shaft of weak sunlight to illuminate the room, but affording a view only of thick bushes and trees beyond.

Boyle and Thorpe stood on either side, Thorpe removing a packet of cigarettes from his inside jacket pocket. He offered one to Ray.

'I don't smoke.'

Thorpe shrugged and popped the proffered fag into his own mouth.

'Too bad. Any other requests?'

Ray felt tears forming in his eyes as the question and the significance of the offered cigarette sank in. He wished he knew what he had done, wished he could get down on his knees and beg forgiveness before whoever had sanctioned this, promising any and every restitution within his ability. But most of all he wished he could see Kate and Martin one more time.

He swallowed, the tears running now, but he was determined that this time his voice wouldn't break.

'I suppose a wank's out of the question?' he said, managing just above a whisper.

'Fuck him,' Boyle said angrily. 'Let's do it.'

They both drew their automatics and simultaneously chambered their rounds before levelling the weapons at arm's length. Ray closed his eyes, his overfull bladder reflexively emptying through his trousers to splash on the floorboards below. He heard the clicks of triggers being cocked, then suffered an eternity of waiting, bracing, wincing, twitching, hyperventilating. It got to the point where he was willing the shots to come, but they never did.

He heard more clicks and opened his eyes to see them reholstering their guns, smirking to each other. The hood was placed over his head again and then they left the room without saying another word. Ray's panting turned into sobbing as he cried tears of relief, fear and utter humiliation, cathartically draining him of the tension that had built up since those two appeared in that corridor outside his classroom, three hours and a lifetime ago.

Mock execution, they called it, with the 'mock' meaning more than just pretend. Its purpose wasn't merely to frighten, but to debase and dehumanise, all the better to underline the present power balance. Ray was left tied there, dripping with his own urine, choking on snot and tears, aware that they could be returning any time for the real deal.

It was too early to feel anger or hatred. He was still shaking, still waiting for the bullets, still mourning the life that he thought was being taken away. He wanted to pace up and down the living room at two in the morning, holding Martin on his shoulder, his confused, colicky howls filling his ears. Under that hood, tied to that chair, he could now see what had been obscured by the fatigue and the stress, the sleepless nights, the hurried, solitary meals. He could see Martin a few months older, smiling, sitting up, crawling. He could see the look of recognition and excitement on his little face when his daddy walked in from school. He could see Ped Brown and Jason Murphy quietly getting on with some work once the new-teacher-baiting novelty had worn off. None of these things had been all that far from his grasp this morning, or last night at the airport, but he hadn't known what any of them were truly worth.

He did now.

LOADING MOD: STABLE CAREER
LOADING MAP: COMFORTABLE HOME [comfho.bsp]
LOADING POWER-UPS: STEADY INCOME
LOADING PLAYERS: LOVING WIFE
LOADING PLAYERS: HEALTHY BABY SON
CONNECTION INTERRUPTED
THE CONNECTION TO THE REAL LIFE™ SERVER WAS UNEXPECTEDLY TERMINATED. DO YOU WISH TO RECONNECT?
Yes/No.

deus nigellus ex machina

Simon stood at the door and looked in. Larry the little drummer boy was hunched over, lifeless on the seat, his hooded head slumped forward. It looked as though he'd been offed already, single tap to the base of the skull and a puddle under the chair. He should be so lucky, the cocky little prick. The puddle looked like it had been recently replenished, which was hardly surprising. They'd left him there a good couple of hours before the 'interrogation', and when he inevitably needed to go again, the poor diddums must have decided he'd nothing to lose. Not his dignity, anyway. Simon wished he could have been in on the grilling, but at this stage it would have jeopardised the mission. There'd be time for the satisfaction of a face-to-face revelation before the end. All good things to him who waits.

He heard footsteps at his back and looked round to see May standing at the end of the hallway, face tripping him. Simon sighed and closed the door. Have to keep the children happy.

'What?' he asked.

'A word,' May answered, nodding to the back door to indicate they should take it outside.

Please not technical problems, not at this stage.

Lydon and Matlock were near the door, standing next to Larry's car. They were arguing, each accusing the other of eating his lunch. It was a choice moment. Between them these two had killed more people than certain class-A drugs, and here they were trading abuse over a stolen Snickers. Nice to hear that they were still conducting it in English, right enough. It was good practice, though there was an element of self-protection about it, especially when tempers were raised. If someone was going to bear you a grudge, it didn't do to betray anything about your identity, and a hot-blooded resort to your native tongue could prove a costly giveaway.

May tramped past them, deliberately out of earshot. Not technical problems, then. Whine coming up. At such times, Simon found it wise to get his own question in first, start them off on the back foot.

'Is everything ready for the road?' he asked. If the answer was anything other than in the affirmative, May knew he could fuck off with his complaint, whatever it was.

'Packed, checked, good to go. Are you?'

'Ready? Yeah.'

'Sure? You don't want to look at our prisoner a little longer?'

Simon felt a chill pass through him like a rippling wave. He said nothing, opting instead for a hopefully inscrutable stare. Even a glib reply suddenly seemed interpretable as evasion.

'Who is he?'

'He's nobody.'

'So what are we doing with him?'

'You know what we're doing with him. The client has reason to believe that some information may have leaked. I thought we went over this.'

'That part, yes.'

'So what's your problem, Brian?'

'My problem, *Freddie*, is that there must be a simpler way of dealing with it. We seem to be taking a lot of unnecessary risks – all revolving around this Ash guy –

and I'm starting to wonder where your head is.'

Simon gritted his teeth. A show of irritation with May would be less suspicious than overdoing the serene patience. 'My head's fine, how's yours?'

'Mine's exposed and I'm starting to wonder why. Ash can identify me and Taylor. The school secretary too; I spoke to her twice.'

'You had the fake 'tache and Gregories, didn't you? She'll give the sketch artist a description of Groucho Marx, on the off-chance they ever get round to asking her.'

'And what about him?'

'He's not going to live to tell the tale. You know that.'

'So why weren't you in on the interrogation? Why's he got a bag over his head? What don't you want him to see?'

'He had to see you two's faces when you picked him up. It would be "unnecessary risk" if we let him see anyone else, wouldn't it?'

May was shaking his head, simmering.

'Why him? Specifically?'

'For fuck's sake, there's no big reason. He's respectable, a schoolteacher. We couldn't use just any idiot off the street.'

'Bollocks.'

'I see you made it through the video-only episodes then?'

'Eh?'

'*Brookside*. Bad language, Brian. Not normally allowed.'

'Don't change the subject.'

Simon looked him hard in the eye. 'I answered your question.'

'I heard you. He's nobody special. So if I put a bullet in his head right now, it would just be a matter of finding ourselves a replacement, yeah? That wouldn't bother you at all?'.

'Yes, it would bother me, because it would be a matter

of great inconvenience and further unfuckingnecessary risk.'

'You know him, don't you?'

'Oh, I see we're finally getting around to saying what's really on our minds. Do you actually want me to answer that question?'

May paused, took a breath. He knew what Simon was saying, the ramifications it implied. Personal information was highly volatile, and thus not shared and definitely not sought. What you knew about someone else could compromise you as much as – if not more than – it compromised him, not least because it could earn you a bullet in the skull. May put his palms up.

'If I had a personal agenda, I'd declare it,' Simon said. 'I'd owe you that.'

'No you wouldn't,' May replied. 'You'd owe us *that*.'

They both smiled. Mutual mistrust had a stability to it, sometimes the only common ground you could rely on.

'One last question,' May said, just as Simon was about to walk away. 'He mentioned a name. Simon Darcourt. Does that mean anything?'

Simon blinked, hoping to obscure any involuntary ocular reaction, the rest of his features in practised neutral expression. Since the airport, there must have been all sorts of confused notions stoating around Larry's baffled wee brain, and it had always been a possibility that he'd mention the name as he fished for explanations, but hearing it spoken aloud was still a jolt, particularly coming from the mouth of a comrade. It had been over three years since Simon heard anyone say it, the last being the TV news reporter covering his memorial service, which he'd watched in a hotel room less than five miles from his former home after taking in the ceremony incognito.

'Doesn't ring any bells. What did he say?'

'He asked if this had anything to do with Simon Darcourt.'

'Dunno. Maybe he's been fucking the guy's wife. What did you tell him?'

'Nothing.'

'Maybe you should have said yes – mess with his head all the more.'

'I'm not sure we could mess with his head any more without using a liquidiser.'

'Now there's a thought.'

They shared another smile. Crisis averted, boarders repelled.

'Come on, Brian, time for the soundcheck.'

May sat silently in the passenger seat, staring blankly at the passing scenery like a kid the first time he's been allowed up front. If he'd been a dog, he'd have stuck his head out the window. The silence was starting to grate. There was never a lot of small talk between any of them, for obvious reasons (they were hardly going to ask each other where they were going for their holidays), but on this trip there seemed to be a tension about their mutual reticence, a hangover from their discussion at the farmhouse. Maybe he was imagining it, or maybe May was just a little wrapped up in himself because they were getting close to showtime on their biggest ever gig. That's what Simon should have been worrying about too, but instead he was still bouncing their discussion around his mind, the words 'Simon Darcourt' continuing to echo in May's fake-but-improving Scouse accent.

He tried to remember May's counter-reaction, whether it suggested he'd seen anything in Simon's eyes when he mentioned the name. It was impossible to know, but worth bearing in mind, particularly given May's evident suspicions surrounding the LDB. Once he got it into his head that there was a connection between them, there were plenty of dangerous extrapolations that might follow on.

It had been an indulgence, one he thought he could afford, and one that was now too late to abandon. Whether or not May was bluffing when he threatened to put a bullet in the prisoner's brain, the drummer boy was now an integral part of the set-up. With May having made his accusation, Simon was saddled with following it through, because if he suddenly drilled the prisoner and gave the order to find a replacement, it was as good as a signed admission that May's speculation was on the money.

'Aw, fuck off.'

May turned his head, shaken from his trance by Simon's ejaculation.

'Arr, 'ey,' May grumbled, noticing the problem.

Simon slowed the Espace as they drew up behind a long line of vehicles crawling its way up the steep incline. The queue was caused by temporary traffic lights about a quarter of a mile ahead, alternating the use of one lane while the other remained closed so that two guys in hard-hats could read *The Sun* and scratch their balls without fear of being run over.

'How can there be a traffic jam?' May asked. 'We're in the middle of fucking nowhere.'

Simon had to bite back a response. Any time he got caught in a tailback, he felt every nerve stretch, every fibre tighten; not merely because of the frustration, but because it so vividly reminded him of Aberdeen. Every fucking morning and every fucking night he'd pootled along, doing horrible things to his clutch as he attempted to maintain an optimum speed of less than one mile an hour, in the interminable procession of SSCs travelling to and from Bridge of Don.

Given that it was such a piddling little backwater with over-optimistic delusions of mediocrity, the town – sorry, 'city' – planners had to be applauded for their achievement in creating one aspect of the place that did resemble modern metropolitan living. Despite a population of less than a quarter mill, they had nonetheless managed to engineer commuter traffic conditions rivalling the most congested cities on earth. This had been achieved through the simple but ingenious device of building the largest commuter dormitory suburb in Europe on the other side of the River Don from where all the aforementioned commuters' jobs were located. Fortunately, no-one had been careless enough to spoil the resultant effect by building a few decent-sized modern bridges, so approximately half of the city's travelling workforce was channelled across two structures originally built to let sheep pass three abreast. There had been a third bridge that Simon only learned about the day it closed, when he turned on the car radio to find out why that morning's tailback began outside his front door, rather than on the dual carriageway as usual. This third bridge had been on private ground, but had been open to the public until the land was sold to a housing developer, whose offer to hand it over gratis to the council was declined. The official explanation was that the structure would incur maintenance costs, but Simon suspected the real reason was that the council's transport convener had some kind of contest going with his counterpart in Mexico City, and this was going to give him the edge.

That hour it took to travel five miles every morning and every night was the only thing worse than work itself.

Every car was a hearse, stuck in that cortege, wending its way slowly towards the driver's own funeral. It was the time his circumstances most mercilessly mocked him, a perfect metaphor for this inescapable, lifeless, soulless, joyless procession. To work, from work, not only enslaved but tormented by this empty time when there was nothing to do but strain against the growing cramp and contemplate the nowhere your life was going.

Aberdeen, fucking Aberdeen – he just wasn't supposed to be there. He wasn't supposed to be doing this job, he wasn't supposed to be yoked with any of it. Aberdeen was for farmers and fishermen and fucking SSCs with no greater ambition for their lives than shiting out smaller versions of themselves and occasionally winning the Employee of the Month award at their mundane and meaningless jobs. It was the kind of place he was supposed to drive into, play a sell-out gig, go back to his hotel, get stocious, pick up one of the marginally less hefty local boilers, shove it in her mouth so he didn't have to listen to her stupid accent, kick her out, go to bed, get up and drive away again, all the time thanking fuck he was only passing through.

He was meant to be living in London; well, maybe New York, Berlin, Amsterdam or Paris by this time, but London was where he was supposed to finally get the right people together for his band. Down there he would have found people who were serious about their music, not a bunch of stupid wee boys wanting to play at pop stars in their dad's garage. University had been a major disappointment in that respect. Too many time-wasters, too many clowns who were more interested in grabbing a share of the limelight than playing a part in creating something special. Not one of them had the maturity to see past their own egos and notice true musical vision when it was right in front of them.

Maybe it was just the wrong time. Musical scenes often developed in cities through a fertile cross-pollination of ideas, influences and personnel, such as the Madchester phenomenon of the early Nineties, or the Bromley contingent that was an incestuous nucleus for The Banshees, The Ants, The Cure, The Creatures, Gen X, PiL and others. It had been just his shite luck to be looking for musical soulmates in Glasgow in the mid-1980s, when the Pied Piper traded in the woodwind for a jangly guitar and led the weak-minded masses down the path of infantile mediocrity.

Nobody cared about musicianship, innovation, structure, experimentation or stagecraft: all it took was three chords and a cheery melody and these fucking morons were getting indie record deals. Half of them could hardly play, and even those that could weren't interested in pushing any boundaries, just treading the same worn-out turf and justifying it with the usual deluded bleating about 'songs' and 'tunes' being the important thing. Any idiot could do what they were doing. A cheap guitar from the Barras, a practice amp, a copy of *The Best of The Byrds*, three like-minded fuckwit mates and you were away.

Any idiot? Every idiot. There were hundreds of them, not one with the self-awareness to realise that they all sounded the same and nothing they were doing was remotely original. The Pastels. The Boy Hairdressers. The BMX Bandits. The Close Lobsters. The Vaselines. Primal Scream, before someone told Bobby Gillespie that rock was trendy *this* month. The Shop Assistants. The Woodentops. His Latest Flame. Fruits of Passion. God, there were so fucking many of them, like fucking lice. It was horrible. All wearing their anoraks, singing songs about sweeties and strawberries and Kylie cunting Minogue.

Awash on that ocean of twee and insipid three-chord

pretendy-pop, it was no wonder he couldn't find anyone with the musical intelligence to understand what he was trying to do. He wrote his university years off, filed under 'Wrong place, wrong time', and set his sights on a more metropolitan future. He intended to head south and take whatever job would pay the bills, subsistence living while he honed his playing, developed his ideas and assembled the right personnel.

But that was reckoning without his dad dying a few weeks before his finals, the true state of the family finances emerging literally in the wake. With the onus on him and him alone to save his mum from losing the house and ending up in some council high-rise concentration camp, he was forced into the previously unthinkable endeavour of applying his degree in the job market.

He had undertaken a BSc in Geography and Earth Sciences because it was the subject he'd been best at (and symbiotically most interested in) at school, but there had been absolutely no vocational aspect to it. These days, he knew, university courses were increasingly focused on specific careers, whereas back then there was still an ethic of 'learning for its own sake', even if that did translate in practice into 'learning for the sake of annual metriculation and thus renewal of the cheap-drink season ticket that was student union membership'. His degree, like most, didn't specifically qualify him for much other than further study, but that hardly mattered because at no point had he ever really imagined his studies leading to a job. The term 'career' for him was going to be something measured in albums and tours, not appointments and promotions. And he didn't even *joke* about ending up a teacher, unlike those other sad bastards who could obviously see further down the tracks than they'd care to admit.

However, when he suddenly found himself having to join the eager hopefuls at the 'Milk Round', he was grateful that the substantial Geology part of his degree did open a few doors. Unfortunately, they were all situated on the front of grey granite buildings in 'Europe's Oil Capital'.

He had tried to look on the bright side. A proper job with proper wages meant that he'd be able to afford some decent kit, even after the slice he'd have to send south. Maybe he'd be surprised and find some willing musical collaborators up there, where they might be grateful to have someone among them with fresh ideas instead of all looking out for the next bandwagon to leap on. Besides, it would just be for a while, until he could get things on an even keel.

Yeah right.

'Just for a while': Death's opening chat-up line in His great seduction, before He drugged you with soporific comforts, distracted you with minor luxuries and ensnared you with long-term payment plans. Join the Rat Race 'just for a while'. Concentrate on your career 'just for a while'. Move in with your girlfriend 'just for a while'. Find a bigger place, out in the burbs 'just for a while'. Lie down in that wooden box 'just for a while'.

The light wasn't quite ready to fade by the time they arrived, so Simon pulled the Espace off the road under cover of some trees and waited. An inventory passed some of the time, though he knew May's equipment-check was merely an exercise in going through the motions. He wouldn't have left the farmhouse if he wasn't one hundred per cent sure everything was operational. Inflating the mini-dinghy killed another few minutes, after which there was more uncomfortable silence, punctuated occasionally by redundant questions confirming technical and logistical details they had already long since worked out, serving only to emphasise the growing tension. It would pass when they had work to do, but it was hard going in the meantime. By the time darkness finally began to fall, Simon was about five minutes off starting a game of 'I Spy'.

They crossed the road and got changed into their wetsuits at the waterside, hitting the floor any time a set of headlights approached. The first one came by when they were both down to their underwear.

'If somebody stops, we'll have to pretend we're shagging, okay?' Simon told May. He looked back, confused and horrified until Simon laughed to let him know he was kidding.

'I'd die of the shame. Rather go to jail,' May said.

'Didn't know you were so uptight that way.'

'I'm not. It's getting seen with someone as ugly as you that I'd never live down.'

'Aye, right. You couldn't pull me in your dreams, pal.'

The smiles were wiped off both their faces when they had to get wet before pulling their rubbers on, northern European waters being less than inviting on a September evening.

'Next job has to be in the Med,' May muttered.

'That's a given.'

May placed the plastic crate containing his gear into the inflatable and pushed it away from the shore as he waded in behind it. The bridge was a two-hundred-yard swim away, on the other side of a small outcrop which masked the moonlit-glinting waves from the road. It spanned two spiked inlets that otherwise would have forced the road against the steep hillside, the waters plunging deep only a few feet from the edge, following the same sharp gradient from the summit to the abyss. The shoreline was jagged through much of the long, snaking, narrow valley, scars of the glacier that had carved it.

Unlike most of the rudimentary and frequently ancient pontoons you'd expect to find in such rural spots, this one was a sturdy and modern affair, one of several erected on this route to accommodate the abnormally large vehicles used in constructing the target. The bridges had to be built so that *it* could be built. Kind of appropriate then, that demolishing one should be a necessary overture.

They worked slowly and carefully, torchlight supplementing the rippling reflected illuminations of what might accurately be described as a Bomber's Moon. May asked for tools and components like he was the surgeon, Simon supplying them like the admiring assistant. Water splashed around their waists, the inflatable bobbing gently next to them, lapping sounds echoing around the sheltered inlet. The buzz was growing, and it felt good, really good. He'd been right. The tension was gone, transmuted into exquisite adrenaline by the purifying sacrament of action. It was always exciting, always, but this one . . . this one felt special. This one felt like a homer, with a personal edge to the thrill that he hadn't experienced since his amateur days.

Back then there was this sense of infinite possibility, the feeling that he could hold the power of life or death over anyone: from the prick who'd just ruined his day to an unknown face in a magazine. And acting on that impulse was an exhilaration that started in your toes and ended in the stars. Better than sex? *Please*. He'd had wanks that were better than sex; he'd had shites that were better than sex. It was obviously the 'ultimate experience' yardstick of people who didn't get much. Oh make no mistake, sex could be good, it could be great, it could even be worth some of the conversations you had to endure before you got it; and then it was over, and you just wanted to be somewhere else, or more accurately you wanted *her* to be somewhere else. The LDB, in one of his more lucid and perceptive moments, compared it to the curse of the mortal condition: in sex (for the male at least), what you work towards, strive towards, crave and desire is in itself the end. Death comes in spurts.

Standing on a stage, facing a mic, hands on an electric guitar, singing a song you'd written – even with three numpties backing you up and a hundred fucking yahoos out front – was *way* better than the best sex he'd ever had. Why else would The Stones be touring into their dotage when they had enough money, power and kudos to have a different sixteen-year-old sliding up and down their poles each hour, every hour for the rest of their lives? But nothing – nothing – could compare with the feeling that electrified every molecule in his body when he was doing what he now knew he did best.

The first time was . . . well, the first time; better than sex, but not unlike it. Same as that first shag, it was unforgettable in every detail but hardly a masterclass in panache or technique, and too clouded by fear, anxiety and the consequences of it going wrong to actually be enjoyable. In his case it was also too personal, too coloured by emotion for the physicality of the act itself to transcend its deeper meaning. The best sex, like the best killing, was with someone who didn't mean everything to you, but didn't mean nothing either; though as a matter of preference he would always choose the latter. Too personal and it could feel a little squalid: rank with the self-disgust that followed getting what you had wanted just a little too much. When it was utterly impersonal you could concentrate more on the moment and your own desires rather than worrying about what the other person was feeling. But it was at its best when it was just personal enough.

Like fine wines, it was difficult to choose a favourite: so many different flavours, nuances, memories, associations, and the fickle palate could revise its evaluations at each time of asking. However, there were certain vintages that would always make the list, such as Jeremy Watson-Bellingham. That one brought a smile to his face every time. He'd deserved to die just for the fucking name alone, but there was more, so much more. It wasn't murder, it was a selfless, public-spirited civic gesture that in a more civilised society would have earned Simon some initials after his name, as opposed to a life sentence.

'Jeremy Watson-Bellingham. JWB. Judgement. Wisdom. Brains. Jump With the Ball. Job? Work Better. And that's what I'm going to help all of you do.'

Tit.

'Your name, sir?'

'Simon. Simon Darcourt.'

'Simon Darcourt. SD. Stand Defiant. Strength and Diligence. Super Dynamic. And yours, madam?'

'Helen Woods.'

'Helen Woods. HW. Hard Worker. Heading Way up. *Hopefully We* can achieve great things together this weekend. All right!'

Tit. Tit. Tit.

JWB. Jobbie. Wank. Bawhair.

The occasion: Sintek Energy's annual conference weekend. The location: Craig Dearg Hydro Hotel, Deeside. The Tit: a management consultant and 'Motivational Guru', into whose hands the company had delivered its staff for an inhumane twenty-four hours, along with fairly unambiguous impressions of what would happen to anyone who didn't participate with maximum enthusiasm.

The introductions were just the beginning of the ordeal,

his 'preparation for self-empowerment through harnessing just a tiny part of the power within the self': viz, glib wee phrases that abbreviated to more or less the same letters as your name. As 'preparations' went, it ranked alongside having Vaseline smeared liberally around your ring by a guy with a sack full of ferrets.

'Initials. Beginnings. We're beginning. We're initialising. Initialising the system, prepping for ignition, counting down to blast-off. And that system is *you*.'

The guy got paid a fucking mint for this.

Throughout one of the longest and most excruciating afternoons anyone ever endured without anaesthetic, he subjected them to an interminable, audio-visually enhanced lecture, the crux of which appeared to be that greater dynamism and efficiency lay via the simple expedient of using new verbs that had previously led an unmolested existence as nouns. Simon had previously heard words such as 'action' and 'showcase' bashed forcibly into this unintended use like square pegs through round holes, but had until then been unaware that one could 'simultaneously desktop multiple homogenised throughput channels' (take more orders), or even 'striplight retro-referenced identifiers' (no idea, but the Tit was looking at the girl who booked ad space, if that helped).

Even dinner provided no respite. Before they could all head off for a change of clothes and a desperate ramraid on the mini-bar, the Tit produced a suitcase from underneath his table and dished out these huge sparkly silver wigs. He ordered that they be worn from then until midnight as a 'team-building exercise', though he declined to elaborate on how a sense of comradeship and a commonality of purpose was likely to be engendered by spending the evening looking like a twat or picking strands of tinsel out of your dinner.

When they sat down to eat, all obediently bewigged like reluctant delegates to a Glam Rock convention, they discovered placecards between the cutlery, bearing what looked worryingly like lyrics. Sure enough, before any of them got even so much as a sniff of a prawn cocktail, JWB, Jumbo Wig Bastard, was demanding they all stand to attention and join in 'the Sintek power-chant', accompanied by a beatbox routed through the dining room's PA system.

'Okay one-two-three. Sin-tek En-er-gy!
There for you and me. Sin-tek En-er-gy!
Oil from the North Sea. Sin-tek En-er-gy!
Okay one-two-three. Sin-tek En-er-gy!'

Seriously.

And it got worse. They were told to turn over their place-cards, finding the reverse blank, and instructed to each compose a rap by the end of the meal. Following the post-prandial coffees, the chanting was to be reprised, with each chorus followed by an individual contribution, cued by the circulation of a cordless mic. Then just in case anyone was misled as to how hideous it was going to be, Jazzmaster White Boy pumped up the volume and gave them an example.

'Well here I am, my name is Je-re-mee,
And my game is enhanced ee-fish-en-see.
I'm the man with the plan, sim-ply the best,
And I'm teachin' you the secrets of success.
So follow my lead, har-ness the power,
And this could be your finest hour.
Okay one-two-three. *Ev'rybody!* Sin-tek En-er-gy!'

To fully appreciate the impact, you really had to be able to see this balding little fatso, sporting the only syrup in the room more embarrassing than the proliferating silver ones, and to hear his nasally supercilious public school accent. Also, for a guy undoubtedly pulling down six figures, you'd have thought the cunt could afford some deodorant.

There were people at Simon's table praying for food poisoning. The meal wasn't up to much anyway, but it tasted of nothing with their thoughts so occupied by the coming horror and their appetites so ruined by the ordure of the task in hand.

The ordeal itself was a bit like being a female prisoner-of-war during a systematic mass-rape. You wanted to avert your eyes and cover your ears so as not to witness your fellow victim's humiliation, already aware of how hard it was going to be to look at each other when this was over.

The Tit got them all clapping their hands as the chant started up again – Okay one-two-three CLAP. Sin-tek En-er-gy CLAP – then repeated his own rap before passing the mic on at the next chorus. The first up was an utter fanny from the personnel department, Grant Hughes, who (difficult as this was to believe) actually made it worse for everybody by being enthusiastic, swaying as he, er, rapped, and throwing in the occasional 'yeah'. Mainly, though, the verses were delivered in mortified mumbling, eyes fixed firmly on the placecard, small smiles of relief on each face as the mic was lifted from his or her hands. Alice McGhee from sales burst into tears one line into her rap, dropped the mic on the table and ran from the room, too distressed to remember she was still wearing the silver wig.

Simon's own contribution was instantly purged from his memory, though nothing could erase the residual sense of embarrassment and boiling fury. It was easier to banish the words than the emotions, and to this day he could still feel a tightening in his guts any time he recalled standing there in front of everybody, sparkly locks bouncing around his face and that fucking beatbox thumping in his ears. And etched permanently in his memory was the sight of Just Won't Bugger-off dancing next to him, jabbing the air with a side-on fist like he must have seen on VH1, going 'ooh ooh' in the background and 'Aw yeah!' after every line.

Obviously, he had to die.

Simon found out where the Tit, or rather his company, M Power, were going to be torturing SSC wage-slaves over the coming weeks, setting his sights on a date in Glasgow a fortnight hence. He had long since sorted himself out with a new credit card under a false name, and booked himself into the hotel that was hosting this latest crime against humanity in the name of ViaGen Pharmaceuticals. Simon had also, by this point, acquired a gun and a silencer, but where was the fun in that? The appropriate tools of the trade for this occasion were therefore purchased at Tam Shepard's joke shop in Queen Street, and at M&S round the corner.

Simon checked in after doing his shopping, popping his head round the door of the hotel's main conference suite to confirm that Jumped-up Wee Bawbag was in da house. Sure enough, there he was, coordinating the 'raft game' that had been Sintek Energy's pleasure on the Sunday morning. It involved everybody kneeling down in a square forma-tion, pretending to row an imaginary raft down an imagi-nary stream while he threw figurative obstacles into their way: 'the dead tree trunk of indecision', 'the boulders of complacency', 'the floating corpse of a wee baldy fat guy'.

Simon treated himself to an excellent à la carte meal in the hotel restaurant, the leftovers of which would probably go into the mass-catering table d'hôte in the function suites.

After that he retrieved his briefcase from his room and had a seat in one of the public lounges, close enough to the ViaGen suite to hear the rap get underway. Through a gap between the partially open double doors he could see silver wigs bobbing to the beat, and the repetition even extended to a distraught female exiting at speed shortly after, make-up streaked with tears, giant pom-pom still stuck on her head.

Simon waited until he saw the Tit heading for the lift, content that his work for the evening was done and that the process of empowerment was well underway. If it was anything like the Sintek do, now that the annoying little fucker had vacated the room, everyone left would rapidly become too empowered to stand up. He gave it a few minutes, then went to one of the lobby telephones and asked to be put through to the Tit's room.

'Hello, Mr Watson? . . . Bewington?'

'Watson-Bellingham,' he replied testily.

'My apologies. It's the handwriting on this thing. This is Guest Services. We've just received a package for you by courier.'

'Oh, right. I'll come down and—'

'That's not necessary, sir. I'll send someone up with it right away. You're in room 432, yes?'

'Ye . . . No. 432? I'm in 327.'

'327? Are you sure?'

'Well it's my room, isn't it?'

'I'm sorry, you're absolutely right. 432's flashing on the switchboard here, got me confused. Your package will be there in two minutes.'

'Thank you.'

'A pleasure, sir.'

He took the predictably deserted stairs to the third floor,

avoiding any potential witnesses in the lifts, then checked the corridor was clear before knocking on door 327. The Tit answered in his trousers and semmit. Simon could hear water running in the bathroom behind him.

'Jeremy Watson-Bellingham?'

'That's me. JWB. Just Wunning a Bath. Ahahaha. You have something for me?'

'Oh yes.'

Simon stuck his gun into the Tit's mouth and pushed him backwards into the room, kicking the door closed behind him with his heel.

'Any noise you make will be your last, you understand?'

The Tit nodded rapidly, eyes bulging almost out of his skull in fear and surprise.

'You cooperate and this will all be over in no time, okay?'

More eager nodding. He was also, Simon realised, gesturing towards his wallet, which lay on the tabletop next to the TV.

'Oh no, don't worry. I'm not a thief.'

The sad sack actually looked relieved.

Simon flipped open his briefcase and removed a pair of tights and a small plastic Teletubby. He withdrew the silencer from JWB's mouth and replaced it with the doll, then secured it by tying the tights behind his head.

'Say "Ah".'

'Mmmff mmm.'

'That's perfect. Now, get undressed.'

The Tit furrowed his brow, possibly thinking about defiance. Simon kicked him in the balls, dropping him to the floor, then knelt down next to him.

'You are going to cooperate, right? I'm not going to have to do that again, am I, JWB? Just Walloped Bollocks?'

The Tit shook his head, tears leaking from both eyes. He

climbed tentatively to his feet and removed his clothes as quickly as his throbbing nads would allow, stopping at his Y-fronts. Simon gestured with the gun, and they came off too.

'Very good. Now put these on.'

He handed the Tit a pair of stockings and sussies, the look on the guy's face getting more and more priceless with each development. Simon turned off the bath taps while the Tit sat on the edge of the bed and pulled on the stockings, the poor mite struggling a little with the suspenders, which were at ninety degrees to the correct position.

'Rose goes in the front, big guy,' Simon told him, indicating the embroidered flower currently at his side.

'Mmm,' he said, which might even have been 'Thanks'.

With the suspenders now attached, Simon sat him back down on the bed, then handed him a set of false breasts and a lacy bra to contain them.

'Jumbo Wobbly Boobs. Even bigger than the ones you've got already.'

By this point, the guy was becoming so baffled that he almost forgot to be scared. He pulled on the falsies but fumbled unsuccessfully with the bra until Simon got him to turn around and did it up one-handed, pressing the gun into his neck in case he attempted to self-empower his way out of the situation.

'Gorgeous. Just needs one final touch now. Can you guess what?'

Evidently he couldn't. Simon opened the Tit's suitcase, resting by the bed on a folding rack, and produced one of his vital team-building components.

'Joke Wig, Big-boy!'

The Tit closed his eyes resignedly. If he hadn't been gagged he'd have let out a sigh of relief. He knew what it was about now, and probably assumed it was a vengeful prank. Probably thought the gun wasn't real either. He got to his feet unprompted, perhaps thinking he was about to be paraded through the ViaGen function suite. Time to disabuse him of that notion.

'Where you going? Sit down and face the window until I tell you otherwise.'

JWB complied, adopting a pitiful slumped posture on the edge of the double bed, his chin almost resting on the false funbags.

'Do you recognise me?'

The Tit shook his head.

'Not surprising. You must do this every week. Every day.'

The Tit nodded.

'Sintek Energy?'

He nodded again, more enthusiastically this time.

'Simon Darcourt. Strength and Diligence. Super Dynamic.'

More nodding, but Simon could tell it rang no bells.

Simon reached into his briefcase for a long silk scarf and used it to tie the Tit's hands behind his back. Then he took another one and passed it around his neck.

'You've guessed what's going on, haven't you?'

The Tit nodded.

'You humiliated me, so I'm going to humiliate you, right?'

More nodding, trying to look as humble and contrite as he could. Behind the Tit's back, out of sight, Simon looped the scarf into a slipknot and attached the free end to the headboard.

'In front of all those people at the conference, right?' he said, walking around in front of his prisoner, nodding as he spoke. 'That would be fair, wouldn't it?'

The Tit kept nodding, Simon too, smiling until he could tell the Tit was trying to smile also. Then he suddenly ceased and began shaking his head. JWB stopped nodding and looked up, concerned.

'Simon Darcourt. SD. Self-Debasement. Squalidly Dressed. Secret Disgrace.' He grabbed both of the Tit's ankles and pulled, lifting him off the bed until the slipknot tightened around his neck. The Tit kicked and thrashed wildly, but all his efforts merely further tightened the noose, allowing Simon to stand back and watch the rest.

'Sexual Disaster. Senseless Death. Suicide? Dunno.'

He didn't always have to kill to get the rush. Just knowing he could was sometimes juice enough, like the aforementioned face in the magazine. He and Alison were going through what in their relationship constituted a good patch, in that she managed to go almost a week without her face tripping her or making mention of 'the future', her catch-all euphemism for marriage, mortgage, babies and a long, slow lingering suburban death. In an attempt to further prolong this unaccustomed cordiality (and hopefully to effect some Pavlovian behavioural reinforcement), he decided to spring for dinner, bed and breakfast at a hotel on Speyside. It was while they were sipping their after-dinner espressos in the terribly-civilised-don't-you-know drawing room that Alison picked up a magazine from the coffee table and introduced Simon to the unique delights of the publishing phenomenon that was *Country Life*. More specifically, amid the offers-over-ten-million property ads and the features on how to cause bigger tailbacks on B-class roads, she drew his attention to the publication's equivalent of page three. There were half a dozen issues to be perused, and each one featured what could only be described as 'the willing sperm receptacle of the month'. The format was a full-page photo showcasing each puppy-fatted, fertile aristocratic offspring, accompanied by a caption that was all but selling her for pedigree breeding (no proles need apply).

'Ariadne Winston-Havers McPherson, 18, pictured here at the family estate of Beinn Ardraig, Morayshire, atop Biffy, her favourite stallion. Ariadne is the younger daughter of Sir Douglas McPherson and Lady Marjorie Winston-Havers McPherson. Sir Douglas leads the Glen Ardraig hunt, with which Ariadne proudly rides, and all members of the family are keen supporters of the Countryside Alliance. Ariadne has just completed her final term at l'Ecole de Mme Aimet in Lausanne, and will be travelling for a year before taking up a place at St Andrews.'

But not if Simon had anything to do with it.

The power-rush was incredible, knowing what he could do, working out geography, methods, probable dates. It lit him up like a Christmas tree, seeming to animate every cell in his body, and as for his libido, *well* . . .

'What's got into you?' Alison had asked gratefully, around two a.m., as she felt him get hard *again* after two prolonged, sweaty, animalistic fucks.

'Must have been the oysters.'

'We didn't have any oysters.'

'I don't know. The country air.'

After the weekend, though, he found that he just couldn't be arsed. Logistically, it was too much of a hassle, and the weather that time of year was too miserable for what would almost certainly be an outdoors job. The idea had been exciting, though. Like going on holiday, as they said, planning and anticipation was half the fun, and in his case he could ditch his plans and go on another 'holiday' any time.

226

He missed that aspect of the amateur days: not just the thrill of acting on impulse, but the constant awareness that he could. Sure, he knew he could still off people on an individual basis, but in practice he was usually just too busy with bigger projects, and besides, he didn't feel the same impulses these days. It seemed a little beneath him, in fact, as though he didn't have quite so much to prove any more. Sign of maturity, he supposed, and of moving on to larger concerns. It was natural that he'd get a little nostalgic for the way he used to work, the times he used to have, but that didn't mean he would swap what he had now to go back there.

There had been a couple of larger-scale operations undertaken for his own motives, and consequently financed out of his own pocket. The only true cost, however, was unnecessary exposure, and the nagging concern of stepping over the barrier into the realm of the clients. The money wasn't missed; if that had been his motive, he could have retired ages ago, but to do what? The same shit as moron lottery millionaires? *This* was living, and that was why it was worth the risk.

Strasbourg was the first, an irresistible riposte to Alain Beloc after he made his *'route de vitesse entre les cours de chaque nation'* remark, which translated roughly to 'come and have a go if you think you're hard enough'. Beloc was coincidentally Simon's MEP since he moved to Draguinan, a fact that should have escaped his politically indifferent eyes but for the bearded little egotist's relentless self-publicity. Sad to relate, the bastard did get re-elected, though he lost his crime-fighting remit, Simon having proven more than hard enough.

He'd been able to justify it to himself as a marketing venture; an ebullient mission statement, if you like. But there was no such business mitigation about Dresden. That had been purely personal, probably too much so, hence his unease at the memory.

They deserved it. There was absolutely no fucking question about that. German Nazi cunts. A squad of them had machine-gunned his grandfather and all of his captured comrades in some godforsaken French forest. Two generations later, a bunch of their pathetic wannabe progeny had given Simon a doing on Sauchiehall Street, on his way home from seeing The Chameleons. Admittedly he had provoked them by being on his own, something the fuckers could never resist, and by the even more inflammatory act of having some dress sense, which must have been like waving fillet steak in the face of the starving. He'd always hated skinheads anyway, even before they sent him to Casualty. They were below vermin; cockroaches. At least vermin had some guile. The entire movement was an exercise in empowering the gormless, amassing specimens so devoid of personal creativity that they were delighted to shed any residual semblance of individuality in order to perpetuate the delusion that they were part of something.

He imagined the recruiting ads:

'Is the burden of independent thought wearing you down? Do you dread the indecision that awaits every time you open your wardrobe? Are you embarrassed by your reticence when you hear other people discuss current affairs, music, relationships, etcetera? Don't worry, you're not alone. Help is just a pair of clippers away! We've helped thousands of sad losers avoid confronting their loneliness and inadequacy, and we can do the same for you. We'll tell you what to wear. We'll tell you what to think. We'll tell you what music to listen to. And most importantly, we'll bring you together with lots of people exactly the same as yourself – it's just like having friends!'

Like cockroaches, they were an extremely primitive and disgusting species whose evolution had stopped aeons ago, but not before robustly equipping them for stubborn survival no matter how far the world moved on and their cultural environment changed. When was the last time anyone saw a mod, a punk or even a football casual? Exactly. But these bastards simply refused to die out. Chances were, after a nuclear war or a collision with an asteroid, the first creature to emerge from the rubble would be wearing eighteen-hole Docs, drainpipe jeans and a green Harrington jacket.

In mainland Europe (where else?) they were actually on the increase, with the former East Germany proving an extremely fertile spawning ground. The German government had officially made denial of the Holocaust a crime, partly as a response to this growing chorus of morons. The neo-Nazis had become fed up with having no answer when the Final Solution was thrown at them as the ultimate and inevitable consequence of their philosophy, so taking their cue from a three-year-old loudly singing 'lalala' with his hands over his ears, they had come up with the ingenious riposte of saying it never happened.

A skinhead 'band' (i.e. four arseholes, three chords, two guitars and a fuzzbox) calling themselves Kristallnacht had been charged under the new law due to the lyrical content of their album, a meisterwerk presumably committed to vinyl using some nascent audio technology that prevented drool from shorting the recording equipment. To raise legal funds for their forthcoming courtcase, they organised a benefit gig in Dresden. They called in sympathetic favours to get free use of the venue, free PA hire, volunteer security and bar staff etcetera. Inspired by this rallying round and sense of communal purpose, Simon drove all the way from the Côte d'Azur to supply them with a dry ice machine too. He and Deacon (Gary Moore to his Phil Lynott on that gig) turned up in an authentically fucked-looking van and just lugged the gear into the hall before the soundcheck. Nobody asked any questions, other than the brain-donor in charge of the lighting rig, who was like a kid on Christmas morning and only wanted to know which button to press to see the magic smoke.

The official death-toll was fifty-five, including, entertainingly, all four members of the band. Less satisfying was the fact that the media coverage pretty much unanimously glossed over the irony of the means of execution, thus blowing the punchline somewhat. Surely just one 'Nazis gassed at Holocaust denial benefit' wasn't too much to ask in return for all that time and effort, not to mention cash. Nerve agent, he now knew, is not bloody cheap. Like most materials in this business, it didn't cost much to manufacture, but the ancillary and logistical fees jacked up the price no end by the time it made it into your hands.

To this day he remained unsure whether it had been worth it, which probably meant it hadn't. It had been an unqualified indulgence, and as such left him with mixed feelings, like the biliousness that might follow pigging out on nothing but cream cakes. Actually, maybe a better comparison was how he'd felt waking up next to some of the mouthy slappers he'd prodded in his uni days: the physical pleasure and the notched bedpost tempered by slight disgust at his own indiscipline and a tiny fear of having given something of himself away. Lust narrowed your perspective until you were only looking forwards at one thing, and the more you lunged towards it, the less you checked your six.

He remembered wishing he hadn't put the RB cards inside the dry ice machines, afraid he had thrown the authorities a bone in admitting authorship of an attack that no organisation would be claiming ultimate responsibility for. Even as he placed the calling cards, there had been doubts, but not doubts enough to stop him. Any hesitancy had been overcome by an irresistible desire to imprint his identity on what was essentially an act of vengeance, something only half accomplished if the avenger could not reveal himself to the vanquished.

In essence, he was trying to kill Frank Morris again. Same thing, arguably, as when he had his fun with Jeremy Watson-Bellingham. Morris never knew why, never knew who. He never endured that richly deserved purgatory of regret, never got to plead forgiveness, piss his pants and beg for a mercy that would not come. And what Simon was mature enough to understand now was that nothing could change that.

'You about done yet?'

May was displaying his tediously reliable aversion to parting with his work. He always seemed to fuss around his fixtures for an inexplicable length of time after the charges were in place, making minor adjustments or, as in this case, testing and retesting the transmission signal.

'Sometimes I wonder if you've got a subconscious desire to be around your little creations when they go off.'

May ignored him, which was also reliable. He didn't let anything distract him, which Simon had found to be a common trait among people who handled explosives; those who didn't share it presumably not enjoying long careers.

Simon's first question was fairly rhetorical. The fannying-about phase signalled the imminent (all things being relative) completion of May's work. It was time to give the signal.

Simon steadied his footing in the water and turned around, opening the waterproof zip-pocket where his cellular was stashed. He heard the splash of sudden movement at his back and turned around to see May levelling a Beretta Jetfire. Fucker had stashed a pocket blowpipe in his wetsuit and was about ten degrees and four milliseconds away from having a point-blank lock between Simon's eyes.

Simon bent one knee, dropping his centre of gravity and moving his torso half a metre to the side, at the same time throwing a forearm upwards to deflect May's aim. The cellular spun away and plopped into the drink. May, having leaned forwards slightly, stumbled and lost his footing as his arm was knocked to the side. Simon gripped May's wrist and pivoted, stepping back with his free foot. The action released May's grip on the gun and flipped him off his feet into the water. As he fell backwards he lashed out with his left foot and caught Simon in the chest. The blow wasn't strong, but the spray blinded him, and when he blinked his eyes clear, he could see only the moon's reflection in the dark waters.

Having initially got hold of May's Beretta by its short barrel, he wrapped his fingers around the handle and cupped his left hand around the trigger-guard, keeping his elbows bent as he trained it directly ahead. May could figure a way of blowing up Mount Everest if you paid him enough, but his small-arms skills barely extended beyond knowing which end to point with.

Simon waited, quieting his own breath as he listened out for movement. May had to come up for air eventually, even if he was already heading back to where they'd left their wheels. He scanned the surface, looking for ripples, bubbles, a surge, anything.

When movement finally came, he heard it before he saw it, coming as it did from his back. The sly bastard had gone behind him right away and then waited for his moment. This time it was Simon who was caught off-balance, turning too close to May's upward-lunging body and allowing him to get a knife to his throat before Simon could aim the gun at his assailant's head. He could, however, jam it into his ribs, just below the heart.

May wanted to talk. Simon knew this because otherwise, right now they would both be dying.

'Something on your mind, Brian old chap?' Simon whispered.

'You were going to kill me. That was on my mind.'

'When?'

'Just now.'

'Well correct me if I'm wrong, but you're the one who came out here weighed down with stashed weapons. What else you got there, a fucking bazooka?'

'You never know when someone might decide you're expendable.'

'Why would I want to kill you?'

'Who the fuck is Ash, Freddie?'

'Oh Christ, not this again.'

'Who is he?'

'What do you want me to say? Do you want me to tell you something about him that would compromise us both? That way I *would* have a reason to kill you.'

'I think my curiosity was reason enough. You're lying and you're jumpy.'

'*I'm* jumpy? I'm not the one who—'

'You're the one who's lying. I asked a reasonable question

233

back at HQ and you cacked your pants. There's something you don't want me to know. Fair do's. But I don't want a bullet in the head because of what you're *afraid* I know.'

'I'm not afraid you know anything. For fuck's sake, how many times?'

'So why bring the gun?' May demanded.

'What gun? This is yours.'

'You had a gun.'

'I . . . Oh for God's sake. Is that what this was about? I was going for my mobile, to give the all-clear.'

'Garbage. Where is it?'

'It's in the water, and it ain't coming back, thanks to you.'

'So I guess we'll never know.'

May increased the pressure on his blade. Simon responded with the Beretta. Their eyes remained locked on each other, barely blinking.

'Can I ask you one question, Brian?'

'Fire away,' May said, his stare intensifying to convey that the pun was intended.

'Do you think I know enough about explosives to pull off MDK?'

May thought about it and smiled.

'Negative.'

'Exactly. So what do you say we back off, slowly?'

'If I can ask a question too.'

'Sure. Take a stab.'

'Who is Ash? Make some stuff up, tell me to keep my nose out of it, but just don't tell me he's nobody, because we both know that's bullshit.'

Simon withdrew the gun and placed both hands in the air, stepping back carefully. Ostensibly a gesture of compliance, it was also a means of buying time. He understood what May was saying. It was the fault of both and neither of them that the Ash issue had got out of hand, but one way or another, it had to be put to bed. Telling him it was none of his business wouldn't do that, as the festering speculation would only continue. A lie would have to be good, while the truth might work as a bluff, May assuming it to be fabricated.

A lie, the truth, which one should he use? He opted for a mixture of both.

'I owe him,' Simon said, placing the pistol down on the inflatable raft, eyes locked on May to make sure he would do the same with his blade. 'I knew him a long time ago, when he was a student. Not here, before your wheels start whirring. He did an overseas year. You'll understand if I don't specify where.'

'I knew it. You're playing with fire, and we're all holding sticks of dynamite. What's this about?'

'That part *is* none of your business. There was a girl involved, you don't need to know the rest.'

'Vengeance is for your spare time. You don't bring it to work.'

'I didn't plan it, Brian. I saw him at the airport when I was here on reconnaissance last month. Bang, there he was, just standing there. What were the fucking odds? We made eye contact. I don't think he recognised me, but that's not something we like to leave to chance, is it? So when the word came through that Mopoza feared a leak, I figured if we had to do him anyway . . .'

'Happy little coincidence for you.'

'Well, when you kill as many people as I do, it kind of skews the odds. Anyway, if I really had a hard-on for settling my score with this guy, do you think he'd still have been alive to show up at that airport?'

May flared his nostrils. He was losing his stomach for the debate, at long fucking last. 'Point taken.'

'Good. Don't suppose you've got a phone handy, amid your wetsuit arsenal?'

'In the crate. Now tell me one last thing.'

'Jesus Christ.'

Simon turned his back and reached into the box. He knew what was coming and didn't want eye contact, even in the half-light.

'This Darcourt guy he mentioned . . .'

'No idea.' Simon located May's phone and flipped it open, speed-dialling Taylor as he turned back around. 'I mean, I can make some shit up if you want,' he added, smiling.

May rolled his eyes and held up his palms. Enough.

Taylor answered after four rings. 'Ready, Freddie?' he asked.

'Roger, Roger. Gig confirmed. Tour truck good to go?'

'Roger.'

'Good. And Roger?'

'Yeah?'

'Is the dressing room prepared?'

'Roger.'

'Okay. Give the groupie his backstage pass.'

'Roger. Oh, and Freddie?'

'Uh-huh?'

'Can you name a rock band without anyone called Roger in it?'

'Of course. Dozens.'

'Well, bear that in mind next time. Roger and out.'

dogging it: the downside

'I'm burstin' for a pish.'

'Again?'

'It's been hours, Lexy.'

'Has it fuck. It just feels like hours 'cause we're still stuck in here.'

'Well it's how it feels in ma bladder that matters, innit?'

'Your ain fault for drinkin' that much ginger.'

'Aw gies a brek. I'm startin' tae taste pish in the back ay ma throat, it's that far up.'

Though he'd used it plenty of times, Lexy had not previously understood why the phrase 'shiting yourself' was used to describe being afraid. He now knew that this was because he had never experienced true fear. Fear up until this morning had been what you felt when you turned up at the volcanic Mr Fennell's class and suddenly remembered you'd forgotten to do your Geography homework; or the sensation when some swine accurately deduced that you fancied a particular girl and then threatened to tell her. These were tinglings, at most that washing-machine feeling in the pit of your stomach. What he had felt in the back of that truck today, however, was the spin cycle, and he was very grateful for having had a major dump prior to his dental appointment, or else the smell might have given them away.

Being desperate for a pee, on the other hand, had actually been a good thing, because if that was all he could think about, then at least it took his mind off everything else. Eventually, however, they'd both had to find some relief before an involuntary puddle betrayed their location.

After the truck stopped and the cars were unloaded, it had been ages before they ventured to have a keek out from behind the blankets. Every time either of them was about to chance it, there would be another noise close by: people walking up into the container or voices passing outside, mostly English, with one Scot and a few foreign. It sounded like there was a lot of loading going on: items being carried in, sometimes by two men at a time, going by the voices; heavy too, from the grunting and straining. Other articles were on wheels, but still required some noisily committed pushing to get them up the ramp and into position. Lexy was imagining them being at the back of Tesco's or somewhere, picturing squeaky-wheeled pallets and stacks of heavy cartons. Whatever it contained, it sounded like a major delivery.

Every time he'd heard an approach, Lexy felt his guts turn to mush as it seemed only a matter of time before they were found out. Men had stood close enough to the pile of blankets for him to hear their breathing, which required him and Wee Murph to silence theirs. Fortunately, this was something he could do without holding his breath, a trick learned playing hide-and-seek-in-the-dark at his cousin William's house. Quiet as he could keep his mouth, there were nonetheless moments when his heart seemed to beat loud enough to be audible from outside. The worst time was when one of the men began grabbing blankets from the pile and throwing them over whatever he had brought inside. Mercifully, he stopped at three, though Lexy was still sure it must have been enough to reveal a shape underneath the pile that remained.

Finally, eventually, the loading had stopped, or was at least suspended. The to-ing and fro-ing ceased, and the voices outside died away one by one.

'I'm havin' a look,' Murph whispered.

'Wait another wee second.'

'We've waited ages.'

'Just another wee second to be sure.'

'Fuck's sake.'

'Shhh.'

'Right I'm lookin' noo.'

'Hing on, I thought I heard somethin'.'

And so on, until Murph lost patience and with a loud tut, stuck his head out from behind the pile.

'It's awright,' he whispered. 'Naebody's here.'

Lexy pulled the jaggy blanket away from his face, tentatively, like yanking it back again would protect him if he was seen. It worked against monsters in the middle of the night when you were about five, but was probably not a viable defence under these circumstances.

The container was full of plastic crates of assorted sizes and colours, surrounding the three large blanket-covered objects in the centre. Out the back door they could see trees, rough grass, cars and the edge of a building, as well as more boxes presumably awaiting transit.

Working out where they were and what was going on took second priority to having a slash. The difficult question was where. Wee Murph didn't let this issue trouble him quite as much, telling Lexy to keep the edgy while he fired into one of the empty wooden crates that had been up the back when they first got on board.

'Aw shite. It's leakin' oot,' he hissed.

'Stop then.'

'I cannae.'

'Fuck.'

There was urine seeping from under the crate while Murph was still peeing like a horse. Lexy had to grab a blanket to stem the flow, then threw another one into the box to soak up what was still hosing out.

'Should've used a plastic wan, ya fuckin' eejit.'

'I couldnae wait.'

'Christ.'

With Murph finally done, Lexy popped the first blanket inside the wooden crate also and replaced its lid, then began looking for a receptacle of his own. Wee Murph moved quietly down the truck, his attention taken more by the containers than by checking out for intruders. Lexy opened a plastic crate, revealing a pile of folded uniforms bearing the name Highland Hydro, as modelled quarterly by the man who came to read the meter. He gave their absorbency a thorough test then replaced the lid, by which time Murph had opened another box.

'Walkie-talkies,' he whispered excitedly, picking one up to show off.

'Put that back,' Lexy ordered, though with neither reason nor authority. He just felt that someone had to be using their heads round here and the chances were it wouldn't be Murph.

'How?'

'Awright, but don't touch anythin' else.'

He knew he might as well have been asking a thirteen-year-old looter in a toyshop. Wee Murph was the kind of boy for whom the 'easily distracted' tickbox had been added to school report cards. Lexy replaced the lid on the raided crate, by which time Murph was already into another one.

Murph whistled upon seeing the contents, letting the note out before remembering the need for quiet.

'Shhh.'

'Fuck. Sorry.'

The blue box was full of paper-wrapped packets marked 'DEMOLITION CHARGE – EXTREME CAUTION'. They looked like slabs of butter, enough to make about ten thousand packed lunches.

'Don't,' he said simply. Wee Murph shook his head. No arguments. It didn't stop him opening another blue box, right enough. More of the butter that went boom, and there were four more crates the same colour.

'Aw fuck, man, this is . . . this . . .'

'I know.'

'Whit we gaunny dae?'

They both looked to the door, thinking the same thing. It was a good thirty yards to the cover of the trees. The sound of running would definitely attract attention, while walking softly increased the time that someone could come out and spot them, especially given the amount of activity surrounding the truck already. Chances were someone might see them through a window too.

'We'd have a head start if we ran.'

'And once they'd seen us, where would we run to?'

'Fuckin' anywhere.'

'That's my point.'

'We could outrun them.'

'Could you outrun a bullet?'

Which ended the debate. Murph sighed, a long, slow exhale, which he cut off when he realised it was making a noise.

'Sorry.'

His deflation only lasted as long as it took for his curiosity to replace it, and he was soon pulling back one of the draped blankets.

'Check this. Whit is it?'

'Christ, I dunno, but I hope it's no' in ma dentist's cata-logue. Bastard sentenced me tae two fillin's.'

It was the biggest electric drill Lexy had ever seen, a glinting, gleaming steel beast mounted on an extendable suspension frame above a wheeled chassis. It was arguably an even more frightening proposition than the explosives, because at least they didn't also boast a rubber-gripped joystick and keypad, bound to draw Wee Murph's eager paws like a magnet.

'Fuck's sake don't touch it. If you turn this thing on, next thing you know they'll be shovin' it up your arse.'

The warning might not have worked if the wee man hadn't right then seen the only other thing capable of holding his attention.

'Grub, man, look.'

Sitting on the floor, just inside the rear door, was a can of Coke and two Snickers bars.

'Wan o' thae guys must have stashed them so his mates couldnae cadge any aff him,' Murph observed, with the expert eye of one versed in the protocols of playground confectionery preservation. At school, you only had to produce a bar of chocolate for half a dozen cadgers to instantly appear, pestering you for a bit as though they'd just parachuted in from Ethiopia. They'd follow you around if you walked away, like a procession of Hare Krishnas, chanting their mantra: 'Gaunny gie's a bit, eh gaunny? Just wan bit, come on, eh, gaunny? Don't be a Jew, man, gie's a bit, eh, gaunny?' If you wanted peace to eat your snack, you had to learn to do it in secret, and you had to make sure no-one knew you were 'carrying'.

'Finders keepers,' Murph said, heading for the stash.

Lexy's instinct was to warn him off, but he kept his

mouth shut on the tripartite grounds that a) The bloke was bound to blame his mates; b) Wee Murph wouldn't listen anyway; and c) he was starving. They scoffed the lot and drank the ginger between them in a matter of seconds, which was just as well because someone came out of the house just as they were finishing.

They stuffed the can and the wrappers in between two of the crates and scrambled back under the blankets. It struck Lexy yet again that this was an utterly pish hiding place – definitely no use at a competitive level – but the crucial factor was that (so far) nobody knew they were there to be found. Unfortunately, there was no 'in den one-two-three' either, and saying you 'had your keys up' was not a known defence against firearms.

Wee Murph was right, though. Since then it hadn't just felt like hours, it was hours. There were people nearby constantly after that; not inside the truck so much, but walking around outside, coming in and out of the building, discussing, arguing or simply hanging about. Waiting.

Every so often there was a long enough lull for them to feel sufficiently confident to whisper, but they didn't dare come out, and nor was there any reason to yet. They were safe where they were for the time being, though they had to hope that the folk in the house didn't run short of blankets when it came time to kip down. For now, the only enemy that did know they were there was the ginger pressing ever harder on their bladders.

'I cannae haud on much longer, man,' Murph pleaded. They were both sure someone was outside, having heard a voice talking on a mobile.

It had been agreed that darkness would provide their chance. They would wait until it was pitch-black and then head for the trees, as quickly and as quietly as they could.

243

Unfortunately, it had been a bright, clear evening, with a full moon in the sky, which made the onset of night stomach-burstingly slow. There had been opportunities a little earlier, when it still wasn't dark enough, but now that it was, there seemed to be an almost permanent presence outside the vehicle.

'Can you die of a burst pish-bladder?' Murph asked.

'I dunno.'

'I'll tell you in aboot two minutes.'

'Shoosh.'

They heard footsteps outside the back of the lorry.

'Lydon,' called a voice. 'Green light. Get rolling.'

This was followed by more footsteps, more voices. The ramp was withdrawn and the roller-shutters pulled closed. Minutes later, the engine started again, covering the sounds of two boys urinating copiously and with blessed relief into a crate of nine-millimetre ammunition.

FRIDAY, SEPTEMBER FIFTH

musical differences

Ray was looking down on himself in the centre of the room, where he sat restrained and motionless. Thorpe and Boyle were hovering around nearby, circling past every so often to check on him. Instinctively, he reached with his left hand and pressed 'n', the key bound to 'say_team: Help! Frozen <LOCATION> nowhere guarded by <NAME> [REDTEAM]Thorpe and <NAME> [REDTEAM]Boyle'. In the Freeze Tag mod, you needed a team-mate to stand next to you for three seconds in order to thaw you out – then you could go looking for some payback. Ray heard loud blasts and looked along the corridor, where a blue female figure was strafe-jumping towards him, making Thorpe and Boyle take the pain. Their puny pistols no match for her double shotgun, they both scattered in search of fresh armour and health packs. She stood above Ray, checking all angles for snipers as her proximity initiated the release process, during which they were both at their most vulnerable. He couldn't see her face, only her back. On the keyboard, he hit 'x', bound to his thank-you message, to find out her name. 'Much obliged, <NAME> [BLUETEAM]?????? m8!' it read.

There followed the familiar, anticipated crash and tinkle of being unfrozen, which was when Ray awoke and instantly sat up. He enjoyed no moment of semi-conscious delirium this time, no gradual remembrance of his waking circumstances. The fucking light was still on for a start, so as soon as he opened his eyes, he could see just how deep in the shit he was still submerged. He looked at his watch. It was after four, meaning he had been out for five hours, more than he usually managed at home these days. It felt like longer; too long, in fact. It felt like he'd slept in and was now running late, with the thing he was late for being the rest of his life.

They'd left him on that chair all day and well into the evening. There'd been no sleep there, no merciful oblivion. Instead it had been like suspended animation, with hours disappearing and individual seconds lasting an unbearable eternity. Every moment was spent wondering what was going to happen next, willing something to happen, something to change, to end this limbo of unknowing; all the while dreading those very same things. He'd tried in vain not to think of Kate and Martin, their names and faces simultaneously giving comfort and torment. He'd wished and he'd fantasised, allowing himself those indulgences as long as he stayed off hope. He wanted to hold them both again. He wanted to escape. He wanted answers. He wanted revenge. He wanted a chaingun, Quad Damage and a shitload of bullets. But he'd probably have settled for dry trousers and a change of underwear.

They had interrogated him, purely an exercise in stomping his psyche, much as the mock execution had been. There certainly didn't appear to be any other purpose to it, as he didn't have anything to tell them and they didn't have much to ask. Ray had posed more questions than they had, though it was a dead heat on who garnered the more information, [REDTEAM] and [BLUETEAM] tied at fuck-all.

After letting him almost literally stew in his own juices for another few hours, they came back, though this time

Boyle was accompanied not by Thorpe, but by the guy who'd driven the people-carrier the previous night. It was hardly a revelation, but at least it narrowed down the theories field, scratching the 'rival factions, caught in cross-fire between' sub-category.

They untied him but replaced the hood, then ordered him to stand up, which he did on unsteady legs. His feet and calves had gone numb, and while putting weight on them wasn't actually painful, the sensation was far from pleasant. The thought of what he might be walking towards didn't help.

Ray was led out of the room and along an L-shaped hallway that turned right after about ten or twelve paces. The floor changed from lino or tiles to wooden boards again. The bag was removed, revealing him to be in a large kitchen, with deep twin sinks and a rusted range that was merely a good clean and a paint-job away from being worth a couple of grand. Through the grimy window he could see headlights and hear the noise of the lorry's engine being revved up. This time, though, he wasn't getting a lift.

Boyle opened a door, beyond which was darkness. He flipped a switch on the wall outside and illuminated the bare shelves of an old-fashioned walk-in pantry.

'Your suite awaits, sir.'

Ray tried to think of a witty comeback, but as the only words bubbling near the surface were 'fuck fuck cunt cunt bastard wanker prick arsehole knob-end', he decided to keep them to himself, for now. The other goon shoved him inside, before Boyle closed and locked the door. Ray then heard straining and an ungodly screech of metal as they dragged the range in front of the door, presumably in case Ray knew how to pick locks using wooden skelfs. He slumped down to the ground, a thin sheet of lino covering the damp-smelling floorboards. High above him, a bare bulb dangled from a grey flex, giving out enough light to induce radiation sickness. He could probably twist it out if he climbed up the empty shelves, but it wasn't like he was planning to kip down for the night.

Not planning to, but his knackered body had other ideas. He remembered sitting with his back to the door, not lying down, so he must have slumped after losing consciousness. His exhaustion existed on so many levels that merely closing his eyes against the intrusive light had been enough: his brain sussed that there was bugger-all reason to be awake at this point and had decided to shut all systems down for a while.

Five hours. Five hours *uninterrupted*. Even with that pigging light on and the cold damp in his trousers, it had been his best stretch of sleep since Martin came home from the maternity hospital. As a result, he no longer felt so resigned or submissive, and didn't just feel awake: he felt revived, purposeful, dynamic even. Unfortunately, he was feeling all of those things inside a locked cupboard.

He got to his feet and climbed up on the lowest shelf to survey what might be resting on the higher ones. He found dust, wood shavings, a Biro and the statutory empty paint tin. Even the bloke in *The A Team* would be struggling to fashion an escape plan out of that lot. Ray stepped down, the floorboards wobbling under the renewed weight and his ankle about five degrees from disaster. Probably rotted through, he reckoned, the thought lighting up the only bulb brighter than the bare effort hanging from the ceiling.

He lifted the sheet of lino and rolled it up, placing it on one of the shelves. The boards below were ancient-looking things: warped, loose, soft and decayed. Ray retrieved the paint tin and wedged it open with the Biro, then squeezed

250

the lid between two of the floorboards and stood on it with his heel. One end popped up without struggle, the bent and rusted nails easily pulling free of the damp joist underneath. The boards either side also came up with negligible resistance, and he placed them on shelves out of the way to let the ample light shine into the resulting hole. There was earth about two feet below, leaving a crawlspace just deep enough to get into. He took off his jacket, placing his wallet and housekeys in his trousers' back pocket, then slithered his way into the gap, hands first.

There were walls at his back and to the left; the kitchen's underside to his right. That was where he wanted to go, but he had to move forward first to get his entire body through the hole, an endeavour not assisted by the support joist that shaved four or five inches off his overhead clearance. He turned his head sideways and edged forward, his hair and left ear burrowing into the dusty earth. There was a smell that reminded him of hoes and old lawnmowers. He could see nothing, his body blocking all the light behind him. His left arm prodded at the darkness ahead, fumbling in the earth to drag himself forward. Somehow, he got both of his feet down through the space and stretched his legs out behind him, digging his toes into the soil. Light was spilling down around him now, enough to make out a wall just a few feet ahead. He used the extra purchase to pull his head back out from under the joist, then began manoeuvring sideways in the direction of the kitchen. The overhead clearance grew as the ground began descending ever more sharply, until he was all but sliding down an incline into the dark. He came to a halt against another wall, from where he was able to look up the short slope at the hole he'd made.

He was in the foundations of the house, in a small

chamber enclosed on three sides by walls and on the fourth by the slope. There was enough light to see pipes leading into the kitchen and electrical cables snaking along the subterranean stonework. More importantly, he could also see a square gap in the foundation wall, leading into the next chamber. The gap, just big enough for a man to crawl through, must have been put there to allow plumbers and sparks into where Ray was now – which suggested that the chamber they came from must be accessible from the surface.

Ray crawled into the space, discovering that the slope did not continue on the other side. Instead, the ground fell away completely beneath the gap. He patted the wall below, leaning down as far as his balance allowed, then a little further than his balance allowed. The ground turned out to be only a few inches further down than his reach, but it was a long few inches to fall when you didn't know that. He belly-flopped ungracefully on to the hard stone floor, where he looked up to see salvation in the shape of a cracked, frosted-glass window, through which moonlight was dimly shining. The smell like hoes and old lawn-mowers turned out to be coming from a hoe and an old lawnmower, among several other derelict gardening implements lining the walls of what was unmistakably a cellar.

Ray took a moment to compose himself and shake the dust from his hair, then held his breath as he tried the doorhandle. It opened amid minor squeakage and major exhalation. Utter negligence on the part of the proprietor, who would have no-one to blame but himself if some moti-vated master-criminal made off with his museum-piece Qualcast.

The door gave on to a short stairwell, leading to the rear

of the house, where weeds and wild grass had smothered the potentially noisy gravel. Ray climbed until his head was at ground level, then flattened himself against the stairs, scanning the area. His car was sitting twenty yards away, to the side of the house. There was a chance the keys would still be in the ignition, it being unlikely his captors were much concerned about passing thieves. The same went for the Rover, for that matter. However, if the keys weren't in the ignition, the sound of the door opening could be enough to drastically cut his head start for having it away on his toes. He could head for the trees silently right then, but in the debit column for that option was the fact that he had no idea where he was, what lay beyond the trees or how long it would be before the goons came to retrieve him from the pantry and discovered he'd gone.

He stayed still a few more moments, listening for any hint of activity. There was nothing to be heard. All through the house, not a creature was stirring, not even a gun-toting bampot.

Ray kept tight to the walls as he made his way around the building, picking each step with delicate care to minimise any sound. His own car was nearer, so he approached it first and peered through the window, but the moonlight was insufficient to make out whether there were keys in the ignition. He placed his fingers on the handle and prepared to pull, then decided against it and gently let go. The night was so still and quiet, the sound was bound to carry. If he was going to gamble, better to gamble with the Rover. In fact, it was inarguably the better bet, as it wouldn't need ten minutes of warming up as protection against stalling, neither of which were conducive to a swift getaway.

Ray made his way stealthily to the larger car and pressed

his face to the glass. The Rover was parked at a better angle to catch the moon, but there still wasn't enough light to see much inside, other than a blinking LED on the stereo. Beyond it was a people carrier, like he had seen the previous night, as well as a van and two Mondeos, each hitched to a trailer-mounted speedboat.

Again he placed his fingers on the handle, pulling until he met resistance and gradually applying more pressure. He could feel the mechanism straining nearer and nearer to release, but knew that however gentle that final increment was, what followed would be as percussive as if he'd just given it a good yank. At that moment, he heard a cough and the sound of footsteps inside the house. He immediately flung the door open and dived into the driver's seat, his right hand reaching and finding keys in the ignition.

'Thank fuck.'

The engine leapt instantly to life and he spun off up the track, one hand on the wheel and the other fumbling around for the headlights. In his rearview mirror he could see the front door of the house, out of which two figures emerged, almost tripping over one another in their haste. His right hand found the headlights as he changed up and floored the accelerator, the illumination arriving in time to save him from shooting straight across the approaching T-junction and into the field beyond.

He hit the brakes and turned hard right, skidding and slewing from one side to the other before getting the machine back under control. A few seconds later, he glanced in the rearview again and saw his own black Polo make the same turn, which was when he knew he was clean away. They'd grabbed it first because it was nearest and, unburdened by trailers, theoretically faster than any of the other vehicles parked outside the house. Theoretically.

Ray slid the Rover into fourth and put further effortless distance between the cars, allowing himself a little smile as he felt the powerful acceleration and imagined his pursuers' faces, hobbling along in his Polo. It was the first and only time he was grateful to Div for selling him the useless piece of shit.

Everybody knew someone like Div, a kind of loveable mess whom all your instincts warned you not to trust, but still you couldn't help doing so; after which you only had yourself to blame.

Actually, that was selling him short. The words 'Div' and 'shambles' were inextricably synonymous in the minds of anyone who knew him, but the evidence could be contradictory. Here was a guy, for God's sake, who these days ran a successful business undertaking the flawless, meticulous and precise relocation of entire computer networks, and yet any time they organised a LAN party, Div was the one who would turn up with half his system missing and need to borrow bits from everyone else. And while Div always gave the impression of being chaotically unreliable, it was difficult to remember an occasion when he had genuinely let Ray down (pace the Polo, but technically even that had now been redeemed).

In this sense, Div was the polar opposite of Simon, who gave the impression of being incredibly together, clinically organised, and yet let Ray down on more occasions than it was healthy to dwell upon. It had latterly occurred to him that the crucial difference was Div gave a fuck.

There were many ways, in fact, in which Div and Simon were opposites, which probably explained why they didn't get along. The weird thing – no, perhaps the appropriate thing – was that it wasn't an entirely mutual antipathy.

255

Simon, tending towards the highly strung, reserved a lot more venom for Div than Div, being more laid back than most other human beings could achieve without opiates, could be arsed mustering for Simon. Div was the only person Ray could remember not being angered to the point of destructive rage by something Simon had done, despite being the increasingly frequent target of his antics and abuse. This was because Div was also the only person who absolutely refused to take Simon seriously, and Simon liked to be taken very, very seriously. Obviously, there was some quality vicious-circle action going on there.

Ironically, the one thing they had in common was also the best illustration of what made them so very different. It was, in a word, Queen. Not the parasite, but the rock band: Freddie and Brian, John and Roger, Scaramouche and Beelzebub, thunderbolts and lightning. Queen was Div's religion and Simon's guilty little secret.

When they all shared a flat in third year (the three of them plus Simon's long-suffering mate Ross), music was often less a shared enthusiasm than a battleground. It wasn't simply a matter of debating the comparative merits of each other's tastes and collections; much of what was said about music wasn't about music at all, but a surrogate outlet for the tensions that were natural between four adolescents in such close proximity.

Ray would occasionally (and very, very foolishly) play the white dove and encourage everyone to agree to disagree. After all, they each had their own stereos in their respective rooms, so volume considerations aside, what did it matter what someone else was playing? Well, it sure mattered to Simon. All it took was Div to stick on a Queen album and Simon would be ripping into him for it as soon as he entered the Neutral Zone (aka the kitchen), demanding to know how he could listen to such garbage and growing all the more frustrated at Div's refusal to offer any explanation beyond that he liked it.

Ray hadn't been very familiar with the Queen oeuvre prior to living with Div, having written them off as the pantomime dames of British rock, listened to on Ford Sierra car stereos by people who bought one album a year, usually at Woolworth's. It wasn't hard to see why they wouldn't be Simon's cup of tea, but a little more tricky to explain the disproportionate ire their music provoked. But that was before Ray had heard the phrase 'Methinks the lady doth protest too much'.

Ray was accompanying Simon on his regular weekend trip to his parents' place in Giffnock to retrieve his laundry. Simon had gone downstairs to get them some coffees and left Ray alone in his old bedroom, where he spotted a pile of records at the bottom of an open wardrobe. Ray crouched down to get a closer look. In the main, the collection comprised valuables and rarities Ray had heard Simon boast about. There were picture discs, coloured vinyl twelve-inch singles, bootlegs, limited-edition gatefold sleeve covers: treasures Simon had tapes of at the flat, but understandably didn't want any harm coming to the originals. Underneath that lot, however, were twelve Queen albums, stacked chronologically from *Queen* to *The Works*. The guy even had *Hot Space*, and had evidently forgiven them for it, given the subsequent purchase of its successor.

The picture was clear. Barring the existence of a sibling he inexplicably failed to mention, Simon had been heavily into Freddie and the boys from an early age; Ray was guessing around *Bo-Rhap*, 75–76, with the earlier material explored retrospectively. Some time after 1984, however, coinciding with his mid-to-late teens, there had been a

Stalinesque purge, possibly the same month as he bought his first Bauhaus twelve-inch or maybe his first can of hairspray. It was one thing to grow out of a band, but this was like the revisionism that followed a military coup. Messrs Mercury, May, Deacon and Taylor had been airbrushed out of all photographs and their works hidden away in a vault.

At least this finally explained Simon's advocacy of grandiose stagecraft, which had always sat incongruously with his, ahem, *official* record collection. He detested the minimalism not just of bands he hated, such as The Smiths, but even of those he liked, such as the Mary Chain. He couldn't take all that standing-in-one-place stuff, looking bored and indifferent, and as for the twenty-minute set, don't go there, man. Ray now understood: onstage, Simon wanted to see the kind of thing Queen did, just as long as it wasn't Queen doing it. He had been raised on the Mercury ethos that 'anything worth doing is worth over-doing', but the problem latterly was that Freddie Mercury was as far from cool as the planet Mercury was from Pluto. To Simon, cool was everything. Image was everything, and the perception of his peers was the thing he worried about most.

Div wasn't winding Simon up with his simplistic expla-nation (well, maybe just a bit or he wouldn't be Div). Div listened to Queen because he liked their music. Loved their music. That was all. His overall rock'n'roll philosophy was also very simple: if it was loud, he generally liked it. This was nothing to do with volume. If you listened to The Clash on a pocket tranny, they would still be loud, just like if you listened to Belle and Sebastian at ten thousand deci-bels, they would still be quiet. Ray hadn't been round chez Div recently, but considered it unlikely he would own any

B&S discs. Granted, Queen weren't the loudest thing in Div's student record pile, but they were loud enough, and that overblown grandiosity counted for a lot too.

Despite all of this, they each had enough in common musically (even that they were admitting to) for them to make the colossal but glorious mistake of starting a band. In retrospect, Ray could see that it was probably motivated by a subconscious awareness that there wasn't quite enough tension between them as things stood, and what the situation really needed was an undertaking guaranteed to push them over the edge.

It started innocently enough, one Sunday afternoon, but then alcohol got involved and foolish things were said and done. They'd spent the preceding Saturday in the QM, watching the 'Battle of the Bands', a monthly opportunity for student hopefuls to strut their stuff in front of apathetic afternoon drinkers. The Entertainments Convenor had cynically proposed this democratic slot as part of his election manifesto, winning him the vote of every chord-strumming wannabe on campus. In that respect, his victory was also his punishment.

The audience at these things tended to be made up of three factions, in ascending order of magnitude: friends of the performers along to offer moral support; folk looking for a quiet drink and a blether, who had failed to see the Convenor's single four-inch-square poster publicising the event in one (out of order) cubicle of the Gents' toilets; and rubber-neckers having a good laugh at the train wreck. Simon, Div, Ross and Ray entered in the second category, but had very soon transformed to join the third.

They were still talking about it late on Saturday night, Simon being inventively scathing about what they'd witnessed and the rest having their own digs when they were able to get a word in. Simon's scorn was unquestionably fuelled in part by frustration that these no-hopers had nonetheless managed to team up and get on a stage, something his own greater talents had thus far failed to achieve. He had been for a few auditions only to find, when he got there, that the existing members of the proposed band were 'total arseholes', which may or may not have been another way of saying he didn't get the nod. Either that or they weren't specifically looking for a lead guitarist/lead vocalist/sole lyricist/stage coordinator/cover designer/rock visionary at that particular moment.

The consensus that they could do better themselves led to Ray's imprudent admission that he had a drumkit back in Houston, and Div's astonishing revelation that he could play bass. He had chosen this instrument, as he claimed in typical Div style, because it had fewer strings than a normal guitar and was therefore less work. This turned out, also in typical Div style, to be deceptive, self-deprecatory mince. Div could play a standard six-string more than competently, but in aspiring to play along with his fave records, he had found it a sight easier to learn John Deacon's riffs than Brian May's.

Ray, for his part, had never laid claim to any musical talent, but he had been fairly blessed when it came to skills involving hand-eye coordination, not that it took much aim to hit a drum. His abilities at computer games, archery (which he took up at uni simply because it was on offer) and arguably even cartoons stemmed from a degree of natural dexterity that he had dedicatedly applied to no useful purpose throughout his adult life.

It was suggested by Simon that they get together first thing on Sunday for a jam session, what with there being a ready-made rhythm section in the house to join the aspiring axe duo of himself and Ross. Despite Ray's gross scepticism about how good an idea it would sound in the cold light of day, sure enough the Dark Man rose at the crack of half-eleven and borrowed his mum's car to ferry Ray's kit in from Ayrshire. They set up in Simon's room (naturally the biggest), Ray damping the kit with towels and jumpers, and got underway as soon as Div got back from his folks' place with his bass and a carry-out.

After half an hour of doing unspeakable things to *Tommy Gun*, they were ready to chuck it. Unfortunately, they persevered, and by half-ten they were all drunk enough to think they were beginning to sound not bad. By midnight, they had agreed to go in for the next month's Battle of the Bands 'just for a laugh', and by two o'clock they had a name. Well, actually, they had four names, with a decision deferred until the next session, when they all knew Simon would get his way.

He did. In preference to Slideshow (Ross, cool and simple), Manic Minors (Ray, after a ZX Spectrum game) and All Dead (Div, from a Queen song, natch), they were to be The Bacchae. No, really. It was the name of a play by Euripides, the title referring to a female cult in naked hedonistic frenzy, which was itself all very rock'n'roll, but the actual name stank. The Bacchae, for fuck's sake. Div said it sounded like something you needed ointment for.

When they first reconvened, the only dose of reality to puncture their plans was the remembrance that they were a fortnight from the end of term, so there was no Battle of the Bands to aim at until at least seven weeks hence. That left time enough – particularly including the Easter holidays – for something truly horrible to get underway.

Perhaps it would have been better if they had been

utterly appalling, as opposed to just bad, as that way it would have soon petered out through lack of enthusiasm and mutual embarrassment. Ray and Ross certainly did their part, contributing sufficient mediocrity and borderline competence to puncture the ambitions of any self-respecting combo, but unfortunately Simon and even Div let the side down badly. Div, once the rust was shaken off, turned out to be a far better bass player than he had let on, and as for Simon, well, the guy could play guitar. There were people who could play *the* guitar and people who could *play guitar*, and with Simon there was no definite article. Between their unevenly matched talents, they had the basis for something that they were fairly confident wouldn't get them bottled off the stage.

To be fair, there was only so far you could go wrong with the classic four-piece line-up, as long as you knew your own limits and had realistic ambitions. And thereby hung the problem. Simon was an undeniably talented musician and had this grand, highly developed vision, but lacked the more immediate clarity to see that they weren't it. He had been cooking up his schemes for conquering the rock world for a frustratingly long time, and had such belief in himself that as soon as he had a quorate line-up, he just assumed the path was set. He also assumed that the rest of them would a) come to realise this; b) toe the line; and c) instantly turn into accomplished musicians.

His impatience was obvious in his insistence on the name. Talk about blowing your wad. *His* band, the band of his vision, were to be The Bacchae. Fair enough, everyone had a rock'n'roll dream. But most would surely bide their time a wee bit, rather than forcing the issue on their first student covers-band after what it would be generous to call one rehearsal. Simon's mind, though, was already years down the line. Within a fortnight, while the rest of them were optimistically talking about their first gig, he was talking about resenting his future fans for what they wanted to take from him.

'I hate all that deliberate hysteria. It really fuckin' offends me to think of these yahoos shoutin' for certain songs, Christ, *demanding* what they want to hear. You've spent ages puttin' a show together, but you've to abandon your playlist because they've decided what they want from *your* set? You're just supposed to perform for them on request. Do they think you're their personal lapdancer?'

All of which was bound to make for a very loud thud when he came back down to earth.

Ray found it difficult to admit to people that their glorified-jam-session-with-aspirations-of-pub-rock was called The Bacchae, while Div refused to utter the name at all. Instead, he began referring to the band as The Arguments, which was far more appropriate, as they spent more time and energy doing that than on actually playing.

There was very little that they didn't all disagree on, but once Simon had unilaterally signed them up for the next BOTB, they had to decide what their set should comprise, and a stushie ensued that made what had passed already seem like a lost golden age of harmony and accord. While the other three traded suggestions that they thought might be mutually palatable, Simon was, as ever, operating on a different plane, and handed out screeds of photocopied lyrics; his idea of egalitarianism being that they all got a say in selecting which of his compositions would make up the playlist. When civil terms of address were re-established, two or three hours later, it was suggested to Simon that they were less likely to go down like a cup of cold sick if they stuck mainly to songs people knew, maybe sneaking one original track into the set if they weren't getting too many missiles thrown at them.

Even Simon saw the sense in this, and the argument shifted from which of Simon's songs they would play to which of Simon's suggested covers they would play. In time, however, democracy prevailed, with results that made a fairly compelling argument for fascism. With all sense and judgement being sacrificed in the name of compromise, it was agreed not only that everybody should get to choose a song, but in the absence of any consensus on a lead vocalist, that they should each get to sing it too.

All four of them. Including Ray. In a twenty-minute set.

The Ents Convener supplied a minimal PA and a drumkit, making it clear that this was because he did not want the hassle of four different bands lugging their own equipment on and off the bar's tiny stage. Despite Simon's whines, they had agreed that this was fair enough, or rather it would have been if one of the amps hadn't blown in a vain attempt to produce feedback during the first mob's ridiculously overblown closing number. Amid Simon's glowering I-told-you-so's, and with the Convenor telling them they needed to be on at their allotted time or miss their slot, they had to make some quick decisions, something of a challenge given that the previous record for reaching agreement on anything was two days.

Ross made the apparently selfless gesture of saying that, as the second-string guitarist, he should be the one to 'bite the bullet'. It was only as the insincere 'Are you sure?'s and 'We'll make it up to you's were being muttered that it became clear he wasn't offering to miss out altogether; merely to go onstage with his axe plugged into the dead amp. Suffering the same muso-psychosis as Raymond the Singing Drummer, he still wanted his moment in the spotlight.

Despite this, they opened almost passably, with Div on vocals for The Cure's *Boys Don't Cry*, a blatant crowd-pleasing gambit and one that was fairly difficult to really fuck up. Div's original, democratically allotted selection had been *Funny How Love Is*, until it was vetoed by Simon's very serious threat to disband the group rather than stand on the same stage as someone singing anything by Queen. After that, Ross signalled the downhill slide as his nerves prompted him to forget the lyrics to the second verse of *A Song From Under the Floorboards*, rescued partially by an improvised guitar solo from Simon that filled the gap almost quickly enough to seem intended.

The three minutes that followed would forever haunt Ray's sense of self-worth. Over the toms, he could see baffled and amused looks as the already guitar-depleted Bacchae played a version of *Lost in the Supermarket* that would have been unidentifiable even to Mick Jones, who had written it. With the drum-mic level set for backing-vocal use, and the mic itself sliding gradually down its decrepit stand, Ray's singing was drowned by his drumming, which was itself suffering from the contortions he was doing to keep his mouth under the bloody thing. Also, the further the mic slid down the pole, the more it picked up the snare and the less it picked up Ray's already tremulous voice. By the end of the first chorus, not only was there no vocal audible, but the amplified snare was smothering the guitar and bass too. People at the bar were holding their ears, wincing before each stroke. Simon, meanwhile, looked ready to bludgeon Ray to death with his Les Paul.

The sarcastic applause that followed was the loudest response to the end of any song all afternoon – until, that was, Simon stepped up to the mic. His singing was no better or worse than any of them, and his guitar playing, as already acknowledged, was the band's greatest asset. The problem was, he couldn't do both at the same time.

He had somehow concealed this from them during rehearsals, presumably by hiding behind Ross's rhythm-playing and Div's bass, chiming in his own chords and solos during non-vocal breaks. How he had hidden it from himself was a mystery of that river in Egypt. Maybe he hadn't been hiding, and could play fine in rehearsals but choked in front of an audience (understandably, given what had just transpired). Either way, with Ross strumming an unplugged guitar, Simon couldn't have been more exposed if he'd been standing there in the buff. He started off playing nothing, and the sparse drums-bass-and-vocal effect might have seemed stylised if Ross wasn't standing next to him like a haddie, strumming silently away. Throwing in his own chords and solos made things a little conspicuous too. Again, Simon might just have pulled it off if he hadn't attempted to remedy the situation by suddenly playing Ross's part. The chords themselves were right, but he simply couldn't strum in a rhythm different to the lyrics, and the resulting 'bouncing ball' effect would have been damn funny if it had happened to four other poor fuckers.

The term following Easter was always the shortest, breaking up after as few as six weeks for end-of-year exams. This was quite a mercy, as life in the flat after what Div called 'the deBacchle' was even uglier than usual. The rest of them didn't set out to make it three against one, but Simon's conduct very soon united them against a common and increasingly volatile enemy. It was made clear from early on that this outrage wasn't something to be laughed off, and it was made even clearer that he was blaming everybody but himself for the fiasco, from his fellow band members to the Ents Convenor and even the long-haired numpty who'd buggered the amp kidding on he was Jim Reid.

In a histrionically huffy gesture, Simon moved back to his parents' place for the run-up to his exams, and nobody was brave enough to ask the rhetorical question of whether he'd also be leaving his share of the rent and amenities bills for the remaining month of their lease. The consensus at the time was that it was a small price to pay.

Ray had assumed that the deBacchle was the death of his great rock'n'roll adventure, but a funny thing happened on the way to the funeral. With no chance of getting a fourth tenant at short notice for the fag-end of the student year, they had been planning to split the difference between them, until Div had a brainwave. His wee brother, Carl, had just finished Sixth Year at school and was starting at uni after the summer, so Div persuaded his parents to spring for the month's rent to give the lad a taster course in student living.

Ray had often noted that people's younger brothers or sisters seemed to have more concentrated versions of their older sibling's features. Carl didn't much resemble Div facially, but in easy-going attitude there was no mistaking the lineage; and when the kid picked up a guitar, it suddenly made sense not only why Div was a pretty good bassist, but also why he had kept his light under a bushel. The younger sibling's concentrated feature was sheer, natural musical talent.

With the exams petering out and the last scraps of grant money doing likewise, despite the mental scarring it was inevitable that they'd start jamming again to fill the days. Even if they'd had cash to blow, they were all staying clear of the QM to avoid the awkwardness of running into

Simon, though in retrospect Ray realised the Dark Man had his own reasons not to show his face round there.

The sense of harmony was immediately obvious, musically as well as atmospherically. Div's voice was a natural complement to Carl's, but this time there was no question of who should be on lead, especially as this guitar hero had no problems playing his instrument at the same time.

At weekends, Carl was hanging out at a place called The Strawberry Club, which was fast becoming the epicentre of Glasgow's mid-Eighties jangly-guitars-and-anoraks scene. It was hosted in a room downstairs from the main dancehall at Rooftops on Sauchiehall Street, an establishment that still described itself as a 'discotheque' in those days. It wasn't quite to the tastes of Div, Ross or Ray, as even self-consciously twee and sugary music was still twee and sugary, but they went along now and again because the QM disco was closed for the summer and the mainstream clubs were full of neds dancing to horrible records in between glass fights. The Strawberry Club carried no such threat, with smiling politeness being an affected part of the scene. People brought sweeties and handed them round, and they spoke with exaggeratedly formal pronunciation, like they'd all been to elocution lessons. It was as revolting as it sounded.

Carl, as it turned out, wasn't just there to dance and chat up girls, much as he enjoyed both. He was at all times being a busy little networker, sufficient to get involved in organising a 'showcase night' to be hosted by The Strawberry Club in the main hall upstairs. At this grand janglathon, a number of unsigned hopefuls would get to share a bill topped by some more established local names, in front of an audience including several invited representatives of indie record labels. And on this bill, of course, would be Carl's own band, as yet unnamed.

The trauma of the deBacchle hadn't quite been exorcised by this point, so Ross and Ray took a bit of persuading, eventually being talked round by Carl's promise that he'd heard a few of the demo tapes and there was 'no way they would be the shitest band there'. Besides, they had six weeks to get ready, which was almost as long as the entire lifespan of The Bacchae from conception to abortion. What they didn't have was a handle, but that was quickly remedied. Div announced with a grin that 'we have to be The Arguments', and received no dissent amid the laughter.

Another thing they didn't have was original material, or rather they thought they didn't have it until Carl judiciously chose his moment to reveal 'a few things he'd been working on'. Haunted by the ludicrously over-ambitious compositions Simon had inflicted upon them, Ray was ready to be sceptical until Carl started playing his twelve-string. The only experience subsequently comparable was listening to a new Teenage Fanclub album: the songs were all so instantly likeable that you could swear you'd heard them before. They were simple, melodic and tantalisingly reminiscent of about ten other bands at once. It needed also to be said that Carl's lyrics were atrocious, but you couldn't have everything.

However, for all his musical eclecticism, there was one thing Carl shared with his Bacchic predecessor: Queen were not to be tolerated. They were old, pompous and bombastic and, worst crime of all, his big brother loved them. Div, therefore, couldn't resist stitching him up. One Sunday, rehearsing in their parents' garage, Div picked up the twelve-string and started playing the euphorically jangly opening chords of *Funny How Love Is*. Recognising it and getting a sly look from Div, Ray joined in with a stomp on the bass drum and booming toms. Carl, naturally assuming they were just jamming, picked out a looping riff on electric, sharing nods and smiles like they did when something was generally agreed to be 'happening'. Then Div stepped up to the mic and started singing, confident in the knowledge that his wee brother had no idea of the song's source. Played as it was, it sounded like it could have been by any number of trippy late Sixties outfits, and the lyrics about coming home for tea were deceptively far away from Scaramouche and Beelzebub.

'Oh man, that was excellent,' Carl said. 'We've got to do it again.' And they got through it twice more before he asked the obvious question.

And so it came to pass that the Strawberry Suckers (© Div 198–) found themselves cheering The Arguments to the proverbial echo for playing a song by the band that best represented the very antithesis of what jangly indie-pop was all about.

Possibly the only other person to recognise the track was the QM Ents Convenor, who had been invited in case he fancied booking any of the acts. He declared their contribution 'Fuckin' top . . . Queen, man – yous have some balls,' and offered them the opening slot on the bill for the forthcoming Lloyd Cole and the Commotions gig. He also confided that 'this scene's doin' my fuckin' heid in. One more bunch of twee cunts gets on that stage an' I'm gaunny lose the place.'

It was an inopportune moment for one of the anoraked denizens to present himself, proffer a white paper bag and say: 'Hello there. My name's Adrian. Would you like a sweetie?' The Ents Convenor decked the guy with a solid right hook before being dragged away and ejected by several bouncers. Rooftops, having about a dozen flights of stairs, was probably the worst venue in the city to get thrown out of, but that had presumably been far from the

Ents Convenor's mind when the red mist descended.

Among the masses (well, a couple of hundred at least) musically inequipped to spot the hand of Mercury was a bloke called Jim Collins, who ran a small Edinburgh-based indie label, Starjet. He wore NHS-style specs that nonetheless probably cost him a mint, and talked like a horse-racing commentator on caffeine, suggesting an endless list of musical comparisons and speculative influences. His strike rate was impressive enough to make Ray wonder whether he had just burgled their flat, though one name was amusingly missing. Collins said he'd get them studio time and release one single as long as it was 'that last one, *Funny*, was it called?'

Of course, he freaked when he found out, but not before the song and its two-track B side were in the can, by which time also the ink was long dry on the contract.

The *NME*'s singles reviewer called it 'a work of three-minute alchemy: turning truly base material into something special'. Div wanted to deck the bastard, but the review (and no doubt the Queen catalogue completists) did help them make it into the indie chart, peaking at eleven. One place higher would have been enough to get them a mention on the ITV *Chart Show*, but as they didn't have a video anyway, it made no odds. Jim was hardly going to spring for something like that considering he wouldn't even pay for a photographer for the single's sleeve.

A mate of Carl's took that picture, a big lanky bloke called Steff. Ray never found out whether he turned pro, but The Arguments definitely didn't. They had a memorable couple of months, as new bands often did back in those days when records stayed in the charts for more than a nanosecond. There were lots of local gigs and a few more mentions in the inkies, the largest a half-column news-story-cum-interview in the *Melody Maker*, written with a predictably snide tone because the *NME* had given the single a good write-up. It was fun, it was exciting and it was a temporary distraction from the unavoidable truth, which was that they weren't a real band: they were two hacks, one journeyman and Carl. Everybody could see that, not least themselves.

The split was amicable, if a little heart-breaking. It wasn't exactly a case of coming this close to glory and having it dashed away, but they'd had a taste of the stuff of schoolboy dreams, enough to know how much they would miss it. They were aware also that they'd only got their fifteen minutes courtesy of sheer luck and someone else's talent, so the chances of a repeat were slim to none.

There wasn't too much time to feel sorry for themselves, as the end of Christmas term was fast approaching and the end of The Arguments had unfortunately come just in time to give them an outside chance of salvaging their degrees. Carl, for his part, didn't even salvage his first year. Within weeks of the split, he had started collaborating with Kenny Redford, with whom he went on to form The Gliders and later the highly acclaimed Famous Blue Raincoats.

Ray remained proud of his own small place in The Gliders' and the FBRs' rock family histories, and looked forward to the day he could elicit a totally blank response by telling Martin all about it. Despite the occasional twinge of regret or jealousy, he had always been very happy for Carl, with the sole reservation that he still sounded far too upbeat all the time. Just once Ray would have liked to hear him sing something about messy break-ups, suicide and death. Even The Beach Boys did *Pet Sounds*, for Christ's sake.

The sun was peeping over the horizon by the time Ray reached a roadsign bearing place names of anything larger than a farm. He knew he hadn't been driving anything like as long as it felt, probably less than an hour, but it had mostly been on some obscure B road, all of whose junctions had been little more than dirt tracks. His old and reliably borked Polo had never reappeared in his mirror after he first lost sight of it, but the fact that he didn't know where he was had kept him aware that he might be intercepted further along the road. Every set of oncoming headlights had him ready to swerve as he anticipated the approaching vehicle suddenly slewing into his path.

Dawn and the sight of an A road allowed him to relax a little, sufficient to stop worrying about pursuit and turn his thoughts to the fact that Kate would be climbing the walls. Jesus, the poor woman. The roadsigns said he was nearing Crieff, which meant he could be home in about an hour, but that was an extra hour more than he'd want to be waiting if the roles were reversed. He reached instinctively for his pocket, then remembered that his mobile had been pilfered and the only change he'd been carrying was in his jacket, back in that pantry. His wallet, however, was still in his trousers. He'd stop at a twenty-four-hour garage and get change, or a phonecard if they were selling them.

Patting his grubby shirt reminded him of the state he was in, and now that there was some daylight, a glance in the sunshade mirror showed his face to be looking like that of a miner coming off shift. His clothes were caked, his face was black and he was still damp with piss. He looked and smelled like a jakey. A lobby dosser, even.

When he reached a twenty-four-hour garage, it happily turned out to be attached to a twenty-four-hour supermarket. There was one not far from his house in Newlands, which he had found himself taking full advantage of in recent months. As well as other sleep-deprived parents,

273

shift workers and hungry hash-heads, it attracted all manner of nocturnal creatures through its revolving doors, and was therefore probably the only kind of place he could confidently show up in his present state without turning too many heads.

He thought about going to the Gents first, to give his face a wipe, but remembered he'd be back there to change anyway, so went straight to the clothing section. He picked up a T-shirt, cheap jeans, Ys, socks, a Mars bar and a can of Lucozade then made for the check-out, keeping a considerate distance from the customer in front. There was a news rack alongside, with the morning editions displayed above the food mags (glutton porn, Kate called them). Ray looked at the headlines, marvelling at how little the world had moved on in the time it had taken for his to turn upside down. Fallout from yesterday's political stories on the broadsheets and a soap star's divorce on the English-based tabloids, all of them seeming to Ray like chip-wrappers, so long did it feel since the stories broke. The *Daily Recorder*, however, had something fresh down the left-most column.

PERVERT
TEACHER
SOUGHT
IN HUNT
FOR BOYS

Ray was about to snort at the familiar sensationalism, wondering what tangential detail was being employed to justify the 'pervert' epithet. Then he realised he recognised the two half-column, school-photo headshots above the headline, confirmed by the caption: 'VANISHED: Jason Murphy and Alexander Sinclair'.

Oh fuck.

He scanned the text frantically, unable to read quickly enough. Phrases leapt out like assassins.

'. . . became worried when they didn't return from school at lunchtime but staff and classmates confirmed that they never got there . . .'

'. . . walked out after losing control of his class. Ash had only been in the job three weeks . . .'

'. . . is understood by police to have been suffering extreme stress. Classmates said he had been taunted by Murphy recently and . . .'

'. . . led his class in a depraved discussion that even involved bestiality . . .'

'. . . forced children to draw pornographic pictures of male sexual organs . . .'

The story was continued inside, where it was accompanied by another photo, a copy of the deer-in-the-headlights pic the school had used for his staff ID.

'. . . still no word at press time . . .'

'. . . police are stressing it is too early to draw conclusions, but . . .'

But but but but but . . .

The photograph wasn't a good likeness, and certainly not of Al Jolson at checkout twelve, but Ray felt suddenly very vulnerable. After what he'd just been through, the comparative threat should have seemed small, but the difference now was that he couldn't go home. The police would be even less likely to believe his story if they were trying to nail him for abducting two kids, while around Burnbrae, the nailing would likely involve a gibbet.

In that psycho-ridden farmhouse, his fear had been of what he had to escape from. Now he had nowhere to escape to.

275

the place of many bampots

'Oh good, a riot,' said McIntosh chirpily.

'Christ, that's just what I need right now, Tosh: you in Pollyanna mode.'

'Ach, come on Angelique, it adds a wee bit of colour to the morning to see the local populace in high spirits.'

'Knock it off or I'll kill you, all right?'

'Heard *that*,' he acknowledged.

They pulled up short of Ash's house on Kintore Road; or rather, short of the placard-wielding crowd spilling on to the road from the pavement on Ash's side of the street. Being held back by a couple of uniformed PCs. Angelique could see Mellis from CID standing outside the semi-circle of headcases, talking to another uniform she didn't recognise.

'Look at these fuckers. I see Mellis; hope he's brought a stack of outstanding warrants. This kinna gathering's usually four-deep with crims.'

'Idiosyncratic spelling of paedophile,' McIntosh observed, looking at the placards protesting variously against Peedafile's, Pedafile's and Pedofil's. Another demanded 'Hang child mullester's', while still another proposed 'Castrait all pervert's'.

'It's not even nine o' clock yet, either. Amazing what can motivate some people to get out of their scratchers when they don't have jobs to go to.'

They walked over to Mellis, who welcomed them to the madhouse with a subtle twitch of his brow.

'Sergeant McIntosh, Special Agent X,' Mellis said loudly, over the hubbub of angry shouting five yards behind. 'What brings you two to this morning's carnival?'

'We're here to talk to a witness who lives in one of these houses, a Raymond Ash.'

'Are you DI de Xavia?' asked the uniform, a sergeant, she could now see. There was surprise in his tone. As per.

'In the flesh,' Mellis said, before Angelique could answer for herself. 'I take it her reputation precedes her.'

'Save it for the Lodge, Inspector,' she warned Mellis, then turned to the sergeant. 'And don't tell me – *you* thought I'd be taller.'

'I . . . eh . . . I'm Sergeant Glenn. We spoke yesterday, about—'

'Oh right. The exploding budgie, aye.'

'Eh?' asked Mellis.

'So what the hell's this about? Has a paediatrician moved into the neighbourhood?'

'You need to stop reading those big papers, Angel,' Mellis said, handing her a copy of the *Daily Recorder* and pointing out the second story on the front page.

Angelique speed-read the text. 'Oh, balls.'

'And big dicks too, according to the weans. Hence this show of enthusiastic public-mindedness.'

'How did they all get here? Are they running buses or something?'

'Looks like it, doesn't it? I'd say it's about half from Burnbrae and half from round here. They're still arrivin' as well.'

'I came by here yesterday,' said Angelique, incredulous.

'Ash's missus said if I didn't want to hang about, first thing in the morning was good because they're up early with the wean.'

'I thought you were going to the school yesterday,' said Glenn.

'No. I phoned there to warn him I was coming, but they said he'd walked out. That's why I tried him here. I figured he'd said "fuck it" and gone home, or at least to the pub. Not sure I'd have lasted the day at work myself if somebody had taken a shot at me the night before.'

'That's *if* somebody took a shot at him,' Glenn added scornfully.

'You're the one who said—'

'About the budgie, aye, but—'

'What's with this bloody budgie?' demanded Mellis.

'Like I told you, Inspector,' Glenn got in ahead of Angelique. 'Ash claimed somebody tried to shoot him. I gave him short shrift, but it turned out there was some evidence that a shot was fired. To wit: some broken windaes an' a deid budgie.'

'*Some* evidence?' countered Angelique. 'I spoke to Forensics yesterday. They found a nine-mill bullet in the wall behind the budgie's cage, and they're still pickin' up feathers.'

'Aye, but in the light of subsequent developments, I've a mind to think the bugger could have fired the thing himself, to get attention. That was my impression when he first came in, and the facts are startin' to back me up. New job, new wean. He's under stress and he wants somebody to notice.'

'A cry for help?' Mellis mused. 'It's possible. From what I've been told, Ash certainly fits the picture of a person on the edge of some kind of breakdown.'

'Who knows what could have been goin' through
mind?' Glenn continued. 'Sick bastard, if you ask me. Did
you hear what he did before he left the class yesterday?
Had them all drawin' cocks.'

'Jesus,' said Angelique. 'Imagine that. Weans drawin'
willies. Whoever heard of such a thing?'

'Aye, but no' at the teacher's askin',' Glenn retorted. 'I
think this guy could have flipped out bigtime.'

'And what do you think?' she asked Mellis.

'I think I know too little to comment. There's two kids
missing, that's my priority at this stage. I'm ruling nothing
out and nothing in. They could be walking through their
mothers' front doors right now. Same as Ash could turn
up here with a lovebite and a hangover.'

'Christ help him if he does,' said Angelique. 'And is there
anything to link Ash with these kids, other than timing?'

'No. Not a thing. Which is what we've all been at pains
to explain to our wee assembly here.'

'Ya big spoilsport.'

'Oh don't worry, they're not letting the facts get in the
way of a good rammy. So what is it you want with Ash?'

'You don't want to know,' interjected McIntosh, for
which Angelique was grateful. Whether or not Mellis
wanted to know, she seriously didn't want to explain.

'You say you didn't go to Ash's school,' Mellis stated
enquiringly.

'No. Why?'

'I spoke to some of the staff last night. The auxiliary or
secretary or whatever, she said the police had come looking
for him but found he was already gone. I'd been wondering
who it was – if he was already in trouble for something, it
would explain the disappearance and I could concentrate
my efforts elsewhere. Then Sergeant Glenn here told me

279

about his discussions with you, and we both assumed it must have been Special Branch.'

'Not guilty.'

'Here, whit yous bastarts gaunny dae aboot this?'

Angelique turned around to see an imposingly corpulent mass of flesh and nicotine prodding insistently at McIntosh's shoulder, a 'Peedafil's out' placard in her other hand. Its otherwise indeterminate sex was identified by the 'Number One Mum' pendant that hung ponderously across a neck as wide as the Kingston Bridge, the trinket looking like it had been reforged from a battleship's anchor with the chain merely resprayed.

'About what?' Mellis asked politely.

'This fuckin' pervert. Yous are aw staunin' aboot like spare pricks, an' this Ash bastart's away wi' two weans. You want tae have heard the language he came oot wi' in ma niece's class yesterday. Filthy cunt, that's whit he is. Whit yous daein' aboot him?'

Those at the rear of the crowd noticed this growing altercation, and began turning to face it instead of the house.

'We're following a number of lines of enquiry,' Mellis told her. 'There's nothing to link Mr Ash to the two boys at this stage.'

'Aye, neither there's no. That's how yous are aw staunin' here, ootside his hoose? Cause he's got fuck-all tae dae wi' it? D'ye hink we aw came up the Clyde in a fuckin' banana boat?'

Most of the crowd was facing their way now, the semicircle changing from convex to concave, smile in front of the house to frown. 'Number One Dad' then emerged from the mob to take his place at his paramour's side, just as large in mass, but more of it intimidatingly solid. Angelique could tell he took family matters seriously, as borne out not only by his pendant, but also by the semmit he wore to reveal, among his many tattoos, a homemade inscription: 'In memory of my deer Father'.

'Is there a problem, doll?' he asked Number One Mum, though he was looking straight at the cops.

'Just these cunts staunin' here wi' their fingers up their holes when they should be oot findin' this paedophile bastart.'

'Sounds like yous need tae get your priorities straight. It's no' a crime tae care aboot your weans, ye know.'

'I would entirely agree with you on that, sir,' said Mellis. 'However, I'm sure Mrs Ash cares deeply about her own child, and having this going on outside her front door can't be very comfortable for either of them, so perhaps—'

'His wife and kid are still in there?' Angelique said with open disgust. 'With all this shower outside?'

'There's a PC in the house,' assured Glenn. 'Jane Beckett. Been there since late last night.'

'Still,' she said, rounding on the Number One Parents, 'how would you like this goin' on outside your house if you'd a three-month-old baby in your arms?'

Number One Mum looked at her like she'd found her on the sole of her shoe. 'Whit side o' the fuckin' rainbow did yous recruit her?' she grunted, drawing her eyes off Angelique. 'Fuckin' PC Munchkin.'

McIntosh put a hand on her arm. 'Angelique, please,' he said imploringly.

'*I'm* calm,' she assured him. Glenn witnessed the exchange with a quizzical look. Mellis smiled back at him, playing on what the uniform didn't know. Big bloody wean.

Angelique turned once more to face their visitors. 'I'd say you've made your point with your protest, but seeing as Mr Ash isn't actually here, I don't think there's much reason to go on intimidating his family, so how's about we all call it a morning, eh?'

'Listen, Chocolate Drop,' growled Number One Mum, taking an unknowing dip in the piranha pool, 'you cannae tell us tae leave. We know wur rights.'

'Angelique,' said McIntosh again, this time sounding more nervous.

'I'm still calm.'

'Come on, you heard the officer,' Mellis broke in. 'Mrs Ash has a right to her privacy.'

'An' we've a right tae protect oor kids fae shite like her husband,' countered Number One Mum, her face getting redder with every word.

'Well,' said Mellis, 'maybe you could do that more effectively if you were with them, rather than standing out here.'

This was the wrong thing to say.

Number One Mum's head visibly shuddered, then she gripped the placard in both hands and swung it at Mellis, who dived backwards, taking Glenn to the floor with him. Angelique dropped and swept the woman's chubby legs with a kick, bringing her to the ground before kneeling on her back and whipping out her cuffs. She had barely got hold of the woman's hand when Number One Dad waded in with a rescue attempt. He caught McIntosh off-balance, batting him aside with an elbow-blow to the face, then bore down on Angelique. She sprang to her feet and sidestepped his swinging right fist, deflecting it with her upturned left wrist to his enormous surprise. The manoeuvre left them inches apart, staring into each other's eyes, which was where it was easy to read what was coming next. He lunged at her with an intended headbutt, meeting instead two fingers of her right hand, splayed to bridge his nose and poke each eye.

Number One Dad howled in pain and took a step back,

holding both hands to his face, but he only needed a moment's respite before rage and (yawn) pride sent him flailing literally blindly at her. Angelique had already checked her step in readiness for launch, so that by the time he bundled into range, she was already airborne for the two-footed kick that would render him unconscious before he even hit the floor.

'Now,' she addressed the gaping crowd, 'as I was saying, I'd like you all to respect Mrs Ash's privacy and kindly disperse from in front of her house. Or do I have to get angry?'

She didn't.

'You all right?' she asked McIntosh, who was cuffing Number One Mum. His mouth was bleeding a little, but he looked more pissed off than anything else.

'This is police brutality, ya fuckin' black bitch.'

Angelique crouched down in front of their prisoner. 'No it's not. But you call me that again and I'll show you what is. Okay, tubby?'

'Fuck me,' was Glenn's contribution, after he and Mellis had picked themselves up from an embarrassingly ineffectual tangle on the tarmac.

'Secret Agent X, Sergeant Glenn. In action. She's a black belt in three different martial arts. It would have been four, but when she was a brown belt she killed the Kempo instructor during training, and he was the only one in Scotland.'

'Don't listen to him,' she told Glenn. 'He's havering.'

The sergeant nodded.

'I didn't kill him, I only broke his collarbone. And it is four.'

Angelique rang the doorbell and waited for PC Beckett to answer. McIntosh, Mellis and Glenn formed a queue behind her on the garden path.

'DS Mellis, would it be possible for you to get some back-up down here?' she asked.

'Eh, aye. Of course. Why?'

'Well, I just figure five polis is maybe not quite enough to be milling around Mrs Ash's living room.'

'Point taken. Come on, Sergeant, we'll wait our turn. Oh and Angel, before you speak to her, you should know: Ash told her nothing about the shooting or dead punters at the airport. He said he'd fallen in the water escaping from a mugger. Didn't want to alarm her, ironically enough.'

'Got you. Cheers.'

PC Beckett led them inside. The phone rang as she closed the door. Everybody looked at everybody else. Mrs Ash emerged from the living room wearing a puke-stained sweatshirt and jogging bottoms, baby in arms, looking like she hadn't slept since the Nineties.

The phone in the hall had a remote handset. Angelique lifted it and offered it to her host, beckoning an exchange for the child.

'It's okay,' she said. 'You'd be amazed the number of things you learn to do while still holding this wee parcel.'

Accordingly, Mrs Ash cradled the child in the crook of her right arm and held the handset to her face with her left, retreating to the living room. Receiving no signals for or against, the three cops followed her in. She sat down before pressing the speak button, gesturing with a nod that they should take their places on the sofa.

'Hello? Raymond! Oh thank God. Where are you? Are you all right?'

She looked defensively at Angelique, who had sprung to her feet upon hearing the name.

'Yes. There's been police here since last night. What's happened?'

Angelique sat down again, biding her time, trying to piece together what she could from Mrs Ash's side of the conversation, which was by far the smaller.

'Oh God. Yeah, there's been a bloody lynch mob outside since first thing this morning. I don't know what the police think. No. But . . . but can't you . . . Jesus. Okay. Okay. I know. Oh Christ, Raymond. No, he's been fine. I know. A bit of posseting. He slept nearly four hours. Okay.' Etcetera. Until, tearfully: 'I love you too. Okay.' She held the phone up. 'He says he wants to speak to one of you.'

Angelique took the handset.

'Hello, this is DI de Xavia.'

'Howdy. Raymond Ash.'

'Where are you, Mr Ash?'

'You'll understand if I'm reluctant to say.'

'Nonetheless, it would be best for everybody if you came home, then we could clear all of this up.'

'You don't have a clue what needs clearing up here. I know nothing about those boys. First I learned about it was in the newspaper.'

'Me too, Mr Ash. There's a lot of things we need to discuss, and I don't need to tell you your wife's very worried.'

'So am I. Look, my money's runnin' out fast, so cut the headgames and listen up. I was abducted at the school yesterday by two men posin' as polis. They stuck me and my car in the back of a truck and took me to an abandoned farmhouse. I can't give you an exact location, but it's somewhere off the road between Kincregie and . . . fuck knows, it's round there somewhere. They all had guns, and there was a lot of comin' and goin', like they're preparin' for somethin'. I don't know what they wanted with me, but I got the impression I wasnae the main attraction. That's

285

probably how I managed to escape. I stole one of their cars. Mine's still there. Black Polo. You find that place and find them, *then* I'll think about comin' in.'

'If you come in now, we can protect you from whoever they are.'

'Who's gaunny protect me from you?'

'Mr Ash, you're not under suspicion for these boys' disappearances.'

'Tell that to the vigilantes.'

With which he hung up.

'Fix Mrs Ash a coffee, would you, Tosh?'

'I'll get it,' said Beckett.

'Tosh'll help,' Angelique insisted. McIntosh nodded, getting the picture. The other cops left the room, whereupon Mrs Ash pulled up her sweatshirt and plugged the little one in.

'You must be telepathic.'

'Experience with my sister-in-law. I can distinguish between hungry crying and non-specific disgruntlement. The fact that he was practically chewin' through your jersey helped too. Do you want me to go as well?'

'No, you're all right.'

They sat in silence for a while, Angelique waiting until the feed was well in progress before asking any questions. Another thing she remembered from James's wife was that you wouldn't get a nursing mother's full attention until the little human pump had relieved some of the pressure in her chest. From the kitchen, she could hear McIntosh on his radio, relaying this farmhouse's sparse location details. It was about an hour north of Glasgow. They were going to get the local force to suggest likely candidates and then check it out with ARU back-up.

'Mrs Ash?'

'Kate.'

'What did he tell you?'

'Same as you. That he'd been abducted and then escaped. Christ, I wish I knew where he was. I know he's okay just now, but . . .' She sighed anxiously. 'It doesn't make sense. Who would want to kidnap Ray? He's not making it up, though. He's scared. I've never heard him like that.'

'There's nothing . . . untoward that he's been involved in? That you know of?'

'Ray? Are you kidding? Neither of us has the time to get involved in more than a cup of tea these days. And any spare time he does get he spends wired to his computer.'

'Doing what?'

'Games. Shoot-em-up stuff. It used to be his business. He ran a PC games network in Allison Street – The Dark Zone – before he became a teacher.'

'What about yourself? Work-wise, I mean?'

'I work for a marketing and PR firm. I'm on six months' maternity leave just now.'

'So it's unlikely they'd be after him to get to you.'

'Hardly.'

Her expression changed, something dawning on her as she ruminated on this evidently absurd possibility.

'You're not interested in these boys, are you?' Kate said. 'You're after something else. Do *you* know about something Ray's involved in?'

'Yesterday was the first time I heard his name. But you're right, I'm not involved in the missing boys investigation. Would you mind if I had a look at Ray's computer?'

'Sure. Hang on, Martin's finishing up here. I'll show you myself in a minute.'

McIntosh eagerly beat Beckett to taking the kid, and was

rewarded with a shoulderful of puke for his enthusiasm. Kate led Angelique up the stairs and into a small, cluttered room, dominated by an impressive PC set-up. The walls were covered with cartoons, all of them hand-drawn. Taking pride of place above the PC monitor was one of a stubby cowboy with a beard down almost to his waist and a sheriff's badge shining through it. Kate noticed Angelique's interest.

'Ray used to draw cartoons for a few local publications. He's been doing it since he was wee. He had a regular one in *The List* a few years back, usually music-related.'

'Are these all his, then?'

'No, a lot of them are copies from Bud Neill. Ray's crazy about him. That's how he got started. His dad had a scrapbook of Bud Neill cartoons and Ray used to copy them when he was a kid.' She pointed to the cowboy. 'He even uses that as his online player model. Lobey Dosser.'

The name meant nothing to Angelique, but she did recognise one of the cartoons, having seen a framed version on the wall at the Tulliallan training centre. It depicted two drunks in a fight, one jumping up and down on the other, bottles lying discarded around them, and in the foreground two uniformed cops. The caption read: 'Now, the smart caper here, probationer, is tae wander roon the corner till somebody reports it.'

'You said he just plays games,' Angelique said, booting up the machine. 'Where's the joystick?'

'Only lamers use joysticks.'

'Sorry?'

'Just quoting Ray. It's his only area of machismo. The kinds of games he plays, you use a mouse. You can use a joystick, but you'd just be frag-fodder.'

'Frag-fodder?'

'Sorry. I try not to listen when he starts, but you can't help picking up the lingo.'

Angelique had a quick scout around the system, checking the usual places: recent browsing history, temporary caches, deleted mail. Personal greetings correspondence aside, it backed up what Kate said: everything was gaming-related, even the techie websites about improving processor and graphics performance. She ran a Fastfind, looking for image file-types. The dedicated cyber-pervs were often known to have their collections stashed away somewhere, and a cluster of .gifs or .jpegs in one folder was the giveaway. In Ash's case, the only image files were in his Internet temporary cache, all belonging to those gaming pages. If he'd been inclined to abduct little boys, she'd have expected to find something more illicit than the Savage UK CTF fixture list, whatever the hell that was.

It was the den of a typical overgrown adolescent, a regression cave where he could retreat now and again with his toys and nostalgia. Outside it, there was clearly a very strong marriage and a child he'd become a teacher in order to support. There was nothing to suggest a reason why he would attract the attention of the Black Spirit, or indeed any other gun-toting ne'erdowells. Neither was there anything to back up Glenn's idea that he was an attention-seeking fantasist, or on the verge of a breakdown, other than the kind most new fathers go through when they realise it's for keeps. The only jarring thing was that he hadn't told his wife the truth about his evening swim, but this was probably because he didn't want her worrying. Same with the dead bloke at the airport. It didn't do for one new parent to let the other think he was totally losing it.

Angelique said her thanks and went outside, where McIntosh had already brought the others up to speed about

Ash's phone call. She stopped Mellis before he could go in.

'This Ash,' she said. 'Does he have any form, do you know, or has he been on the wrong end of anything before?'

Mellis nodded. 'For what it's worth, yeah. Breaking and entering. Donkey's years ago, though. Nothing since.'

'You've got a file?'

'The jacket's with DI Carmack at Burnbrae.'

'Lot of use that is to me.'

'Don't sweat. You'd be better talkin' to Angus McPhail at Partick. You know Gus?'

'Aye. Thought he'd retired.'

'Christmas he bows out. It was his collar.'

She dropped McIntosh off at HQ then headed for the West End, her old student stomping grounds. Partick copshop saw more than its fair share of the bizarre, having Glasgow Uni on its patch, which was why Raymond Ash had ended up there in the final year of his degree.

'It was just a student prank that got out of hand,' Gus McPhail told her, having looked out the station's records of the case. She sat opposite, a hand over her own folder containing notes and updates on the Black Spirit. 'They broke into the university museum. They didn't steal anything, just, ehm, rearranged a few of the exhibits.' He smiled as he spoke. It was the kind of case he didn't mind recalling.

'Wait a minute, I remember this. I was a student here too. I was in first year at the time, but it was the talk of the whole campus. Was it not some kind of protest?'

'Well, catch-all excuse for anything students get up to, isn't it? I think it was part protest and part just because it was there to be done. The uni had spent a whole load of cash on a new security system for the museum.'

'And the students were saying the money could have been better spent elsewhere, I remember. I think I was at a meeting about it. You go to everything like that in first year.'

'So these two decided they'd break in to prove the system was keech anyway.'

'How did they manage it?'

'Computer hacking, distraction, what have you. They were quite clever, but . . . well, they didnae need tae be *that* clever. That was the point. They didnae just succeed in provin' the security was keech – they proved that if somebody had wanted to screw the place, it would have happened already. Anybody could have done it – they were just the first to bother.'

'So how did they screw up?'

'They didnae. Nobody knew whodunnit.'

'How did you catch them, then?'

'An anonymous tip. Well, supposedly anonymous. It was called in from the guy's parents' hoose, but it was a young bloke's voice and he had nae brothers. He gave himself away.'

'Ash?'

'Naw, the other fella. Simon Darcourt, his name was.'

The name rang a bell, but she couldn't place it. Maybe she remembered hearing it in her uni days, but she was sure it was more recent than that.

'Why did he do it?'

'You answered that one yoursel' a minute ago. It was the talk o' the steamie. Everybody was goin' on about how smart and how ballsy these guys had been, and if you ask me, it was killin' him that they all didnae know it was him.'

'Wouldn't be the first time that's given us a body.'

'Aye. You hear them sayin' aboot serial killers that

deep-doon, they want to be caught because they want somebody to stop them. I think some of them want to be caught so they can finally take the credit.'

Their discussion winding down, Angelique asked for a photocopy of the case file, still wondering why that name was familiar, as well as trying to construct a scenario that could tie a student prank to an abduction more than a decade later.

Gus handed her the pages and she opened her folder to accommodate them. She caught him staring at the cover, on which there was a reproduction of the Black Spirit's eponymous calling card.

'Right bad yin,' he said.

Not half, she thought, then remembered that he shouldn't recognise it, that the image was classified. 'You know this? You've seen this before? When?'

'This mornin',' he replied. 'Ridin' up Woodlands Road on a two-legged horse.'

'Fuck off.'

'I'm serious.'

'And I'm outta here.'

That was the problem with not just the Glasgow polis, but the city in general: everybody was a fucking comedian.

Angelique drove down Gibson Street, bringing back memories of the university sports centre at the top, and of the good work undone in the late-night takeaways further down. She checked the tank: running on fumes as per. With a trip out Crieff way in the offing, she'd best fill up. There was a station not far away; quarter of a mile along – as it happened – Woodlands Road.

She coasted through the roundabout and indicated as the petrol station came into view on the left-hand side.

Before she got there, however, she glanced to her right and almost ploughed into the oncoming traffic as a result of what she saw.

'Fuck me.'

Angelique righted her swerve and pulled the car quickly into the kerb, before leaping out and crossing the road with the engine still running. She must have driven past here a hundred, a thousand times; filled up at that station at least a dozen, and though she'd noticed the black statue at the foot of the hill, she'd never actually looked at it.

She was bloody well looking now.

It was a two-legged horse, which should have been striking enough, but it was what it bore on its back that had almost caused her to flip the motor. In front was Ash's bearded cowboy with the shiny sheriff's badge, and riding behind him was none other than the grinning ghost, the smiling spook, the Black bloody Spirit. It wasn't exactly as on the calling cards, which had omitted the brow of his hat to make the figure look more shapeless, but it was undoubtedly the same: a towering black figure with two oblongs for eyes and a gaping grid of teeth below.

There was a plinth underneath. Barely breathing, Angelique bent forward and read the inscription:

Statue erected by public subscription on
May 1st 1992 to the memory of
BUD NEILL
1911–1970
CARTOONIST & POET
Creator of Lobey Dosser, Sheriff of
Calton Creek, his trusty steed El Fideldo,
resident villain Rank Bajin, and many
other characters.

She thought Gus had said 'right bad yin' as a comment on the Black Spirit's deeds, but she had misheard.

Rank Bajin. Resident villain.

Jesus Christ.

'They were quite clever, but . . . well, they didnae need tae be that clever . . . Anybody could have done it – they were just the first to bother.'

The Black Spirit's MO to a T.

'I think some of them want to be caught so they can finally take the credit.'

She couldn't wait until she reached the office to make the call. Instead she got Rowan on her mobile and asked him to relay Enrique's number on the spot. Enrique answered after an even-more-agonising-than-usual number of rings.

'Enrique, it's Angelique. I need to know: does the name Simon Darcourt mean anything to you?'

There was a moment's silence, or maybe it was a month's.

'Simon Darcourt,' he repeated, considering. 'Simon Darcourt. Yes. He died on flight 941 out of Stavanger.'

'You know the names of *everyone* who died on that plane?'

'No, just Simon Darcourt, Jesper Karlsen, Jostein Groen and Marta Nillis.'

'Why them?'

'Because they're the ones whose bodies were never recovered.'

lobbing clogs into the loom

Lexy rolled over and pulled the covers tighter, thinking with some relief that, as it was still dark, his alarm wouldn't be going off for ages yet, so he could snuggle down again. He looked for the red LED read-out on his bedside table to find out exactly what the time was. That was when he remembered that he had no idea where his bed, table or alarm clock were in relation to his current location.

He was lying down on the lorry's floor, wrapped in a removal blanket; jaggy but warm.

'Shite.'

He reached around for the torch Wee Murph had given him, pilfered from one of the crates, but couldn't find it. Murph was still asleep, his breathing audible close by. Lexy remembered feeling sleepy from the movement of the lorry and the warmth of being buried behind the pile. The pair of them must have nodded off, and worryingly, he had slumped down and wriggled his way out from their hiding place in search of a comfier position.

'Murph.'

'Mmm-waah.'

'Murph.'

'Five mair minutes, Ma.'

'Murph, wake up.'

'Mmm-wuuh-mmm . . . Aw fuck.'

'Murph, where's your torch?'

'Aw fuck, man. I was dreamin' there.'

'So was I. I was at hame in my bed, but I fuckin' woke up here. I cannae find my torch.'

'Put the light on then.'

'Very fuckin' funny.'

'Sorry, man, I'm no' awake yet.'

Lexy could hear Murph rummage among the blankets, then with a click there emerged a beam of light. His own torch was revealed to be sitting about a foot from his knee.

'Christ,' said Murph with a yawn. 'Why did you have to wake me up, man? I was havin' a dream aboot Linda Dixon. I was gettin' a feel ay her diddies an' everythin'.'

'Dreams is as close as you'll get.'

'Well, right noo I'd settle for just seein' her again if it meant we got hame.'

'I know what you mean, Murph,' Lexy said, wisely stopping short of the whole truth, which was that he wanted his mammy.

'Here, we're no' movin'.'

'That's why I woke you up.'

'What time's it?'

Lexy pointed the torch at his watch. 'Half eleven.'

'Shite, man. We've been asleep for 'oors. I wonder where we are?'

'Dunno, but they've no' come back in for their gear yet, otherwise we'd be fucked. I ended up lyin' oot here, in plain sight.'

'Whit did ye dae that for?'

'Tae get away fae your fartin', probably.'

'Cannae help it. It was the beans.'

Wee Murph hadn't let on about the torches before the truck set off again last night. Instead, he had waited until they were well underway and then scared the crap out of Lexy by holding one under his chin and suddenly switching it on, going 'Muahahahaha' at the same time.

Once Lexy had scraped himself off the ceiling and been cajoled out of his subsequent huff, the pair of them put the new-found lighting to use in a further hunt through the crates, reckoning they were safe from interruption as long as the vehicle remained in motion. The search came to a sharp halt when they discovered the baddies' store of provisions, containing several loaves, three six-packs of scoosh, a variety of tins and, crucially, a can-opener. With neither of them salivating at the prospect of cold Cream of Mushroom, they had opted for pork'n'beans, helping themselves to a tin each along with a few slices of dry bread. It was after this banquet that tiredness started taking over from adrenaline, though it was a miracle Wee Murph didn't blow all the blankets away with his exploding arse before the pair of them nodded off.

'Half eleven, man,' Murph said. 'It's nearly Friday lunchtime. Ma maw an' da'll be worried sick.'

'The polis'll probably be oot lookin' for us.'

'Man, we need tae get oot o' here.'

Murph stood up and began walking towards the rear of the truck, the beam of his torch pointing the way.

'Where ye gaun?'

'There' a wee hole in that shutter. I'm gaunny have a keek through it.'

'You'll never get your arse up that high.'

'Very good. I says a keek, no' a keech.'

'I know.'

Lexy followed on behind, using Murph's beam for guidance. They had agreed not to use both torches at once in order to save battery power. Murph was pressing his face against the shutter, where there was indeed a tiny hole between two of the slats, probably made by rust.

'Let's have a look.'

Murph stepped aside and allowed Lexy a shot. He closed one eye and squinted through the gap: he could see trees and bushes, with a steely grey colour visible behind through breaks in the foliage.

'No' much tae go on,' said Murph. 'We could be roon the back o' the school for aw I can see.'

'Hing on, I 'hink that's watter.'

'Watter? Where?'

'Through the trees. I 'hink we're by a loch or somethin'.'

'Gie's another swatch.'

Murph returned to the spyhole. 'Dunno, man, that could be the side ay a warehoose. Or a big puddle.'

'Doesnae matter where it is as long as we're stuck in here, though, does it?'

'Nae sign o' the baddies, but. I think they've ditched this.'

'They wouldnae ditch the truck if it's got aw their gear inside it.'

'I'm no' sayin' they'll no' be back. I'm just sayin' they're no' here the noo. Let's see if we can get this 'hing opened.'

'Got you, Murph. Let's fin' somethin' tae wedge up the shutters.'

Murph trained his torch around the walls and over the crates.

'The drills,' Lexy remembered.

They pulled the blanket away and examined one of the machines.

'Could we drill oor way oot?' Murph asked.

'Aye, if ye can get through a hole six inches across.'

'Aye, awright, I only asked. Whit aboot drillin' through the lock?'

'The lock's doon at the flair. The lowest these 'hings can

298

reach is aboot two feet. We need tae look for somethin' tae use as a crowbar.'

'What aboot thae spare hingmies?' Murph asked. 'Look.'

Murph pointed his torch at the drilling machine's chassis, where there sat a rack accommodating three smaller heads of different lengths and girths. Unlike the fearsome, huge, razor-toothed ball of steel currently attached to the shaft, these resembled chisels, presumably for more precise cutting.

They grabbed one each and returned to the door, where they spent a few sweaty and frustrating minutes failing to force the tapered blades between the floor and the rollers.

'Hing on,' Lexy said. 'Gimme that wan as well.'

'How?'

'I'll show ye.'

Lexy took the smaller of the makeshift chisels and rested its tip against the desired point of entry, then began hitting its base with the other shaft. This was more of a success, in as much as it gouged a groove in the wooden floor and allowed the drillhead underneath the shutter, but when he tried to apply some weight, it just slipped back out amid splinters and dust.

'Fuck.'

'Try again, you're gettin' there.'

'Okay.'

After a few more minutes of Wee Murph playing the spider to his Robert the Bruce, Lexy gave up while he still had ten fingers.

'It's nae use. It's stuck solid.'

Wee Murph inevitably had a few goes himself before coming to the same depressing conclusion.

'Tight as a camel's arse in a sandstorm,' was how he put it, giving Lexy a much needed giggle.

'Right enough,' Lexy reflected, 'if they were leavin' aw this gear lyin' aboot in the back ay a lorry, they'd make gey sure it was well locked up.'

'The padlock's probably the size ay a binlid.'

'Shite, man, whit we gaunny dae?'

'Whit aboot the guns?' Murph asked. 'They still there?'

'I'd doubt it. There was that much comin' an' goin' yesterday.'

'Aye, but they were loadin' stuff, no' takin' it away. C'mon.'

Murph made for the other end of the truck, pointing his torch at the draped blankets covering the lattice. He stuck his head behind the sheets, Lexy only able to see the end of the beam dancing against the inside of the cloth.

'Are the two of them still there?' he asked.

'Aye. I 'hink they were a breedin' pair, but.'

Lexy came closer as Murph pulled up the blankets, the torchlight revealing more metal than Margaret Gebbie's smile.

'Fuck me.'

There were six machine guns and six shotguns, all lashed tightly to the lattice using Velcro-fastening straps.

'D'ye want to try shootin' the padlock aff?' Murph asked gleefully.

'Naw. That only works in the films. If you fired wan o' thae 'hings at solid metal, it could ricochet roon here an' blaw your heid aff. That's if it didnae set aff aw the explosives.'

To Lexy's surprise and relief, Murph seemed to take this on board without a fight.

'Somethin' very bad's goin' doon, innit, Lexy?'

'Aye.'

'I wonder who they are. The IRA or somebody. The UHF, wan o' them lot.'

'They didnae sound Irish.'

'Well, mebbe they're thae muslin mentalists ye keep hearin' aboot.'

'Could be,' Lexy agreed. 'We never got a look at them. Sounded English, but.'

'Whit's that got tae dae wi' it? Hauf the Soothside o' Glesca's muslins.'

'Bad bastards, whoever they are. Aw these guns. Aw this gear.' Lexy sighed, the enormity of it weighing upon him, and with it a realisation that added to his burden: 'We've got tae dae somethin'.'

'Aboot whit?'

'Tae stop them, I mean. Whitever they're plannin', folk are gaunny get kill't. That's what I'm bettin', anyway.'

'Whit can we dae? We're stuck in here.'

'Aye, but we're stuck in here wi' aw the gear they need. I 'hink it's time we began actin' oor age.'

Wee Murph grinned. 'Ye mean start vandalisin' stuff?'

'You read my mind, Murph.'

They agreed that it would be in the best interests of remaining lead-free if they made the damage inconspicuous. Neither of them fancied messing about with the explosives, and even if they had known any way of disabling the stuff, the fact that half the packets were now swimming in pish was a further disincentive. Instead, they set to work on the drill rigs. The machines themselves were formidably sturdy beasts, but Murph identified the point of least resistance as being the control panel. Lexy balanced his torch on one of the lattice strats while Murph removed the cover panel from around the joystick and keypad, using a screwdriver from a small toolkit he'd found in the same crate as the torches. He ripped out all the wiring, stabbed some holes in the circuit board, then screwed the cover back in place.

'Totally Donalded,' he declared, before repeating the procedure on the next one. Lexy, meanwhile, pulled back the blanket from what they had assumed was a third drill, but which was in fact a mobile electricity generator for powering the other two.

'Better be careful wi' this,' Lexy warned.

'Ach, bollocks tae it,' Murph disagreed, flipping open the cover and setting to work inside with one of the drill-heads. 'Hand us that other drill hingmy,' he requested. Lexy complied. Murph bent over the contraption once more. Neither of the drillheads returned, but he did emerge with a rubber fanbelt and a clutch of loose components, which he chucked into the wooden crate at the front that he had first used as a toilet.

Murph then made for the weapons cache, pulling a machine gun from the lattice and holding it at waist height.

'Whit ye daein'?'

'Check it out, man. "Come an' meet my leetle friend." Gerrit?'

'Christ's sake, don't fuck aboot wi' thae 'hings.'

'It's awright, they're no' loaded. Aw the ammo's in the crates. Hey, check this. Daow naow naow naow.'

Murph was now pretending the weapon was a guitar, and started singing a song, something about bikini girls with machine guns.

'You're aff your heid.'

'Heh, imagine you made a guitar oot a machine gun. It would be mental.'

'No' wide enough.'

'An electric wan – wouldnae need a soundboard.'

'It would need a neck wide enough for six strings,' Lexy pointed out.

'It would look cool but, wouldn't it?'

'No' really. Guitars are ancient, man. My da listens tae bands wi' guitars. The Manic Street Preachers an' aw that geriatric stuff. Pure Arran sweater music, man.'

'Aye. I heard you got a free pipe an' slippers wi' their last CD. Ma auld man's worse. He listens tae this band The Clash, fae aboot a hunner year ago. Tooooommy guuuun,' he sang. 'That's wan o' theirs. Gerrit? Tommy gun.'

'Speakin' of which,' Lexy said, nodding towards the wall-mounted arsenal.

'Aye, right enough.'

'Where's the ammo again?'

'That crate there, or the wan next tae it,' Murph advised.

'Right.'

'Whit?'

'I've got an idea for gettin' oot o' here.'

Lexy took a magazine from the ammo crate and handed another to Lexy, then removed a machine gun of his own from the wall. Murph slammed his clip into the empty breach like he had seen in the films, then bent down to pick it up when it fell out on to the floor.

'Wrang way roon, Murph. The bullets come oot pointy-end first.'

'Cheeky bastart. It's dark in here, remember. Whit's the plan?'

'Gie's a hand an' I'll show you.'

Each pocketing one more magazine for good measure, they resealed the lid on the ammunition crate – the first place they reckoned the bad guys would look – then set about moving the contents of two crates of explosives to their own former refuge beneath the blankets. Not an ingenious hiding place, Lexy knew, but the purpose was to create confusion and buy them time: the plan was to run, not fight.

'But where are we supposed to hide when they come back?' Murph protested.

'Ever heard the story of the Trojan horse?'

'Naw.'

'What aboot *The Hobbit*?' Lexy tried, thinking of Bilbo's unseen escape in a barrel. Both of their English classes had done it in First Year.

'Naw.'

Lexy sighed. 'Forget it. When you hear somebody comin', just jump intae a crate, awright?'

'Sound.'

'And in the meantime . . .'

survivors' mutual counselling group

Ray looked at himself again in the sunshade mirror. He could use a shower and a shave, but at least he no longer looked like a vagrant. Whether that was desirable under his current fugitive status remained to be seen, what with the police not likely to be putting out any APBs in search of a piss-smelling bin-raker.

He felt better, that was for sure. He'd managed to give his face a good scrub and shake most of the dust from his hair, but really wished he could do something about the stubble. On TV, people always had a five o'clock shadow when they got huckled, so he felt dressed for arrest. The innocent and unsuspected members of society were always crisp-collared and clean-shaven, and that was what he wanted to look like right then.

The car would help. Step out of a top-of-the-range number like that with jeans, T-shirt and a bit of growth and you looked like a pop star or an Internet millionaire. Same get-up coming out of, say, a fucked black Polo, and you looked like precisely the dubious sort likely to abduct thirteen-year-old schoolboys.

Anyway, he knew that being recognised was among the least of his worries. Scrubbed, manky, shaven or not, he looked nothing like the photo in the paper, and even if he did, who was likely to notice the match? He'd seen wanted pictures and Photofits a hundred times, and forgotten the face as soon as he turned the page and saw some actress falling out of her dress at a movie premiere. The only people actively looking for him were the cops, the armed psychos and the bampots who'd gathered outside his house. The bampots weren't going to find him here, and would most probably be at the Special Brew by now; while the cops weren't going to spot him inside a big, posh motor that belonged to someone else. That said, he couldn't hide out in a supermarket car park forever, not least because the armed psychos *did* know what registration to be scoping for.

Kate had been strong, one of the few things he had to be grateful for over the last forty-eight hours. If she had gone to pieces, he'd probably have followed. He knew that the second he started feeling sorry for himself was the second he'd remember he was just an ordinary shmo with a job, mortgage, wife and kid, and thus utterly inequipped to cope with all of this.

There was a strong urge to just go home. The police and the bampots would have to be faced, but he felt sure he could deal with both once he'd had time to hold Kate and Martin again. What he couldn't deal with was that his abductors knew where he lived, and the last thing he wanted was to lead them back home. Admittedly, they could be waiting for him there already, but right now so were the cops, meaning Kate and Martin would be safe as long as he remained on the run.

To protect his family, he had to stay away from them: it was just the latest absurdity in this through-the-looking-glass world he'd been dropped into. He'd been shot at, kidnapped, mock-executed, interrogated, imprisoned and then finally escaped in time to find he was suspected of abducting two teenagers. In the case of this last, once the shock had passed, his initial reaction was that it was a coincidence of the type that could only happen when your luck was already in minus figures. Two boys from his school had gone missing and so had he. That was the only connection. He had a damn good alibi, but unfortunately the witnesses concerned might be a little reluctant to come forward, nor was he in a big hurry to ask them.

However, as he sat in the Rover and wondered emptily what his next move should be, he found some smoking embers of logic in his frazzled brain questioning whether so many wacked-out occurrences could really be unrelated. If he had disappeared from work without telling anybody – say because Martin became ill and they ended up at the hospital overnight – on the same day as two boys from the school went missing, then *that* would be a coincidence. Disappearing from work without telling anybody – say because two pricks put a gun to his head and stuck him in an abandoned farmhouse overnight – on the same day as two boys from the school went missing, was almost certainly not.

The boys' disappearance had to be linked to his, just as his disappearance was now definitely linked to the two gunmen taking pops at him on the Cart bridge. And if probability dictated that these bizarre events could not be coincidental, then what did that imply for the most bizarre event of all, particularly given that it had been the first of the sequence? It was absurd but true that two strangers had turned up with silenced automatics and tried to shoot him en route to picking up a chicken passanda and a lamb jalfrezi. It was absurd but true that two more numpties had kidnapped him halfway through the Second Years' morning double period, then wheeched him and his car away in a juggernaut. It was absurd but true that there were now protestors outside his home accusing him of being a paedophile and possibly a child-killer.

He had seen Simon Darcourt walking out of Domestic Arrivals at Glasgow Airport. That was also absurd.

But . . .

It took about three hours to drive north from Crieff, keeping within the speed limit at all times, this being the worst day of his life to get stopped by the boys in blue. He had to fill up on the outskirts of Aberdeen, which added some time too. With most of his cash spent at the supermarket, he was left with the options of lifting more from the machine on the forecourt or paying by card, both of which would record his location and time of transaction. However, if the cops were going to those lengths to track him down, they'd catch up with him soon enough anyway, and it wouldn't tilt the odds in his favour any if he had no petrol.

One plus point of the pit stop was that he noticed the northern edition of the *Recorder* wasn't carrying his story. This shouldn't really have been a surprise, it being the city where the local paper legendarily led on the Titanic disaster with the headline 'North-East Man Lost at Sea', but it was a relief nonetheless.

Ray made it to the estate around four. There was every chance she wouldn't still be there, but if so, maybe there'd be a forwarding address. It wasn't like he was spoilt for alternative options.

He recognised the place from after the memorial service, and remembered the route from the church as flagged by roundabouts and supermarkets. He didn't know the number or even the name of the street, but he recalled the house's position opposite a T-junction and the fact that it was a darker shade of red brick than its neighbours either side. At the time, Ray remembered thinking how it was *so* not Simon, and wondered how he could possibly have fitted in. His snobbery was bound to have been viciously double-edged: it wasn't just that the estate was decidedly un-rock'n'roll and thus erred unforgivably on the side of respectability, but Simon, having grown up in a Victorian-built sandstone villa in Giffnock and spoken often about the importance of living somewhere with a sense of individuality, would have considered it vulgar as well as bourgeois.

In one way, it was actually the perfect neighbourhood for the Dark Man, as Ray always believed his greatest fear must be that he'd end up somewhere he belonged, where he'd have no-one to feel different from or superior to.

Ray didn't fancy the place much himself back then, but wasn't so dismissive now. Even if he wasn't fired or jailed, he knew he was never going to have the secluded mansion with the recording studio in the basement and six-seater Jacuzzi in the en-suite, so a pretty, clean and quiet suburban neighbourhood on the edge of the countryside was nothing to be sniffed at, especially with a wee one at your feet. There were lots of kids playing on the pavements, bikes left unguarded outside front doors, garages open invitingly to reveal toys, garden swings and washer/driers. It was very 'choose life' and twee to the point of smug, but it was also obvious that crime and fear didn't stalk the place either.

Ray parked in front of the house and took a breath, working out how to play it in the happy event that she was still there. Obviously a knock at the door, a brief hello and then asking whether her deceased bidey-in might actually be still alive and running about with the bullet-brigade was not on. He'd just have to get her talking and see what was there to be found. There'd been a small gathering at the house after the service, and they had spoken then for a few minutes in the kitchen, Ray having gathered up the used disposable plates and brought them through from the living room in an attempt to make himself useful. He had been feeling awkward and hypocritical about being there, not just given his history with the deceased, but because the wake had been announced as being 'for any family and friends who wish to attend' and despite technically not fitting either category, he had been dying for a pee and thus tagged along. Clearing up the debris from the sausage rolls had seemed the least he could do for the use of her lavvy and a drink of Irn-Bru. They didn't speak for long, but there had definitely been a connection and a sense that they might have a lot more to say to each other under different circumstances. Either that or Alison was just very good at talking and listening to people. Living with Simon, she'd definitely have needed to be the latter.

Ray got out of the car and walked to the driveway, where for the third time in as many days he found himself looking down the barrel of a gun. This time his assailant didn't miss.

Ray dropped to his knees, clutching his chest, the damp seeping into his fingers through his T-shirt.

'Ya got me,' he said, looking up in time to see the gun being levelled for the *coup de grâce*.

'Connor,' said a female voice. 'No.'

But it was too late. The trigger was pulled and Ray got a faceful of cold water, accompanied by an impish laugh.

'Connor.'

Ray wiped his eyes and got a good look at his assassin. On any other day, he'd have found it pretty freaky, but today it simply belonged: he was looking at Simon

Darcourt in miniature. The guy wasn't dead, he had merely shrunk.

'Ha ha ha – all wet,' mini-Simon said, grinning.

Ray, for his part, was grateful for the soaking, it being the equivalent of a slap in the face after which he could be sure he wasn't seeing things.

'God, I'm really sorry.'

He turned his head to see Alison McRae, Simon's one-time significant other, hurrying across the grass towards him. She looked better than he'd remembered, and she'd looked pretty good then; at least as good as the bereaved can look at a wake. She was about five foot ten, long sandy blonde hair, with angular features, a face that looked coldly but perfectly sculpted until she smiled, when it warmed up a treat. There was a vivid sparkle to her eyes that had been understandably missing back then. Ray wished he could take a picture back to show Kate: proof that there was such a thing as a maternal glow, once the sleepless nights and physical ravages had been left behind.

'It's no bother,' Ray said. 'He's a crack shot.'

'Crack pot more like. Aren't you, monster?' she said, picking him up in her arms. It was affection and defence: Ray may have been soaked and apologised to, but he was still an unknown quantity. He got to his feet, hoping she'd clocked the upmarket car and subtracted it from the vagabond effect of the face-fuzz and cheap threads.

'Can I help you?' she asked. Some people had a way of making that question sound a lot like 'fuck off', but fortunately she didn't seem to be one of them.

'I don't know if you remember me. My name is—'

'Raymond. Sorry, I didn't recognise you at first. You were at the funeral.'

'That's right. Eh . . . you said to drop by if I was ever

311

in the area. It's been a wee while, I know, but I was passing through, so . . . Is this a bad time?'

'Yes. I mean no. I mean yes I said that and no, it's not a bad time. I think I owe you the use of a towel at least.'

'Man all wet.'

'Yes, he is, Connor. And whose fault's that?'

'Mine,' he said gleefully.

'Come on in.'

Ray bent to pick up the water pistol.

'No, just leave it there. It's not even his. It belongs to Wendy next door. I think she's inside getting her tea.'

Alison led him through to her living room and gestured to him to take a seat. 'What you doing up in this neck of the woods?'

'I was visiting a friend,' he lied. 'Dropping off some computer gear.'

'Oh. Are you still in that line?'

'Em, unbelievable as it may sound, I'm an English teacher these days.'

'So why aren't you in school?'

Ray held his breath for a second, trying to decide whether this constituted suspicion or merely chitchat.

'Holiday weekend for Glasgow schools. Friday to Monday.'

'Missing it?'

'Oh aye. I live for it.'

She smiled, much to his relief. 'I'll fetch you that towel.'

Connor took her absence as his cue to begin handing Ray toys from the floor, one after the other. There seemed to be no purpose to Ray's role other than to accept them, though putting them down on the settee was cheating, and resulted in them being handed over a second time. Ray gave his best shot to accommodating the pile, all the time beguiled by the child's likeness to, presumably, his dad. He was like George W Bush, in that he looked more like his father than his father looked like his father. Wheels began whirring. Maybe Alison wasn't going to get a towel, but was about to walk in with a gun and blow him away to protect the secret he'd stumbled upon. Given his current environment, however, it seemed a little out of context.

'Oh, he does that to visitors,' Alison said, returning with the towel. 'He normally waits until you've got a cup of tea in your hand, right enough. Would you like one?'

'I've never wanted one more in my life,' he said, honestly.

They each had a seat in the kitchen while Connor watched TV next door. The kid's viewing lasted less than ninety seconds before he was in after them, offering Ray more toys. Alison red-carded him and sent him back outside, where she could hear the aforementioned Wendy returning to the fray.

She sighed with relief as he bombed through the door, wincing only a little as it slammed loudly behind him.

'You got any kids, Raymond?'

'One. Martin. He's three months.'

'You poor bastard. They get better.'

'So I keep hearing.'

'I *know*. When they can walk and talk they're a lot of fun. Actually, once they're old enough to realise you'd have them in a square go, things get a lot easier.'

'I've a cheek to complain. You're on your own.'

'Yeah,' she said, contemplatively, perhaps thinking back. 'I got a lot of help. The girls either side have kids.'

Ray couldn't wait any more. 'Forgive me for prying, but I have to ask. He's . . . there's something very familiar . . .'

'He's his father's double, I know.'

'How old is he?'

313

'Two and a half. You can do the subtraction. Simon's wee legacy.'

Ray nodded, taking a moment to erase the notion that the Dark Man might be about to walk through the door and say 'Daddy's home'.

'Did you know, at the time, I mean, when . . .?'

Alison handed him a mug of black tea and placed milk and sugar on the table in matching earthenware.

'I had no idea. God, when I found out . . . Some irony, let me tell you. Simon didn't want kids, safe to say. I did, but I didn't think I'd ever be having his. In fact at that time I didn't think we'd be together much longer. Turned out I was right.'

Ray poured some milk and stirred his tea. 'Nobody plays silly-buggers quite like fate,' he said, feeling eminently qualified to comment.

'No kidding. Connor was conceived the very night before Simon died. I know that because it was the first time we'd had sex in months.'

Ray did his best not to spit the tea he was drinking, but his widening eyes betrayed his reaction to her sudden candour. Alison had a very serious look on her face; not defensive, but earnestly adult-to-adult. This was still a friendly cup of tea in the kitchen, but they weren't going to be discussing the weather or even their kids any more. Alison stared at the floor for a moment, slightly embarrassed.

'When you were here before, things were too hectic to really talk,' she said, looking up again. 'But I recall you said if I ever needed to speak to someone about Simon . . .'

Ray nodded, remembering. That was the part where he thought they'd made a connection.

'At the time I didn't really think about it. Wakes are a

great time for platitudes; I garnered quite a collection. Emotionally and, as it turned out, hormonally, I was all over the place, and I thought you were just being polite. But once the dust had settled, I began to understand what you meant. And I think I would probably have called, except that once I found out I was pregnant, I had other things to concentrate on. Good things.' She smiled a little, then the seriousness returned. 'Simon wasn't a very nice person, was he?'

Ray said nothing.

'Don't worry, you don't have to tread eggshells. That was what you meant, though, wasn't it?'

He nodded, trying to look solemn rather than enthusiastic.

'You lived with him too, for a while. You knew him.'

'When we were young.'

'But that was what you meant.'

'It was nothing specific you said after the service, just an impression I got. I couldn't picture you clutching his photograph and crying yourself to sleep. I just thought . . . there might come a time when you needed to talk about him, warts and all.'

'He was a bastard,' she said flatly. 'That's what I'd have needed to talk about, if I hadn't been suddenly very distracted. And the reason I knew that was what you meant was that I remember being surprised when you told me your name. You were the last person I'd have expected to attend.'

'I didn't get a very good press, I take it.'

'I heard a lot about you, let's put it that way. And very little of it was good.'

'I can imagine.'

'But you still came.'

'I didn't hate him. It all happened when we were too young and daft to know better. I wasn't going to rubber his death.'

'I did hate him. I do hate him. More and more, every day.'

Alison got up. Ray thought this was because the conversation had strayed into dangerous ground, but was wrong in assuming it heralded the end. She excused herself and disappeared for a few minutes, then returned to say she had asked Wendy's mum to look after Connor for a while. With the coast clear, they took their teas through to the living room and sat at either end of the settee. The TV was still on, with the sound muted: *Neighbours*, inexplicably still going after all these years. It had been cult viewing in his student days, having made the jump to post-modern-ironic-kitsch status after about two episodes.

Alison put her mug on the carpet, clearing a space among the discarded toys.

'After Simon died, I went through the usual rose-tinted remembrance at first. Hard not to, especially when everybody's saying sorry for your loss and telling you how great he was. Even when I thought about how unhappy I'd been, I was more inclined to remember the good times we'd shared. Then gradually I began to look back a bit more objectively and realised that they were simply good times we were both present at. We didn't share them. Simon never shared anything. You could be around him when he was having a good time, and you'd be having a good time too, but . . . oh, I don't know.'

'I do,' Ray assured her.

'A few weeks after he was gone, I remember trying to think of an occasion when Simon ever did anything for me, you know, that took him out of his way, or put his own needs second. I came up dry.'

Ray felt chilled by the remark. Div had said roughly the same thing a few months back, when they were talking about old times and he got fed up with Ray sticking up for Simon. 'Can you honestly tell me a time when that bastard did anything for anybody else, when he made any kind of sacrifice?'

Ray couldn't. He was about to offer Div the time Simon lent Ross twenty quid because there was a problem with his grant cheque, but then remembered how the story panned out. When Ross's money did finally come through, he and Simon kept missing each other for a few days, so the debt wasn't repaid. Simon, who was awfully fond of telling his friends how friends ought to behave, clearly believed Ross should have taken steps to remedy this sooner, and sent him an invoice through the post, thus transforming it from a minor embarrassment to something extremely ugly. The fact that Simon had owed Ross close to fifty quid for half the previous term was, in Simon's familiar justification, 'different'.

'He was an only child,' Ray said neutrally. 'And he had a minor problem with the Earth's orbit.'

'You mean he didn't buy the theory that it went round the sun?'

'Exactly.'

'We always forgave him, though, didn't we?'

'He was easy to forgive. It made for a bad habit.'

'That's what I kept asking myself, after . . . you know. Why did I keep forgiving him when he was always going to crap on me again? It was easy, though. He had charm to burn, and it was always tempting to put whatever he'd done behind him because his good side seemed such a special place to be. It was the same at his work. Anybody else would have talked their way to a P45 years ago. Simon rubbed everybody up the wrong way, but never got the bullet. That's how he ended up in the marketing department.'

'He worked in marketing? I didn't know that.'

'Yeah. He was always sounding off about how useless the marketing department was, and one day he must have said it a little too loud. Instead of an apology, he was made to go and work there for a fortnight, a kind of "mile in my shoes" thing. Of course, when he got there . . .'

'Everybody wanted to be his friend.'

'You got it. But the punchline was that it turned out he was right. Well, they weren't useless, but he was better at it than half the incumbents and he'd only just walked in the door.'

'He always knew the importance of image.'

'He looked bloody good, and he knew it, if that's what you're getting at. He was attractive, in every sense of the word. That was part of the problem. We're so much more forgiving of the beautiful people because we like having them around. They make the place brighter and more interesting.'

'*Hearts are not had as a gift but hearts are earned/By those that are not entirely beautiful,*' Ray quoted.

'What's that?'

'Yeats. "A Prayer For My Daughter." His way of saying the same thing. The beautiful people get things a little too easy and they can be a wee bit cold as a result. Present company excepted.'

Alison gave a qualified-looking smile, not entirely comfortable with his remark. He hoped to fuck she didn't take it as a come-on.

'I'll accept your compliment with good grace, but I would never categorise myself among the beautiful people. I know I'm not four foot nothing with a hump, but . . . you know what I mean. It's the desire to be, the knowingness that makes the difference. Simon seemed to have this constant alertness to how he was being perceived – ironically complemented by a complete lack of self-awareness.'

'Sounds like the ideal marketing executive then.'

Alison laughed, but there was sadness in it. In fact, everything she said hinted that she was skimming the surface of a far deeper bitterness than she was prepared to dip into. Simon, he guessed, had hurt her far more than he had hurt any of those who'd burned their fingers in those petty, self-absorbed adolescent days. To Ray, Div, Ross and everyone else back then, even though he seemed to loom so large in their lives, ultimately he was just a pain in the arse with a colossal ego.

Ray looked again at the TV. It had changed to the news, something Simon never watched. The Dark Man had to have been the university's least militant student, with absolutely no interest in politics, as though it was not only irrelevant, but somehow inapplicable in his case. He poured merciless scorn on Ray and Ross for taking part in student demo marches, whether they were about the Poll Tax, grant cuts, apartheid or whatever, and changed the subject at the first opportunity whenever such matters were being discussed. He liked to portray this as proof of his superior insight into the futility of their enthusiasms, but Ray suspected the truth was that Simon genuinely didn't give a fuck about anything until it was directly in his way.

They talked on, Ray telling Alison all about his student days, including the sorry tale of the deBacchle. Alison reciprocated with Simon's version of the same events, evidencing a talent for revisionism that would have won him a job on *Pravda*.

'Did Simon get involved with any music up here?' Ray asked.

'Yeah, that's how we met. I saw him playing in a band, at a place called The Sheiling. It was a popular hang-out for students and recently former students, if you know what I mean.'

'Aye.'

'I can't remember what the band were called. It was the kind of place you just turned up and watched whoever was playing, then there'd be an alternative club until the early hours. Oh no wait: Book of Dreams, that was their name. Post-Goth, pre Nine Inch Nails kind of stuff. They were pretty good, I thought. I said as much to him afterwards in the bar as an ice-breaker, then we got talking. And the rest is misery.'

'What about the band?'

'The usual. Musical differences. He kept falling out with the other members, especially the singer, Angus. Simon had successfully auditioned for them, because they were already a going concern. Their previous lead guitarist got a job in Texas.'

'The band?'

'No, the state. This is oil town, remember. Simon, being Simon, wanted a bigger say in what they were doing.'

'Don't tell me: he had a better name for them too. Something pertaining to Euripides.'

'Bang on. Eventually, they got fed up and punted him. It really was a shame. Musically, he fitted in great. They sounded damn good and he was a big part of that, but he didn't want to be *part*, he wanted to be all. Ironically, the band did change their name soon after, because they

320

thought Book of Dreams didn't sound dark and scary enough. They became Chambers of Torment.'

'No way. As in . . .? Angus was Angus McGheoch?'

'The same.'

'God. I saw them at the Barrowlands two years ago. Sell-out tour. I guess their subsequent fortunes didn't go down well with Simon?'

'What? You mean getting himself thrown off an express train to success, acclaim and rock notoriety? No, Simon wasn't bitter.'

'So did he chuck it after that?'

'Effectively, yes, but not in spirit. He kept talking about what he was planning, and a few times he thought he'd found sufficiently like-minded recruits, but . . .'

'They disappointed him.'

'Yeah. Well, sometimes. But mainly the problem was that he'd rather sit around drinking and talking than actually doing anything about it.'

'Him and a million other thwarted dreamers. It helps put off accepting the inevitable.'

'After which, unfortunately, the thwarted dreamer becomes a grumpy old git, ranting in front of *Top of the Pops*. There came a time when he forgot there was a difference between being an iconoclast and just being a miserable bastard.'

'I can't imagine living round here helped much either,' Ray suggested.

'You mean the Burbs, or Aberdeen? Doesn't matter, I suppose: he hated both. But Aberdeen especially. With a passion.'

'I can picture him in full rant. Usually very entertaining, if you didn't have an emotional attachment to the target.'

'Entertaining for a while, anyway. I mean, I'm from

Edinburgh and I've been here since I was a student, so I'm the last person who needs to be informed of Aberdeen's shortcomings. It isn't the warmest or most picturesque place in the world, I know. The locals tend to be a bit reserved compared to other places you could mention, but you get used to that and it's not actually the locals that are the problem. It's that half the population don't want to be here. Have a look down this street: you'll see For Sale signs outside one house in four. People come here because this is where the oil biz is centred, but it's not exactly Manhattan and it's probably a few hundred miles from their roots, their friends and families. As soon as they can get work elsewhere, they're off, so it doesn't make for a cosy sense of community.'

'But you still like it, presumably?'

'Connor was born here, and this is a nice neighbourhood to bring him up in. Low crime, lots of countryside, *terrible* accent, but nothing I can do about that.' She smiled. 'I feel settled. I like my job, I like my house, and I've got a lot of friends here. Plus, I'm a great believer that what you find in places is what you bring to them. People bring resentment because they've been uprooted, so it's no wonder they don't find it very welcoming. Simon brought all manner of bitterness with him, and it became easy for him to blame everything he didn't like about his life simply on being here.'

'He didn't have his heart set on an oil industry career, as far as I can remember.'

'No. But what he really resented was that it wasn't a matter of choice. You know his dad died shortly before his finals.'

'Yeah. I was very sad to hear it. I met his old man a few times. Lovely bloke, his mum too. They worshipped the ground he walked on.'

'They spoiled him rotten, more like it. His mum told me she'd had four miscarriages before she carried him to term, and she was in her late thirties by then, so he was extremely precious to them. I don't think Simon ever fully adjusted to the fact that his "most privileged" status didn't extend beyond the family home.'

'Tell me about it,' Ray said, thinking of his flat-sharing days. Everybody could be difficult to live with, especially under the added pressures of student life, but some of Simon's domestic conduct bordered on the pathological. Never mind an absolute and binding refusal to lift a dish-cloth or spring for a pint of milk, he used to do things that gave the impression his flatmates didn't exist; or at least didn't count. Other people's towels, for instance, provided a handy and varied supply of floormats for standing on when he got out of the bath. If he brought a girl home and decided his own bedsheets were a bit whiffy, he'd just lead her into someone else's, provided they were fresher and their owner wasn't home yet. And, least forgivable in an all-male adolescent household, if he ran out of blank tapes, he'd just record over whatever compilation cassette had been left in the kitchen's communal boombox. Asking for an explanation or a justification was merely an exercise in Beckett-esque futility.

'Why did you use my towel to mop up the floor?'

'Because it was wet.'

'Why did you take that girl into my bed?'

'You weren't using it.'

Better to find a nice solid wall and bang your head against it.

'When his dad died, he left a lot of debts,' Alison continued, 'and Simon really had to take the first job he could to bail things out.'

'He was very dedicated, then.'

'To his mother, yes. That was one of the few psychological weapons I was ever able to use to get the upper hand: he hated the thought of being in her bad books, so I'd threaten to tell her when he was being particularly loathsome.'

'You clipe.'

'I'm not talking about him leaving the toilet seat up, here.'

'I can imagine.'

'Can you?' Her tone was suddenly challenging, indignant. Don't presume to understand, she was saying.

'I'm sorry, I didn't mean to—'

'No, I'm sorry. The thing is, I've never really spoken to anybody about a lot of these things. Not to anyone who would understand. I barely know you, but you probably know better than anybody what I'm talking about. Other people, I'd start telling them things but they'd end up cajoling me into defending him, even friends of mine who I *know* hated Simon. They didn't want to be disrespectful of the dead, I suppose, and certainly didn't want to be encouraging the bereaved to start pissing on his grave.'

Alison gave a hollow laugh. 'Christ, I'm saying bereaved because there's no courtesy term for the state I was left in. Is there such a thing as a common-law widow?'

'To be honest, I was surprised to learn Simon had settled down for so long.'

'I think laziness was as big a factor in that as anything else. It would have been too much bother to move out. Besides, Simon knew he could have his cake and eat it with me. I provided all the comforts and conveniences of home, but without the monogamy trade-off. I don't know whether he thought I was too stupid to suss or whether he knew I'd always be daft enough to forgive him, but he got around, let me tell you. It tended to be when he was feeling sorry for himself, like he was owed a casual shag as compensation for whatever he believed he was missing out on in life.'

'Sounds like the early onset of midlife crisis. I've had a fair dose of it myself since the wee one was born. Hasn't manifested itself the same way, right enough. I don't have the energy.'

'You're married, aren't you?'

'Aye. Kate, my wife's name is.' Ray feared he would fill up at the mere mention.

'Simon would never have married me. Not that it seemed a big loss by the end, but, well, there was a time when I thought . . . Stupid. I thought I could mellow him, or maybe just that time would if I hung on long enough. Eventually I realised Simon wasn't going to marry anybody. Marriage is for squares, daddy-o. We lived together all those years, but it was mainly out of habit. There was no trace of commitment, and I was either too blind or too desperate to see that. We were renting this place for more than three years until Simon died. Actually buying somewhere would have been a surrender, you know?'

'You've bought it now?'

'Yeah. The owners were oil people, uprooted to the Middle East. They'd told us the place was theoretically up for sale, but there was a price slump, so they were happy to have the rent cover the mortgage until things picked up. I bought it with compensation money. There was a fund; I think the airline and the Norwegian government were the main donors.'

'And Simon didn't have a hefty life insurance policy all paid up?'

Alison laughed. 'Yeah, that would have been him all the

way. Actually, maybe he did, and there's a baffled insurance agent trying to track down a beneficiary called *Morag*.' She pronounced it with scorn, looking Ray in the eye to check whether he understood.

'Morag, was it? I was going to ask. I was Larry.'

'No point in asking . . .'

'None at all.'

She shook her head, both of them laughing. They were referring to Simon's initially irritating but ultimately rather disturbing habit of referring to people by names he had given them, instead of their own. They weren't nicknames, because nicknames had to have some kind of frame of reference, usually shared among a social group. Some of Ross's pals, for instance, called him Sneckie, due to his hometown being Inverness; while Div used to call Ray Apollo because he was always calling Houston. Simon's names had no such derivation. He just one day started calling Ray Larry and Ross Hamish. He neglected to rename Div, which was an early indication that he had been the first among them to achieve non-person status.

Ray tried steadfastly to ignore it and to refuse to respond, but Simon was dedicatedly persistent, and utterly deaf to protest, as though he couldn't see what Ray's (or indeed Larry's) problem was. He would even introduce Ray as Larry in company, and when challenged, offered no explanation other than 'you're just Larry – can't you see?'

'He thinks he's fuckin' Jesus, noo,' was Div's take on it. 'Changin' folk's names. "Simon, I will call you Peter."'

Ray's retrospective interpretation was that it was his way of defining people entirely on his own terms, in subservient relation to himself. It was as though Simon didn't see others as autonomous entities, but mere functionaries who existed only in the context in which he regarded them.

'Did you guys have a nickname for him?' Alison asked.

'A few, yeah,' Ray replied, offering a conspiratorial grin. 'Mostly of Div's suggestion. The one that stuck, though, was the one he actually quite liked: the Dark Man. It came from Darcourt, obviously, and he revelled in that mysterious, brooding edge it suggested, but for the rest of us it was more a reference to his general state of mind. He didn't tend to have a song in his heart and a skip in his step, you know?'

'Only too well. And you saw him in his carefree youthful years, believe me. After his mother died . . .' Alison sighed. 'It was like living with a one-man zeitgeist.'

'When was that?'

'Nearly five years now. Couple of years before Simon. Pancreatic cancer, poor thing.'

'He must have been devastated.'

'He was. He was with her right at the end, and . . .'

'What?'

'I don't know. There was something, definitely something he wouldn't talk about. He wasn't so much depressed as consumed with this black, black simmering rage.'

'So would I be if I'd lost both parents.'

'Oh no, absolutely. But there was something more, I was sure. And whatever it was, it was so preoccupying, he hardly talked about his mother until after it had lifted.'

'God. How long did that take?'

'Couple of months. When it did pass, it was sudden, like he'd just snapped out of it. I suspected it was because he'd started an affair. He went away on business for a few days and came back with a smile on his face. There were a *lot* of business trips after that, usually at weekends, which I thought was a dead giveaway. Simon giving up his weekends for the betterment of Sintek Energy just didn't compute. Mind you, what also didn't compute was that he was horny as a goat whenever he returned from one of these jaunts. Not that I was often up for entertaining him, but the cheating partner traditionally doesn't want anything to do with her indoors, does he?'

'So I'm led to believe.'

'That's why I could never be sure. Plus, an affair wasn't exactly Simon's style. Affairs take commitment, especially given the logistics. I don't know, I gave up trying to figure him out a long time ago. I mean, the last couple of weeks before he died, he seemed really kind of energised, as opposed to Mr Existential Gloom, and I thought we might be turning a corner. But there's nothing to say he wouldn't have been back to his cornered-wolverine persona by the end of the month.'

'Did you see anyone at the memorial service that looked a likely candidate?'

'For a secret lover? I don't remember seeing anyone looking particularly distraught at his loss, including myself. If it wasn't for all the official hoo-ha, I fear it might have been a sorry wee affair. There were a lot of people from Sintek, and my friends there to offer me moral support, but it wasn't wall-to-wall with folk offering heartfelt testimonials. I was about the nearest thing left to a next of kin, apart from some distant relatives on his dad's side, in France. That's why the service was up here in Aberdeen.'

'Stuck in Aberdeen forever. That wouldn't have pleased him much.'

'He'd be spinning in his grave if it wasn't that . . . well, he isn't in his grave. The service and the headstone were just ceremonial. Simon's body wasn't recovered from the crash.'

Ray felt something lurch as she said this. His common sense was telling his imagination to behave, but as his common sense wasn't exactly having a blinder this week, his imagination was telling it to fuck off. He hoped his reaction wasn't obvious, and pretended to be distracted by the TV in order to evade inquiry. It was on to the Scottish news by now, footage of a picket line giving way to the newsreader back in the studio.

'What do you tell the wee yin about him?' Ray asked, trying to get her talking again while he calmed the whirrings in his brain.

'He's too young to ask much. He knows he doesn't have a daddy like the other kids, but he's not really curious. *Yet*. I suspect Simon's reputation will have to be rehabilitated when that happens.'

'Quite right. He should count his blessings. Mine will be able to see for himself what a shambles his old man is. Still, I suppose I can always tell him about my wee place in the great rock'n'roll—' Another glance at the TV sharply truncated Ray's musings. The screen showed a reporter standing outside Burnbrae Academy. The sound was off, so Alison wasn't going to hear his name mentioned, but Ray guessed his own face would be staring back at him any second.

'Eh, sorry, do you mind if I put the TV off? I keep looking at it and I feel very rude.'

'No bother,' Alison said. She patted around herself on the settee. 'Sorry, I've no idea where Connor's put the remote.'

Ray surveyed the floor, the carpet barely visible under the spread of discarded toys. On screen, the report cut to a police press conference at which two pairs of distraught parents sat behind an array of microphones and tape recorders.

Ray stood up to switch it off manually, but when he pressed the button, it merely sank into the set.

'That's why I need the remote. Connor's knackered the Off switch. He likes seeing the wee light change from red to green, so he pressed it on and off until it broke.'

Photographs of the two boys filled the screen, the same ones as had appeared in the paper. His would be next, any second. He looked balefully again at the pile of assorted plastic on the floor, before being saved literally by the bell.

'That'll be Connor back, or maybe Lindsey wants a word. Excuse me a second.'

Alison turned her back to walk out of the door just as Ray's face filled the screen. It was the same crappy shot as in the paper, but sitting in the same room, it would have been difficult for Alison not to notice a resemblance. The bulletin returned to the school, where the reporter gave his soundless, straight-to-camera summing up.

After that, it was back to the studio and over to the sports desk. Ray exhaled at length and flopped back in his seat as he heard Alison in muffled conversation at the front door. It was getting on for time to make his excuses, though the thought that he didn't know where he would be going next made the settee all the more comfortable. The downside was that, while Alison had been content to entertain him as a uniquely qualified confessor, she was overdue to start asking some questions of her own.

He heard two lots of footsteps. A visit from the neighbour would make a good moment to leave. Ought not to intrude, best leave you ladies to it. That sort of thing.

The door opened, Alison leading a petite and very serious-looking Asian woman into the room.

'Mr Ash,' she said. 'Thought I'd find you here. Angelique de Xavia. We spoke on the phone this morning. I think it's time we had a wee chat about that chap at the airport.'

target acquired

Angelique hadn't believed in any kind of deity since she saw *Clash of the Titans* at a kids' matinee and made a revelatory deduction about the comparative value of one load of hoary old Bronze Age myths over another. However, she sure knew what the God-botherers meant when they said He giveth and He taketh away.

She was standing in a corridor outside the interview suite at Grampian Police HQ, her mobile still warm in her hand from her conversations with McIntosh and then the Chief, Murray. It was good news, she knew. Great news. Vindication, validation and relief, all of which should have been as welcome as they were satisfying. So why did she feel like throwing the phone against the wall and then smashing every window in the building?

He giveth: thanks to her persistence, hard work, deduction and a spot of sheer ingenuity, it now sounded very much like they had the Black Spirit by the balls.

He taketh away: after all of the above, it still wouldn't be her hand that got to do the squeezing.

While she had been driving north to Aberdeen, they had found the derelict farmhouse and gone in with full ARU back-up, by which time not only was the show over, but the circus had packed up and left town. There was still plenty of evidence of what had gone on there, though. They discovered the chair Ash had been tied to, complete with piss-puddle beneath, as well as the kitchen pantry and his subterranean escape route. Outside there were tyre tracks from a number of vehicles, plus sufficient food refuse to indicate that the place had been occupied for a few days; either that or it was the site of a very large picnic lunch. Ash's black Polo was found less than a mile from the site, burnt out to erase any forensic traces. The car he had escaped in turned out to have been stolen more than a month ago, but had been decked out with fake plates. Boasting a typical Black Spirit flourish, the registration borne by the fakes was traced to a car once belonging to Doctor Harold Shipman, the current holder of a British record Simon Darcourt presumably had his sights on.

The terrorists' evacuation had happened fast, presumably very shortly after discovering that their prisoner had absconded and their location was therefore compromised. They had cut their losses and split in a hurry; so much of a hurry, in fact, that they forgot to pick up all of their goods and chattels, and that was going to be their undoing.

'They've dropped the ball, bigtime,' was how the Chief put it, fond as he was of imported American clichés. 'They left some photocopies in a drawer under the kitchen table. Detailed schematics. We know what he's going to hit, and we'll be ready for the bastard this time. Got to hand it to him, though, he's got some balls.'

'Why, what's the target?'

She almost had to sit down when he told her.

'The Stadium of Light.'

'Isn't that in Lisbon?' Angelique asked. She knew fine where it was, but she needed a moment to stop her head spinning. It didn't sound like Maclaren and Wallace would be getting any whisky.

'Sunderland, woman.'

'Begging the question of what they were doing around Crieff?'

'Lying low, I'd say. If you're planning something like this, better to be hanging out a few hours' drive away from the police force covering your intended target, wouldn't you agree?'

'Planning something like what?'

'I shudder to think,' Murray said, by way of confessing ignorance. 'But the where and the when are in no doubt.'

Angelique swallowed. 'Is there a match tomorrow?' she asked, knowing with a low dread that the answer would be in the affirmative.

'An international, no less. Sold out. It's a friendly: England versus Denmark. They're playing all over the shop these days while Wembley gets rebuilt. And one of the local MPs will, of course, be in attendance, the stadium being close to his constituency.'

'One of . . . The Prime Minister.'

'Of Great Britain, on Sonzolan independence day. Kick-off at three.'

'Christ,' she breathed, the enormity starting to truly hit home. Never mind the PM, he was just one guy; but a foot-ball stadium full of tens of thousands of people was as close to the ultimate terrorist nightmare scenario as you were likely to get, nuclear weapons aside.

'It's Black Spirit style and Black Spirit scale, all right,' she agreed. 'But will he hit it now, considering . . .?'

'We've still done our job if he doesn't. Chances are they'll remember about those photocopies at some point, but they might not, or they might remember too late. They might just risk it, because they don't know for sure whether we've found the plans or even the farmhouse. Whatever happens, our people will be ready. Low-profile, but ready. And thanks to you, they'll all finally have a picture of the man they're looking for.'

'They? Our people? What happened to us? *We* the people?'

'Sorry, Angelique. Lexington's come in over the top. You know how it is. This is huge, big as it gets, and he's got jurisdiction. It's between London and the Geordies now.'

'Mackems,' she corrected, hearing Millburn's voice in her head.

'What?'

'They're not Geordies, they're Mackems. And none of them did a fucking thing to track this bastard down, but they're just going to waltz in and take the collar?'

'We're all on the same team, Angelique. Besides, you're up in sheep land and it's after dark already.'

'I could be in Sunderland in six hours. Five.'

'They're already in briefings down there. Look, you've done a hell of a job. Lexington asked me to . . .'

Angelique stopped listening when he slipped into autopatronise, then went about winding down the conversation as quickly as she could. It was at times like these that she despised cellular phones. All there was to do at the end was press a minuscule plastic button, when the occasion called for slamming an ancient bakelite handset into a brass-lined cradle with a force that would shake the building.

'You okay?' asked a passing PC.

'Fuck off.'

'Ooh, sounds like *some*body's got PMT.'

'Listen, sheep-shagger, if I had PMT, they'd be scrapin' your sack off the ceilin' with a spatula right now, okay?'

This time he didn't tarry to argue the point.

Angelique took a walk to the bathroom and allowed

herself a few moments to calm down. She gave her face a splash with cold water before heading back to the interview room where she'd left Ash, someone she knew she'd do well to remember had put up with a lot more shit than even her this week. With that thought, she diverted via the drinks machine and grabbed a couple of cans. The guy had looked like he could seriously use something a little stronger, but it was better than a boot in the balls, as Maclaren would say.

'Cheers,' Ash acknowledged, with genuine warmth. Mock executions didn't half make you grateful for the little things, she thought. 'So what's the story?'

'Oh, an everyday tale of politics, egos and bullshit,' she replied.

'Eh?'

'Never mind, feeling sorry for myself. Pathetic. You came up trumps, that's the story. They found something very useful at the farmhouse, as well as corroborating evidence of your account.'

'What about the kids?'

'Nothing. Unrelated, would be my guess.'

'Could you tell the papers that? I'd quite like to go home without running the risk of being castrated.'

'We'll try.'

'But I take it these guys are still on the loose.'

'Not for much longer, thanks to you.'

'How so?'

'I'm sorry, it's classified.'

He sighed. 'Any danger you can tell me what it all has to do with Simon Darcourt? Because, you know, anythin' that gave me a Scooby what the fuck's been goin' on would be much appreciated.'

'That's classified too,' she informed him. 'But to be

honest, I'm not feeling particularly loyal or dutiful right now.'

It's not every day you discover your late ex-flatmate is one of the world's most wanted terrorists, responsible for the murders of literally hundreds of people. Ash had been wrestling for a few days with the part about Darcourt also not being quite as late as was erringly suggested by events such as his funeral, so it could have been that he was all out of astonishment. Fatigue admittedly may have played a part in reining in any histrionics, but either way, he took it very calmly, something Angelique felt moved to remark upon.

'I'm all out of astonishment. And I'm very tired,' he explained, confirming her seldom-doubted vocational suitability.

She had started him off with the calling card, laying it down on the interview-room table. 'I know you're familiar with this individual,' she told him.

'Rank Bajin,' he had identified. 'Nefarious villain and good father to four sons. Fond of oratund loquacity and toasted cheese. Is he the latest suspect for the missing schoolboys?' he asked with weary sarcasm. 'Because frankly, that's not his style. As far as I remember, he even helped return Fairy Nuff's children when Big Chief Toffee Teeth kidnapped them.'

'I think you should be taking this a little more seriously,' Angelique warned.

'You're showin' me cartoon characters and you're accusin' *me* of takin' the piss?'

'Touché,' she acknowledged. 'Allow me to get to the point. Was Simon Darcourt familiar with this image, to your knowledge?'

'Aye. I pinned it on his bedroom door when we were flatmates. His nickname was Dark Man. You know, Darcourt, Dark Man. It seemed appropriate. He thought so too. Why?'

Which was when she told him the whole bloody story. He sat and listened, calmly, nodding every so often, as though at his own thoughts rather than her revelations. At one point, tears began welling up in his eyes, but there was no protest, no incredulity. No resistance.

'On any other week, that would have fair knocked me oot my stride,' he offered, supplementary to his previous explanation for seeming markedly underwhelmed. 'I think if I got a shower, a hot meal and a decent night's kip, I'd probably wake up in the morning and freak out about it. Right now, the scary thing is it makes perfect sense. Well, you know, in an appropriately fucked-up and twisted kind of way.'

'How's that?'

'Simon's got what he always wanted. Renown, power, money, kudos—'

'Kudos?' Angelique queried with open disgust.

'It's a post-rock'n'roll world, Detective Inspector. No points for being good when everybody wants to be *bad*. And it doesnae get much badder than mass murder, especially if you can pull it off with a bit of stagecraft. He's world-famous. No, he's got something more than fame: he's got world notoriety. Garth Brooks is world-famous, but who'd want to be Garth Brooks if you could be Iggy Pop, Lou Reed and Marilyn Manson rolled into one?'

'Sounds more like Charles Manson.'

'My point exactly. Charles Manson, David Koresh would be another example. Guys who wanted the power, the adulation, the iconic status of rock stars, but couldn't get it the way their idols did. They got it somehow, though, didn't they? And now Simon's got it. Feared on one side of the law, respected on the other. Subordinates jumpin' to his command, women hangin' off him no doubt, money, international jet-set lifestyle, and the power of life and death in his hands. He gets to walk taller upon the earth than us mere mortals. The reason it makes sense is that in a way he always did.'

'What do you mean?' Angelique asked.

So Ash told her, recounting all he knew about Darcourt, from their first meeting as students to what he'd learned from Alison McRae earlier that same day. If there had been any lingering doubts about whether this was the man they were looking for, Ash's story blew them away. Loath as she was to admit it, the person he described was even a ringer for the one in that much maligned psych profile.

'His accomplices will be regarded as mere bit-part players in the greater drama that is his life . . .'

It was all there. Raging egotism, sociopathic lack of empathy, a previously respectable figure with no criminal background (student pranks notwithstanding, and that merely underlined his desire for notoriety at any cost). *'His sin is not anger, but pride . . .'*

There was even the death of a mentor/authority figure; in practice this seemed to have been two figures, the impact possibly even more ferocious through the death of the second unleashing something repressed since the death of the first.

'I once heard of a psychological condition called alixothymia,' Ash said, as a silence grew amid their contemplation of each other's unsettlingly complementary tales. 'It describes people – killers, I suppose – who do hideous things, and they keep doing these hideous things, apparently never sated. But for whatever reason they first started, the reason they keep doing it is because if they stopped, they'd have to turn around and look at what was behind them. They keep going because it's the only way of outrunning the horror of their crimes.'

Angelique nodded, understanding what he was trying to say. He was searching for some kind of mitigating explanation, possibly out of a surrogate guilt.

'I've been following the Black Spirit's trail of devastation for years now,' she said, 'and in that time I've developed a wee psychological theory of my own. Want to hear it?'

Ash nodded. He was beginning to look a little crushed. Cold – if, as he put it, fucked-up – logic had made him calmly receptive to the evening's devastating truth, but only now were its bloody implications beginning to thaw and seep into his conscience.

'He's a wanker,' she told him. 'That's my theory.'

Ash smiled sheepishly. 'I'd have to concur.'

'That's what it all boils down to in the end. Everything else is just hair-splitting definitions of precisely what *kind* of wanker he is. And I've got a theory on that too. Care to take a guess?'

'A total wanker?'

'Close enough. The exact answer was "a fucking wanker". And that's why he arsed up. Wankers never change. Do you know how the Partick polis found out who broke into the university museum?'

'Yeah. That fucker told them.'

'How do you know that?'

'Same source. Pretty much my last conversation with him, for obvious reasons.'

'He couldn't take it that people didn't know what he'd pulled off, could he?'

'What I'd pulled off, in the main, but yeah, you're right.'

'Fast-forward to him as the ingenious and audacious terrorist. He leaves these Rank Bajin calling cards as part of his ego trip, so that the authorities make no mistake in apportioning blame; or credit, looking at it from his point of view. None of the foreign cops are likely to recognise a 1950s Glasgow newspaper cartoon character, so he's not giving anything away immediately, but he's still trying to offer a clue, isn't he?'

'Well at least he's graduated from phoning up the investigating officer.'

'But it's got to be gnawing away the whole time that once again, nobody knows it's him, same as after the museum.'

'What good is fame if you no longer have an identity?'

'Exactly, so when he comes back home, it's gaunny gnaw all the harder because this is where he used to be just another nobody. Then by coincidence, he sees you at the airport. It's the kind of thing that should put him on his guard, remind him that this is a small place and there's people here who remember his face, whether or not they think he's dead. But he's a wanker, so he just cannae resist goin' after you, 'cause he wants you to know who he is now, wants you on your knees before him.'

'Prior to puttin' a bullet in my brain, no doubt, once he's had his fun.'

'Well, yeah, afraid so. He's a wanker, not an idiot. But he took an unnecessary risk just so that he could play headgames with you, and it backfired because you escaped and led us right to his wee temporary HQ.'

'So now you're gaunny slap the cuffs on him, and then *everybody* can find out who he is. You're probably doin' him the biggest favour of his life.'

'Not me personally, but I know what you mean.'

'Not you personally?'

Angelique paused, feeling the anger start to well up again. Murray was right, she knew. They were all on the same team. It just felt a bit like she had beaten four defenders and rounded the goalkeeper then rolled the ball across the six-yard box for someone else to sidefoot it home.

'It's out of my hands,' she said. 'The big boys have taken over, so I just have to run along like a good girl. Anyway, it's jurisdictionally out of range; geographically too, seeing as I'm up here in the northern wasteland.'

'Does that mean you'll be headin' home?'

'You anglin' for a lift?'

'Well, seeing as you impounded that nice car, and mine's in Perthshire.'

'More like in pieces, I'm afraid. They torched it.'

'Every cloud has a silver lining.'

'Not your pride and joy, then?'

'Not quite.'

'I can give you a lift, but I wasnae plannin' to leave until the morning. It's well after twelve and it's been a long day. I was gaunny grab some kip for a few hours.'

'That sounds pretty good. Can I call my wife?'

'Sure. You can use my mobile. I'll go and sort us out with some rooms at the section house.'

'If there's none spare, right now I could sleep in the cells.'

'There'll definitely be none of those spare on a Friday night. The section house will be more comfortable – marginally. You could get that shower too, though I'd reckon you're on to plums with the hot meal.'

'Doesnae matter. Food I can get any time. Sleep, on the other hand . . .'

what great oafs from little arseholes grow

Simon checked out of his hotel in Glasgow at exactly 20:30 hours, after a light meal and a hot shower. There were some who advocated the most spartan and ascetic living conditions at times like this, in order to stay lean and sharp, but Simon considered it psychologically important to remain well acquainted with what he'd be missing if he or anyone in his charge fucked up.

Taylor collected him out front in one of the Espaces. May had the other one, having dropped him off the night before. After they'd finished at the bridge, they'd waited for Lydon and Matlock to arrive at Glen Crom with the tour truck, then gave them a lift back down the road once they had planked it. It was almost six by the time he got to bed, which was according to schedule: sleeping by day would keep him frosty for the long nightshift ahead. Aware that the phrase 'Do Not Disturb' was interpreted by housekeeping staff the world over as a dare, Simon had bolted the door and moved the dresser in front of it to reinforce the point.

Taylor and he were the vanguard in what began building into a small convoy as they got nearer to Dubh Ardrain, with vehicles pulling out from laybys at their back, prompted by confirmatory flashes of the Espace's headlights. May was first, then Simonon and Deacon, each towing a speedboat, then finally Headon and Cook in the vans. All but the lead Espace diverted up the reservoir approach road, where the tour truck had been concealed, half a mile past the rigged pontoon. There they would tool up and await the go-ahead.

Upon Simon's instruction, Taylor pulled into the final layby before the entrance to the complex and watched the cars drive inside, one by one. He looked at his watch. It was almost midnight, almost time for the shift changeover. He was waiting for the backshift workers to be clear and well on their way home before making a move. There'd be another changeover at eight, but nobody would be leaving from that one. The nightshift's other halves would get a phone call soon after, apologising and informing them that their partners were being required to work a double shift to sort out a major technical problem, for which they'd be getting plenty of lovely OT. Because let's face it, that's all they really gave a fuck about, wasn't it?

Taylor looked ahead at the steel gate and the crappy Sixties low-rise office building just inside it, then across to the pine-built visitor centre a couple of hundred yards along on the other side of the road, nearer the water. Simon could tell what he was thinking.

'Not much to look at, is it, Roger?'

'Oh, I don't know. It looks like money in the bank, to me. That's always a pretty sight.'

'A mine is just a hole in the ground until you walk out with the gold. Remember that.'

'Roger.'

Simon rolled his eyes. They both laughed.

Dubh Ardrain. Gaelic for Black Ridge, Black Promontory, Black Mesa, something like that anyway. And it really wasn't much to look at, not from the road. You could drive past it and not know it was there. Even a visitor centre and several large signposts probably weren't enough to tip off many of the passing tourists as to what lay concealed. It would be easy for them to think the pine building was a lochside aquatic wildlife centre, just another take-it-or-leave-it, scones-and-souvenirs drop-off point on the road through the glens.

As opposed to the reception area for one of Scotland's greatest engineering feats. Three hundred thousand tonnes of concrete stacked high in the buttress above, quarter of a million cubic metres of rock removed from the mountain below. Thirty kilometres of tunnels and aqueducts. Miles of road widened and strengthened merely to accommodate the construction traffic and the transport of the giant internal components. A man-made cavern you could fit Hampden Park inside, housing the twenty-metre-high turbines that pumped out six hundred megawatts of electricity, generated by harnessing the dual powers of water and gravity.

It wasn't internationally recognisable, like the Forth Rail Bridge, probably because power stations didn't sell many postcards; in fact, its existence wasn't even widely known throughout Scotland, never mind beyond. But once Simon was finished with it, it would be the most spoken place name on every television channel, every radio station and every newspaper on the planet.

After about ten minutes, the backshift's cars began to leave. There would be eight of them. Simon counted them all away and then picked up his radio.

'May, this is Mercury. Come in.'

'Reading you, Mercury, this is May.'

'Okay, they're all out. You've got two coming your way heading for Crianfada; the rest went off towards Cromlarig. A Ford Mondeo and a Honda Accord. Once they're past, do your thing. Everybody else, that's your cue too. Mercury out.'

Simon screwed the silencer on to the end of his pistol,

eyeing the security guard's kiosk. A few moments later, a paunchy old man emerged and ambled lazily across the concrete to the gate.

'Time to rock'n'roll,' Simon declared.

Taylor put the Espace into gear and drove the last hundred yards to the entrance, causing the security guard to stop halfway through sliding the gate closed for the night. Simon got out and walked towards him, hailing him with a wave.

'Can I help you?'

'Aye. Would you mind holdin' on to these for me?' Simon said, producing the gun from behind his back and shooting the guard twice in the head. 'Cheers.'

The man had barely hit the ground before Taylor was out of the Espace, pulling polythene from the backseat to shroud him in. Simon slid the gate open again before bending to retrieve his spent shells, while behind him Taylor rolled the corpse on to the sheeting. Taylor lifted the body into the vehicle, leaving a few drops of blood glistening on the tarmac underneath. They each grabbed a handful of earth from the landscaped flowerbed next to the booth, sprinkling it on the ground to absorb the moisture and cover up the stain.

Murder, concealment of the victim and removal of evidence: it was all over in less than a minute, expertly and emotionlessly executed. Simon felt nothing, not even excitement. Well, perhaps a frisson, but nothing compared to what was to come. When you knew you were about to fuck a girl six ways from Sunday, the first grope of her breast didn't really set the heart thumping, did it?

Not like it did when that was all you knew. Not like it did the first time.

* * *

Revenge, they said, was a dish best served cold. Simon would concur, having burned his mouth on his first home-cooked effort, which had been thoroughly overheated but still half-baked. It was a recipe etched in bile and marinated in poison, a naïve attempt to sate a craving that could never know satisfaction if it was fed for a thousand years. Trying to stem an anger like that with one death was like trying to drain the ocean with a sponge.

What restitution could possibly be enough for the death of his father once he knew the hideous truth behind it?

Simon had always understood the symbiosis between the simultaneous failings of both his father's health and his father's business; the vicious circle of debt, stress, illness, absence and further debt. But what he only learned at his dying mother's bedside was that all of it had been precipitated by some wee parasitic ned who was mercilessly bleeding Darcourt's Brasserie for protection money.

His father had requested that Simon never find this out, due to his shame at facing death in failure and ignominy, not wanting to pass such a psychological debt on to his son as an inheritance. Simon's mother, however, told him she felt guilty that Simon had been forced to sacrifice his aspirations so young in order to bail her out, and was aware how miserable his life in Aberdeen was making him. Her growing fear was that he was nonetheless inheriting the legacy of failure his father wanted to save him from, but because of what he *didn't* know, rather than what he did.

'I don't want you to think your dreams can only end in failure because of what happened to your dad,' she said, before telling him the truth.

Frank Morris was the cunt's name, at the time just another of the pitiful apologies for gangsters Glasgow had to put up with; guys who'd last less than a day in a real underworld, and whose vision barely extended beyond their postal district. He ran protection rackets on half the restaurants in the city (or more accurately half the non-Chinese restaurants, as they had their own breed of leeches), and attached himself to Darcourt's when his dad moved the brasserie from where it started on Victoria Road to a larger prime site on Sauchiehall Street.

Simon's dad had arrived from France in the Fifties, with just the shoes on his feet and the promise of a chef's job at the Central Hotel. He worked his arse off and saved every penny until he was able to open a place of his own, and built up his business from nothing over almost thirty years. Frank Morris took less than eighteen months to demolish it.

The protection payments started off huge and got bigger. His dad worked harder to keep up, but according to the first rule of protection rackets, the more money he made, the more money Morris took. In attempting to stay afloat, he pushed up prices, which drove away custom; he laid off staff, which meant service was poor; and he was forced to cut corners in the kitchen, which quickly destroyed the place's priceless reputation. Three decades of excellence, three decades of skill and endeavour, all eaten away in no time by this piece of council-scheme trash and his team of wee hard men.

Because of Frank Morris, his father had died broke as well as broken. Because of Frank Morris, his mother had to face cancer without the companion she most needed. And because of Frank Morris, Simon was stuck in Aberfuckingnowhere, whoring for Sintek Energy, instead of lying in an LA hotel suite, watching some blonde groupie lick coke off the end of his dick after a sell-out gig at the Hollywood Bowl.

After his mother's death, Simon found himself descending into the darkest depression of his life, consumed by thoughts of anger and frustration, compounded as he learned how much kinder the fates had been to Frank Morris over the intervening years. Having already exerted a grip on the city centre's entertainment sector, he'd been well placed when the drug trade moved from the housing schemes to the nightclubs during the 1990s. It was said by some that he was seeing a slice of every fourth Ecstasy tablet consumed in Strathclyde region; others said every second. And he ran it all from his 'Castle', a detached sandstone villa on the periphery of the Marylea housing scheme where he had grown up.

Simon entertained revenge fantasies, naturally, but these only served to reinforce the sense of hopelessness that must have tinged his father's humiliation. He was an oil-biz marketing exec. What the hell could he do to a drugs baron, even if it was only an ageing, neddish, Glasgow one?

His mum had wanted to save him from thinking that his dad's failure had been his own fault. His dad had wanted to protect him from knowing that he'd been brought to his knees by a wee lowlife he was powerless to fight back against. Both had done so because they didn't want this knowledge proving a psychological hindrance to the pursuit of Simon's own ambitions, but it was already too late. His dad's legacy of debt had banished him to the northern wastes, and by the time his responsibility to his mother was finally lifted, the damage was long done. He was stuck in a wage-slave job, watching his life trickle away, and he couldn't act against the man responsible because he was too intimidated, just like his father before him. His inheritance was therefore complete.

The greatest insult, and surely the one that had stung

his father all the way to his grave, was that all of this should be visited upon him by a piece of scum not fit to look him in the eye. Frank Morris was a nothing, a wee toley shat out of an alcohol-and-nicotine-ridden whore of a mother, raised on chip fat and superlager in some council-scheme gulag. Anybody can be a hardcase when there's a whole team of you picking on one guy. Simon's father was a thousand times the man Morris was, and Simon dearly wanted to prove it.

So dearly, in fact, that it reached the stage where he could barely think of anything else, until one evening, sitting in the life-sapping traffic, he asked himself what was really stopping him? The answer, he realised, came down to two fears: death and prison.

Yeah, he thought, what a towering threat: to lose everything he had now. Would killing Morris really be worth sacrificing this idyllic existence?

It was a moment of absolute liberation, when he understood the true value of the choices before him; understood, perhaps for the first time, that he *had* choices. Even consumed by grief and anger, he had been ready to accept that there was nothing he could do, there was nothing someone living this suburban suit-and-tie life could do, because people like Morris existed in a different world, beyond the people carriers and the privet-bordered concentration camps.

But there *was* something he could do. He could kill the bastard. If that was what he really wanted, he could kill the bastard. If he was a better man than Morris, and of that he had no doubt, then he could find a way, no matter what the guy's reputation and no matter how many knuckle-dragging neds were under his command.

His depression lifted immediately, leaving his mind like

a clear-blue dawn after a month of storms. When he woke up each morning, he found himself springing out of bed, powered by the energy of suddenly having a purpose to his life after so many sleepwalking years. Unfortunately, he still had work to go to, but it was a lot easier to get through the days when there was something else beyond them other than the slow drive home, a microwave ready meal and a couple of hours' mindless telly before bed. Besides, his job was to prove invaluable in realising his plan, devised after several weeks' research and a couple of weekend reconnaisance trips to Marylea.

The point of greatest vulnerability, he was quickly able to identify, was 'the Castle', Morris's solid stone edifice of self-congratulation. The proud old building had stood there for decades before the council planners decided to infest the surrounding area with the vermin decanted by Sixties inner-city slum demolition, and the rat colony that was Marylea had gradually expanded to encroach upon it. Morris had grown up there, and, like all the other wee urchins, came to regard the house as the last word in grandeur, unaware that their very presence was decreasing its value at the rate of the altimeter on a nose-diving jet plane.

When he made his grubby little fortune, instead of shipping out to Milngavie or Eastwood like the rest of the nouveau-riche schemies, Morris bought the home of his pitifully limited dreams (after sufficient vandalism and intimidation forced its previous owners into an unplanned sale). Not for him the upmarket neighbourhood and the veneer of respectability down at the local golf club. He was a ned to the last, and wanted to live in 'the big hoose' over-looking the Marylea estate, so that the scum he came from among could see him as the lord of the manor, king of the castle.

The rear of the property backed on to woods, affording some privacy in marked contrast to the uninterrupted view the front offered to the nearest rat-cages sitting across Marylea Road. The back garden was where Morris liked to relax by spending time with his pigeons, accommodated in a large dovecot that ran almost the length of the back fence. Everybody's hobbies seemed silly to the uninitiated, but this one had to be among the daftest. The things didn't even race. The 'sport', if you could call it that, between competitors was for your own birds to seduce someone else's back to your dovecot, whereupon they became your property until such time as their fickle affections were bought by still another flea-bitten doo.

Morris was said to be out there every night, talking to and preening his favourites. Simon's reccy trips to the woods behind the Castle bore this out, each occasion witnessing Morris stand at the dovecot, holding birds in his hands and, bizarrely, putting his mouth to their beaks and blowing until they puffed up like feathered beachballs. Morris was a scrawny, scruffy little man, wearing a hideous and manky old flannel jacket that presumably had some kind of effect on the birds, because no-one above the gutter would even approach the thing without tongs. He looked somehow too small to be all the things he had come to mean to Simon, but that merely served to underline the insult that had to be corrected. This little prick looked like he ought to be cadging the money for a tin of Special Brew in George Square, and yet he had ruined the lives of everyone in Simon's family.

A rifle would have been easiest, but not ideal, as such weapons could be as difficult to get hold of as they were easy to trace. Noisy, too, unless he could acquire a silencer, something else to put him at the mercy of another crook who could pass on what he knew to the cops or the gangsters, whoever he most needed to keep sweet.

He remembered that during their uni days the little drummer boy had been part of an archery club. Simon's contention that such weapons were obsolete had kicked off a discussion about the stealth factor and their possible use in the perfect crime. The LDB's idea for an untraceable murder weapon was a crossbow bolt made of ice, fired through the eye into the brain, as the shot would be silent and the evidence would just melt away.

The flaw, as far as Simon could see, was that unless the shot was perfect, the ice would shatter if it met any substantial resistance. He also remembered reading about a hunter in the States getting a real, steel-tipped bolt through the eye but still surviving, having been lucky about which part of his brain it embedded itself in. Simon knew he would only get one shot at this, so he couldn't afford any such margin of error. The method, however, had a lot to recommend it, crossbows not being so difficult to come by; and while the purchase could still theoretically be traced, that would only happen if the police had a clue what the murder weapon had been.

Simon's solution was a variant on a technique already well known to the sniping assassin. While hollow-pointed bullets had been used to maximise damage since their spectacularly effective introduction by the British Army at Dum-Dum in India, an even messier effect was to be had by filling the cavity with mercury. What happened was that, upon impact, when the bullet itself slowed, the mercury didn't, instead exploding forward and outward with devastating consequences. A shaft of mercury suspended in ice would have the same effect on Morris's brain as bunging it into a Moulinex, as well as allowing for silent delivery and leaving no explanation as to how it got there.

To construct a number of these little deathsicles, he enlisted the unknowing assistance of the Sintek lab, on the premise that he was organising a photoshoot to create a new image for a forthcoming trade ad campaign. Columns of metal suspended in ice, representing the oil locked in stone beneath the North Sea, something like that. No bother, they said. They had a freezer capable of rendering temperatures below minus fifty, so they could not only produce what he was requesting, but make sure it would tolerate the hot studio lights for a good while before there was any danger of it melting. Nor was it too much trouble to supply him with a cryogenic flask to transport the slugs in, keeping them immersed in liquid nitrogen.

Covering all the bases, Simon even went to the bother of organising the supposed photoshoot, and it tickled him that Sintek were still using the image in corporate publicity to this day. 'Unlock the power' was the slogan.

Simon unlocked the power at dusk on a balmy late-summer Sunday evening. As on his reconnaissance trips, he parked his hired car on the other side of the woods, near the on-ramp for the eastbound M8, and made his way on foot to the spot he'd picked, overlooking the rear of the dovecot. The crossbow was an appropriately French-made Eigle-Hawk, capable of firing its bolt at more than three hundred feet per second, and was fitted with a fifty-yard parallax scope, through which Simon viewed Frank Morris's last living movements. The ned emerged from the house as before in the appalling flannel jacket, and showed his true class as he nipped the fag he'd been smoking, popping it into his pocket before approaching the birds. The guy was a million-aire, but was still saving the rest of the dowt for later.

Simon removed one of the deathsicles with a small pair of plastic tongs and placed it into the slide. Having been practising the shot for weeks from various ranges and angles, he had achieved a one hundred per cent accuracy record from distances of less than forty yards, and he estimated his current range at around thirty. However, those figures had been achieved when his hands weren't sweating or his heart banging like a Lambeg drummer outside a chapel. It wasn't fear he was feeling, just tension. As he looked through the scope at Morris's head, there was no moral dilemma, no questioning the path his life might be about to take. His only worry was that he'd miss.

Simon watched him pick up a bird in both hands and lift it slowly to his face. Morris took a deep breath and so did he.

Morris put his mouth to the bird's beak and blew, remaining motionless, eyes closed, like it was the tenderest kiss between lovers. In that moment, Simon's heart was suddenly stilled and his hands steadied.

This was his becoming.

Simon pulled the trigger and Morris was dead before he had breathed out. His head jerked once, his arms each gave an involuntary shake, like a marionette, then he fell backwards and the pigeon took flight.

Simon watched him for a moment, lying flat on his back on the unkempt lawn. It looked as though he might spring back up again any second, but for the blood seeping from his eye socket and the twitching of his feet.

He had done it. It was over. And he felt . . . he felt . . .

'Ever get the feeling you've been cheated?'

Was that it?

No swell of emotion, no rush of catharsis, no euphoria, no regret, no revulsion. Just a dead guy on the grass, whom no-one had even noticed yet, and the sounds of birds still tweeting among the trees in the darkening twilight.

It wasn't right. He *had* been cheated, and the worst of it was, he had cheated himself. Morris was dead, but that was all. He hadn't known why, he hadn't known who, and he hadn't even suffered. He didn't deserve this instant, clinical, silent death; Simon should have been in his face, pulling his still-living brains through his eye socket with a crochet needle, looking him in his good eye and making sure the last words he ever heard were the name of François Darcourt.

After which, he later understood, Simon would still have felt the same. It was just another of the many ways in which murder was like sex. All that effort, all that planning, all that panache in going about the deed, but in the end it all leads to one final moment, after which there is only emptiness. It is then that there is some consolation to be had in knowing that you took precautions, so at the very least your sense of anticlimax won't be compounded by unwanted consequences.

It being his first time, Simon was naturally paranoid about what clues he might have left, what amateurish mistakes he must have made; concerns that were multiplied on the Monday morning, when his boss ordered photos of the murder weapon blown up to poster-size for their stand at the forthcoming OilExpo at the Aberdeen Exhibition Centre. But there were no consequences; not legal ones anyway. Only a hollow feeling and the signs of his depression returning, now that his energising project had failed to deliver what he'd expected of it.

He was soon to realise that nothing could have delivered what he'd expected, because his expectations had been unrealistic. What he ought to do was more accurately evaluate

355

what killing Morris *had* delivered, which was the best few weeks of his life. More immediately, however, he found insult added to his sense of disappointment when he learned from the newspaper that someone else had bagged the credit – and not *just* the credit – for his work.

'It is understood by police that Sunday night's murder of Glasgow gangland figure Frank Morris was ordered by a rival drug dealer. Police say their sources have indicated that there was a contract out on Morris worth as much as £30,000, which is already believed to have been paid to the hitman responsible.'

Incredible. Truly incredible. If Simon had waited another couple of weeks, someone would have beaten him to it and saved him all the bother. It said a lot about what a tinpot gangster Morris was, too. Glasgow was a small place, its underworld even smaller. Morris was bound to have known there was a price on his head; and yet Simon was able to sneak up on him in his own back garden. Typical narrow-minded ned complacency. He was safe as long as he was in the Castle, because in front of it was *his* scheme, his turf, and no enemy would dare try taking him on there.

But talk about fucking cheek! All that effort, all that ingenuity, just for some chancer to say 'Aye, it was me, big man. Thirty thousand sheets, soon as you like, please.' The point was, Simon *hadn't* waited another couple of weeks and he hadn't been saved the bother. He had done it himself, and somebody else was coining it in as a result. It was The Arguments and Chambers of Torment all fucking over again. In both those cases, he'd had all the ideas, all the vision and done all the work: taken a bunch of no-hopers and moulded them into something they could never have been without him; only for them to enjoy all their success and take all the credit once he was out of the picture.

Well, it wasn't happening a third time. This was a matter of honour and a matter of principle. It was also, as it turned out, a matter of thirty Gs, and he was fucked if some ned was tucking a greenback meant for him into his Kappa jogging trousers.

The phrase 'a rival drug dealer', to anyone who had read a Scottish newspaper in the past ten years, meant Bud Hannigan: another jumped-up schemie, but one with sufficiently more brains and ambition to make him a far bigger player than Morris could ever have hoped to be. If it was true that the contract had been redeemed, there was little question it would have come out of his pocket.

He decided to hire another car and take a drive down to see Hannigan at the snooker club he owned, where he was known to hold court of an evening. Simon told the goon on the door he had information that someone was ripping off his boss, but would only divulge exactly what he knew to the man himself. He was patted down for wires and weapons, but the only thing he was carrying was the cryogenic flask and plastic tongs. It was probably curiosity over these that got him an audience, as Hannigan was too important to be entertaining any scrote who walked in claiming to have information. No doubt these were normally paid off by underlings if their gen was up to much, and given a good kicking by the same if it wasn't.

Hannigan received him from behind a large mahogany desk in his office, a room preposterously lined with oak panelling despite being in a two-storey, Trumix-and-chipboard, Seventies-built dump. It was like the castle-inside-a-condo from that Steve Martin movie, with the motif Thirties Gangster rather than Medieval Gothic.

'Mr Smith,' Hannigan said, without getting up. 'Common name in my business. What do you have for me?'

Simon opened the flask, releasing a suitably mysterious plume of smoke as the nitrogen evaporated, then removed the remaining four bolts with the plastic tongs. He placed them on the desk, one by one.

'What are they?'

'The question is not what are they, but where is the fifth one?'

'Do tell,' Hannigan said impatiently.

'Well, the water part is long gone, but the mercury part is in the Royal Infirmary morgue, being scraped off the inside of Frank Morris's skull.'

'What would Frank Morris's skull have to do with me?' Hannigan asked, ever the cagey gangster.

'I could think of thirty thousand things it had to do with you.'

'I'm sorry, you've lost me,' he said, with the same smug smile he probably turned on for the cops when they asked him questions they both knew the answer to.

'Sorry to waste your time, then,' Simon said, picking up the bolts again and replacing them in the flask. 'I just thought you might want to know about it if somebody had taken you to the cleaners.'

'I got what I wanted, Mr Smith. From where I'm sittin' it looks like you were the wan who got taken to the cleaners.'

'True enough, but it's not me who's got a reputation to consider. I mean, I wouldn't like to think there were people in this city who thought I was fair game to take the piss out of.'

That got Hannigan on to his feet.

'What do you want?'

'My money.'

'You're talkin' to the wrong guy, then.'

'So who should I be talking to?'

Hannigan sighed, thinking it over. He was trying to remain as confidently blasé as before, but it was obvious the insult and the repercussions Simon had hinted at were starting to boil inside. Hannigan looked at the goon who was manning the door, giving him a steady nod.

'Come on,' the goon said, taking Simon by the arm and leading him out of the office into the corridor.

'Wait there,' he told him, then disappeared back into Hannigan's absurd oak-lined sanctuary. He re-emerged after a couple of minutes.

'Mickey Fagan,' the goon said. 'Used to be quite high up in Morris's crew. Got his jotters for skimmin' even mair than the other thievin' wee wanks that work for him. He tell't us he was gettin' his ain back, but the fat bastart just needed the money.'

'I'm not takin' the piss here, but what proof did he offer before you gave this chancer thirty K?'

'He was the first to tell us it had happened. We knew before the polis. Mickey said he stabbed him through the eye, oot the back where he keeps his pigeons. Mickey's still got friends on the crew, obviously.'

'Where does he live?'

'Foxhill Avenue, Nettleston. Number ninety-eight.'

'Alone?'

'D'ye 'hink anybody would live wi' that fat ugly cunt?'

'Takes all sorts.'

'If he's gettin' any, he's payin' for it. You plannin' tae drop by?'

'Briefly, yeah.'

'Bud says your money'll be already spent. It's been a week. Fagan owes a lot of people. Heavy people.'

'Aye. He owes me. But it's not just the money I'm bothered about.'

'Didnae think it was.'

'Fat bastard, did you say?' Simon asked, already deciding how this man he'd never met would die within the next few hours.

'Aye. Greedy in mair ways than wan. Why d'you ask?'

'I'm going to need some heroin. About three grammes. Pure stuff, not the shite on the streets.'

'Pure is expensive. Three grammes of pure is *very* expensive.'

'I'll take it off what you owe me.'

The goon gave him a dark grin. 'Come back here in an hour. What's your mobile?'

Simon, still running on balls and brass neck, was about to parrot it out automatically when he remembered that he was just a marketing exec playing at being a hitman, and it was the marketing exec's name and address on the mobile bills.

'I'll be back in an hour for the H. I'll let you know how to get in touch once my business with Mr Fagan is complete.'

Simon thought the bluff sounded confident enough, but was still worried the guy might start laughing at him as he walked away.

'You know, you don't look the type,' the goon said instead. 'For your line, I mean.'

Simon turned around. 'And how long would I last if I did?'

The goon delivered on the smack, which Simon tested for

adulteration in his car with a bottle of mineral water. Pure heroin dissolves clear and tasteless in cold water; all that nonsense with lighters and teaspoons was only necessary because of the shit it was cut with. The sample was a little cloudy, but was probably about as clean as anyone in this city had ever seen it.

He drove past Fagan's house to make sure he was home, looking for the light of a TV against the curtains in the drab wee council semi, sitting in a street of identical drab wee council semis, amid a scheme of identical drab wee streets. Having ascertained that the thieving chancer was home, Simon took a detour to a petrol station and bought a cheap baseball cap (mandatory delivery-driver attire), then progressed to the nearest Indian takeaway for a curry. He brought the food back to the hire car and opened the tinfoil container on the dashboard, stirring the heroin into the rich massala sauce before replacing the cardboard lid and putting it all back inside the poly bag.

It took Simon three goes at ringing the bell before Fagan grudgingly dragged himself away from *Who Wants To Be A Millionaire?* and answered the door.

'Chicken Tikka Massala, pilau rice, keema nan, Bombay potatoes,' Simon said, holding up the carry-out.

'Whit? I never ordered this.'

'I know. Mr Khan says it's on the hoose, tae make up for the wee misunderstandin' last night. Hing oan, you *are* Mr McGraw, aren't you? Ninety-nine Foxhill Avenue?'

'Whit? Eh, aye. McGraw, that's me. On the hoose, you say?'

'Aye.'

'Magic.'

'There's your curry, then.'

'Cheers.'

Mickey Fagan, you *had* thirty thousand pounds. You now have enough heroin to kill Keith Richards. Thank you for playing.

So his graduation from revenge killer to professional assassin was as inadvertent as it was instantaneous, though its fortuitousness was a factor of time, not destiny. It became very obvious very soon that he and murder were star-crossed, and it had merely been a matter of them finding one another.

Simon had improvised the means of Fagan's untraceable death in a twinkling, then proceeded from concept to realisation in a near effortless matter of hours. And what had really taken him by surprise was that he got a greater rush from killing Fagan, a man he only clapped eyes on at the moment he handed over his deadly gift, than he had from killing Morris, with whom he had a decade of scores to settle. The latter had been all gut-tangling emotion; the former nothing but raw power, coursing through him, energising him, making him feel he could do anything – and kill anybody. It was the most vivid, thrilling, invigorating sensation he had ever experienced, and he already knew he'd want more.

Besides, 'professional killer' sounded a far cooler way to think of himself than 'marketing exec'.

He stopped off one last time at the snooker club, where he left instructions on how he could be contacted. The hotmail address he quoted didn't exist yet, but he was pretty sure the username would not have been taken. If his services were required, Hannigan had to email him: the message would be meaningless, but the number of letters in each word would provide a newly bought pre-pay mobile number for Simon to call, once he'd nipped to the supermarket and bought a new pre-pay of his own. After that, details could be offered: names, locations, motives, money.

Nothing happened for quite a while; long enough to begin to feel like it had all been a delusional fantasy, and in a more coldly rational light, long enough to think that they hadn't taken him seriously, and might even throw him to the cops if it would somehow benefit them. Mitigating against that was the fact that they had comped him three grammes of uncut smack, but it was still difficult to reconcile the ice-cool figure who'd negotiated that deal with the suitful of frustration stuck in the Persley Bridge tailback every morning.

Then one Wednesday night he was checking his email and felt his whole body electrify when he saw that a message was coming in from the new account, addressed to thebacchae@hotmail.com. Never have the words 'Retrieving message 1 of 1' had such life-changing significance; when Simon saw them, he knew nothing would ever be the same again.

When he called, it wasn't Hannigan who answered, nor even one of his underlings. The voice was accentless middle-class English, newsreader neutral.

'I got your details from a Bud,' the voice said, by way of introduction and explanation, then rhymed off the info with no pause for formalities. 'Paul Noblet. Forty-six. Planning officer, Teasford County Council, Yorkshire. Interested party believes Noblet's successor would be more sympathetic to his petitions. Accident or no fee. Fifteen offered; that's minus twenty per cent commission. Interested?'

Simon had more bother sorting out a pseudonymous PO box to receive the unmarked bills than he had despatching the unfortunate Mr Noblet. The lot of the professional killer was far less arduous than he could have possibly imagined. No briefcases, no dossiers, no hasty assembly and dismantling of high-powered rifles inside towerblock windows, and not even a binding obligation to dress in black.

The targets were not heavily guarded statesmen or senior underworld figures, but ordinary men (occasionally women, but generally they tended to be the ones holding the invoice) who someone else considered it advantageous to be rid of: husbands, lovers, bureaucrats, rivals, bosses, creditors, none of whom had any idea what was coming. Simon took it as an unspoken gauge of improving western living standards, among the items and services that not just the rich could afford: in the Sixties it was television sets; in the Seventies it was foreign holidays; and these days it was assassination.

He regarded it as a point of professional pride as well as a valuable security consideration not to repeat the same method, and even made a principle of not using firearms, like Queen had made a principle of not using the otherwise ubiquitous synthesiser on their first ten albums. This kept his imagination finely tuned, as well as providing constant fresh perspectives on the risks of detection; the simplicity of a bullet in the head could engender sloppiness borne of complacency. Like Queen recording *The Game*, eventually he decided he did need a gun, but by this time he knew that in the end, the method didn't matter: if you had the will, everything else was merely detail. And if you didn't, then it made no odds what weapon was in your hand. It was the will people were paying for – that and the security of being several clandestine removes from the man who wielded it.

What they'd make of the fact that that man was still nine-to-five-ing for Sintek Energy, he didn't like to contemplate. Flexi-time arrangements made for a few midweek sorties, but he was constantly reminded of Billy Connolly's song about the Territorial Army: *'And we'll have the revolution on a Saturday, 'cause I've got to work through the week.'*

Until Marseilles, that was. He was tipped off that something was different when he carried out a traceroute on the incoming email, something he always did to confirm the source: the quoted address varied, but the English middleman's relay server was always the same. The traceroute revealed that it had arrived via a French ISP, confirmed by the accent that answered the phone.

You know you've really arrived when you start your first European tour.

The target was a Parisian businessman, Jean-Pierre Lacroux, who had humped one too many secretaries and good-time girls for his wife's liking, and now she fancied his life insurance as compensation. He was given a copy of the bloke's itinerary for a forthcoming business trip to Marseilles, including flight times and hotel details, hotel rooms having proven a happy hunting ground thus far.

Simon arrived the day before Lacroux and checked into the same hotel. He hired a car, made the purchases he required, had an excellent dinner and then retired to his room for some shuteye, a good night's sleep always bulwark number one against stupid mistakes.

He was woken by sunlight shining through a gap in the curtains, which even without the attendant grogginess would have been confusing, as the last thing he had done the night before was close a set of blinds. The room had shrunk, as had the bed, while the number of doors had been reduced by two. More disturbingly, his travel bag and

365

all of the room's furniture had disappeared, a glimpse through what turned out to be a porthole behind the curtains revealing that so had not only the entire city, but the land as well.

The cabin's door opened, and in walked two men who both had to bend to get through it.

'There's someone who'd like to speak to you, Mr Darcourt,' one of them said, his voice the same as had relayed the now apparently bogus details about Monsieur Lacroux.

Simon followed them through several corridors and a steel-glinting kitchen up to the sun-kissed deck of a luxury yacht (luxury as in the ten million notes category; the word, he now appreciated, having been previously rather over-liberally applied). His sense of geography told him he had to be somewhere in the Med, but there was a seaplane moored off the aft and he felt woozy enough to have no idea how long he might have been unconscious, so he couldn't be sure. He was led to a canopied area, where a bottle of champagne sat in an ice-bucket on a table, next to two flutes. To the side of it was a TV and VCR, and in front of it were two sunloungers facing the prow, backs to Simon.

'Marcel, pour Mr Darcourt and myself some champagne, would you?' said a voice, revealing one of the sunloungers to be occupied. 'And Mr Darcourt, please come here and have a seat.'

Simon walked around the table as one of the man-moun-tains poured the drinks, the bottle looking like a miniature in his hands. There was a bald, podgy little man in sunglasses sitting waiting for him, a laptop resting on his thighs, a telephone at his elbow on a short wooden table. He was caucasian but not white, Simon unable to discern whether his skin was merely dark from the sun or from ethnicity. The man smiled and gestured to Simon to take a seat. Simon, still in his T-shirt and boxer shorts, felt a microscopic bit more comfortable to observe that his host was dressed only in a pair of extremely ill-advised G-string trunks. Proof, he very quickly appreciated, that this was a man who was far too powerful for anyone to dare offer any sartorially constructive criticism.

'I've had my eye on you,' he said, his accent as unplace-able as his origins. 'And I think we might do business together.'

The man-mountain Marcel handed them both their champagne, serving the bald man first.

'I'm sorry, I'm at a bit of a loss here,' Simon said. 'I don't believe I've had the pleasure.'

'You haven't. And if you're angling for my name, nor will you. But to ratify future communications, you should refer to me as Shaloub N'gurath. On a sunny day like this, however, you can call me Shub. Cheers.'

They talked for hours; or rather, Shub talked for hours, with a garrulousness that suggested he maybe spent too much time floating on the ocean, where visitors had to be brought, drugged, by overnight seaplane. However, for all his loquaciousness, he nonetheless had a disciplined gift for not telling the listener anything concrete, never mentioning names, locations or indeed any specifics what-soever. If Simon had walked into the first police station on dry land, intent on alerting them to this uniquely dangerous Blofeld-alike, he would have been hoofed into the street as a time-waster half an hour later. 'No, I don't know who. No, I don't know where. No, I don't know how. But there was this guy on a boat. No, I don't know where it was. No, I don't know what it was called.' Boot. After which Shub's people would have picked him up and . . . well, he wasn't going to be walking into any police stations, he was damn sure about that.

'Criminals cannot help but talk,' he told Simon. 'That is why I do not employ criminals. I employ professionals, and professionals do not talk. They do not talk to each other, they do not talk about each other. In this world, happy is the man who does not know his comrade's name, for he does not have to worry that his comrade will slit his throat tonight. Most important of all, professionals do not talk to the authorities. Do you know why?'

It seemed a rhetorical question, but Shub was staring intently at him as though demanding a response. Simon couldn't think of any way of articulating something so monumentally obvious without resorting to platitudes that would make him sound like a schoolboy. That was when he realised he was floundering because it was something of a trick question.

'Because professionals don't get caught,' he answered.

'Very good,' Shub said. 'Professionals do not get caught. However, I am experienced enough to know that nobody is perfect. Accidents can happen. How is it your own poet puts it, Mr Darcourt? *The best laid plans of mice and men . . .*'

'*Gang aft agley.*'

'Go often wrong, yes. The professional knows when the situation is retrievable and when it is not. If it is not, he knows when to walk away, and he knows to clean up the mess. If you compromise yourself, as far as I am concerned, you have compromised me. Remember that, any time you consider taking a risk. If you fear you are contaminated, it is your responsibility to amputate and cauterise before the infection spreads. You find yourself on the run? You do not

368

run to me. If you can stay hidden, stay hidden, but always remember my people will be looking for you too. And this is what will happen when they find you. Marcel.'

Marcel wheeled the sunloungers around so that they were facing under the canopy, where he put a cassette into the VCR and switched on the TV. The picture warmed from black to show a male face, sweat-drenched, contorted and hyperventilating.

'Sound, please,' said Shub. Marcel pressed the remote. Simon could now hear fevered breathing, and a whimpering beneath it.

The camera pulled back to reveal that the man was strapped naked to a steel table like he had seen in the yacht's kitchen, resting upright against a portholed wall. On either side of him stood one of the man-mountains, dressed head to toe in white plastic overalls, each of them holding a two-handed power drill.

Marcel placed the champagne bottle on the table and tossed the ice overboard, returning with the bucket in time for Simon to vomit into it a few seconds of videotape later. This, he felt, was ample evidence that Shub's point had been made, but he was wrong. Shub sipped champagne and stared at the screen, motionless, unflinching, for a full ten minutes.

'If the authorities reach you first, we will get to you wherever you are held,' he said, holding out a beckoning hand into which Marcel placed the remote control. 'We will break you out if possible, to find out what you told them. We broke this guy out. If that's not possible, we can get to you inside. There's a lot of things we can do inside too, but ideally we'd bring you back to the boat. These are double-length tapes. It lasts more than three hours.' Shub turned up the volume until the screaming and the sound of the drills was deafening, turning to observe Simon's stomach-wrenching discomfiture. 'I'm sure you'd agree,' he shouted above the noise, 'a bullet in your own head would be much quicker.' With which he suddenly switched off the TV, silencing the cries, the drills and the grinding, leaving only the lapping of waves and the calls of gulls.

'Professionals do not get caught.'

Simon heard the rumble of the truck and the hiss of its air brakes before he glanced in the rearview and saw May's Espace come round the bend ahead of the convoy.

'Showtime,' he said to Taylor, who hit the accelerator and led the procession into the entrance tunnel.

Simon lifted the two SPAS-12 shotguns from the seat behind and slotted gas pellets into each one's grenade launcher.

'Steady hands, Freddie,' Taylor said. 'Remember the *Twilight Queen*,' the cheeky bastard referring to their first abortive approach to the Black Sea cruise liner. This had ended in four of them having to dive off their speedboat after Simon accidentally launched a CS gas canister from his weapon when they hit an unexpectedly large wave. Fortunately, the wind was blowing away from their target and they were able to reboard unseen and resume attack a few minutes later.

'You worry about the driving and don't fly over any speedbumps like you flew over that fucking wave.'

'Roger.'

Simon glanced in the wing mirror. The truck was in the tunnel at their backs, behind the vans and one of the speed-boat-towing Mondeos. May and his Espace would be bringing up the rear, after locking the main gate behind

370

them. The shield door would remain open for now, at least until the morning shift came on at eight.

He ordered Taylor to stop about ten yards before 'the crossroads', as the staff referred to it, where the entrance tunnel intersected a second cutting, accessing the tailrace on one side. On the other, there was an offshoot ramp leading to an observation deck above the central cavern, which was where they took the tourists to get a medium-distance look at the machine hall. The entrance tunnel was wide enough for two lanes of traffic, which allowed the truck to pass them and pull in ahead, its rear level with the intersection.

All engines were cut and no words were spoken as the team assembled at the rear of the lorry. The sound of the generators covered any noise they were likely to make, but by this stage nobody needed to be told what to do. They formed into coordinated groups, checked their weapons and pulled on their filter masks.

Simon checked his watch. The new shift would be in the control room for Changeover Report, which in theory was supposed to be a detailed breakdown of current operational status, but in practice meant a cup of brew and a blether about who was going to win the football tomorrow. In Simon's experience, terrorists were about the only people in this world who turned up for their job and just got stuck in, rather than scratch their arses and read the paper for half an hour before thinking about doing a hand's turn.

He and Taylor led the incursion squad into the central cavern at a soft-footed jog, leaving Cook, Deacon, Steve Jones and May (when he caught up) to unload the truck. They split into three groups at the machine hall's main floor level. Simon led Matlock and Lydon up the near stairs, while Taylor, Headon and Strummer strode quickly and quietly beneath the control room's observation window to the flight at the end. Simonon and Mick Jones headed below to the turbine's lower access levels, in case somebody was down there getting an early start and fancied trying to be Bruce Willis.

Simon led his team silently along the upper corridor, almost reaching the control room door by the time Taylor and his men came into view from the other end. Once in place, he and Taylor readied their weapons, while Strummer gripped the doorhandle and the rest took position either side.

Upon confirmatory nods from both Simon and Taylor, Strummer counted down from three by holding up fingers. On Go, he pulled the door open long enough for them to each pump two gas pellets into the room, then slammed it closed again, the three of them bunching up against it as the inevitable desperate ramming began.

If anybody in there kept his head, he might grab the phone and dial for help instead of joining the melee battering at the door, but by the time the switchboard had answered and asked which service he required, he'd be as unconscious as his colleagues.

They waited until the thumping ceased – a matter of seconds – then opened the door. Simon stepped over the tangle of bodies while the others began removing them, two to a man, taking them to the storage chamber, where they'd be bound and gagged with heavy-duty tape then locked behind a reinforced steel door. Matlock had asked why they had to use a non-lethal gas instead of just getting it over with, but that was why he was unlikely ever to enjoy inner-circle status. No matter how well you've planned something like this, it never hurts to have some leverage in case of emergencies – especially when you've just cooped yourself up inside a giant hole in the ground.

The phone had indeed been removed from its receiver, and was dangling from the desk. Simon put it to his ear.

'. . . repeat, which service do you require, sir?' asked an impatient female voice. 'Another toddler playing with the phone, I'll bet,' she said more quietly, to whoever was sitting next to her at the switchboard. Simon lifted the filter mask from his mouth. He could smell the gas immediately, but it was dissipating rapidly since the door had been opened.

'Hello? Sorry about that. It's Dubh Ardrain control room, yeah. Somebody jumped the gun a wee bit, thought we had a fire. No, it's nothing. Sorry to trouble you. Okay, cheery-bye.'

Simon disconnected the call by putting his hand down on the cradle, looking at the receiver to take note of the number printed on it in punch-tape. He took out his radio and relayed it to May. Radios would be fine for use around the main cavern, but those working topside would have five hundred metres of rock between them and their comrades, and the only means of communication would be to call the control room directly on their mobiles.

He walked to the semi-circular windowed buttress and looked out upon this gigantic facility over which he now had complete control. Six huge cylinders protruded robustly from the floor of the machine hall, yellow-walled, three metres tall, but they were merely the tips of icebergs. Out of sight beneath, the turbines plunged a further seventeen metres, accessed by four lower levels. Above them, the cavern ceiling arced to a height of twenty metres, flanked by gantries and traversed if necessary by a mobile platform suspended across the centre. A giant lighting rig illuminated the place, itself clinging to the overhead rock with dozens of stubby limbs.

At the mouth of the entrance tunnel, he could see May and Cook rolling the first of the drills towards the nearest aqueduct's maintenance access door. One of three, the aqueduct ran from the turbines through five hundred metres of Ben Larig to the vast reservoir on top of the mountain. The reservoir was once merely a corrie loch, pooled at the bottom of a natural basin amid the expansive promontory that was Dubh Ardrain; the water another remnant of the glacier that had carved a trench through the mountain range, leaving the snaking scar that was Loch Fada and Glen Crom below. Further tunnels and aqueducts had been dug into the stone shoulders of the mesa, diverting the surrounding streams to flood the basin and expand its capacity to almost fifty square kilometres. And holding the billions of gallons in place up there was a concrete gravity buttress dam, four hundred metres long and fifty metres high.

Dubh Ardrain was a reversible pumped-storage system, allowing it to use its own stored power to pump water back up from Loch Fada into the reservoir at times of low demand. However, being constructed during the Cold War, an aspect of its intended purpose was to continue generating power in the event of a nuclear attack; hence the disproportionately enormous reservoir, allowing for sustained continuous generation without the need to reverse the flow. The threat of atomic annihilation had lifted since then, but the prudent practice had remained of maintaining capacity topside, especially during the comparatively drier summer months.

All six turbines were currently channelling the day's usage back up the mountain, but their capacity would shortly be reduced by one third, when Simon powered down Aqueduct Three. Inside each tunnel was a mobile maintenance and inspection platform, which they would be using to transport equipment to the surface, and these tended to work more efficiently when there wasn't several thousand gallons of water flowing rapidly around them. For emergencies, there was also a stairway cut into the aqueduct floor on one side, but that wasn't quite so handy when you were lugging several hundredweight of drills and generators around with you.

Deacon and Steve Jones emerged with the second drill as May and Cook headed back to fetch the generator. It had seemed almost insultingly ironic that they needed to bring their own electricity supply to a place like this, but the inconsiderate bastards who'd built it had inconveniently neglected to put an easily accessible power outlet at the head of the dam.

Headon and Mick Jones returned to cart away the last of the unconscious hostages, Taylor stepping aside in the doorway to let them through.

'That's eight,' he said. 'Everybody accounted for. No strays.'

'Good. I'm going to power down Aqueduct Three now.'

'Is there a signal or something for when it's clear? I don't remember you saying.'

'Yeah. The door unlocks and you can open the fucking thing. Clear enough?'

'Crystal.'

Taylor exited, no doubt muttering insults under his breath. Simon turned to the control console and deactivated pumps five and six. They would need a few minutes to fully shut down, then it would take another five for the aqueduct to drain. He returned to the window and looked down again, listening for the lowering note as the turbines gradually slowed to a halt, smiling with a private satisfaction. He had been here in another lifetime, just another glaikit Geography student on a field trip, and had marvelled at it like he was standing on the bridge of the Starship Enterprise. Now he was in the captain's swivel chair.

He watched May and Cook wheel the generator out of sight, heading for the vacuum-sealed door leading into the freshly drained aqueduct. Deacon and Steve Jones stood behind them with the first of the drills, waiting for the platform to be sent back down. Strummer and Matlock would go up with the second, followed later by Lydon and Simonon with the explosives and detonators.

Simon took some time to savour the moment.

Burns was wrong. The plans that 'gang agley' were not the best laid: that was *why* they ganged agley, for fuck's sake. This, however, this work in progress, this plan in action, was why the Black Spirit was the most wanted man in international terrorism: whether they wanted his abilities or his head on a stick, they all knew he was the best in the business. The only thing better laid than his plans would be whichever young mademoiselle was lucky enough to catch his eye in Monte Carlo less than twenty-four hours from now.

The control room phone rang, shaking him from his reverie: May on the surface, checking in.

'Control,' Simon said, picking it up.

'It's May,' confirmed the voice. 'We've got a problem.'

'What?'

'The generator's fucked. Worse than that: it's been sabotaged. Drill parts jammed inside, cables cut . . . It's a mess.'

'Sabo . . .' Simon's mind started racing, but the time for speculation was not now. There was only one pertinent question to be asked. 'Is it fixable?'

'It'll take time. And parts, too.'

'Well, where are we going to find spare electrical parts in a power station? Bring it back down. We'll get Deacon on to it.'

'Roger.'

'No, Deacon. Taylor knows fuck-all about—'

'I meant Roger as in acknowledged.'

'Just get down here.'

'Roger.'

Simon slammed down the phone, the possibilities piling up in his head despite his attempts to stay focused. May was his first suspect, the bastard having been as jumpy as an arachnophobe in a room full of tarantulas since the farmhouse. Being the one to 'discover' the damage was a classic double-bluff, and he had broken the golden rule by sniffing around Simon's personal information, so had he jumped the dyke? Was the bastard wired? Were there a hundred troops topside waiting to huckle the lot of them? Or did he still think Simon was planning to kill him and had therefore thrown a spanner in the works so he could use the resulting confusion to cover his exit?

That said, it somewhat minimised the impact for the damage to be revealed at the earliest juncture, when there was still plenty of time to repair it; plus, if May was planning to get off his mark, topside wasn't the smartest place to make his getaway. Even if he had a motorbike secretly stashed at the reservoir, he'd have to travel three miles down the winding mountainside track to reach the main road, where the bridge west was out and the only open route would take him back past the power plant. On the other hand again, it was a good few hundred yards to the main gate from the machine hall, and if they were standing around waiting for him to descend on the automated platform, that would give him a few minutes' start.

Simon ran from the control room, hurrying down the stairs then making the rest of the journey to Aqueduct Three at a brisk walk, not wanting to appear panicked.

'Something up, boss?' asked Deacon as Simon brushed past him and through the vacuum door. He heard the sound of the pulley as soon as he entered, and looked up along the insulated lighting panels to where he could see only the underside of the descending platform.

Simon reached for his radio. 'May, this is Mercury, come in.'

He could hear the hiss of his own transmission echo in the tunnel above, just audible over the steady hum of the pulley, rendering May's response redundant.

'Receiving. What is it?'

'Forget it. Mercury out.'

Simon exited the aqueduct and went to the nearest drill, whipping off the blanket that was covering it. There was no visible damage, but if they had a saboteur in their midst, it was improbable he'd have stopped at the generator.

'I want these checked out before you take them anywhere,' he told Deacon. 'Somebody's been messing with the generator. May's on his way back down with it.'

'Messing with it? Deliberately?'

'Looks like it.'

Deacon had a troubled look, something else on his mind. 'What?'

'We were missing some stuff back at the truck, when we tooled up.'

'What stuff?'

'Radios. I mean, everybody's got one, but I was sure we had a couple of spares pre-tuned to the frequencies. They may just have been moved between crates, but now that you say . . .'

'Christ. Okay, I'll look into it. You worry about the drills.'

'I'll need power before I can—'

'I know. There's an adapter cable in the truck for plugging it into the mains.'

'I'll get it,' Steve Jones volunteered, with an eagerness that would normally have scored him points but today made him the highest new entry on the suspicion chart.

'I'll go,' Simon told him. 'There's something else I need to check out.'

He stomped off towards the entrance tunnel, heading for the lorry. Lydon and Simonon were sitting among the crates laid out around the crossroads, drinking cans of juice.

'Tea break, is it, boys?'

'We're third in the line for the lift,' said Simonon apologetically, in that half-arsed American accent that he obviously thought covered up his European origins. Simon's own guess was boring old Belgium, which was why he had singled him out for that moniker. Only problem was that the bloke in The Clash's first name was Paul, and Simon kept calling him George.

'I don't care if you're third in line for the throne. Look fucking lively, the gremlins are out in force. Is anything missing? Where are the explosives?'

'Blue crates. We're sitting on them.'

'I need the cable adapters for the drills. Quickly.'

Simonon stood up immediately and made for one of the yellow crates, the colour code for miscellaneous supplies. Lydon followed suit, though with a moment's delay for a last swig from his can: the difference between slavish obedience and nonchalant cooperation measurable in a mouthful of scoosh.

'Shit,' Lydon said, upon delving into his box.

'What?'

'Uniforms. They're all damp. And they smell of piss.'

'The magazines were wet too,' said Simonon. 'I thought it was just condensation.'

Simon looked into the back of the truck. There were dark streaks on the wooden floor where the crates had been dragged, as well as vivid tyre marks from the drills, all of it caused by fluid. He climbed up the ramp and walked inside, making for the spare small-arms cache on the right-hand wall. Pulling back the blanket with an anxious tug, he was relieved to see an array of weapons still attached to the wooden lattice, though it occurred to him that he didn't know how many there should be.

'Deacon, this is Mercury, come in.'

'Deacon, receiving.'

'John, how many spare guns should we have?'

'Six of each.'

'Oh, right. That's okay.'

'Yeah?'

'Yeah. That means we're only missing two fucking machine guns.'

Simon lashed out with an angry boot at one of the wooden crates sitting at the cab end of the lorry. The lid flipped into the air and tumbled down on to the floor, revealing a fanbelt and several empty tins inside, as well as a pish-soaked grey blanket like the ones piled up in the corner.

'What is this, a fuckin' dosshouse?' he muttered. Then the ramifications quickly began to sink in. 'Shite. Lydon, Simonon, get up here,' he commanded, taking hold of his shotgun with both hands at waist height.

Simon gestured towards the pile with a nod as they came

up on either side. Lydon drew his pistol while Simonon approached the blankets. The Belgian counted down from three with his fingers, then hauled the pile away from the wall.

Fortunately, nobody fired.

Stacked up behind the blankets was what looked like half their supply of demolition charge.

'Our explosives,' George observed redundantly. Lydon restricted his utterances to a half-cough, half-sigh, in relief that his trigger finger hadn't twitched and blown them all to kingdom come.

'Begging the obvious question of just what you clowns were sitting on.'

All eyes turned to the crossroads. Simon pumped a round into his shotgun and began walking, slowly and deliberately, down towards the blue crates sitting on the tarmac. He stopped next to the nearest one, while Lydon and the Belgian, pistols drawn, took position close by. Simon flipped the lid off, revealing a stack of damp, paper-wrapped charges, then repeated the drill three more times to the same effect. He looked back at the stack against the inside wall of the truck. It wasn't half of their stash, but had to be a third. There were two blue crates left. Simon stood over the one on the right, Lydon and the Belgian its partner.

It was Simon's turn for the silent, gestured countdown, made on the fingers of his left hand as they bent in sequence to resume their grip on the barrel of his SPAS-12. On zero, they began firing: Simon pumping four rounds into his crate, Lydon and Simonon a dozen slugs between them into theirs.

The sound brought reinforcements running from the machine hall as Simon placed a boot against the crate and forced off the shot-punctured lid.

It was empty, as was the other.

They stood wordlessly, staring into the crates as their arriving colleagues formed a semi-circle in the mouth of the entrance tunnel. Simon looked at his watch. The timing of Saturday's events meant that at least three spare hours had been necessarily built into the schedule. It wasn't time to panic – yet. But they suddenly had a lot of work to do, starting with solving a serious rodent problem.

The silence was broken by Simon's radio, a message from Deacon.

'I've had a quick butcher's at the consoles on these rigs. The wiring's cut and the circuit boards are like Swiss cheese.'

Simon breathed out very slowly, using all his experience to stay calm and focused.

'Is it fixable?' he asked, just about preventing his voice from breaking up.

'I think one of them is. I can wire up *some*thing. Might not be programmable, but . . .'

'*Some*thing that can drill a hole?'

'Yeah. That's all though, so we're looking at double drilling time at least.'

'Then why are you pissing about talking to me?'

'Roger. Deacon out.'

Simon designated everyone who could do more than wire a plug to assist Deacon in repairing the equipment, allocating the rest to seek-and-destroy parties to hunt for their uninvited guests. They cleared the truck of spare weapons and ammunition, now that they had more than unsuspecting electrical engineers to contend with; Simon helping himself to a machine gun to supplement his SPAS-12 and his automatic.

He watched the search teams troop off in their different

directions then picked out a can from the provisions crate, drinking it slowly as he leaned against the rear of the truck. He was starting to feel a tightening in his stomach, which the lukewarm Irn-Bru was unlikely to relieve.

In his head he could hear drills, but they weren't the kind Deacon was working on.

SATURDAY, SEPTEMBER SIXTH

opposing force

Ray was in a jail cell without bars, only the refraction of light from the corridor betraying that there was a force-field preventing his exit. He was dreaming again, he knew: playing in his sleep because it was as close as he could get these days. Jailbreak this time: a mod in which if you got fragged, you were imprisoned in the opposing side's cell block until a team-mate managed to bust you out. Rescue was on its way: standing just beyond the force-field was the female who'd thawed him out yesterday: 'Athena' player-model, her hair tied back in a ponytail, but with Angelique de Xavia's face.

'Time we got you out of here,' she said.

Ray opened his eyes. Angelique was standing in the doorway of the section-house bedroom, holding a steaming mug of coffee and a generously stacked bacon roll.

'Come on, sleepyhead. Here's that hot meal, but don't freak out until you've finished the coffee.'

Ray blinked a few times, feeling extremely groggy.

'I'll leave these here and I'll be back in five,' she said, placing the items on his bedside table and withdrawing.

Ray struggled into a sitting position, knowing that he'd nod off again otherwise. Contrary to his confident predic-tion, he'd found sleep difficult to come by, given what was going through his head, and he hadn't needed the shower or the hot meal to precipitate freaking out. They said you shouldn't give your stomach too much to digest close to bedtime, but that went double for your mind, and what he'd just been fed was the mental equivalent of a five-course blow-out. There was something else too, some indistinct niggling sense of insecurity that kicked in every time he felt close to reconciling himself to Angelique's shattering revelation. It was as much his failing attempts to pin it down that kept him awake as the feelings of anxiety that it caused.

Eventually he must have given in to sheer exhaustion, but it felt like that had only happened about half an hour ago. He sipped the coffee, which was pretty good, and had a mouthful of the roll, which was magic. Cholesterol therapy. Before he started work at Burnbrae, it was sausage and bacon rolls that had got Kate and himself through the mornings, she eating with one hand and steadying Martin on her breast with the other. It suddenly felt a long time ago, a long way away. He was missing them both so much, the sense of longing flooding into him in concentrated doses when he wasn't having to worry about imminent death or resurrected psychopaths.

Angelique returned bearing more gifts: this time a couple of towels and directions to the shower.

'You're an angel.'

'Angel X.'

Ray's unease didn't dissipate once they were underway, despite the fact that Angelique's car was taking him home; maybe even *because* it was taking him home. Short-timer's disease: the closer you get to finishing your tour of duty, the more nervous you become. The silence wasn't helping either. It wasn't awkward, but in between bouts of small talk, there was nothing to keep his mind from his worries.

'Do you mind if we have the radio on?' he asked. 'I feel

like I've been away for a month and I could do with catching up.'

'Sure,' she replied, reaching for the dial. They were greeted with a blast of the truly loathsome *Ibiza Devil Groove* by EGF, something Ray was grateful not to have heard for a good three years.

'A wee kick in the Balearics there, ha ha ha, from the Silver City FM crypt,' whined the DJ.

'Should never have been exhumed,' Ray muttered.

'What's wrong with it?'

'If I start telling you, I might never stop.'

'It's good to dance to.'

'I want out of this car.'

Angelique laughed. 'What is it about boys and music? They're always so serious about it. It's like they're fighting a war or something.'

'Aye. A war against shite.'

'There's a place for everything. It's all music, isn't it?'

'You're gauny stick up for the Spice Girls and All Saints in a minute, then I really am gettin' out of the car. I don't care what speed it's travelling.'

'And if you died, it would be natural selection. No place for you dinosaurs here in the future.'

'That's a bit harsh.'

'You're the one who said it was a war.'

The song mercifully faded, giving way to the half-hourly news, which led with a story on fishing quotas.

'Don't suppose two missing Glasgow schoolboys is considered a story up here,' Ray remarked. 'Have you heard anything more?'

'Afraid not.'

They listened to the rest of the bulletin. Like yesterday with the papers in the supermarket, it felt like the world's events were dragging along at a far slower pace than Ray's life. The only event that seemed genuinely 'new' was the collapse of a road bridge near Crianfada, eliciting a snort from Angelique.

'What?' enquired Ray.

'That'll be on my desk when I get back. Anything suspicious was to be reported to me while we were all on the look-out for the Black Spirit. You should have seen some of the shite I got. I bet the bastards who make the arrests didn't have to investigate any fertiliser thefts.'

'You still hurtin' about endin' up bein' the bridesmaid?'

'It's traditionally not the bridesmaid who gets fucked.'

'You know what I mean,' Ray insisted.

'Yeah I do. And I am. I ought to maintain a sense of perspective about it, though. They're mounting one of the biggest police operations in British history today. I don't know what starring role I thought I would've had amid a cast of thousands.'

'Are you allowed to tell me what the big plot is yet?'

'No.'

'Who am I gaunny tell?'

'Nothing personal. But if it got out, there would be panic and everything could fall to bits.'

'Panic?'

'We're talkin' about a major public event. Crowds and hysteria don't mix.'

'So why isn't it being cancelled, whatever it is, if you know that's what he's gaunny attack?'

'Because we might never get another chance like this. If we cancel, then he knows the game's a bogey and he'll disappear again.'

'Hell of a risk, given his track record.'

'Not if we're ready for him. He's used to being unexpected

and invisible – that's part of his track record too. This time, we know where he's headed and we know when. We also know what he looks like, at long last, thanks to you – though he knows that as well, and he's probably already booked an appointment with a plastic surgeon for when this is over. He doesnae make many mistakes, so we have to take this chance because it could be a bloody long time before he makes another.'

'He *doesn't* know that,' Ray countered, thinking of all that business with the hood back at the farmhouse.

'Know what?'

'That you know what he looks like. He knows I escaped an' he knows I'd tell the polis what I saw, but I didn't see *him*. He made sure of that. He's got no way of knowin' I've sussed he's still alive.'

'Even better. He's unlikely to disguise himself today, then.'

But for Ray, the insecurity was back, fast turning from a niggle to a full-blooded kick to the kidneys. There had always been something that didn't quite add up, and now that he was beginning to see what it was, he understood why he was still scared.

'If he was so intent on messin' with my head, why didn't he reveal himself back at the farmhouse? Wouldn't that have been his big moment? I mean, if he was gaunny kill me anyway – which I think we're both agreed on – why deny himself that quintessential wanker pleasure?'

'Maybe he was savin' it. I mean, he didnae know you were gaunny bugger off in the middle of the night, did he?'

They turned to look at each other.

'Oh fuck,' they said, in stereo.

'He did know,' Ray confirmed. 'I was *supposed* to escape.

Christ, why didn't we see that? This guy's a master of planning, covers all the bases, pulls off all these amazingly complex operations, but he locks me up in a wee daft pantry with conveniently loose floorboards, leadin' to a direct route out of the house? And for fuck's sake, the night before, there's two gunmen come after me: they're professional bloody killers but they cannae hit me from five yards? A newbie on AOL with a three-hundred ping wouldnae have missed from that range. It was a set-up. The gunmen didnae miss, because they werenae supposed to *hit*: they were sent to put the wind up me, so I'd tell the polis I was bein' chased by armed assassins.'

'And the polis would then give greater credence to your story when you turned up a few days later, claiming to have been kidnapped.'

'Exactly. That carry-on at the bridge was just to plant the seeds for what was comin' next. Which was for them to abduct me purely so that I could escape and lead the cops to the farmhouse.'

'Where they conveniently discover a load of photocopied blueprints and promptly go chargin' off to Sunderland.'

'Sunderland? The England friendly?'

'Doesn't matter now, does it? Because it's *not* Sunderland: that's the point. Christ on crutches.'

Angelique pulled the car over into a layby and drew to a halt. Ray knew he wasn't going home any more, in her car or anyone else's.

'This was his plan all along, wasn't it?' he said. 'He needed a decoy. If he hadnae seen me at the airport and decided to indulge himself, he would have abducted some other sucker for the same role.'

'He'd have been safer abducting somebody else. So he's still a wanker.'

'But a clever wanker. He's sent all the polis to the Stadium of Light while he gets on with his felonious little plans elsewhere.'

'And we're back to square one,' Angelique said gloomily.

'Maybe not. How many collapsing road bridges do you get on the average weekend?'

'Good point. Where did they say that was?'

Ray couldn't remember, having been distracted at the time by Angelique's snort. 'It'll be comin' up again in the travel report,' he said, turning up the volume control on the radio, where the sports bulletin had reached rugby and was therefore coming to an end. They waited with gritted teeth through the incongruously cheery weather forecast, then finally got what they needed, the bridge story being the lead travel item.

'There is still access to Crianfada, but the road to Cromlarig is closed and, according to police, is likely to remain so for several days until a temporary structure can be put in place. The only route into Cromlarig at the moment is via Strathairlie, and the AA are warning that if you're approaching from the South, that represents almost a three-hour diversion, so if you're planning to attend today's Highland Games, you'd better get your skates on. Meanwhile on the A9, a slow-moving extra-wide vehicle with police escort is causing tailbacks of up to . . .'

Crianfada. Cromlarig.

'Have you got a road map?' Ray asked.

'Glove compartment. Where's Cromlarig anyway?'

'West Highlands. About three hours north of Glasgow, maybe a bit less west of here. But that's when the bridge hasn't collapsed, obviously.'

Ray popped open the fibreglass hatch and fished out a well-thumbed road atlas, flipping impatiently from the grid reference to the appropriate page. He placed it on the dashboard so that they could both have a look, but there really wasn't much to see.

'Maybe the bridge collapse *is* just a coincidence,' Angelique said, having pored over the map for a while. 'Christ, what is there for him in the Highlands? There's hardly even any people there to kill.'

'What's nearby?' Ray asked. 'Any airforce or army bases that wouldn't be on the map?'

'The military bases *are* on the map – just none on these pages anywhere near Cromlarig. It's tourist country. Lochs and mountains and tartan and shortbread.'

'Isn't there a nuclear submarine base up there somewhere?'

'Nearest one is the Holy Loch, and that's about fifty miles from Loch Fada, on a different road through the glens too.'

'Could there be another one that the government have kept secret?'

'No,' said Angelique, pointing to the page. 'Not here anyway: Loch Fada's landlocked.'

'Good. It would be nice to rule out nuclear weapons, don't you think?'

'What about nuclear power?'

Ray looked again at the map. 'No. The nearest nuclear station would be Dounreay. All there is here is . . . oh fuck.'

'What?'

There it was all the time, staring out at him, waiting for him to notice, waiting for him to make the connection.

'Dubh Ardrain,' he said, pointing between the village of Crianfada and the town of Cromlarig. A yellow 'T' icon (tourist attraction) sat next to the snaking blue of Loch Fada along the stretch where the bridge had collapsed.

'What's that?'

'One of the biggest power stations in the country.'

'But not nuclear?'

'No. Hydro-electric.'

'Why would he be interested in that?'

'Today, I don't know, but he always was.'

'Was?'

'Since we went there as students, on a Geography field trip.'

'I thought you did English.'

'I did Geography too, just in first year. That's where I met Simon. He was very taken with Dubh Ardrain, and believe me, it wasnae often Simon was impressed by anythin' that didnae have an indie label or a bra around it. I remember him sayin' he'd love to shoot a video there one day, inside the hollow mountain.'

'But what could he do there now? Even if he blew the place up, the only people he'd kill would be the staff, and he prefers a bigger bodycount for his efforts. Shit, hang on – it's a tourist attraction though, isn't it?'

'Not today. The road's closed, remember? Tourists cannae get there, and neither can anybody else: such as the polis or any other emergency services, apart from those based in Cromlarig or further north in Strathairlie.'

'Which probably amount to Hamish Macbeth, a district nurse and a bucket of water for the fire service. Better check it out.'

'We better had.'

'What's with we? You've got a wife and baby to get back to, remember?'

'Aye, and I've got a better chance of protectin' them both if it's me who's comin' after *him*.'

'He's had his fun with you, Ray. He's got bigger fish to fry now.'

'Has he? I can identify four of his men – that part they know for definite. Me escapin' was part of the script, so are you tellin' me they're not plannin' to tie up their loose ends later? As for Simon havin' his fun, that's not over either. He's still got a score to settle.'

'I thought he was the one who fucked *you* over.'

'He did, but . . .' Ray sighed. 'Simon had – *has* – a rather Simoncentric view of the world, so he never saw it that way. Plus there's . . . ach, it's a long story.'

'And we've got a long drive. Including that three-hour detour.'

'There's a watersports centre at Crianfada. We could make the last leg by boat instead.'

'Good thinking. That's three hours less, but it still can't be that long a story. 'Fess up.'

Ray didn't tell her everything, obviously. Just the more salient parts, many of which she already knew from the file and her conversation with the polisman who'd lifted them. It had been second term, final year, without doubt the most purgatorial in anyone's university career: the finals are close enough for you to be constantly worried about them, but still too far off when you're impatient for it all to be over. Second term is also post-Christmas, making it the most miserable, cold and dreich in any year, let alone your fourth. Consequently, there was even more recourse to the QM bar and the Grosvenor Café, and a greater likelihood of crossing paths with the Dark Man again.

In fact, this was fairly inevitable, given that they still shared quite a few friends. On top of that, Ray remained uncomfortable about the way things had ended, and felt there was something mutually cowardly about avoiding each other rather than sitting down to clear the air over a beer or at least a coffee. He didn't actively seek Simon out, but did stop doing a one-eighty if he walked into the bar and saw him already seated.

What made this a little easier was that Ray was receiving corroborative reports from mutual friends that Simon had 'calmed down a lot', and that this dampening of his volatility was largely down to his current girlfriend. It was also, some surmised, possibly a consequence of having a relationship with a female that lasted beyond the following weekend and the next chance to pull someone new.

The inexorable reunion happened one Tuesday night in the QM bar, when Ray was already shoehorned in at the back against the windows overlooking the disco, and therefore had no means of escape when Simon and his remarkedly pacifying companion walked up to join their table. Cutting off even the rubber-ear or cursory nod options was the fact that the two girls sitting to Ray's left were just heading off to catch a film at The Salon, so got up and offered their seats to the new arrivals.

With the benefit of hindsight, and particularly given his current informed perspective, Ray could feel justified in saying that Simon was one of the few people on the planet capable of making magnanimity seem ostentatious. Everyone at that low and rickety table knew what had gone down between them, doubtless the new girlfriend included, so instead of a tentative hello, Simon leaned over and offered a warm handshake, before introducing him to 'Felicia' as though he was a brother. Simon even did him the courtesy of calling him Ray and not Larry. In retrospect Ray could see him as Ralph Fiennes in *Schindler's List*, staring at himself in the mirror and trying on 'I forgive you' for size. At the time, though, the effect was just another instance of Simon's charms working their magic. Ray felt forgiven, though it didn't occur to him to evaluate who, if anyone, had actually sinned. And yet again, he felt ten feet tall to be back in Simon's court.

The king's new consort sat between them, and it was easy to see why she hadn't been dispatched as swiftly as her many predecessors. For one thing, she had a smile on her face and she wasn't dressed for a funeral, unlike the succession of self-loathing gnarly Gothettes that had dallied briefly on Simon's arm. Her personality was different too, in as much as she had one. Ray, still in chronic virginal frustration, had oftened wondered of Simon's previous conquests whether their abject dullness made them easier to bed; it certainly made them easier to dump. Rina, as everyone else called her (Felicia being her given Simon name, which she was naïve enough to interpret as innocent affection) sparkled with conversation, humour and energy, and was refreshingly non-deferential towards her esteemed host. Ray had been used to Simon's always being the last word on most matters, especially music, but Rina could be wittily withering not only of his opinions, but of the subject's dubious importance in the first place. That was why he couldn't help but smile in recognition when Angelique took the same derisory line.

Looking at the two of them that night, Ray concluded that the comparative longevity of their relationship (six weeks and counting) was due to Simon having finally met his match and liked it. However, within weeks, arguably days, Ray would learn that he was wrong on both counts. She was more than a match, and Simon didn't fucking like it.

Simon and Ray's relationship, on the other hand, was perhaps the best it had ever been. There was a great feeling of maturity about being able to put their differences, grudges and, let's be honest, embarrassments behind them;

together with a sense that they would be better friends for all of it. They blethered endlessly, the way they used to, making each other laugh, exchanging thoughts and ideas. The only jarring note was that the subjects of The Bacchae and The Arguments were conspicuously diverted around like road accidents. Ray was the only one who skirted close to the issue, but the signs he got in return let him know that Simon wasn't ready to laugh about it yet.

Ray got to know Rina very well too, at first through sharing Simon's company, but increasingly through sharing Simon's absence. He might have 'calmed down a lot', but he hadn't changed: Simon was consistently late for meeting both of them, except for when he never turned up at all. It was a downside of Simon's otherwise charming capacity to find certain people (temporarily) fascinating that he was very easily diverted, and it wasn't unusual to coincidentally run into him hours later in the company of a different crowd. If you asked why he didn't show up to meet you, he would tell you it was because he had met them instead, an answer which he expected the listener to find as satisfying as it was logical.

Even when he did show up, he would often spend the first drink with Rina and then gravitate off to a conversation in a different part of the room/bar/party, leaving her in the company of his unappointed deputy. This wasn't something Ray was inclined to complain about, because he couldn't imagine any other circumstances under which he and Rina would be spending much time together, and his only concern was that she was unlikely to see it as a fair exchange. If Ray had found it exciting but occasionally vertiginous to be in Simon's exalted company, then being around Rina felt like swinging on a chairaplane round the top of the CN Tower.

She was a year younger than him, but she was the type of girl who made Ray feel as though he was a teenager in the company of a sophisticated adult. Admittedly, most people could make Ray feel that way, probably as a result of his birthday falling in February and him consequently being the youngest kid in the class from Primary school upwards. However, Rina never gave the reciprocal impression that she was thinking of taking him to McDonald's later if he was a good boy. They got very pally, particularly as Ray became more comfortable being her friend and less inclined merely to play the humble fool for her amusement.

But while she and Ray were getting along like best buddies, her patience with Simon was fast wearing thin. Ray recognised the symptoms because he'd been there too. The disaffection happened by degrees, and in Rina's case the process seemed to be happening at an accelerated pace. First came fascination, which Simon underwent frequently and promiscuously among those who took his interest. Next came the charm, as he made you realise that his interest in you was more enduring than in the others, because you were something more than them: a counterpart who gave as good as you got; who had as much to say (and as much wit to say it) as he did. The problems arrived at the third stage, when Simon started to feel threatened. He wanted you to go on being that interesting and witty person, but on his terms, an adjunct, not an equal. That was when he gave you a name, to tell you 'this is who you are'.

Rina had been less bothered by the naming than Ray, but no less resistant of Simon's attempts to contain her. That was why he kept buggering off to talk to other people. He wanted the best of both worlds: Rina on his arm (and in his bed), without her stealing the limelight, without her diverting attention from him.

'I think part of him wants back to the daft lassies who'll just worship him, but another part of him knows I'm worth more than them, and doesn't want to give me up,' was how she put it.

Despite their growing friendship, Ray would have to own up to a certain culpability in diverting Simon's attention from Rina, now that he'd had his 'interesting person' status renewed, and this was massively exacerbated when they came up with a new shared project. Ray would later put the museum thing down to a certain nihilism instilled by all that final-year, second-term psychosis, but in truth it was merely another instance of late-night drinking spawning an idea so intoxicating that the next morning failed to sober them of it.

Simon, being dedicatedly apolitical, was the last person to be motivated in his deeds by the desire to make a 'statement', and regarded what they were planning as a kind of situationist artwork. Ray did have a degree of genuine anger over the university's decision to splash out thousands on a new security system for a museum that nobody had ever tried breaking into anyway, but was mainly driven, after the idea had become planted in his head, by the 'because it's there' factor. To that he might add the 'why does a dog lick his balls' factor: once he realised he could do it, there seemed little reason not to. Consequences didn't enter into it. For one thing, ending up in jail would save him from sitting his finals, but even that was barely worth a thought. Consequences only happened to those who got caught, and he, like every other crook in history, wasn't planning to be.

They told no-one, well aware that a juicy titbit mouthed

at Kelvingrove Underground station could make it to the other side of the Hillhead campus before you did. The plan, indeed the whole notion, spawned from a chance remark Ray made to Simon as they discussed the university's latest profligacy. The previous term had witnessed the announcement of a six-figure outlay to have the main building and its landmark steeple (The Tower of Guilt, as it was known among students, particularly those with essays due) sandblasted back to its original white. This was an extravagance compounded by it being the architect's original intention that the stone should gather soot and render his creation black. Now, despite bare shelves in parts of the library, they wanted to shell out on a computerised security system which, as Ray fatefully put it, 'I could disable with a Commodore Amiga and a nine-hundred baud modem'.

Contrary to popular misunderstanding, much computer hacking does not require technical expertise or a facility with arcane pieces of machine code (though both of these do help), but is based around the simple device of sussing other people's passwords and then negotiating the system from there. Mothers' maiden names, dates of birth, children's birthdays . . . People are either too lazy to think of something securely esoteric or too scared that they'll forget what it was; and that's now, when the world revolves around PCs. In Glasgow back in the late Eighties, it was shooting fish in a barrel.

'It's just a question of finding the point of least resistance,' Ray explained to Simon.

The point of least resistance, in this case, was called Wullie Ferguson, the university museum's thick and bad-tempered nightwatchman, because any security system – computerised or not – was only as effective as the stupidest person who had to operate it. Auld Wullie was known to every student who'd ever raised his or her voice after midnight within a half-mile radius of the museum, barrelling from his office like a ruddy-faced cannonball at the slightest provocation and threatening expulsion as a ready sanction, like he was one step down from the university chancellor. The only time he was known to have a smile on his face was after Rangers victories, and it needed no solicitation for him to inform you that he was an Ibrox season-ticket holder. Using the aforementioned Amiga and primitive modem – one you still had to clamp the telephone receiver to – Ray successfully gained full access privileges on his first test run, the remote computer rejecting 'Rangers', 'Loyal' and '1690' before opening its doors to 'Souness'.

Gaining physical entry to the premises was achieved using the less technological method of starting a fire in a nearby skip and waiting for Auld Wullie to go into Red Adair mode, at which point Ray and Simon snuck into the building via his office.

It was plausibly rumoured that Wullie spent much of the night asleep once the unions were closed and there were no drunk undergraduates to shout at, knowing from decades of experience that this was an adequate level of vigilance in a place nobody had ever attempted to steal from. Ray and Simon therefore waited close to his door until they heard snoring, then set about their fun. In a measured, poignant and well-thought-out demonstration to highlight the university's inappropriate financial priorities, they rearranged all of the stuffed animals so that they looked like they were shagging each other, then carefully removed several paintings from the walls and replaced them with photocopies of that poster showing the tennis player scratching her arse.

Danger: criminal masterminds at work.

Exaggeration built the legend. By the end of the week, it was the Egyptian mummies that were shagging each other and the burglars had rearranged the whale bones into a cage, inside which they had imprisoned a bound and blindfolded Wullie Ferguson.

The adrenaline rush of carrying it out was, Ray had to admit, even greater than that of being onstage with The Arguments, but the aftermath was far less pleasurable. After a gig, he could feel the excitement for days, and enjoyed reconstructing moments in his head, wishing he could remember every second. After the museum, it was dread that lasted for days, and as he reconstructed his deeds, he was wishing he could remember more clearly where they might have left clues.

They hadn't, though. Not ones that the university or the local polis could read anyway. Dire pronouncements of punishment were made, like that was going to make them want to own up, but the more the uni authorities stamped their feet, the more stupid they looked and the more clever the burglars. Eventually they learned to quit digging, realising that the best thing to do was ignore it, write it off – students will be students – and let interest fade. As a result, the story had all but died down when the polis suddenly showed up at Ray's flat to huckle him; by which time he was so used to the idea of having got away with it that when they asked for him by name, he thought something awful must have happened to his parents.

The polis, to their credit, were a lot more down-to-earth about it than the uni, as represented by the vice chancellor, who was practically chewing the reception desk at Partick cop shop. They saw it for what it was: a student prank. No thefts, no breakages, no vandalism, and the only harm was to a few egos. This was, of course, after they had scared the shit out of the pair of them by giving them third-degree interviews, an overnight stay in the cells and generally treating them like they were a menace to society.

The president of the Student Rep Council – fortuitously a fan of The Arguments – intervened to stay the university's hand, threatening demonstrations if it carried out its stated desire to expel the pair of them. The vice chancellor was made to see sense over how he'd be digging himself back into his previous hole if he martyred the culprits so close to their finals, but he still insisted charges be brought, so Ray and Simon got their day in court, their stern admonishment and their names in the files.

They had to appear together in the dock, which was the last time they ever spoke. The case didn't come up until during the Easter holidays, and by that time their relationship was irredeemably poisoned by words and events that could not be unsaid or undone.

The police had no evidence other than their easily elicited confessions, so the only way they could have found out was if someone had grassed. Ray reckoned that if Simon had told anybody, it would have been Rina, but she swore the first she knew about it was when the arrests were made. This left only one possible culprit, who was as shamelessly prepared to spill his guts to Ray as he had been to the cops.

'Come on, they were gaunny find out anyway.'

'No, they quite obviously weren't.'

'The suspense was killin' you, Larry. Admit it. I did us both a favour, got it over with. We've got exams to worry about, without that hangin' over us.'

'Aye, now I just have to worry about goin' into the job market with a criminal record on my CV.'

'Don't be daft. It was just a bit of fun. They're hardly gaunny throw the book at us.'

'They werenae gaunny throw anythin' at us when they didnae fuckin' know we did it.'

'Fuck's sake, man, chill out. This way we all get a laugh about it. We can tell folk the whole story at last.'

'That's why you grassed us up? So you could act the big man?

'Come on, it must have been killin' you as well.'

'Away an' lie in your pish.'

'Ach, Larry, don't be such a big wean.'

'Aye, sure, cheers for the advice, Simon. An' here's some for you. If you ever plan on a life o' crime, learn to fuckin' button it, eh?'

Ray needed a shoulder to cry – or at least whine – on, so was as pleased as he was surprised when Rina phoned that night and asked him to meet for a drink. It wasn't just a friendly show of solidarity, more an expressed need for mutual support. She and Simon had had a huge argument too: the subject had been the same, prompted by her multi-level disapproval of what he had done, but this was really just a route into a whole mass of other angers that had been building up.

They met in a pub close to her flat, a spit-and-sawdust joint where they could be sure Simon would never enter because it was unlikely to contain anyone worth impressing. The conversation began about him, naturally, but by the end of the first pint had moved on to them talking about themselves and then about each other. It was good, *really* good, the kind of intimacy that makes you feel you're building the foundations of a truly special friendship. Ray was sure it was going to be one of those nights that went on until chucking-out time, so was a little deflated when, after a second drink, Rina suddenly reached for her bag – and it wasn't her shout.

'I've got a nice bottle of wine back at the flat. Do you want to head round there instead?'

'Yeah, sure,' he said, equally relieved and delighted that the evening wasn't coming to an end. And at that point he was still daft enough to think wine was all they were going back for.

Ray had reached the stage where he had started to regard his stubbornly enduring virginity as a kind of Mephistophelean trade-off. If he had been told on that dreich first Monday he turned up to matriculate that by the middle of fourth year he'd still not have had sex but *would* have had an indie-chart hit single, he'd probably have taken the deal. Sooner or later, everybody (just about) got to have sex, even people like Norman Tebbit. That was why man invented alcohol. But not everybody got to be in an indie rock band, even if only for a few months. Problem was, those months were now over, and during them he had been extremely disappointed to find that one side of the deal didn't have an unavoidable effect on the other. He was in a rock band, for fuck's sake. People in rock bands had sex. People in rock bands couldn't *help* having sex. All the girls in their immediate orbit should have instantly turned into adult sophisticates with hang-up-free carnal appetites.

Maybe some of them already were, but if so they never got off with Ray. He had always managed to locate and home in on the ones who shared his own immature self-image, meaning they were cringingly uncomfortable with their developing sexuality, while Ray was hardly the confident and experienced type who could put them at ease and lay them down by the fireside, baby. It wasn't just the physical side of his relationships that had consequently proven unsatisfactory. He had, in effect, paired up with a series of girlfriends who were too much like himself, and between them they had multiplied their common problems and insecurities rather than helped each other cancel them out. It therefore didn't take long for them to recognise in each other the things they liked least about themselves, and that would be all she wrote.

Always being the runt of the litter at school, Ray had never been in with the in-crowd, and while he was independent enough not to be like those who compromised themselves in often demeaning ways to gain entry, he still carried a few scars to his self-esteem. That was perhaps one of the reasons he was so tolerant of Simon. No crowd was as 'in' as his, and Ray had found himself an integral part of it. With Rina, though, he had at last begun to see how he looked through someone else's eyes, and not found himself staring at a wide-eyed, over-eager, twenty-one-year-old teenager, but someone she wanted to talk to. Someone she wanted to spend time with.

Someone she wanted to spend the night with.

Ray had heard any number of stupid expressions in his life, but ahead of even 'compassionate conservatism', 'better than sex' reigned supreme as the all-time champion. Anyone who said something was better than sex couldn't be doing it right. Nothing, he decided that night, was better than sex, and he had subsequently failed to encounter anything that dissuaded him.

As Rina took his hand and led him to her bedroom, even before they had done anything, it felt more exciting than playing onstage, more thrilling than breaking into the museum. And the sense of anticipation was so intense because he knew they *were* going to do something. He was playing with one of the big girls today, and he was a big boy now. Or at least would be, very soon.

Ray didn't consider there to be anything remotely sexy or even charming about his virginity, which was why he had no intention of sharing the significance of its passing with the woman who was doing him the unparalleled honour of taking it. Nor did he want his overall inexperience to be conspicuous, as there was definitely nothing sexy or charming about a technically incompetent lover, whatever crap the problem pages spouted regarding enthusiasm being the most important thing. Ray had no shortage of that, as well as years of imaginings to prepare him, but a more valuable source of guidance had been the corner-shop back in Ayrshire, where throughout the early Eighties, requesting 'something from under the counter' got you sorted out with some highly educational Scandinavian materials, even in Betamax.

It was, without question, the greatest experience of his life to that date. Every kiss, every touch, every caress, every sensation surpassed even his most fevered early-teen imaginings, and the best part was that Rina seemed to be enjoying it more than a little too. By some miracle, he didn't come immediately upon seeing her naked body, or at any of the other absurdly over-stimulating junctures along the way; though the time-honoured male mental-distraction technique did come to his rescue during Rina's more vocal moments. For a lot of guys, this involved tasks such as listing album tracks in the correct order or alphabetising the names of football teams; Ray was probably the first to enhance his sexual longevity by trying to remember, in order, the names of all twenty levels of *Manic Miner*.

He knew it had served its purpose when Rina, apparently

post-orgasm, pulled his head down closer to hers and whispered in his ear: 'Let yourself go. I want to feel you come.'

Were ever any words sweeter?

Ray might have fumbled, bluffed and improvised his way through the rest, but for this part he knew exactly what to do, again thanks to those illicit and much maligned porno vids. As he felt the deliciously unavoidable moment rapidly approach, he quickly withdrew, whipped off the condom (untimely ripped from its long-term rest home/grave in his wallet), then straddled Rina's chest and ejaculated on to her face.

Even before the first warm jet was airborne, he already knew he was in the throes of disaster. There had been a look of confusion in her eyes as he pulled out and removed the johnny-bag, but it all happened too fast to abort take-off.

'What the hell are you doing?'

Ray felt the greatest moment of his life turn instantly into the worst, suddenly recognising this video-induced delusion as a flimsy edifice he really ought to have seen through. He remembered Dennis Potter's anecdote about a Hollywood producer saying: 'You know when you're just about to come in a girl's face, and the phone rings?' and belatedly appreciated that Potter found the whole thing grotesque, not merely the fact that the Hollywood shark would answer the phone.

Time froze, which was just as well, as Ray's heart had stopped beating.

Then Rina burst into laughter: helpless, convulsive laughter that shook the bed.

She reached for a hanky from a box near the headboard. Ray didn't feel relief yet. He knew that sexual discretion was not always highly prized among students, particularly disappointed females, and envisaged the whole campus knowing the story by the end of the week.

'I'm really sorry, I . . .'

'Have you been with a lot of girls who are into that?'

'No.'

'So what made you think I was?'

Ray hung his head, nothing left to lie for. When he looked down, he could see Rina's breasts, which reminded him that this wasn't as bad a moment as he might have begun to think.

'You're the first one I've been with.' He could feel tears forming, but didn't want to wipe them away for fear that he would only draw attention to them.

'No way,' she said, still laughing. 'No way that was your first time.' Then she noticed the tears, which had begun to run down his cheeks. 'Oh Christ, you're not kidding, are you?'

Ray shook his head.

'Well don't look so sad about it. I wasn't that bad, was I?'

He smiled back, sheepishly.

'Come here,' she said, pulling his head down to rest on her chest.

'I'm sorry, Rina, really, I—'

'Don't worry about it. Just don't do it again. Well, not unless I ask you.'

At which they both laughed, and Ray knew it was going to be all right.

This was confirmed by them doing it (obviously not all of it) again after a few giggly minutes of billing and cooing, this time to the unlikely musical accompaniment of Adam and the Ants on Rina's tape deck. This was, she explained, a bit of wish-fulfilment on her part, as Marco,

Merrick, Terry Lee, Gary Tibbs and Yours Trulee had represented the zenith of stylised sexuality during her early Eighties pubescence, and she had youthfully imagined their music would be playing when she was grown-up enough to be finally doing it herself. Rina's previous sexual partner, whose name she could at that point not bring herself to utter, had been vocally appalled at the suggestion, an over-reaction she suspected was down to a number of albums she'd spotted in a pile back at his parents' house.

(Ray's own fantasy first-time soundtrack had been The Ronettes' heartbeat-booming *Be My Baby*. He'd have liked to be able to say that this was inspired by *Mean Streets*, but the truth was that he hadn't seen it by that point, and the notion in fact came from watching *Moonlighting*, specifically the episode in which Maddy and David finally got it on.)

'So you were *my* first too, in a certain way,' Rina told him in a near whisper.

'I like that,' he replied, stroking her hair. 'And I'm grateful old Adam isnae popular with the guys these days.'

'He was only unpopular with one,' she said, biting her lip in shy reaction to her oblique candour.

Ray held her that bit tighter. He was unsure what he was supposed or expected to find in the revelation, other than that she trusted him enough to make it, and that part knocked everything else into a cocked hat.

'You didn't have to tell me that, Rina. It's none of my business.'

'I wanted you to know, because I wish you'd been the first.'

'Attempts to come in your face notwithstanding.'

'Well, you were definitely the first to do that.'

412

They both laughed.

'So are we going to be boyfriend–girlfriend?' she asked.

'I do hope so.'

'Because if we are, you'll have to stop calling me Rina. It's a silly playground name that I've never been able to get rid of. My real name is Katrina.'

'Katrina,' Ray repeated.

'But I'd prefer if you called me Kate.'

Angelique phoned her boss on her hands-free to let him know where she was headed and why. Understandably, he wasn't recommending the entire Sunderland operation stand down on the basis of a suspicion that Ray was too gormless to have escaped the farmhouse through his own initiative. They had evidence, and it was incumbent upon them that they act on it, especially when it pointed to thirty thousand potential victims in a football stadium. Even Pinochet couldn't match those numbers.

Crianfada was a blink-and-miss-it wee village: just a few houses, a sub post-office and a pub. The nearby water-sports centre was the only reason most people would even notice the name, but even the sailors, windsurfers and divers tended to bed down along the road at the larger tourist destination of Cromlarig. Ray suspected Angelique had indeed blinked and missed it when she skited through the place at speed, as though having forgotten that she was imminently about to run out of road.

'First things first,' she said. 'I want a look at this bridge before we do anything else.'

They pulled up in front of a row of cones, beyond which two candy-striped barriers had been erected, just in case anybody had thought the 'ROAD AHEAD CLOSED' signs a hundred yards back were referring to some other thoroughfare. There were three guys in fluo-rescent yellow jackets and heavy black wellies standing next to the barriers, one of whom immediately set off towards them as they got out of the car, the unwelcoming look on his face suggesting they weren't the first to require individual assurance that the situation was indeed as described on the signs.

Angelique held up her warrant card to save him the speech.

'Who's in charge?' she asked.

'Douglas is the engineer,' he replied. 'Come on through and I'll get him. He's down in the drink just now. And watch your step or you'll find yourself in with him.'

They were led through the barriers, beyond which the road simply disappeared as though a bite had been taken out of it, leaving jagged teeth-marks in the tarmac. Across the gap, the two-lane blacktop continued on towards Dubh Ardrain and Cromlarig with the undisturbed innocence of a calmly retreating shoplifter.

The engineer emerged from below, helped up from a ladder by one of the wellingtoned fraternity. Angelique introduced herself while Ray tried not to look like a spare tool.

'I'm fairly baffled at this stage,' he heard the engineer telling her. 'If there was widespread fatigue in the struc-ture, I'd have expected it to come down when a heavy vehicle passed over it; an oil truck maybe. But there was nobody around. It passed inspection a year ago, and now it just appears to have spontaneously collapsed.'

'And what could have caused that?'

'Hard to tell. I'll know more when I can get some of the materials analysed. The problem is, a lot of the debris has already been washed further out into the loch.'

'Is sabotage a possibility?'

'Until I know more, anything's a possibility. Sabotage, aye, that's a possibility. I'm not sure it's a plausibility, though. Who would want to demolish the road to Cromlarig?'

'How aboot the Blairlethen shinty team?' asked one of the welly brothers. 'They always get skelped when they go there.'

Angelique said her thank-yous and they headed back to the car.

'You think it looks like Simon's work?' Ray asked as they pulled away.

'Did it look like subsidence to you?'

'More like Godzilla had popped by for a nibble.'

'My thoughts as well. How are your sea legs?'

'I can just about handle a pedalo. Or the rowin' boats at Rouken Glen.'

'You'll be fine. We've got to get a closer look at this place.'

'Out of interest, just what are you plannin' if we get a closer look and we *find* something?'

'Depends what we find, but my prediction would be to stand back and call in the cavalry.'

'And how are the cavalry going to get there?'

'We'll cross that bridge when we come to it.'

'There is no bridge, remember? That's my point.'

The watersports centre was on the near side of Crianfada, a low wooden building with a large car park and a concreted slipway. There were half a dozen sail dinghies lined up on the shore, alongside four jet-skis and a rack of windsurf boards. Ray could see a couple of windsurfers in the water right then, out beyond the two moored motor-boats that were bobbing at the edge of the loch in front of the building. Angelique had a worryingly long look at one of the power launches, then proceeded into the reception area, where a sandy-haired teenage girl hailed them both from behind her desk with a smile.

Ray hung back as Angelique did the talking, taking a stroll around the reception area's centrepiece: a scale three-dimensional model of Loch Fada and Glen Crom, from Blairlethen at one end to Cromlarig at the other. Dubh Ardrain power station was marked out on the glass of the display case, though there was little to represent it on the model unless you already knew the significance of the sprawling corrie loch and the dam holding it back.

There was a rack of tourist leaflets next to a bench against the window, advertising the usual highland and island attractions, including a tour of Dubh Ardrain. At the end of the bench was a pile of copies of the local newspaper, a flimsy free-sheet covering a radius of at least a hundred miles but a population of only a few thousand. Having yesterday stared with alienated detachment at the irrelevant headlines in the national press, he could hardly think of anything less pertinent to his current predicament.

But he was wrong to a near-absolute degree.

'GAMES HOMECOMING FOR SCOTS LEADER' said the front-page headline.

'NEW First Minister Andrew MacDonald will be on home ground as the guest of honour at this year's Cromlarig Highland Games. In twenty-four years as the area's MP and more recently MSP, Andrew has never missed the annual event, but this will be the first time he has attended since his election as First Minister in March, and the red carpet will be rolling out to meet him.

The trappings of his new office mean that Andrew will be arriving from Edinburgh by helicopter, a far cry from those days in the Seventies when his Hillman Hunter was a familiar site around the glens . . .'

Ray checked the date on the paper, which stated only 'September', the free-sheet being a monthly publication. The travel bulletin replayed in his head.

'If you're planning to attend today's Highland Games, you'd better get your skates on.'

'Angelique,' he called, lifting a copy and placing it face-up on the model display case. 'I think you should see this.' Angelique excused herself and turned away from the desk. 'The leader of our nation is headin' to Cromlarig this very afternoon for the Highland Games. Another wild coincidence, huh?'

Angelique gawped at the front page. 'The leader of . . . The First Minister.'

'Not as prestigious as the Prime Minister at a football international, but you said it's his style to go for the less expected target.'

'It sure is. Not a head of state, but the closest thing Scotland's had for a long time. Your pal Simon's certainly got a sense of irony.'

'How?'

'General Mopoza threatened an attack on "the British state", quote unquote, and if you're right, it looks like our man's planning to take out a potent symbol of its gradual break-up.'

'Wrong,' Ray argued. 'On three counts. One, that bastard is not my friend. Two, you need a sense of self-awareness before you can have a sense of irony; and three, there's nothin' ironic about targetin' Andrew MacDonald.'

'Why not?'

'Because he was Defence Secretary at Westminster during the Sonzolan conflict.'

Angelique's eyes widened. 'Of course. And he *always* goes to these bloody Highland Games in his constituency, doesn't he? It's the human-interest angle they wheel out about him every time. I remember him takin' flak for it from the tabloids during the war. Swanning off to drink whisky while "our boys" were in action, all that stuff.'

'So Simon would have had plenty of notice to come up with his plan.'

'If it was his plan,' Angelique questioned. 'Could have been Mopoza's idea.'

'No chance. Killing Scotland's man-in-charge would be far too pleasing to Scotland's biggest ego for him not to have thought of it himself. On top of that there's Dubh Ardrain: arguably Scotland's greatest engineering achievement, so who better to vandalise it.'

'We don't know Dubh Ardrain is part of the equation now though, do we. If MacDonald is the target, Darcourt could be planning something for the Highland Games. Security would be comparatively light, the way he likes it.'

'Dubh Ardrain *is* part of the equation,' Ray insisted, removing the newspaper to clear their view of the model. 'Otherwise, why would he take out the road before it reached the power station? It would have been far easier to block the route closer to Cromlarig. The road and bridges on the other side weren't widened or strengthened, because all the heavy plant was coming from the south. Simon doesn't want anybody to be able to reach Dubh Ardrain from this side, because this is the direction the cavalry would be coming.'

'And the ambulances,' Angelique added grimly. 'But

what can he do at Dubh Ardrain that's going to affect MacDonald down in Cromlarig?'

Ray stared at the model, looking back and forth at the two locations Angelique was talking about. They were four or five miles apart along the tight and winding glacial glen, the power station hidden beneath the mountains and the postcard town sitting at the north-western shore where the long and narrow loch came to an end. At that scale, it looked like a landscape from *Civilization* or *Populous*, strategy games for the budding megalomaniac.

'No explosion at the power plant could be strong enough to do more than shake a few sporrans at the Games,' Angelique said, articulating Ray's very thoughts, with the exception of the sporran remark. 'And I can't think of any way he could use the electrical capacity, so what does that leave?'

Only one thing, Ray deduced, by process of elimination. If this was *Populous*, as a competing deity, you would have a number of cataclysmic means to visit destruction upon the town that had incurred your wrath. Simon, however, had only one, and it was the deadliest in the game.

'Water.'

'Water? How?'

Ray looked at the model once more. He already knew what he was going to say, but felt he needed a moment to let the insanity ferment before sharing it round.

'Like Anne Elk, I have a theory. You're not going to like it.'

'Just run it by me. And who's Anne Elk?'

'Never mind. I think he's going to blow the dam.'

'What would that do?' Angelique asked, then had another look at the scaled-down landscape. 'Oh fuck.'

'Yup,' Ray confirmed. 'However many million or billion

gallons of water there are in the reservoir would come beltin' down the mountainside into Loch Fada, hittin' the opposite shore here where the glen bends inwards, which is gaunny channel the whole lot down between the mountains like a canal.'

'Won't it just raise the water level? I mean, Loch Fada's long. Surely it could accommodate—'

'Eventually, yes. But you'd get a massive wave effect first. And to amplify that effect, Loch Fada is artificially shallow along this stretch.'

'Artificially?'

'They hollowed out a mountain to build this place. Where do you think they put it all?'

Angelique bit her lip. 'You were right,' she said. 'I don't like your theory. I just wish it was because I could find a big hole in it.'

'So do I.'

'Hang on, I've got one. If they flooded Cromlarig and they've taken out the road south, how are Simon and his pals supposed to get away afterwards?'

'Boats,' Ray remembered. 'They had two speedboats on trailers back at the farmhouse. Have we come to that bridge we need to cross yet?'

Angelique got out her mobile phone. 'It sure sounds like it. Time to call in that cavalry. And before you say anythin', jet fighters don't need to cross bridges. Let's see how he likes an airstrike up his arse.'

'He'll like it fine. He's inside a mountain, and the entrance tunnel's got a shield door that was designed to withstand nuclear war.'

Angelique began dialling. 'I'm beginning to wish I hadn't brought you,' she said.

'Me too.'

Ray watched her walk outside for privacy – classified privacy no doubt – and turned back to the model. Over at the counter, the receptionist was keying something into her computer, cheerfully oblivious of what had just landed on the shoulders of her visitors.

Even before Angelique returned to tell him, Ray knew what was coming. The First Minister was officially opening the Games at three, and Ray's watch said five past twelve. The nearest sizeable police or army presence was at least two hours away on the wrong side of a big hole in the only road that led to Dubh Ardrain from the south, with the alternative route involving a three-hour detour.

'We *are* the cavalry, aren't we,' he asked as Angelique walked back in.

Her face confirmed it. 'I was going to say *I* am, but thank you for volunteering.'

'Are they at least going to evacuate the town?'

'Not yet.'

'Not *yet*? What, are things not quite cliff-hanging enough for them so far?'

'Two good reasons, Ray. One, this theory of yours is still just that until we see somethin' solid to back it up. And the other is that he wouldnae be the Black Spirit if he wasnae ready for it. He's taken steps to prevent anyone intervening while he and his chinas are at work, so he's got contingencies against us findin' out where he is. It's not a major leap to assume he's got a contingency against us findin' out what he's up to as well. He could have a remote camera or just a bloke up a hill with binoculars, but if we start evacuatin' people now, he could just blow the dam ahead of schedule. He might not get the First Minister, but he'd get two or three thousand others.'

'I take it the VIP won't be running the same unknown risk as his constituents?'

'He's been told, but he's still comin'. He's travellin' by helicopter, so they've the option to abort at any time.'

'Lucky him.'

'It makes sense. If Darcourt thinks everything's hunky-dory, at least that gives us—'

'Less than three hours,' Ray stated. 'That's what it gives us. Less than three hours for the two of us, unarmed I might add, to get inside a heavily guarded subterranean fortress and take down one of the world's most dangerous terrorists.'

'And yet you're volunteering.'

'Well, just like you, I've got two good reasons. One is that they're gaunny hunt me down and kill me anyway. Kate too, for a motive that I think I made clear, and probably Martin just for what he represents. Simon might forget, but he never forgives, and when he saw me at the airport it would have reminded him of a very big unsettled score.'

'What's the other reason?'

'I fancy our chances.'

'You *do*?'

'Yeah. You might be up against the Black Spirit, Angelique, but I'm up against that fanny of a flatmate. He might be a world-feared terrorist these days, but I'll bet he's still a wank.'

third-degree Burns

Simon looked at his watch, aware that if he maintained the current frequency, he was in very real danger of developing a twitch before this was all over. The problem was, there was nothing else to occupy his time other than watching it trickle away, the spare hours being steadily eroded while the buttress walls were steadfastly not. He lifted his radio from the control-room console and called May.

'What's the situation? Any progress?'

'Yes. We're approximately ten minutes further forward since the last time you asked, ten minutes ago.'

'Watch the fucking lip, okay? Can you get Deacon to give me some kind of ETA?'

'No. Deacon's busy trying to fix the equipment. Why don't you just pick a time at random and add the duration of these calls. That way your guess would be as accurate as his.'

'I should have shot you while I had the chance, if you weren't going to be any fucking use to me anyway.'

'You'd be better shooting whoever fucked our equipment.'

'I will, I promise, if we ever find the bastards. There's about twenty miles of tunnels around this place, plus access shafts, vents, surge chambers. It's a shitey place to be playing hide-and-seek if you're "it".'

'There's also the possibility that they aren't here at all.

If they got out of those crates while we were taking the control room, they could have doubled back out of the entrance tunnel.'

May was right. They hadn't posted anyone on the front gate because the next shift wouldn't arrive until around eight and they needed all hands elsewhere at that stage. Their gatecrashers could have snuck out and might already have flagged down a passing car. To make matters worse, the road collapse was bound to be public by now, meaning that the first vehicle they were likely to encounter would be a cop car on its way to or from the accident site.

'It's been a couple of hours,' Simon said, thinking aloud. 'If they'd raised the alarm, I think we'd know about it by now.'

'I wouldn't be so sure. These backwoods cops would hardly just come screaming up here if they'd been told we were heavily armed.'

'That's a very good point,' he conceded. 'We should put somebody on look-out topside and lock the shield door until the morning shift is due.'

The landline phone rang on the console, as if he didn't have enough on his plate. If it was someone from the National Grid, he'd have to retrieve whoever was in charge from among the hostages. It was something he had planned for, but he wasn't expecting it to come up until daytime, as the plant was in non-supply mode overnight.

'Radio silence,' he told May, then lifted the phone. 'Control room, Dubh Ardrain,' Simon answered.

'Maybe we should consider aborting while the going's good.'

Simon walked to the window and looked across the machine-hall floor to the gathering around the sabotaged equipment. He saw May staring back up at him, holding the receiver of a wall-mounted telephone. May wisely didn't want the conversation relaying around every radio in the team, but it was well seeing the bastard didn't have the balls to suggest this face-to-face.

'That's a little premature, *Brian*. We've a few problems to solve, but nothing's desperate yet. I think it's a bit early to hit the ejector button.'

'It's never too early to walk away, *Freddie*, but it can be too late. And you know what too late means, don't you. You've been a guest on the good ship Black and Decker too, I assume.'

Simon took a breath. It was understood (if seldom discussed) among the inner circle that they all had Shub in common, but nobody knew how close anyone else might be to the man in the middle. Some might never have met him; others, particularly lower down the food chain, might not know he was their conduit into a given operation. This was the first time anybody had directly acknowledged so much, and it certainly helped explain why May had been so jumpy about whether Simon knew Ash.

'I didn't hear that and you didn't say it,' Simon told him. 'That's about the biggest favour I can do either of us right now, agreed?'

'Agreed.'

'If we walk away, we're finished, and I mean even if we walk away clean. Never mind reputations. You're only as good as your last job, so a failure on this scale wipes everything else from your CV. There isn't a seniors tour for our game. If you fuck up, you disappear, forever; and if you're lucky, you perform the vanishing act yourself.'

'We've all made provisions,' May said.

'So you see yourself lyin' on a beach somewhere, livin' off your savings? Fuck off. You'd go nuts.'

'Yeah, those cocktails and blowjobs would really start to wear me down.'

'Don't kid yourself, Brian. I know what kind of blowjob gets your rocks off, and we've got one lined up right here.'

'She seems to be playing hard to get, though. And her over-protective big brother could be paying us a visit any minute.'

'That's why I always make sure we have options. MacDonald will be there until at least five, so that's two extra hours, if we need them, to hit our primary target. Knowing you, your demolition plans are probably very belt-and-braces, so we can space the bores a bit wider and put more explosive in each one.'

'If you're going to cut corners, I'd recommend instead that we concentrate more explosive on the central buttress. Take that out, and the water should do the rest.'

'See? Power of positive thinking, Brian. Whistle a happy tune while you're at it and we're laughin'.'

'Fuck you. And what if the cops show up outside?'

'We've got eight hostages now, about twenty more due in a few hours, and we're holed up inside a mountain with a nuclear shield door. Even if we end up with half the British Army outside, there's not a lot they can do except negotiate, which suits us fine. We ask for a helicopter. We set a deadline. The negotiators try and stall to get more time, which is cool because it's time we want.'

'For what?'

'Worst-case scenario is we miss MacDonald because we're late, but we'd get the dam rigged eventually. Whether it's three in the afternoon with nobody knowin' we're here, or three in the mornin' with a column of tanks outside, sooner or later that dam is gonna blow. And when it does, anybody standin' in front of this place will be hangin' ten all the way to Cromlarig.'

'*If* Deacon gets the gear fixed,' May reminded.

Simon wanted to kill him, but knew he'd just be shooting the messenger. That was why he was on tenterhooks and calling for bloody progress reports every ten minutes. At the planning stage, he always tried to isolate the individual elements that the operation was reliant upon, because a failure in any single one could be calamitous. They therefore brought extra explosives, extra ammo, extra guns, extra Dubh Ardrain uniforms. They even brought two drills, for fuck's sake, and factored in enough time in case they were for any reason reduced to one. Simon had planned for the authorities being alerted and he had planned for a siege. He had even planned for the scheme being rumbled and Cromlarig being evacuated. His response to that was contingent upon early (both appliances) – or at least punctual (single appliance) – completion of the drilling; while his response to everything else was contingent on the drilling taking place at all.

No mouse and no man planned for sabotage. Maybe that was what the lecherous, drunken Ayrshire bastard meant. After all, he wrote it out of remorse after demolishing a nest with his plough. Whoever had done this to Simon wouldn't be writing any poems about it, but they would certainly be fucking sorry.

He lifted his radio.

'Everybody listen up. We're going to Def-Con Two. I'm closing the shield door. Simonon, grab your goggles and get topside. Look-out duty's starting early. You keep one eye on the road and one eye on Cromlarig. May and Steve Jones, you go topside with Simonon. May, you booby-trap the reservoir approach road; remote-detonator. Jones, you'll stay up there with your finger on the button. Use your discretion. The cops are unlikely to be driving a tractor and the farmer doesn't represent a threat. Everybody else, unless Deacon tells you otherwise, you're joining the search. I'm shutting down both turbines so we can use our ears as well as our eyes. That means radio silence too. Unless it's an emergency, the first message I want to hear is that you've got these fuckers. Mercury out.'

'I'm brickin' it, man,' Murph whispered.

'Shhh,' Lexy replied, the quivering in his breathing surely enough to confirm that he felt the same. Though he was cold, his fingers were sweaty where he gripped the machine gun, the metal warmed by his constant touch. Wee Murph had started off holding his weapon like a guitar; now they were both holding them like they were teddy bears, cuddled for comfort in the darkness of a long night where the only adults around were not going to tuck them in and tell them it would all be okay. Lexy was beginning to wish they hadn't brought them at all. Neither of them knew what they were doing with the things, and he was terrified one of them would go off by accident, which would at best give away their position and at worst save the bad guys the bother.

He was starting to shiver, though it was hard to tell how much was through cold and how much through fear. They had been stuck in the damp, dark drainage tunnel for ages, terrified they could be discovered any second, but too scared to move because they could be walking straight into capture.

It had felt okay at first, sitting there in the light of Murph's torch, a rush of blood in his ears, thumping in his chest and nervous giggling from the pair of them out of relief that they had made it this far and found a half-decent hiding place. Though it had seemed a lot more, it had probably only been a matter of minutes between getting out of the crates and reaching this spot, and Lexy felt like he'd been holding his breath the whole time.

It had seemed a miracle they didn't feel the crate throb to the rhythm of his pounding heart as they lifted it out of the truck, though there was a loud, low sound filling the place and covering up any noise he might have made. Once on the floor, he had waited nervously for the chance to get out, hearing voices or the sound of boots on concrete every time he was planning to edge it. After a while, he became convinced he was imagining the noises simply out of his own understandable anxiety, and was about to just get it over with when he definitely felt something brush against the crate. He had tensed up into a ball before it even occurred to him to ready the gun, by which time the lid had been pulled off and Murph was standing over him.

'Fuck's sake, were you sleepin'? Hurry up.'

He hardly had time to look around, enough only to observe that they were in some kind of cave, before they ran for the first doorway they could see, light shining out from it on to the dim, smaller passageway that intersected the main tunnel. The doorway led, via a short corridor and a left turn, to another tunnel, walled on one side by concrete and the other by bare rock, the passage running parallel to the one the truck was parked in. Striplights overhead lit the way, Lexy wondering what kind of cave could have such an extensive electrical supply. Forward of the crossroads, the passage continued out of sight as it bent gently to the left; but behind, instead of leading to the entrance, it sloped downwards towards another parallel doorway, this one closed.

'Bad guys went that way, intae the big cave,' Murph said, pointing.

'Okay,' Lexy acknowledged, then followed him in the opposite direction. The door opened with a creak of metal, leading them on to a steel platform inside another tunnel, this time even bigger than the main one, but with water running through it beneath their feet. It was dark, only the light spilling in from the passageway illuminating the circular chamber. The sound was louder here too, as though it led directly to whatever was making it.

'It's an underground stream,' Murph announced, but Lexy doubted it. The tunnel was straight as an arrow and the water, barely a foot deep, was running down the centre of a semi-circular concrete channel. It looked like some kind of sewer or drain, clearly designed to accommodate a lot more fluid than was currently trickling through.

Lexy read the sign on the front of the door they had come through. It said 'Tailrace access 4', and above it were the words Highland Hydro and a logo built around two Hs, rendering one a simplified mountain with blue water on top, and the other a pylon.

'It's a hydro-electric plant. Mind we did it in Geography.'

'Maybe *you* did. We've got Miss Galloway for Geography, so the only thing we pay attention to is her tits. Can we get oot this way?'

'Naw. If this is a hydro station, it'll lead tae a loch or a river or somethin'. It's shallow here, but it'll lead under water for a good bit at the end. Plus I think they put mesh up tae stop fish an' that comin' in.'

'Whit's at the top end, then?'

'Turbines. That's whit the noise is.'

'So where we gaunny go?'

Lexy looked along the platform. It didn't lead anywhere, so it had to just be for keeping an eye. However, the sign did say 'access'. More than that, it said 'access 4', meaning there were at least three others. He leaned over the edge and saw that there was a built-on ladder hanging from the far end of the steel grid, allowing the workies down into the water.

'Doon here, an' alang. 'Mon.'

'Where tae?'

'The next wan o' these.'

'Where's that gaunny take us?'

'I don't fuckin' know. Have you got a better idea?'

Murph's silence answered the question. Lexy climbed down and dreeped the last few feet, shuddering as he hit the ground in concern that the jolt would set the machine gun off. He looked up and watched Murph practically slide down the thing like it was a chute in a playpark.

'Careful. Watch the gun doesnae go aff.'

'If you're that feart, take the bullets oot it.'

'Aye, an' if we run intae the bad guys I'll just ask them tae gie us a minute while I put them back in.'

Lexy pulled his torch from his pocket and switched it on, Murph following suit a couple of seconds later.

'No' baith at wance,' Lexy said. 'The batteries.'

'Fuck's sake, you're worse than ma maw for naggin'.'

'Shhh.'

'That as well.'

They made their way up the incline, the water noticeably widening to fill more of the channel as they progressed. For a while they walked closer to the sides, trying to stay above it, but before long they were ankle-deep.

'Fuckin' freezin' man.'

'I know.' Lexy pointed upwards with his torch. 'We're nearly at the next ladder.'

'Hing on, I'm confused.'

431

'Whit?'

'How come the watter's gettin' deeper, but we're walkin' uphill? Is this like the Electric Brae or somethin'?'

'It's gettin' deeper 'cause there's a flow noo. Did you no' hear it? They must be drainin' somethin'. Maybe one o' the big pipes fae the dam. They're no' generatin' though. That's for sure.'

'How, whit would be happenin' if they were generatin'?'

'We'd be gettin' flushed doon this pipe by a thoosand gallons o' watter.'

'Shite, man. Don't say that.'

'Better hurry an' get up that ladder then.'

They had to haul themselves up slowly by their hands for the first few bars, then made the rest of the ascent far more rapidly. Lexy's gun clanged against the metal of the ladder as he climbed on to the platform, giving him another minor heart attack. He stretched down a hand to help Murph up the last wee bit, then went to the door at the end, which turned out to be locked.

'Aw, away tae fuck,' Lexy moaned, shining his torch up and down the blocked exit.

'Whit aboot thon wee tunnel?' Murph asked.

'Whit wee tunnel?'

'Back doon there.' Murph pointed his torch down at the side of the channel, from where they'd just come. There was a small opening at about waist height, which Lexy hadn't seen, having been focusing his torch and his eyes squarely on the platform ahead. There were times when he had to be grateful that Murph had the attention span of a two-year-old, always on the look-out for new distraction. Of course, that was what had got them into this shite in the first place, but it was a bit late to be worrying about that.

They climbed back down and pointed their torches into the smaller tunnel. It was big enough to crawl into on all fours, though this was at the cost of damp trouser-legs, as the concrete-lined floor had water running along it too.

'I think it's a drain,' Lexy said.

'Llmmm-mmmm,' Murph replied, putting his tongue under his bottom lip in the now standard insult that followed a totally obvious remark.

'I'm just sayin'. If it's a drain, this is the outlet, so there must be an inlet.'

'It doesnae look big enough for an adult tae crawl through,' Murph observed.

'They could, but they'd be slower. I 'hink this could be our best shout.'

They crawled along, Lexy first, splashing through the cold water, the sound of the turbines still drowning all other noise. Murph's torch confirmed that the entrance was out of sight behind them due to the curvature of the tunnel, but they kept going until Lexy could see light up ahead, shining in from above. He shut off his torch and told Murph to do the same, before crawling close enough to get a look up. He could see a mesh panel, presumably in the floor of a brightly lit room, from where the turbine noise was louder than ever. Just past that, the tunnel bent sharply to the left, leading to other drains, other rooms.

'Go back,' Lexy whispered.

'How?'

'If we sit aboot haufway, we've got two escape routes. If somebody starts crawlin' in fae either end, we bomb it for the other. Meantime, we sit tight.'

And they did, in the dark with their torches mostly off, getting colder and more nervous as the time steadily passed. The running, climbing and crawling had been a lot

433

easier than the waiting, but they both knew this was the least risky option, particularly after Murph turned his stolen walkie-talkie back on and they heard the baddies' reaction to their handiwork.

'*You'd be better shooting whoever fucked our equipment.*'

'*I will, I promise, if we ever find the bastards.*'

That wasn't the worst moment, though. The worst moment was when the turbines shut down, joint equal with every moment since. A hush fell over the place, so still that they could even hear the flow of the water back in the tail-race tunnel. Their breathing seemed now to be amplified by the walls, and it was easy to imagine the drainage tunnel carrying the sound directly to the men searching for them. Murph's 'bricking it' remark was therefore as dangerous as it was unnecessary. Lexy would have been justified in returning the 'lmmm-mmm' insult, though perhaps not at such potential cost.

The tension built with every silent second, until Lexy was almost hoping for discovery to at least end the uncertainty. Until, that was, the uncertainty ended, with a faint glow of light in the darkness behind Murph.

'Oh fuck,' he couldn't stop himself from saying.

Murph turned his head to look too. By this time there was a play of light and shadow where the tunnel curved out of sight, accompanied by a sound of shuffling. Both of them froze, until spurred back into motion by a loud burst of static from Murph's walkie-talkie, which Lexy had fruitlessly asked him to turn off. If their pursuer hadn't heard them already, then he'd definitely have heard that; maybe it had even been his intention.

'All units, this is Strummer. They're ahead of me in a drainage tunnel, headed into turbine area, lowest level.'

Lexy slung the machine gun around his back by the strap

and began scrambling along the tunnel, panic causing him to lose his footing and sprawl face-first on to the wet ground.

'Fuck's sake, hurry,' Murph said, almost falling on top of him at the rear.

Less hurry, more haste, sounded in Lexy's mind in the voice of his old Primary Six teacher. He picked himself up and proceeded more steadily, reminding himself that they could move faster in this confined space than an adult, at the same time as trying not to think how long it would be before the adult had a clear line of fire.

He reached the mesh and got into a crouch, then pushed upwards with his hands. It wouldn't budge.

'Fuck.'

'Use the gun, man,' Murph urged. 'Go ram it.'

Lexy took a firm hold of the weapon in both hands, pointing the muzzle away from his body, then slammed it upwards with every fear-multiplied ounce of strength he could muster. It flipped open on a hinge, then slammed shut again through its own weight. Lexy heaved to once more, this time following through with the butt to prevent a repeat, then levered it fully open and pulled himself up. He stepped clear and bent down to offer Murph a hand, but the wee man shot up through the hole like he had a trampette down there.

Lexy slammed the cover closed and looked around for something to place on top. They were in a short, curving, dead-end passageway with a bank of dials on one wall and several large chemical drums against the other.

'Come on,' Lexy said, running to one of the drums and attempting to push it. Murph joined him on the other side and between them they slid the hulking aluminium barrel on top of the drain.

Lexy panted from the effort and took hold of his gun again, turning just as a man in khaki combat trousers and matching jacket rounded the curve in front of them. He looked like a Nineties refugee, except Lexy didn't imagine The Gap ever sold machine guns as accessories.

Reflex took over; it had to, because Lexy's brain had no idea what to do. He dropped to his knees next to the drum, aimed his weapon and pulled the trigger.

It wouldn't move. Murph, still standing, had the same degree of success.

Everybody in Khaki levelled his machine gun at chest height. 'A hundred lines, boys,' he said. 'I must not leave the safety catch on. Now drop the guns.'

They both complied without delay, tossing the weapons to the floor and raising their hands without being prompted.

'Oh Christ,' said Wee Murph, his voice choking up.

Lexy was too scared to cry. His heart sounded like a trance mix and he was breathing in and out about twice a second.

'Mercury, this is Mick Jones,' Gap Man said, his voice coming at them both from his mouth and Murph's radio. 'I've got them.'

His accent didn't match his name, and neither did his tanned and swarthy face. Wee Murph would probably have said he looked Turkish, but that was because Murph said everybody foreign looked Turkish, it being the only foreign destination he had ever visited.

'Mercury here. The guns?'

'Those too. You won't believe it. It's a couple of kids.'

'Couple of wee neds, more like.'

'Will I bring them in?'

'No. Unfortunately for these little pricks, we're well fixed for hostages. I don't like people fucking with my property. Execute them and get yourself topside. You're added to the look-out roster. Use any lift: all the aqueducts are dry now. Mercury out.'

Lexy felt a slumping sensation in his stomach, as though his heart and lungs had collapsed inside him. He looked at the barrel of the machine gun, then at the man's eyes, where he saw no doubt, no conflict.

No mercy.

'You were a good mate, Murph,' he said, his voice dropping to a broken whisper as tears clouded his sight.

'You an' aw, Lexy.'

'Nothing personal,' their executioner told them, and pulled the trigger before Lexy could close his eyes.

Simon heard the two bursts of fire echo up through the machine hall from their source somewhere below, and felt the beginnings of calm settle about him. Just one problem finally being solved was enough to thoroughly alter his perspective: when there is zero progress on all fronts, a sense of hopelessness unavoidably sets in; but all it took was a single element falling into place to restore both confidence and optimism. It was more than a matter of having one fewer thing to worry about: it reminded him that such worry was an essential part of the job. Going right back to that fake passport for flight 941, there was always one factor that didn't get sorted out until nail-bitingly close to curtain-up. In this case, it would be a pretty major factor, but it would happen in the end, and it would happen because he worried enough to make sure that it did.

Literally eliminating the unforeseen rogue elements had been the turning point; the intruders had been the source of all the problems, so it seemed almost poetic that their

437

deaths should herald the onset of the solutions. He'd have to confess that it had therefore been a heart-in-mouth few seconds between the order and the kill. A turning point, yes, but one that could have turned either way. If Jones had chosen that as a highly inappropriate moment to grow a conscience, then it really would have been a sign that the mission was doomed.

As it happened, Jones didn't let him down, but you could never be sure with the kiddie factor. People could be so absurdly sentimental about it, especially face-to-face. Christ knew how many kids were going to die when the water hit Cromlarig, and nobody had a problem carrying out the op, but put one right in front of them and there was always a danger that their brains would spontaneously turn to mush. In fact, it wasn't merely absurd; the hypocrisy was sickening. People always made such a disproportionate fuss over the child victims, and bugger the rest. What was the cut-off point, Simon wanted to know, where they ceased to be eligible for special sympathy? Puberty? The age of consent? Or was there a sliding scale of tragedy about their deaths: maximum points for babies and toddlers, down to minimum in mid-teens, when they're moody and objectionable and therefore mourned but not missed?

These two certainly weren't going to be a great loss in the grand scheme of things. Two fewer sales for Limp Bizkit: what a fucking tragedy.

He'd order Lydon and Matlock to dispose of the bodies later, as their first lesson in the importance of keeping the truck locked and their eyes open. And unless they were suitably contrite, their second lesson would be a couple of bullets in the back of the head. Months of planning and reconnaissance, every component double-checked, every trace erased, every precaution taken, yet all it required was two inquisitive little bastards to sneak on board and the entire mission had been jeopardised. Jeopardised, but not thwarted, which luckily for them was the only thing that mattered right then. The turning point had come. Time and expertise, he knew, would do the rest.

And they did.

Over the next few hours, one by one the elements clicked tightly into place like a rifle being assembled. The production line at Deacon's improvised electrical workshop started rolling at around four, beginning with one operational drill and followed shortly after by the generator. Drilling got underway topside at four-forty, supplemented a little over an hour later by the second appliance, Deacon's initial pessimism proving misplaced.

The control-room phone started ringing just before six, the first of the dayshift workers based south of the road collapse waking up to the news on the radio and calling in to make his understandable excuses. Simon had the head engineer, one Michael Livingston, brought upstairs at gunpoint to take the call and to make a whole lot more. Livingston had to inform the visitor-centre staff that the place was closed and they had the day off, as well as ringing the nightshift's other halves regarding the compulsory overtime. He would also be required to field the inevitable calls from the Grid regarding the facility's temporary lack of output, in response to which he could accurately assure them that the water would definitely be in full flow by around three o'clock.

Simon was aware, he explained, that all of this provided Livingston with the opportunity to raise the alarm through some subtle form of subversion: calling someone by the wrong name, perhaps, or making an obscure reference that would communicate a surreptitious SOS.

439

'So I just want you to know that if the authorities do show up, even by coincidence, the first thing I'll do is shoot you in the balls. Then I'll shoot you in the knees, and then the soles of your feet. And I promise I won't finish you off until I have to leave, which in a hostage situation could be quite some time. The alternative is that you're a good boy, you say your piece, we get our work done, and you all get to go home to your loved ones. Of course, you'll also get to give statements and descriptions to the cops, but we'll be long gone by then, so we won't hold that against you. You have my word.'

'What is it you want here?' Livingston asked, curiosity temporarily edging out fear.

'The less you know, the less reason I've got to kill you. Agreed?'

'Agreed.'

Simon had heard it said that some actors gave their best performances when they were at their most nervous. Livingston could now be considered among them. His voice barely wavered throughout, and it was unlikely he'd be able to think up anything esoteric while his thoughts were dominated by the protection of his family jewels.

With no word of police interest from Simonon topside, the shield door was reopened at 7:45, in time to admit those dayshift workers lucky enough (ha) to live at the right end of the loch. At 8:30, a headcount was carried out, minus the stranded Crianfada contingent. With all staff accounted for, the shield door was closed once again and the newly restrained dayshift group were placed with the rest of the hostages in the now thoroughly reeking storage chamber. (Toilet trips for hostages were filed under 'Negligence' in Simon's book. Aside from the security risk, people tended

440

to feel a sight less defiant when their trousers were soaked with their own pish.)

By midday, drilling was almost complete, with May estimating they would be fully ready to rock'n'roll at around half past one.

Simon resisted the temptation to say 'I told you so'. His abstinence was assisted by a reluctance to tempt fate, but he knew this was just irrational superstition. All the pieces were in place. The rifle was fully assembled, and would very soon be locked and loaded. After that, he only had to pull the trigger.

Nothing could go wrong now.

team deathmatch:
leet good guys [LGG] v terrorist llamas [TL]

In the beginning, there was *Doom*.

Well, strictly speaking, in the beginning there was *Castle Wolfenstein 3D*, and if you wanted to get truly archeological about it, then in the beginning there was *3D Monster Maze* for the Sinclair ZX81, requiring the optional 16k RAM pack, which was so heavy that its own weight frequently hauled it off the interface and crashed your machine.

To say it wasn't much to look at was an undeserved kindness that cleverly avoided the ancillary issue of it having absolutely no sound. What it did have, however, was a first-person, three-dimensional perspective; even if it was a first-person, three-dimensional perspective of an amorphous black blob that was recognisable as a dinosaur only to those who had read the cassette-sleeve and were sleep-deprived to the point of hallucination from staying up all night trying to play the fucking thing. The game was, nonetheless, genuinely creepy, with the lack of sound arguably adding to the effect: when you *know* there's an invincible enemy stalking you but you can hear nothing and can see only a long corridor stretching out ahead, the atmosphere can get absurdly tense. Throw in the constant anxiety that the ZX81 is about to crash and you've got the original high-adrenaline 3D gaming experience, which any history of the first-person shooter genre would ultimately lead back to.

The technology had advanced exponentially over Ray's

lifetime, and with it, so had the boundaries of the programmers' imaginations. There were new genres, indeed whole new concepts developing, as ZX Spectrum gave way to Amiga, Amiga to PC, 486 to Pentium, CPU to GPU. *Doom* looked as primitive now as it had made its black-and-white antecedent look then, but when it came along in '94, it provided an experience far more frightening and ten times as involving as any horror movie; and it was enjoyed all the more by those who had once felt the hairs on their necks stand on end while exploring those black-and-white corridors, trying to evade ASCII-rendered death.

For more than twenty years, Ray had been roaming those computer-generated mazes and getting as much from them as an adult as he had as a geeky teen. This was not, he would fiercely contend, because he had never grown up; he had, and could point to the wife, wean, job and mortgage to prove it. It was because the games had grown up with him. If he was still playing pixelated and antiquated teen-era fare such as *Jet Set Willy* or *Skool Daze* for hours on end, then yes, he'd be referring himself for therapy (the occasional late-night drunken resort to a ZX Spectrum emulator for nostalgia purposes didn't count), but gaming had turned into something much more. Between the virtual environments within the games and the social sub-culture surrounding them, it provided what often seemed like a whole other world. Sometimes it was a world Ray knew he was retreating to, but mostly it was a place that augmented the world he was already in, a place to visit in order to meet old and new friends and to have a good time. Not for nothing was his favourite newsgroup called games.pub.

'But don't these games make you violent?' he was unavoidably asked, by people who had never played; just like it was people who never watched horror movies who wanted 'video nasties' banned back in the early Eighties. Ray regarded this as such a frank confession of the questioner's stupidity that he considered it futile to even respond. His favourite maps back in the early *Quake* days were The Abandoned Base (DM3) and The Cistern (DM5), because both contained the vastly entertaining combination of the Lightning Gun, the Pentagram of Protection and large quantities of H_2O. The funniest and most satisfying trick in the game was to grab the LG and the invulnerability power-up, then hop into the drink and pull the trigger, instantly frying everyone else who happened to be in the water. Pretty soon players began to interpret the distinctive sound of the Pentagram as 'Everybody out of the pool', but now and again you still caught out a few newbies or someone who just couldn't get clear in time.

Doing this made Ray laugh, gave him a buzz and earned him lots of kills. It did not make him want to bring a three-bar fire along to the Pollokshaws Baths so that he could lob it in and frag the swimmers.

Horror movies made you a serial killer, porno vids made you a rapist and playing online games made you a psycho. And people said *Ray* was living in a simplistic fantasy world.

'But don't these games make you violent?'

In the past, if he had been forced to answer that question, he'd have pointed out that he hadn't committed an act of violence since he got into a fight at Primary school. If asked right then on Loch Fada, however, his answer would be: 'I fucking well hope so.'

Angelique cut the speedboat's engine and let it drift as they rounded a truncated spur and the dam came into view on the mountain above. They were both clad in wetsuits, diving masks around their necks, O₂ tanks on the floor of the vessel next to the binoculars, torch, crowbar and two spearguns, these last being the only available weaponry. They weren't for hire, the receptionist had nervously stressed to Angelique as she handed them over; they belonged to one of the centre's instructors, who had brought them back from the Caribbean. Ray had found them very useful in the underwater areas of *Sin*, but not as effective as a rocket-launcher or a shotgun.

He had been scuba-diving once before, on holiday two years ago. Angelique assured him that it was just like riding a bike, but Ray was acutely aware that if you fell off a bike, you generally tended not to drown or develop hypoxia. The holiday being somewhere a lot warmer than the Highlands in September, it was the first time he'd ever worn a wetsuit. It was also the first time he'd worn a kevlar vest. Angelique had two in the boot of her car, placed there yesterday when she was supposed to be driving herself and a colleague to the farmhouse. Her encounter with the Sheriff of Calton Creek had led to a change in plan Ray was now seriously regretting, but not as much as he was regretting his own soul-searching trip to the frigging airport on Wednesday. But for that, he'd have known nothing about any of this until it made the TV news. And what would he have done to help then, he asked himself? Buy the charity record for the disaster appeal?

Angelique at least looked like she knew what she was doing, though she had no idea how reassuring it was for Ray to see that she had tied her hair back in a ponytail, making her look even more like the Athena player-model who kept coming to his rescue. Dressed head-to-toe in black rubber, and with that lithely petite build, she also resembled one of the black-ops assassins from *Half-Life*. That was reassuring too, as those sneaky wee besoms took a hell of a lot to put them down.

She lifted the binoculars and looked up at the dam, then handed them to Ray to see for himself just how depressingly correct his hypothesis had been. There was a gantry on the front of the buttress, about halfway up the walls, and on it he could see four men, split into pairs, each pair standing beside a bulky item of machinery from which clouds of dust were billowing.

'They're drilling,' he said.

'Looks like it,' Angelique agreed. 'A buttress wall like that would probably just deflect the blast if you put a bomb in front of it. If you really wanted to rupture it, you'd have to put your explosives deep into the concrete. Shield door is closed too.'

'You absolutely sure they couldnae be just givin' the walls a clean? Bit of sand blasting, maybe?'

Angelique reached for her mobile, giving Ray a wry and regretful smile.

Her conversation sounded like a rehash of what she and her boss must have discussed earlier, without so many ifs but plenty of buts. Evacuation, if it was going to happen, would have to be immediate, as they had no idea how close the terrorists were to finishing their preparations; but there was every likelihood this would mean everyone in Cromlarig drowned in a tailback rather than at home or at the Highland Games. Back-up, and lots of it, was on its way from every available source, but the clock was hard against them. They could get a helicopter full of highly trained soldiers there in forty-five minutes, but its approach would be visible for miles, especially from up on that mountain, negating any element of surprise and possibly precipitating the same response as an attempted

446

evacuation. Alternatively, they could put down in the next glen, but that would at least double their road-journey time and give them less than an hour to do whatever they thought they could.

The alternative was nonetheless considered better than nothing (and certainly better than anything that brought the disaster forward), so the order was given and Angelique was assured that the assault team would be airborne within minutes. For the next couple of hours, however, it was still up to them.

'You got any experience of this sort of thing?' Angelique asked.

'What? Runnin' around in caverns and corridors, takin' on a team of headcases armed to the teeth? I'm a virtual expert.'

'A vir . . . Oh that's right. Games. *Tomb Raider* and all that stuff.'

Ray bit back a response. If *Quake* was the new Punk, *Tomb Raider* was the games world's Mariah Carey.

'You can't start again if you get killed,' Angelique helpfully reminded him.

'I'll try and bear that in mind.'

It was team deathmatch, Ray thought, Rocket Arena rules: no health packs, no spare armour, no respawns; if you die, you stay dead, first team to get wiped out is the loser.

The only way to get through this, the only way to avoid freezing up with mortal fear, would be to think of it as a game, and play it with all the skill, tactics, savvy and common sense he had learned to apply from his first ZX81 to his last *Q3* league match. He had to use what he knew, because little as that was, in this context it was *all* he knew. The US military had famously used a modified version of

Doom to train their Marines, so if even bad-ass soldiers could learn something from virtual fragging, surely so had Ray. He just wished he'd played a little more of the anti-terrorist mod *Counterstrike*.

'So what's the plan?' he asked. 'Sneak inside, kill all the bad guys with our mighty spearguns and then take in the caber-tossing down in Cromlarig?'

'You got the sneaking part right. But given the weapons and numbers imbalance, I think we have to make the most of the fact that they don't know we're here.'

'Sounds good to me,' Ray agreed. He thought of *Thief*, in which stealth was always advisable over combat. If you killed a bad guy, his mates would come running; they were bigger than you, had more weapons than you and there were more of them. Sneak in, stay quiet, stay hidden, stay alive.

Angelique picked up one of the Dubh Ardrain leaflets they had brought from the watersports centre, which very helpfully included some topological schematics of the facility to supplement Ray's own hazy memories. They were going in through the tailrace tunnel, that part was decided, but that part only.

'We can't win a stand-up fight with these guys,' said Angelique. 'It wouldnae just be suicide, it would be Cromlaricide. I think our best chance is to let them get on with it while we make for the dam, hopefully unseen, then ditch their explosives before they can detonate.'

'Do you know how to defuse a bomb?'

'I shouldn't need to. We're not lookin' at some sophisti-cated device for blowin' up a public building here. This is a demolition job. They'll wire the charges for detonation and pack them into the boreholes – all triggered via a remote, 'cause I cannae see anybody volunteerin' to stay up there an' push the plunger, can you?'

'Not unless he's a hell of a surfer.'

'So if we can get up top, it would be a case of pullin' the rigged charges back out the holes and chuckin' them as far down the hill as we can throw. Then, when they press the button, the blasts'll take a big chunk out the hillside, but the dam itself should stay intact.'

'Won't they have somebody guardin' their handiwork?'

'I would expect so, but they're no' gaunny stay there right up until kick-off, are they? When Darcourt decides it's showtime, they'll pull back inside the mountain, where they'll be plannin' to wait out the big flood until it's time to leave on their speedboats. That gives us a window.'

'It also gives us a ringside seat. We'll have no way of knowin' how big this "window" is. These charges could go off while we're up there playin' frisbee with them.'

'Then we'd better be quick.'

Angelique popped her mobile and the Dubh Ardrain leaflet into a waterproof pouch at her waist, before clipping the torch to her belt, strapping on her oxygen tank and pulling her mask up over her eyes. She gave Ray a quick refresher briefing on the first principles of using scuba gear – breathe in, breathe out, repeat – then slung one of the spearguns around her shoulder and handed him the other. 'Don't forget the crowbar,' she said, before biting on the mouthpiece and flipping backwards out of the boat.

Ray watched the splash and the ripples, feeling his stomach tighten and his heart begin to accelerate. The talk, the hypothesising was over, and it was now time to literally take his life's biggest (and possibly final) plunge.

Stop it, he told himself. You're running this on the Real Life™ engine, and it's incompatible with your system spec.

He looked down, his view slightly refracted through the

glass of a mask. On his chest he had undamaged armour. On his skin he had an environment suit supplemented by a full tank of O_2. And he already had two weapons in his inventory: a speargun and a crowbar.

Game on.

LOADING MAP: DUBH ARDRAIN POWER STATION [dubh1.bsp]
LOADING GAME MEDIA: INDUSTRIAL DRILLING RIGS
LOADING GAME MEDIA: EXPLOSIVES
LOADING POWER-UP: BULLETPROOF VEST
LOADING POWER-UP: WETSUIT
Angel_X[LGG] ENTERED THE GAME
Lobey_Dosser[LGG] ENTERED THE GAME
AWAITING SNAPSHOT . . .

It was the classic in-game infiltration technique: blast a hole in the grate guarding a submerged tunnel, then make your way into the enemy base silently and undetected, ready to take the bad guys by surprise. In this case, the grate was actually only a mesh to prevent salmon swimming into the tailrace, so the quieter appliance of a crowbar replaced blasting; and unlike most game scenarios, they were able to pull this off without having to evade the molestations of mutant sharks, or even mutant salmon.

The daylight ran out quickly as they swam up into the tunnel. While they could still see each other, Angelique gestured to Ray to follow her upwards to the ceiling, which they each kept a hand on as they proceeded blindly into the darkness. All Ray could hear was his own breathing, and all he could feel was the motion of the water in Angelique's wake, the only way of knowing she was still there in front.

Suddenly, Ray's hand was in air rather than liquid as it brushed the concrete, and another few yards brought his head above too. The gentle slope had reached Loch Fada's surface level, and would take them above the waterline from here on in. A light appeared up ahead, Angelique switching on her torch now that its beam wouldn't be completely swallowed.

Once the water was only waist-deep, they stopped to ditch the crowbar, masks and tanks, submerging them so as not to leave an obvious trace of their entry. Theoretically, they could find them again if they waded back down to the same depth, but to Ray it seemed to underline the one-way aspect of their mission. If they got out of here at all, it wasn't likely to be the same way they came in, and combat lay in the way of all other exits.

The tailrace extended ultimately to the turbines beneath the main cavern, and beyond those were the aqueducts leading to the dam. All of those areas would be guarded, so they were pinning their hopes on the cable vent shaft, which, according to the leaflet, they would reach after the surge chamber but crucially before the machine hall. The shaft led vertically all the way up to the summit, emerging a few hundred metres in front of the dam. That was the upside. The downside was that it was a ladder-climb all the way, imposing a sitting-duck vulnerability that Q2 had taught him to appreciate. In the game, they rarely extended beyond ten metres. The vent shaft topped three hundred.

The tunnel was unsettlingly quiet, the splashes of their footfalls amplified and echoing. Fortunately there was dense stone all around them, so they were unlikely to be heard by anyone unless they were actually in the tunnel. Angelique's torch danced about the walls, mainly to their right, the side of the entrance road and therefore the side broached by access doors and punctuated by observation platforms. Ray kept wanting to look behind each time they passed one, expecting attack to come by surprise from the rear. In FPS games, gantries like that were usually occupied by baddies, and if they weren't it was because your passing by was designed to trigger their sudden appearance.

Angelique stopped in her tracks, holding up a hand.

'What?' Ray whispered.

She pointed her torch by way of explanation, picking out the outlet of a smaller tunnel on the wall of the tailrace. They had seen another below the previous gantry, so he was wondering what was special about this one. When he drew level with Angelique, he found his answer written in blood. The concrete below the outlet was darkly streaked where it had drained into the tailrace and been washed away. Angelique reached down and put her hand inside the outlet, her fingertips red and sticky when she withdrew.

'Just a residue,' she whispered. 'It's drained away, but it's still pretty fresh. A few hours. I'm checkin' it out.'

'Rather you than me,' Ray whispered, before remembering that the passive role wouldn't be much fun either: Angelique was crawling off into the drainage tunnel with the only light source.

Ray squatted next to the opening, once again blind, clutching the speargun as his only defence against invisible enemies. After a while he heard shuffling and panting, heralding Angelique's slow return. With a wince, he realised that she was dragging something, and was instantly less grateful to her for that bacon roll. She emerged backwards, feet first, shuddering once she was upright.

'I don't think you're gaunny want to see this, but I couldnae get a decent look back there.'

Angelique reached into the drain with both hands and put her foot against the wall, pulling a body out arms-first and laying it gently down on the damp floor of the tail-race. There was a light clatter on the concrete as she did so, and Ray caught sight of a gun-butt strapped around the corpse's shoulder.

'Oh Christ,' he gasped, as Angelique played her torch up and down the body's gory length. There was a large gap in the lower chest, ribs visible through the ragged flesh, the area ringed in a black scorchmark. Above that, a join-the-dots trail of bullet holes led from below the left shoulder in a diagonal to what was left of his face; half of his jaw and most of his right cheek having been blown away.

Angelique bent down and pulled the machine gun away from him, revealing the weapon to have enjoyed as good a day as its owner.

'His gun exploded,' she said. 'Looks like he tried to bag somebody then got a big surprise when he pulled the trigger. After that, whoever he was aiming for was a jolly bad sport and finished him off.'

One point deducted for fragging yourself or a team-mate, Ray thought.

[LGG] 0 [TL] –1

'How?' he asked.

'Sabotage. Only explanation. Which makes the picture here suddenly a lot more interesting. You'd need to be pretty close to the action to manage a trick like that. It would have to be an inside job.'

'An infiltrator? Somebody undercover?'

'No. If there was somebody undercover who'd managed

453

to infiltrate *this* outfit, then we wouldnae have needed you to suss out what the plan was, and there'd have been a zillion cops waitin' for them here last night. Maybe all isnae sweetness and harmony among the naughty boys.'

'A double cross?'

'Troubled times. If you cannae trust a mass-murdering terrorist mercenary these days, who can you trust?'

Angelique unclipped a walkie-talkie from the corpse's belt, transferring it to her own and switching it on.

'We're now tuned to Radio Wanker. All this stone won't help, but we might hear the odd titbit.'

Ray looked again at the face. Now that his attention wasn't monopolised by what was missing from it, he realised he recognised what was left.

'This is one of the guys from the bridge.'

'The budgie-murderers. That's one case closed today, anyway.'

'What?'

'Never mind. Help me get him back into the drain. Somebody went to the bother of hidin' him, presumably so his mates don't realise they've got an enemy in their midst. That goes for us too.'

The radio began showing signs of life, their increasing proximity to the machine hall measurable in bursts of static and semi-audible snippets of communication until they were soon receiving complete transmissions. Whoever said eavesdroppers seldom learn anything to their own advantage was probably eavesdropping on the wrong conversations, and definitely didn't work at GCHQ. It might have been more accurate to say that eavesdroppers seldom learn anything to put their minds at ease.

'Mercury, this is Matlock. I'm at Turbine Five, base level.

There's a whole lot of blood down here, but no bodies.'

'I don't fucking believe this. Where the fuck is Jones?'

'He's topside.'

'No, the other one.'

'I thought you sent him topside too.'

'I just spoke to May. He hasn't seen Jones topside. He wasn't on the drilling detail.'

'Which one?'

'The one I'm fucking looking for. Mick. And not one of you fucking half-wits said a fucking thing because everybody just assumed he was with somebody else. Strummer, I thought you were with him at the time.'

'Strummer, receiving. I found them in a drainage tunnel, but I couldn't keep up. When I heard Jones had cornered them, I went back out via the tailrace.'

'So please, one of you, tell me that Jones did *not* somehow fail to take out two schoolboys from point-blank range.'

'It's beginning to look like it.'

'Fuck me. Well if they're still alive, they've still got our radios, so remember: careless talk saves lives. Find them. Mercury out.'

They listened to the exchange standing perfectly still, barely breathing, the volume down as low as was still audible so as not to carry beyond their position. Ray felt his hairs prickle as he heard Simon's voice for the first time in all those years. The accent was softened and his pronunciation more crisp, like he was speaking to foreigners, but it was unmistakably him. The other voices confirmed that he *was* speaking to foreigners; though like the assassin on the bridge, this was indicated by a neutrality of accent rather than any stumbling English.

'Schoolboys,' Angelique whispered portentously.

'I was just thinkin' the same thing. That truck was parked

outside Burnbrae Academy while they went in and got me. Schoolboys are inquisitive.'

'Resourceful too, by the sound of it. It must have been them who sabotaged that gun. And if they've sabotaged one . . .'

'That sounds like a dangerous assumption,' Ray warned.

'You're right. Just thinkin' out loud. *Hoping* out loud. Let's stick to what we know for sure. Personnel: there's Darcourt, callin' himself Mercury. Jones is the dead one, but there's another Jones as well. There's also Strummer, May and Matlock. That's five at least.'

'Twelve. Minus the stiff.'

'Twelve?'

'The codenames: Mercury, May, Strummer, Matlock, two Joneses: Queen, the Sex Pistols and The Clash. Rock bands, all of them four-piece.'

'Yeah, that's where the code names came from, but it doesnae mean—'

'You wouldnae have two Joneses if you didnae need all twelve names. There's eleven still out there, Angelique. Those five plus Taylor and Deacon, Simonon and Headon, Lydon and Cook.'

'What about Vicious?'

'Simon thought Sid Vicious was a tit.'

'But he's cool with Freddie Mercury?'

'You'd be surprised.'

'Okay. Eleven of them out there, and they're now actively lookin' for intruders. At least we know the odds. Come on.'

Angelique quickened the pace as they resumed their ascent, then drew to another halt when they reached the surge chamber. She played the torchlight around, picking out platforms either side as the tunnel widened into a

456

hexagon, its walls extending out of sight into the rock above. There was a tall lip where the tailrace met the chamber, meaning that a certain volume was required to accumulate before it would spill over and begin draining down into the loch. On the other side, there was water filling the hexagon two or three feet below the lip, and, according to the leaflet, this was because the tunnel plunged sharply before the chamber, creating a steep upslope to slow the rushing waters exiting the turbines. The shaft overhead took further sting out of it, then it spilled steadily out of the chamber and down into the tail-race.

They climbed the ladder on to the platform on the left, where Angelique found a switch and illuminated the chamber via inset lighting panels. Two doors were now visible on opposite sides of the pool. The one on the right said 'Machine Hall'; its counterpart 'Transformer Chambers'.

'That's what we want,' Angelique said, indicating to the left. 'The cable shaft goes from the transformers to the pylons up top.'

Above the entrance to the tailrace, Ray could also now see a wheel-operated valve on one wall. Next to it, a notice warned: 'Maintenance procedures only. Automatic override during generation. Manual override in Control Room.'

He gazed down at the lip, where there was a rubber-lined indentation running the width of the tunnel.

'What are you looking at?' Angelique asked, having already gone through the door then stuck her head back out to see what was keeping him.

'A valve. For sealing off the tunnel, I think.'

'Why would anybody want to do that?'

'Maintenance, according to this. And how about if there

might be guys with guns coming down here looking for the late Mick Jones?'

'Good shout. Close it. It's one fewer angle they can attack us from.'

'Whereas in the cable shaft, there'll only be two: above and below.'

'Just hurry up.'

The wheel moved at a finger-blisteringly grudging pace, which Ray at first put down to the initial stiffness that accompanied the turning of any such circular device, from valves to jar-lids, but there was no sudden easing, and the whole procedure passed at the same rate until the door was sealed. Fortunately, the only grinding came from Ray's bones, so at least it didn't make any noise. He gave his aching shoulders a shake, then walked quickly through the door into a dark and narrow passage, lit only by the rooms it connected.

After the darkness of the tunnel and the low, striplight flicker of the surge chamber, the transformer room made Ray feel like a pit-pony, stumbling dazed into the brightness. There were three massive machines housed in the chamber, bare rock on the walls and corrugated aluminium insulating the ceiling, reflecting back lighting already so bright it was easy to believe the entire station's output was required to power it.

The transformers sat to his right, against one of the rock walls, fed by grey steel pipes and tubes like they were gigantic iron lungs and the patients inside had paid for the gear with their Kensitas coupons. Great red coils, twice his height, jutted upwards from each like defensive spines on metallic dinosaurs, and all around Ray the air hummed with an electric buzz that seemed to vibrate his very bones.

He couldn't see Angelique, and was about to call out

when he remembered how suicidally stupid that could be. Looking up, he observed nine thick, black cables, three from each transformer, threaded through steel guidance loops as they were drawn into a gap in the ceiling. There were three cables on each wall of the overhead shaft, and a ladder on the fourth, but no Angelique. There had to be a stairway somewhere to access the bottom end of the vent, and that was where she'd be.

A door came into view as Ray walked past the first of the transformers, opening outwards as he approached. Thank fuck, he thought, having endured a momentary insecurity unnervingly reminiscent of turning around in a department store and discovering his mum was nowhere to be seen. The memory made him think of *Lost in the Supermarket*, not a very comforting recollection either, given its immortal rendering by The Bacchae.

'Machine Hall Access' was denoted in heavy black type, legible now that Ray had rounded the transformer and the opening door was at a less obtuse angle. Beyond it was a closed second door, at ninety degrees to the first, bearing the legend 'Cable Shaft Access', the significance of which hit his brain about half a second before a bullet hit his chest.

Ray fell backwards, grunting with pain, his memory reminding him he was wearing kevlar and his nerve-endings loudly disputing the benefits. Two men had come through the passage, the first reflexively responding by drawing a pistol and firing a single shot. By the time Ray opened his eyes, the man had crossed the floor and was standing above him, legs astride, pointing the pistol at his head, a shotgun slung across his back. His eyes were narrowed, finger on the handgun trigger. Nobody had fucked with *his* weapon, that was painfully sure.

'Say your prayers, asshole,' he taunted, before his eyes suddenly widened in incomprehension. 'Ash?' he asked, incredulous, the query giving the still reeling Ray time to recognise him as one of the goons who'd abducted and later mock-executed him. Boyle, he'd called himself then; but which rock-star handle was he going under now?

'Howdy,' Ray responded, breathless. The second man moved into view alongside, pointing a machine gun. Ray didn't recognise him.

'What the fuck are you doing here?'

'I missed you guys,' he replied. He kept his eyes firmly on Boyle because he knew if he looked elsewhere, he'd be bound to look up, and then they'd both be screwed. Both? Everybody.

'Who is this prick?' the second gunman asked. 'Is he a cop or what? May said there was something funny about him, something Mercury was holding back.'

Boyle nodded, bemused. 'I think we need to get the two of them together and ask a few questions, don't you, Mr Matlock? Get him on his feet.'

The second gunman hauled Ray upright, grabbing the speargun from him and throwing it to the ground. Boyle looked at it witheringly.

'Who were you hoping to kill with that? The Little Mermaid? Come on.'

Boyle turned to lead the way, Matlock at Ray's back, giving him a shove in the shoulder blades like he didn't know which way was forward. Ray heard a thump, as though somebody had dropped a large cabbage, and felt something spray his wetsuit at the shoulder. He and Boyle turned around simultaneously to see Matlock teeter unsteadily on his feet, eyes expressing confusion. There was a spear jutting through the front of his neck, pointing downwards at an acute angle, blood pouring off the end of it like it was a burst pipe. His right hand reached up in exploratory fashion, as though a fly had landed on his throat, before he collapsed like a suddenly discarded puppet.

Boyle looked upwards for the source just as the source dropped behind him in a flash of black. He spun around to point the pistol, but there was already a foot travelling to meet his wrist. Ray heard a crack of breaking bone as the weapon spun away from Boyle's hand and skidded on the solid concrete. He then had to dive clear as Boyle's head jerked backwards and his body was thrown clean off his feet by the force of the next kick. The gunman's heels flailed at the floor as he tried to regain balance, but he only succeeded in sustaining his momentum a few feet more, slamming the back of his head against one of the transformers with a dampened clang. Boyle slumped down into a sitting position, more by accident of the angle at which he'd landed than any control he was able to exercise. His head rolled to one side, eyes open, blood pouring from his nose into his slack-jawed open mouth, enough to drown him if he wasn't already dead.

[LGG] 2 [TL] –1

Boyle wasn't the only one gaping. Ray was agog, looking back and forth between the two gunmen and their sole assailant.

Angelique breathed out a long sigh and gave him an almost apologetic look in acknowledgement of what she had wreaked.

'Don't fuck with the Glesga polis,' she said quietly with a shrug.

'I think now would be a good time for me to apologise for anything remotely disrespectful I might have uttered over the past twenty-four hours,' Ray told her. 'And can I just say thank you, too.'

'Don't mention it. Grab that pistol, and don't forget your speargun in case we meet the Little Mermaid. Then let's get these bastards out of sight. If somebody finds them, I don't want it to be right underneath this shaft.'

'Anything you say.'

They dragged the bodies into the passage connecting the transformer room to the surge chamber. Ray helped himself to one of the walkie-talkies and lobbed the other into the water.

'Ditch the weapons too,' Angelique said. 'Apart from the pistol he fired. We know that works.'

'You're telling me.'

'The rest we can't trust.'

They tossed the other three guns into the hexagonal pool, then Angelique led the way up to the vent shaft access.

'I'll go first,' she said, as they reached the ladder. 'You climb as fast as you can and do not, under any circumstances, look down. If someone does spot us in this shaft, we're dead anyway, so it's no' gauny matter whether you see it comin'. What's the time?'

Ray looked at his watch. 'Ten to two.'

'Right. Try and think about what you'd normally prefer to be doin' this time of a Saturday afternoon.'

Ray did. And it involved avoiding ladders when someone was trying to shoot him.

The sound from the transformers covered that of their climb; the vibration having devoured the gunshot, a few metallic footfalls were mere garnish. Ray's fear of falling off was salved partially by the protective rings encircling the ladder, while the fear of what might be imminently pursuing them below was with every step being superseded by that of what unavoidably awaited at the top. Seeing how many bundles of explosives you could lob before the enemy clocked you and detonated the rest sounded like a shite idea for a teamplay mod, but he was already logging on to the server and it was too late to hit ESC.

'At long fucking last,' Simon muttered to himself, walking across the machine hall to where May had just emerged from Aqueduct One, nearly forty-five minutes after the rest of the drilling detail. Over the past half-hour Simon had been regularly tempted to take a trip topside to see what was keeping him, but was restrained by the experienced knowledge that the bastard took even more time when he knew you were looking over his shoulder.

The look-outs had been pulled down, no evidence having emerged of any evacuation at Cromlarig or any attempted incursion by the authorities. All they had to worry about now was what had happened to Jones and the two barn doors he'd been ordered to hit.

Taylor and Matlock had been first on the case, joined later by the rest of the newly relieved drilling crew. There was no word so far, though with so many tunnels and so much electricity running through the place, it was possible they had already found their answers but been unable to relay anything back. If it turned out the teenage saboteurs were somehow still alive (as opposed to Jones merely having freaked out and taken their corpses off to a quiet corner to do something that didn't bear thinking about), then in truth it wasn't the biggest worry he might have had to deal with at this stage.

Simon met May with a warm smile. It never helped to give the moody bastard the impression you were anything less than delighted with his efforts.

'Ready for curtain-up?' he asked.

May gave a satisfied nod. 'The fat lady's doing her vocal warm-up exercises. She threw us a few artistic tantrums, but she promises she'll be onstage at three.'

'Well, she's got an excellent manager. What about the pattern?'

'I started off with the alternative, concentrated configuration at the central buttress, but when Deacon got us the second drill, I estimated we had time to revert to the original. I was right.'

'Whatever I'm paying you, remind me to double it next time.'

'Yeah, right.'

'You managed not to cut any corners?'

'Just one. We didn't cement the charges.'

'Will that affect the blast?'

'No, it was just a security measure, so that they couldn't be tampered with. As we were running late, the stuff wouldn't have dried in time anyway.'

'Oh dear. So we're wide open if someone manages to suss our plan, break into the mountain and breach all our defences in the next half-hour.'

May returned Simon's grin. 'Wide open, yeah. How's things this end? I hear there's some problem with Jones.'

'That's what I get for sending a man to do a boy's job.'

'What?'

'It's nothing to worry about. He found our saboteurs: couple of kids. He was supposed to kill them and then head up top, but he's disappeared. So have they.'

'Doesn't sound like nothing to worry about to me.'

'If they're alive, their chief concern will be staying that way. They're not gonna give us any trouble.'

'We don't know what – or who – they've seen, though. We can't leave witnesses behind.'

'We won't.'

'But—'

'We won't, okay? Once we've blown the dam, there's no need for a quick getaway. The chaos round here is gonna last long enough for us to find them and Jones, dead or alive. You stick to worrying about the main event. Is everything functional? No more nasty surprises?'

'My equipment never left my sight. I only kept the charges in the truck. It's all checked and ready. We need a landline, though.'

'There's one in the control room. What's the deal?'

'The charges in each borehole are all wired to individual relay detonators. I've got a remote transmitter up there connected to a cellular. Can't trust radio signals with all this rock. When the time comes, you just dial the number. It picks up on the third ring, so you can test it as long as you stop before that.'

'Let's test it now. What's the number?'

'Mother of Christ.'

'What?'

Simon turned around to face what May was suddenly staring at. It took a lot to provoke an expression like that on someone so tediously poker-faced, and even more to distract him when he was talking about his toys. This would do it though, every time. Matlock was staggering towards them from the door leading to the Transformer Chambers. He was soaked in blood from his neck to his thighs, and what looked like an arrow protruded downwards from his neck.

'Fuck. Somebody help him.'

Matlock collapsed before anyone could reach him, dropping to his knees and then on to his side, an arm supporting his head so that no pressure was brought upon the arrow. May and Simon got there first, Deacon and Cook at their backs.

Simon knelt down next to his kebabed comrade. He was still breathing, but only just.

'Can you speak? What happened?'

Matlock barely managed a whisper, struggling to channel enough breath even for that. He sounded like a fish gasping its last, the smack of his lips louder than his words. However, audibility and intelligibility were not proportionally linked. They might not be hearing him too well, but they were all soon reading him loud and clear.

'Ash,' he breathed. For half a second it might have sounded to the others like merely another choking noise, but Simon immediately felt his blood freeze. 'A . . . cop. Girl. Vensha . . . ven . . . sha.'

'Where's Taylor?' May asked anxiously.

Matlock shook his head, as perceptibly as he could manage. 'Girl.'

'The girl? She killed him?'

Matlock nodded.

'She's a cop?' asked Simon.

More nodding.

'Where did they go?'

Matlock swallowed, seemingly readying himself for the effort of telling them, but instead, when he opened his mouth, all that issued was a splutter of thickened arterial blood, followed by a pitiful final exhale.

Simon's head was buzzing, trying to work out the ramifications, but it was like doing a mathematical equation where the numbers and variables kept changing. What didn't help was that his men were articulating the same questions as were in his mind, adding to the number of voices simultaneously demanding answers.

'How could Ash be here?'

'How could he know?'

'How did he get in?'

'What happened to the decoy plan?'

'If the cops didn't buy it, why is there just one of them, as opposed to one hundred?'

'Did he say Ash is a cop?'

'No, the girl's a cop. What did he say she was called? Vensha?'

'I thought he said vengeance.'

Throughout this maelstrom, May said nothing. Instead he just fixed Simon with a look that not so much accused as tried, judged, sentenced and executed. Then he finally made his own, single and piercingly salient query.

'If he knew we were here, what else does he know?'

The question translated Matlock's whisper.

'Vent shaft,' Simon said, the implications sinking deep even as he formed the words. 'He came from the transformer room. That's where the cable shaft is.'

'Where does it go?'

'The fucking topside,' spat May. 'They're headed for the dam.'

Looks were exchanged: suspicions, insecurities, the first signs of panic.

'All right, listen up,' Simon said firmly, keeping his voice barely below a shout. He had to show he was in control, otherwise he wouldn't be much longer. 'Deacon and Cook, you take the lift and check it out. Headon, you stay at the bottom of the aqueduct so we get a relay on these fucking radios. May, control room, right now.'

'Yes *sir*,' May acknowledged, with a sneering sarcasm that was only just the right side of mutiny.

Angelique was wiping the sweat from her eyes as they came through the door at the centre. The skies had cleared overhead and it was turning into a beautiful late-summer's day; beautiful, that was, other than the terrorists, the corpses, the explosives, the intended mass murder and the imminent threat of being vaporised. She'd caught glimpses of the view as she hurled the charges from the platform: Loch Fada shimmering silver-blue beneath the mountains, windsurfers dancing on the surface. It was the kind of spot you'd happily lug a picnic basket up a three-hour climb to reach, just for the pleasure of sipping a beer and dodging the wasps as you sat on the grass, sun kissing your shoulders and maybe some obliging chap doing the same to your neck.

This had some of those elements, she'd have to concede, but not really enough to be truly relaxing. She ought to be thankful for small mercies, though: she did have the obliging chap, rendering services far more welcome than a snog even if he had been her type. Angelique had a lot to be grateful to him for, in fact, but prized above the information and initiative he'd supplied was simply that he'd kept the heid. He was probably just giving a passable impression of calm to mask an unprecedented level of personal terror, but if so that made two of them, and she knew all it would take was for him to lose the place and her 'experienced professional' front would collapse too.

They had started from the centre and were working their way to the sides, reckoning that if they suddenly ran out of time, the dam might better survive two diffuse blasts than a big one in its middle. The charges in each borehole were threaded together like a string of pearls, with a trigger mechanism at the end nearest the opening. It crossed her mind that under these circumstances, the bomb designer might not have implemented the standard safeguards against interference, but she wasn't about to play the odds by disconnecting the detonator. Besides, if the bad guys pressed their button and nothing happened, they'd have the option to repair the damage and have another go.

They had cleared just over half the boreholes when she heard the door open. Angelique had a loop of charges in her hand, and was wiping her eyes in readiness for another two-handed fling. She turned around and drew her pistol, dropping the explosives, but the first guy through the door had a start on her and opened fire with his machine gun before she could even aim. Instead of a rapid stutter of bangs, however, there was only one as the gun exploded in his hands, the left of which was blown off by the blast. He dropped to his knees, doubling over his truncated limb as a second gunman emerged behind. This time Angelique had time to aim, but her target ducked behind his injured comrade just before she fired. She got off two shots, both of them ripping into the torso of the impromptu human shield as his less than selfless companion retreated inside the wall of the dam.

'Ray, we've got to get the fuck off this thing,' she called out. 'Get into the aqueduct. It's the only chance.'

Ash took the time to hurl one more chain of explosives from the platform, then ran for the entrance door at the opposite end. Angelique picked up the string of charges at her feet and was about to do likewise when another idea occurred to her. She ran for the door the gunmen had come through, her pistol drawn, the explosives slung round her shoulder. It opened to a short stairwell inside the wall, leading to the aqueduct's airtight access port.

Angelique bounded down the flight and hauled open the door. Below her, the escaping gunman was descending on an automated platform, speaking frantically into his radio. She took hold of the explosives in both hands and lobbed them down into the tunnel, where they whizzed past the gunman's head, causing him to look up. Angelique ducked out of sight, anticipating a volley of shots that never came, then charged back out on to the platform, heart and lungs totting up a double-time invoice as she made for the next aqueduct.

'This is Deacon. They're ditching the charges, chucking them over the edge. Cook's down. His fucking gun blew up. Those fucking kids, it must have been.'

Those fucking kids, yes. Those pesky fucking kids. 'Everybody get that?' Simon relayed. 'Ditch any weapons you took from the truck. Right away.'

He turned to May. 'Blow it. Now.'

'Deacon's not clear yet.'

'Fuck Deacon. Blow the dam.'

'Why don't we just kill these fuckers and put back the charges?'

'Who's gonna do that? They're up top, an' they know we're comin' now. They could pick us off one by one.'

'There's only two of them. We could . . .'

Simon drew his pistol and held it tightly in both hands, pointing the barrel between May's eyes. 'Blow the fucking dam.'

May shook his head, staring with a defiance that had gone well beyond insolence and into the mockingly smug. 'You're forgetting about that question you asked me, back at the bridge. You can't do this without me.'

'All I have to do is dial a number.'

'Yeah, but what number, *Freddie*?'

Simon shot him twice in the head, then unclipped the mobile phone from May's belt. Like the predictable idiot wouldn't have tested the receiver while he was topside.

'The one on your last-number redial, *Brian*.'

Lexy could feel himself starting to cry again. He wanted to hold it back and yet at the same time he wanted to let it out. The result was a choked snuffle and a tight closing of his eyes, which squeezed out tears from both.

'Whit's wrang, Lexy?'

'Sorry, Murph. That guy. I just cannae get ower it. I kill't somebody, Murph.'

'Don't be stupit, man. You were a fuckin' hero. D'ye 'hink he'd be sittin' there feelin' bad aboot it if he'd kill't us? Aye, that will be chocolate.'

'I know, but it was just so horrible.'

'He'd probly have died anyway, even afore you shot him. Did you see what his ain gun did tae him? An' it coulda been me that jammed that wan, couldn't it? So it was a joint effort. But you were the man on the spot. You finished him aff afore he could dae anythin' else. That took some guts, man.'

'Dunno how. I was pure paralysed. I thought that was us when he fired. I mean, we'd nae way o' knowin' if it was wan o' the guns we'd knackered, or whit effect it would have.'

'Well it wasnae gaunny have an optimisin' effect, was it? I mean, in the manual, it's no' gauuny say: to get the most from your weapon, be sure to jam a big daud of metal down the barrel.' Murph put on a posh English accent, forcing Lexy to laugh.

'Thanks, Murph,' he said.

'Whit fur?'

'Gettin' us through this.'

'*Me* gettin' us through it? You're the brainy wan.'

'Am I fuck.' Lexy felt his hackles rise. Even after everything they had faced over the past few days, there was still nothing scarier than being accused of being brainy. If they survived to go back to school, he might be wishing Gap Man had finished him off.

'Aye you are. It's awright. I'll no' let on.'

They had taken refuge in yet another tunnel, a dry one this time. After hiding the body, they had crawled back into the drain themselves and headed in the opposite direction, beneath the turbine access decks. The drain ended – or rather began – at Turbine One, the furthest along, and hearing no activity on their radios, they decided to chance coming up. There on the lowest access deck, they had found a knee-high hatch, and opened it to reveal a short crawlspace and the top of a ladder. The crawlspace had to be negotiated backwards, even by them, in order to get on to the ladder, which led a couple of metres down into a tunnel flanked by huge cables on either wall.

'What's the time?' Lexy asked.

Murph's torch lit up. 'It's just comin' up for . . .'

Suddenly the whole tunnel shook, cable brackets pinging from the walls like they were drawing pins, amid a rumbling, crashing sound they could feel as well as hear.

'Whit the *fuck* was that?' they asked in unison.

The shaking continued for a few seconds, both of them crouching into balls on the floor of the tunnel as more brackets dropped and the sagging cables swung and thumped against the walls.

'Earthquake,' Wee Murph ventured.

'Bomb mair like. Those explosives.'

472

'Oh fuck, aye.'

The shaking and rumbling finally ceased, though there seemed to be another sound in the air, like a continuous presence. Maybe it was just the after-effect in his ears, like when he had his headphones up too loud. They stayed still and quiet for a while, anticipating another shake, not daring to believe it was all over. None came, but the other sound got stronger, and it definitely wasn't just in his head.

'I think we should make a move,' Murph said.

'But the bad guys—'

'Think aboot it, Lexy. That was a bomb, as you says. So whatever they were here tae dae, I 'hink they've done it. They're gaunny be aff their marks, in't they? Probly away awready.'

'Just a wee while longer. To be sure there's nae mair blasts.'

'Two minutes, then, awright?'

'Awright.'

Lexy was counting by elephants in his head so that Murph couldn't cheat. He'd reached thirty-three when they both felt water running around their feet.

'Oh fuck.'

'I don't know much aboot hydro-electric stations, Lexy, but I know there's no' meant tae be water in a tunnel full o' cables.'

'It's awright. They're insulated.'

'Aye, so we're aboot a quarter ay an inch o' rubber away fae gettin' deep fried. Let's get tae fuck oota here.'

Lexy offered no argument. The water had risen to his knees in a matter of seconds, and the speed at which it was rising seemed to be on the increase too. By the time they had both got up the ladder and out of the crawlspace, it was seeping out of the hatch behind them. The floor outside was already wet from water flowing up out of the drain that had been their escape route.

'Good job we never stayed doon there,' said Murph.

'Tryin' no' tae think aboot it.'

They made their way quickly up through the turbine access levels, employing only a cursory minimum of checking out each stairway and corridor, as the rising threat at their backs was more pressing than any potential danger up ahead. On the second-lowest deck, they passed through the first of two open balconies – the other directly above – from where they could see up into the main hall, as well as along the sides of the other turbines. The two in the centre, Three and Four, looked like ginger cans somebody had toe-ended, and their corresponding balconies were a crippled mess of concrete and steel. Above them, the railings guarding the gantry on the cavern's ground-floor level were mangled, and there were fragments of metal embedded in the facing rock. Water was spraying out of cracks and holes in both turbines, but it had to be coming from elsewhere too, as the entire excavation was filling up below the balconies. Silence was no longer going to be a consideration, as it took a firm voice to be heard above the sound of the deluge.

'This place is fucked, man,' Wee Murph observed.

This time Lexy did allow himself the indulgence of going 'Lmmmm-mmmm.'

It was marginally quieter when they reached the main-floor level, only because they were on the other side of the turbines from the excavated area; the sound of rushing and pouring was still echoing off every wall. They waited just below the top of the stairway, now scoping very carefully for bad guys. There was another stairway ahead and to the left, leading to the Control Room, according to a sign. It was housed in a building shaped like two Lego blocks sitting on top of three, running the length of the machine hall. At its centre was a bay window affair, flanked on the left-hand side by another observation gantry. Lexy was sure he could see a figure up there, but when he looked again there was nothing.

To the right of the stairway, there was a slope, the concrete leading down out of sight behind a railing to something dug further back into the cavern than the end of the turbine pit; or turbine pool, as it could now more accurately be described. Hard left, past the jutting tops of the turbines and a perilously exposed area of open cavern, was the entrance tunnel.

'Bollocks,' Lexy said. 'Cannae see anybody.'

'Zat no' a good thing?'

'Don't think so. I can still see two cars an' two motor-boats. I don't think they're away yet.'

'Shhh,' warned Murph.

'Whit?'

'Listen. You no' hear it?'

Lexy listened, though he didn't know what for. All he could hear was water.

'Cannae hear anythin'.'

'There it's again now. Shhh.'

This time he did hear it: a thumping, low and dense, with a metallic edge to it.

'It's comin' fae doon the slope,' Murph said. 'Somebody's there. Stuck, mibbe.'

'Whit if it's the folk that work here? We havenae seen any o' them.'

'They could be locked up, aye. Let's check it oot.'

'It could be the baddies, but.'

'Well if they're stuck, they'll be easier tae shoot,' Murph reasoned.

'Awright for you to say. You've no' shot wan yet. Nothin' easy aboot it.'

'You know whit I mean. Come on.'

They scrambled, crouching, across the gap to the top of the slope, then ran down it full tilt, the fact that they were charging towards a dead end hitting Lexy only once he was in full flight. On the left at the bottom there was a heavy steel door with a handle like a cog. The thumping resumed again as they reached it, and there was no question it was coming from inside.

'Who's there?' Murph asked. There was no reply, only more thumping.

'Who's there?' he repeated, to the same response, accompanied by a muffled human voice.

'Just open it, Murph,' Lexy said, levelling his machine gun. 'I'll be ready.'

Murph looked at Lexy then nodded. 'Okay. After three,' he said, gripping the handle. 'Wan . . . oh fuck.'

Murph pulled the door open and immediately dived inside. Lexy looked round, spotting a man at the top of the slope, machine gun in hands. He dived into the gap behind Murph, who slammed the door closed a micro-second before bullets began thumping into the steel, leaving a streak of rounded indents, like boils.

Lexy found himself lying face-down on the floor next to two guys on their backs, ankles and hands tied, mouths gagged. Around the room there had to be about thirty more of them, but these two had shuffled their way to the door and kicked it to try and attract attention; something the overpowering smell of pish should have managed on its own.

Murph was facing the door, his machine gun trained on it, finger on the trigger. 'Come in here an' we'll blow you away, ya bastart,' he shouted, his voice maybe a little too squeaky to strike much terror into the gunman's heart.

Whether it did or not, the gunman didn't bother coming in, but instead merely locked the door and walked away.

Lexy peeled the tape from the nearest hostage's mouth and began doing the same for his other bonds.

'Polis are gettin' awfy young these days,' the man said.

'We're no' polis.'

'I know. We heard the explosion, thought they must have done their business and been off. That's why we were bangin' the door.'

'We thought the same. Nae luck. I take it there's nae way oota here?'

'Bloody storage chamber. Reinforced steel door, another remnant of our facility's glorious Cold War history.'

'Is that a no, then?' Murph asked, untying another hostage.

'No,' said the newly ungagged bloke. 'There's a drainage channel here. We couldnae get doon it because we were all trussed up.'

'Magic,' said Murph wearily. 'Another drain. Where is it?'

Two more of the hostages began shuffling on the floor in the centre of the room, clearing a space and revealing the grate.

'Right,' said Lexy. 'Let's get everybody untied. I'll watch the door. Murph, you lead the way. An' I'll bet you're glad we saved the power on thae torches noo.'

Murph stood over the drain, facing down and frowning. 'No' really,' he said. 'Look.'

Lexy took a step nearer, his view having been obscured by two of the hostages. Water was starting to bubble out of the grate and flow across the floor of the chamber.

477

'Aw, shite.'

Ray had been scrambling down inside the aqueduct when the charges were detonated. The blast shook the tube and threw him from the inset stairs to the centre, where he began rolling, sliding and tumbling towards a rippling pool at the bottom, which he sincerely hoped was a good few feet deep. Striplights whizzed past his head at all angles as he fell, creating an effect reminiscent of a flume he'd ridden on the Costa del Sol. The steep, rapid and unflinchingly straight descent, however, was more like the kamikaze chute, standard fixture of all such water parks, designed to subject the rider to five seconds of naked terror before ramming his trunks up his arse and garroting his testicles.

The memory served to remind him of the suggested survival technique, which was to lie straight back and cross one foot over the other. Ray did this, and soon began aquaplaning over the damp tunnel floor, the wetsuit saving him from being flayed alive in the process. He splashed deep into the water at the bottom, shooting maybe ten feet under, probably mere inches from the twin turbine intakes at the base of the shaft. If they had been on, he'd have been liquidised; but then again, if they'd been on, he wouldn't have been able to access the aqueduct in the first place.

He surfaced with a gasp and looked upwards for a door. He remembered from the cut-away diagram on the tourist leaflet that there was access to the aqueducts from the machine hall and from the turbine sub-levels, as well as up top at the dam. There was a door visible about ten feet up the pipe from where he was treading water. Unfortunately, also visible was a foaming white mass rushing down the tunnel to meet him.

The water's initial impact plunged him back under and threatened to keep him there until he found less resistance and even something of an up-current closer to the wall. He surfaced again and spat out a mouthful, shaking his hair from his eyes with a flick of the head. The rising level was lifting him closer to the door, but he knew he had to get there before the water did, or else it would automatically seal.

Ray pushed his way around the wall until he was at the stairs, where it took a few flailing attempts to climb beyond the water level, especially with hundreds of gallons more pouring down around him. After a couple of heart-stopping slips which threatened to plonk him back whence he came, he reached the door and bundled through it on all fours. He found himself on his knees in an airlock chamber, facing a second door, which he lunged for and barged open before remembering that he should perhaps have closed the other one first. Water flooded into the chamber from behind and washed him out into a narrow corridor, where it proceeded to rapidly cover the floor and climb the walls.

The force of the flow pushed him along the passage on his front until he came to a staircase, on to which he gratefully clambered, spitting what felt like a lungful of water as he did so. There was no time to reel, to feel dazed or even fear, and still less to weigh up his options in light of who might be lying in wait. The water was rising and so must he. Taking a deep breath, he got to his feet and began climbing the stairs, reaching another curving corridor at the top. He knew it wouldn't help to look back, but felt he had to anyway. The water was coming up the stairs almost as fast as he had, and was only a few steps behind. Nonetheless, behind it was, and that was all that mattered. Or at least that was all that mattered until he turned back around and saw more water coming to meet him, this time pouring down the next flight of stairs.

'Aw for fuck's sake.'

Ray gripped the banister rails one by one as he made the next ascent, the rubber around his feet providing a welcome degree of purchase on this concrete waterfall. The sound of rushing and crashing got louder as he reached the top, where he found himself at one end of a balconied walkway, affording a view along one side of the whole flooded excavation. The water level was already higher than the balcony floor, flowing in ankle-deep under the bottom rung of the safety railings and pouring down inside the turbine housing to meet the stuff he'd been climbing to escape.

The next two turbines along were wrecked, their maintenance and access areas mangled and collapsed, and the force of the blast had impacted where he was standing too. Further along the corridor, the railings were buckled and the floor was tilted upwards almost the width of the passage where something had smashed into it from below, the peak of this tilt being the only part not submerged.

Ray waded his way carefully up to this point, which was where he was able to see that there was no corresponding downslope on the other side, because there was in fact no floor on the other side. The steel inside the concrete had been severed, and the remainder of the balcony floor was folded back against the next stairway, blocking the route up. Behind him, there was a bubbling sound as the water from below came up over the top of the staircase.

Is this it? he couldn't help but ask himself. No sudden blast as he hurled charges from the dam, no bullet or knife, but drowning here unseen in the bowels of this man-made cave? He thought of Kate, that first night they made love.

480

Adam and the Ants. No bullet or knife. He thought of Martin, all the hopes he had, the songs he wanted to play him, the books he wanted him to read.

What would he be when he grew up?

Ray breathed in through his nose. All around him was the smell of wet stone: incongruously warm, inexplicably comforting.

'Make it that there's a river runnin' through the caves, an' we're wadin' through it until it gets too deep an' then we have to duck under an' haud oor breaths an' swim through the dark an' come up in a big pool except still in a cave, right?'

Ray looked over the mangled and now almost submerged balcony railings into the rising, foaming black pool, and knew that he still had a chance. He remembered the sunken city level in *Duke Nukem*, trying to ignore the fact that he'd snuffed it the first couple of times attempting to find his way out of the submerged skyscraper. It was only a matter of yards, and this was the one area in which Real Life™ gave better odds than FPS games; the latter only letting you hold your breath for about ten seconds before you started to drown.

Ray dived over the railings and began swimming around the turbine, striking out for the next platform along, which would have been sheltered from the blast. He knew the water would be above the level of the balcony by the time he got there, but was not tempted to wait for it to lift him all the way to the machine hall's gantry. The only easier target than a player on a ladder was some lamer bobbing below you in a big open pool of water.

As he approached the turbine housing, he took a breath and dived under the surface. The lights had all shorted out below the waterline, but the giant rig on the cavern ceiling allowed him to make out where the balcony was. Once

481

under, he propelled himself in a breaststroke, looking for light spilling down the next stairwell, above which the fluorescent strips should still be functioning. He swam in above the sunken railings and followed the corridor ceiling, a glow visible at the end.

His chest tightened as he rose up the staircase, a moment of despair setting in when he reached the top and found himself still submerged, but on this level there was a second flight zigzagged against the first. He turned around and kicked both feet off the wall for renewed momentum, already breathing out in a stream of bubbles before surfacing with a great gasp five steps below the dry corridor floor.

Simon stood in front of the closed-circuit monitor relaying the view from the security post at the main entrance. He'd been staring at it for a few minutes now, unable to take his eyes off the view, though it mocked him with its silent tranquillity. It showed the locked steel gates, the approach road and the landscaped flowerbeds, but what he saw was humiliation, failure and defeat. What it did not show was an engulfing torrent of water sweeping into Loch Fada, on its way to wipe out Cromlarig at the end of the glen. The dam was not breached, though every other fucking thing seemed to have been.

He thought of Shub and his drills, then looked to the Glock pistol in his hand.

No. Not until he'd got some payback, anyway.

Simon turned to the window and gazed into the machine hall, where water would soon fully swallow the crippled turbines, filling up the hollow mountain but unable to wash away his failure. He felt it ironic, nonetheless, to be surveying such enormous devastation and regarding it

with anything less than pride. It was, it had to be acknowledged, one hell of a mess; the thought making him appreciate that though the water couldn't wash away his
mistakes, perhaps it could yet cover them up. Failure was
a matter of degrees.

Terrorism, like politics, was about perception. The
outside world didn't have a clue what was intended to
happen here. All they would know was what they would
find: the mighty Dubh Ardrain power station destroyed,
and thirty-odd staff drowned in the very waters they once
harnessed. Mopoza could take the huff if he liked, and
would probably withhold payment, but if he had any sense,
he'd make out this had been the sum of the plan all along.
It was still one hell of a strike against the General's enemies,
in the heartland of the man who had been in charge of the
forces that overthrew him.

But jobbie-polishing aside, it was still merely a fraction
of what it should have been. For that Simon wanted
answers, and he wanted them written in blood. He picked
up his radio.

'Any of you fuckers still alive, report to the Control Room
right away.'

He watched them from the window a few minutes later,
a paltry rump making their disparate ways across the
machine hall before grouping at the foot of the stairs: Jones,
Lydon, Simonon and finally Strummer.

'Is this it?' he asked rhetorically, stepping out into the
corridor as they approached.

'Yeah,' said Jones. 'Deacon and Headon got it in the blast.
I don't know about May, though. I thought he was with you.'

'He was,' Simon said, holding open the Control Room
door.

'Where is he now?'

483

'Right here.'

'Oh fuck.'

The four of them gathered around May's body as Simon closed the door.

'What happened to him?' Strummer asked.

'What does it look like? I shot him.'

'What for?'

'He disappointed me.'

'He disa . . . You fucking—'

'Oh, shut up,' Simon commanded. 'What you ought to know, Joe, is that Mr May was taking a very unhealthy interest in my personal background, and who's to say he wasn't taking a similar interest in all of yours?'

Strummer's eyes narrowed. 'I think he was just as interested as all of us in knowing who the fuck this Ash person is and how he got here.'

'Aren't we all,' Simon agreed. 'So I'd suggest we get hold of him, and then we can all get everything out in the open. The cop too. We need to find out how much the authorities know, and how the fuck they know it. I want them taken alive.'

'This whole place is going to be underwater soon.'

'So you'd better hurry up, then.'

'Even if they're alive, they could be anywhere.'

'They could *be* anywhere, but it's where they'll be headed that matters. And these self-righteous goody-two-shoes fuckers are nothing if not predictably principled.'

Ray ran up the next staircase on the balls of his feet. The noise of the water was covering his sounds, but he knew it would cover everyone else's too, so he ducked back against the wall when he got to the top. After this passageway, he would reach the final flight, which would take him to the machine hall, where death or glory awaited, depending on how the terrorists had fared in the blast. He unslung the speargun from around his shoulder and took it in both hands, then set off into the corridor at a sprint. He managed two paces before his feet were whipped from under him in a flash of black.

When he turned around on the floor, he was looking down the barrel of a pistol. Fortunately, it was Angelique's finger on the trigger.

'Thank Christ, you're alive,' she said, offering a hand to get him to his feet. They hugged each other and laughed with nervous relief.

'So how we doin'?' Ray asked.

'Still intact.'

'More than can be said for this place. What happened?'

Angelique looked a little embarrassed. 'Oops. My bad, as the Yanks say. I threw a load of the explosives down the aqueduct. Seemed like a good idea at the time. Probably took out some of the bad guys, but . . .' She shrugged, like she was talking about a supermarket car park prang.

'No use cryin' over spilt milk, eh?'

'Well, it's not all my fault. I'm not the one who sealed off the tailrace.'

'Oh fuck,' said Ray, remembering. It was designed to channel the outwash of all three aqueducts at once, so would have drained the place in no time if he hadn't wheeled it shut. It still might, if they could open it.

'There's a manual over-ride in the Control Room,' he said.

'Okay, then that's where I'm headed.'

'What about the bad guys?'

'They're runnin' away. I think it would be fair to say that they don't like it up them.'

'Don't like a square go, mair like. Fuckin' llamas.'

Angelique gave him a baffled look. 'What the hell's a llama, apart from a long-necked South American quadruped?'

'Gamer slang. A lamer is somebody who's just shite, but a llama is someone who, regardless of whether they're lame or leet, will always be a wank.'

'Sounds like our boys. They're pullin' out in the huff.'

'How d'you know?'

Angelique held up her radio.

'Mine's at the bottom of a pipe,' Ray said.

'Yeah, sorry. You picked the wrong aqueduct – there were more charges still in place above the one you took.'

'It was the express route down, at least.'

'The bad guys didnae fancy your chances, anyway. They've written us off as dead and they're sneakin' out to lick their wounds.'

'Magic. So we just tread water – literally – until they're gone?'

'Not quite.'

'How did I know you were gaunny say that.'

'There's hostages bein' held in the storage chamber at the end of the cavern. One of the bad guys asked Darcourt if they should machine-gun them before they left. His exact answer was "save your bullets – they'll all be drowned in about ten more minutes".'

'Fuck.'

'The storage area's down a ramp at the—'

'Yeah, I know,' Ray interrupted.

'We can wait a few minutes, but if the coast isnae clear upstairs soon, we'll have to take a chance. God knows how many of them are trapped down there.'

'I'll call it a bonus mission. Let's do it.'

486

They set off at a jog before cautiously climbing the final flight, down which more water was inexplicably pouring.

'How can . . .?' Angelique asked.

'Place is like a Terry Gilliam cartoon. Pipes, channels and tubes everywhere. And don't complain to me, bombergirl.'

They emerged behind the exposed top section of the turbine, crouching together as they took a tentative look down the hall. There was further damage even at floor level, blast debris having smashed into the far end of the control building, beneath the Control Room's external gantry. Loose and broken bricks lay on the floor, amid fragments of metal and concrete. Insulation panels had been blown off the wall, leaving heavy cables exposed against the brickwork where they ran from beneath the floor, all the way up the rockface to the lighting rig on the ceiling.

Around Ray and Angelique the water was ankle-deep, pouring over the edge into the excavation, where the level was rising to meet it, now only a few yards lower. To their right, they could see it flowing down the slope towards the storage chamber; to their left it was covering the cavern mouth and running downhill into the entrance tunnel, where crucially there were no longer any vehicles.

'Okay,' said Angelique. 'This is it. You get them out of there. I'll get the tailrace open.'

Simon heard the quiet footfalls in the corridor and held his breath. They sounded fast, nimble and light; he guessed female, the cop. He backed against the wall behind the open door and gripped the SPAS-12 with both hands, left on the barrel, right on the trigger.

The door moved a little as she came through it, upon which she was confronted by the sight of May's body, Simon having moved him to the centre of the floor, face up, for this very purpose. The corpse took her immediate attention just long enough for him to step out from behind the door and say 'Psst'.

He fired as she turned, aiming for her kevlar-protected chest, the point-blank blast throwing her backwards into the air and over the control console. Her handgun – another Glock, so in fact it was probably Taylor's handgun – clattered against the window and thumped to the floor alongside her. Simon leapt across to kick the pistol further away, but she was in no state to even reach for it yet. Her eyes were closed as she winced and moaned, the spray of pellets embedded in the vest having no doubt broken a few ribs. Simon drove the butt of his rifle into her throat, causing her to grab her neck and roll over in reflex. He looked at her face, pretty beneath the pain. Must get her out of that wetsuit, he thought. It would be conducive to her interrogation, and after all he'd been through today, the least he deserved was a ride.

Later, though. Meantime, there were other carnal desires to be satisfied. He kicked open the door to the observation deck and took hold of the cop by the ponytail, dragging her out on to the gantry. Her feet kicked as she struggled to push herself along, trying to take the weight off her hair. Down below, he could see Lydon, who gave him a thumbs-up.

'Bring him,' Simon ordered, pointing to below the platform.

Ray walked with his hands in the air, two gunmen behind him, one in front, joined by another when they reached the top of the slope. His mouth was bleeding from the gunbutt blow he'd sustained, but he could be certain he was about to receive a lot worse. The picture was clear. When they didn't shoot him right away, he knew he was going to be brought before the king, to give Simon his big gloating, wanking moment before he personally pulled the trigger.

From the gunshot Ray had heard, it depressingly didn't sound as though Angelique had been subject to the same sport. There was always the possibility that she'd been the one who got the shot off, but in his heart he knew it was the other way around: if they'd been lying in wait for him, then they'd have had the drop on her too.

He had to shuffle through the water, which was now up to his shins, prompted by the occasional prod from a gunbarrel. Behind him he could still hear the thumps and muffled cries from the storage room. There were children's voices among them, he was sure, screaming for help with what air was left in the place.

Ray looked up as the party passed beneath the Control Room window. On the gantry ahead, he could see Angelique lying on her back; and, standing over her, pointing a shotgun, face turned away but figure unmistakable, was Simon.

The same narcissistic tosser as ever. He was throwing a fucking shape, frozen there in a carefully struck pose, waiting to turn around and reveal himself to Ray, who was presumably supposed to be impressed/gobsmacked/start wanking in sheer admiration/whatever.

'On his knees,' Simon commanded, still not turning round. Ray was thumped brutally between the shoulder blades and fell face-down with a splash. A hand grabbed the strap of the speargun and lifted him to his knees, the goon removing the weapon and dropping it contemptuously into the water in front of him.

'Who were you going to kill with that? The Man from Atlantis?'

Ray said nothing, just looked up. Get it over with, for fuck's sake. Springsteen doesn't get a build-up like this.

Simon turned, at last, his face composed into a calm smile.

'Hello, Larry,' he said.

Ray spat some blood into the water by way of response. Simon ignored it, tried to look slightly quizzical.

'Don't you recognise me?'

'Call me Raymond, ya fuckin' wank, or I'll just ignore you. I thought I'd told you that. And you can cut the fuckin' theatrics as well. Yeah, you're the big terrorist. The Black Spirit. Rank Bajin. Wow. I swear to God I'm impressed, but if I'm no' comin' across that way, it's because I've had kind of a rough day. How's yours been?'

Simon shrugged, trying to pretend his blood wasn't boiling.

'Disappointing.'

'Chin up, mate. You've had worse Saturdays, surely. What about the time you made a cunt of yourself in the QM bar, tryin' to sing and play guitar at the same time?'

Simon raised a pistol with his right hand, his left still resting the shotgun against Angelique's head. He held the handgun sideways, which was him to a T: there was no benefit other than it looked cool.

'I think the era you're talking about is the one you'd probably file under the time of your life, *Raymond*. At least one of us has moved on from there. And at least one of us will move on from here.'

'Cannae see the progress, to be honest. Makin' a cunt of yourself seems to be the recurrin' theme. Back then it was musical incompetence. Today you've just changed your instrument.'

'I can play *this* one pretty well, Larry, as you're about to find out.'

'But not until you've finished wankin' aboot it, eh?'

Simon laughed, patronising Ray's defiance.

'And what have *you* got to wank about, in your ordinary, anonymous little life?' he asked. 'Tell me that. What the hell have you achieved? A fucking schoolteacher. Wife, mortgage, and a kid now, I understand. You really shine out in the crowd, Ray.'

'Aye, I suppose I should have strived harder for distinction. Maybe if I'd killed a few hundred people, that would have made my life more worthwhile. Instead I've just had to settle for havin' a few folk around that like me. Friends. Do you remember the concept? Or how about conscience? That one ring any bells?'

'Conscience. What a load of bollocks. What is a conscience, but an attempt to protect your standing in the fucking tribe, the investment you've made in a reputation. Just another chain to hold you back from making your life what you want. I don't have those chains, Ray. The world is a far more interesting place when you're not bound by an identity.'

It was Ray's turn to laugh.

'Are you guys gettin' this?' he asked, looking round. The goons remained stone-faced, but there was plenty going on behind their eyes, he could tell. 'No identity, Simon? Don't talk shite. What you want more than anythin' else is for people to know who you are. That's why you've been pissin' about playin' games with me all week. You never took my advice about learnin' to button it, did you? Did you tell your mates here about your track record for blabbin' to the polis?'

Ray looked for a response from his guards, but they remained impassive; irritatingly disciplined. Any problem they had with the Dark Man would presumably be dealt with when other business was concluded. Simon could see that Ray had understood this, and it was hard to imagine anyone looking more smug. The fact that he was doing so after such a monumental failure confirmed everything Ray and Angelique had supposed. Getting Ray on his knees before him meant more to the wanker than anything else here today.

'That's the whole point, Raymond,' he said. 'I've left that person behind, and I'm somebody else. I can play whatever games I want with you, because Simon Darcourt no longer exists.'

'Oh aye, that's right, I forgot. It's not the first time you've tried to erase the past and reinvent yourself. I saw all those Queen albums in your wardrobe, mate. You're a fraud. If Simon Darcourt doesnae exist, it's because you never knew who you really were. I know who Raymond Ash is.'

'No,' Simon said, cocking his pistol. 'You know who Raymond Ash *was*. So tell me, just before we're done here, is there anything you'd like me to pass on to dear Felicia when I pop by later?'

Ray swallowed. All his anger and defiance was drained, little good that it had done him while it lasted. The thought of Kate brought home the completeness of his loss, and of Simon's victory. It should have been a consolation that his last acts on this earth had saved all those lives, but at that moment he'd have traded every one of them for his own, his wife's and Martin's.

He hung his head disconsolately and looked down into the gloomy water, hiding his face to deny Simon the sight of his submission. He was submerged to his lap where he knelt amid the four gunmen, two in front and two behind. The speargun was inches from his knees, pointing forward. Dead ahead, running down the wall, were the cables powering the overhead lighting rig. And golly, must that thing use a lot of juice.

'No,' he finally answered, looking up and reaching his right hand subtly forward under the water. 'But I've got one last thing I'd like to ask you.'

'Fire away.'

Ray's fingers felt the handle of the gun and dragged it gently back along the floor until the grip was against his palm.

'Have any of your men here ever played The Cistern or The Abandoned Base?'

'What the fuck are you talking about?'

'I thought not. Too bad.'

Ray squeezed the trigger and sent the spear whizzing, unseen and unheard beneath the surface, pulling his hand immediately back out of the water. The spear ripped into one of the cables, which instantly discharged enough electricity to kill all four of his guards with a flash, a fizzing and a very nasty smell. Ray, in his neck-to-toe wetsuit, was wearing the Pentagram of Protection.

[LGG] 9 [TL] –2

Up above, he glimpsed the briefest flash of black-clad limbs, before the lighting power shorted out and the cavern was plunged into total darkness. After a couple of seconds, the emergency system kicked in, bathing the place in a dim glow from a series of wall-mounted panels. They might even have been on the whole time, unnoticed under the blaze of the rig, and automatically switched to a back-up circuit after the main supply got terminally rerouted through the four llamas.

He watched Angelique disappear into the Control Room as he climbed to his feet, surveying the carnage. Simon was out of sight, but Ray didn't fancy his chances with a pissed-

off Angel X on his tail, especially as she now had possession of the shotgun. The four corpses lay around Ray like
petals on a flower, with him the stamen. Their hands were
practically welded to their weapons, as he found out when
he knelt down to try and lift one. He placed a foot on the
corpse's chest, taking hold of the machine gun with both
hands, and was about to give it a good tug when he heard
a splashing surge behind him.

Ray turned around to see Simon rise from the knee-deep
water and lunge towards him, pistol in hand. He slammed
into Ray's body like he was a Superbowl quarterback,
knocking him off his feet, his momentum carrying both of
them sideways until they crashed against the mangled railings overlooking the drop. Ray was pinned by Simon's
weight, his feet off the ground and his back leaning over
the edge. There was nothing he could do to regain balance,
so he directed all his strength to gripping Simon's right
wrist and forcing the muzzle of the pistol away from
himself. Simon punched him in the face with his free left
hand, his feet pushing against the floor to bend Ray further
over the balcony. The sound of the pouring water seemed
deafening, but maybe it was just the blood inside his head
as he strained with all he had to keep hold of that wrist.

Simon tried punching him in the side instead, and in a
reflex response, Ray brought a knee up from amid the
tangle. This further weight-shift was enough to buckle the
already straining barrier, and the pair of them tumbled over
the edge as it collapsed beneath them. Ray, being closer,
was able to grab a handful of metal as he fell, but Simon
was tossed head-first into the water, six or seven feet below.

Ray heard a grinding, rumbling sound as he hung on to
the stump of the barrier, water cascading over his hand
where he gripped. His feet dangled above the dark surface,

which now appeared to be swirling, clockwise. The sound vibrated through the concrete floor, making him sure it was imminently about to disintegrate.

In the meantime, he had a more immediate problem. He twisted as he dangled, turning around to face the water, where he could see Simon swimming towards an exposed, jutting shard of the crippled turbine. Simon got an arm around the metallic outcrop and was able to take a grip with one hand, steadying his aim with the other as the growing swirl tugged at his body.

'I've one last question for *you*, Larry,' he shouted, finger on the trigger. 'How does it feel to know you'll never see your son grow up?'

Ray looked him in the eye one last time.

'You tell me, Simon.'

Even across the foaming, spraying water, Ray could see the doubt, the confusion, the questions suddenly written on Simon's face, but he never got to ask them. A second, more powerful rumbling shuddered around the cavern, upon which Simon lost his grip on the shard and was pulled into the quickening swirl. He fired two shots but missed by more than ninety degrees as he was spun wildly in the current. After that, he let go of the gun, needing both hands to try and stay above the surface. Both hands, however, weren't enough.

Ray looked down at his feet, which were now at least a yard higher above the water than when he first fell. The rumbling had been caused by the tailrace reopening, causing rapid changes in pressure all through the submerged levels as the excavation began to rapidly drain. He scanned back across the spiralling pool, but could not see any sign of life. Then the artist formerly known as Simon Darcourt resurfaced one last time, before being swallowed up and flushed away like the piece of shite he was.

[LGG] 10 [TL] –2

'Suck it down,' was Ray's parting shot.

'You talkin' to me?'

Ray looked up to see Angelique standing over him, bending to grip his wrist with both hands.

'You took your time,' he complained, judiciously waiting until she had helped him back over the edge before doing so.

'I lost him when the lights went out. I thought he'd gone back into the Control Room.'

'I could have used your leet skillz.'

'Who am I compared to you? Four guys with one shot. Sign of a misspent youth, I reckon.'

'No. You need to misspend your teen years, late adolescence and much of adulthood to learn tricks like that.'

'Come on, let's get those hostages. And grab a gun; we don't want any more last-minute surprises.'

Ray forcefully prised a machine gun from one of his electrocuted victims, the process of looting a fallen foe again proving a lot more bother than online, where you just walked over them and at the most pressed your 'Use' key. He checked the safety was off and took hold of the weapon in both hands, the first time he'd ever held a real gun. It was cold and heavy, a thing of ugly brutality. He remembered the aftermath of Columbine, factions in the US media blaming *Quake* and Marilyn Manson. Computer games and rock'n'roll.

Aye, right.

They made their way down the slope together in silence, exchanging dread looks at the lack of noise emanating from behind the steel door. Then they heard a definite thud, the dampened sound of metal on metal.

496

'Hurry,' Angelique said, running the rest of the way and lunging for the door handle.

'Hang on,' Ray warned. 'You might want to—'

But it was too late. Angelique turned the handle and the door flew open, throwing her backwards as several hundred gallons of water and at least two dozen flailing bodies washed out of the room. The water came up to Ray's feet where he had sensibly remained, a few yards up the slope. He sent Angelique a smirk that was rewarded with a single finger, then began wading down to assist.

Ray was offering a hand to the nearest spluttering hostage when out of the corner of his eye he caught a glint of metal. 'Gun,' he shouted to Angelique, both of them instantly pointing their weapons at the backs of two drookit figures who were getting to their feet, machine guns swinging from straps around their shoulders.

'Drop them,' Angelique commanded. 'And turn around, slowly.'

They complied without argument, which was when Ray could see that they were actually *on* their feet, but a good half-metre shorter than everyone else. The kids looked back and forth at their captors.

'Don't worry, we're the good guys,' Angelique assured them.

'Whit aboot the terrorists?'

'We owned them,' Ray said, grinning.

Suddenly, one of the kids gaped, face filling with astonishment.

'Mr *Ash*?' he asked, incredulous.

'Fuck, Lexy, so it is,' confirmed the other.

'What are you doin' here? I mean . . .'

'We're havin' a serious truancy crackdown at Burnbrae. You pair are in a lot of trouble.'

'No way,' said 'Lexy', which would make him Alex Sinclair; the other one Jason Murphy.

'Naw. He's an undercover agent, aren't you?' Murphy ventured. 'You were just at the school as part of an operation, in't that right, tae track these guys doon? I mean, nae offence, we knew you werenae a real teacher.'

attaboy, clarence

The car pulled into Kintore Road just after ten o'clock. Ray sat in the back with Angelique, a police driver up front at the wheel. Neither of them had said much all the way down, but he was grateful for her company nonetheless. In such an aftermath, it would have been difficult to be with anyone else, and she probably felt that way too.

Ray pointed out the house in time for the car to stop just before his front gate. The living-room curtains were drawn, a dim light playing behind them. The driver opened her door, clearly intending to get out and escort Ray, but he told her not to bother, and thanked her for the trip. Angelique reached for her doorhandle as Ray opened his.

'A word before you go,' she said, climbing out of the car and out of earshot. She winced a little as she got to her feet, clutching a hand to her ribcage.

Ray stood up and faced her across the roof of the Rover.

'Make sure you get some rest,' she said. 'Baby or not. You're gaunny be givin' statements for about a week.'

'I'll try.'

'And, ehm . . . It's up to you, obviously, an' I wouldnae want you to be anythin' less than truthful, but if you could maybe see your way clear . . .'

'To not mentionin' the fact that you destroyed a few million quid's worth of power station?'

'Eh, that, aye.'

'It all happened so fast, officer. The details are a bit of a blur.'

Angelique grinned. 'Sleep tight, Ray.'

She got back in the car, which pulled away and left him standing before the garden path leading to his wee mortgaged house, his beloved wife and his infant son. His 'ordinary, anonymous little life,' Simon called it.

Ray called it home.

He put his key in the lock and smiled.

burnbrae academy: the sage wisdom of wee murph

'I heard he's a fanny. I'm gaunny rip it right oot him.'

'Naw, Ger, seriously. I don't care how hard you 'hink you are, or how long you've been suspended. I'm warnin' you: do not, under any circumstances, ever, *ever* fuck wi' the new English teacher.'

one last rock'n'roll song: *synchronicity II*

'Hell of a result, de Xavia. No arrests, though, I notice.'

'You better be takin' the piss.'

'It just looks better on the records.'

'You *are* takin' the piss.'

'I suppose they're a lot less bother this way. Plus, they never sue.'

'How many bodies have been recovered?'

'Ten, including the security guard. There were six around the machine hall, one – well, parts of one – at the dam and the divers found two more washed out into the loch.'

'We guessed there were twelve on their team. The rest must have been obliterated by the blast. Wait a minute, you say only two in the loch?'

'That's right. One with half his chest missing, apparently, and another with a broken neck.'

'There wasn't one with a spear through his throat? I left him in the tailrace too.'

'I believe he was found in the machine hall.'

'And Darcourt?'

'Not so far. The currents caused by that outflow can be pretty strong. The divers are still working, but they said his body might never be recovered.'

'Where have I heard that before?'